THE LOST KING

AN EPIC MEDIEVAL FANTASY

MICHAEL CUELL

First published in the UK in 2017.

Website: www.michaeljcuell.com
Twitter: @michaeljcuell

Print ISBN: 978-1-9998584-0-7
Kindle ISBN: 978-1-9998584-1-4
Epub ISBN: 978-1-9998584-2-1

Cover and text design by Mousemat Design Limited
www.mousematdesign.com

Printed in the UK by Biddles
www.biddles.co.uk

To my wife Caroline
who has supported this book from day one,
and my daughter Hermione who inspires
me every day: this journey is for you.

1

"Somebody please…help me!"

His voice was shaken, its strength lost by his muffled sobs. He had always hoped that one day his voice would be as deep and powerful as his father's, but right now he could barely muster a feeble whimper. He felt so ashamed. Not just for the voice, but also for his failure to act when it counted. At the time when his father had needed him the most, he had failed to defend him; he hadn't even put up a fight. So now he felt ashamed. His only saving grace was that the pain he was suffering, both physically and emotionally, was so overpowering that it was able to fight off the shame, quickly battering it into a corner of his heart, where it would wait to torment him another day.

Arundel Stal was just ten years old, not even remotely close to his prime. His entire life had been spent in the comforting confines of the Great Palace of Ryevale, under the care of his father, King Andreas. He was close to his father, closer than many princes were to their king, and he had certainly lived an easier life than many of his ancestors before him, when they were growing up.

He knew his father hadn't meant it to be this way, of course.

"A hardened upbringing creates a hardened mind, the requirement of a King," his father used to say. Often, they were just words.

Those who lived in the realm of Galbraxia, and especially the city of Ryevale, would see the King as a man hard as stone, a noble yet stern leader, who governed his people with a fair but firm hand. They knew him as a commander of men, a man who could not be broken. But Arundel was the only one to see a different side to King Andreas. He saw the softer side of his father; he basked in his warmth and the love he showed for his only child. They had a bond that no other could understand or share.

Arundel's mother, Hytheria, had died during his birth, a loss that he would not fully grow to understand until he had seen at least two winters; but one that would break his father's heart in an instant. However, instead of pushing them apart, as it would for so many, the loss had brought them closer together. Arundel was the last remaining memory that King Andreas had of his beloved wife, while Andreas was the only link that Arundel had to the mother that he had known intimately for nine months, yet never met. So it was that the man, known to most as a great King, was known to his son, behind closed doors, simply as a great father.

Having spent all his years living with the comfort of warm log fires, hearty feasts that filled his young belly and the finest animal furs that provided him with the secure feeling his mother could not, his current situation plunged him into an unknown world, which he was not sure he could survive. Yet that was the point. He understood that, even at the tender age of ten. He knew that he was there for one purpose only, with no kindly intent. Arundel, son of Andreas, the King of Galbraxia, was no longer within the walls of the Great Palace. Instead, he found himself bound to a tree deep within the Weeping Woods, alone, left there to die.

The trees had been growing for thousands of years; some said that they were the oldest living things in the realm. To the East, they skirted a host of villages that he knew very little about, not even a name, merely their existence. To the North was the Last Port of Galbraxia, a small town once alive with trade and enriched with money from that trade: many had travelled from there across the Tavarian Sea to what was now known as the Forgotten Lands. However, as ties with those lands had faded, trading with them ceased and so the Port fell into poverty and now stood a mere shell of its former self, a degraded reminder of a time long forgotten.

To the South stood Staverstock, a fortified city built into the hills of Alvern. This was once the last line of defence during the days of war with King Havanas, ruler of the realm of Carazan, which lay beyond the hills. Staverstock's years of war were long gone, but it was still used by the soldiers of Galbraxia for training purposes.

To the East lay the city of Bragmout, the keepers of the bridge. Bragmout stood on the edge of the Endless Ravine, a huge crevice in the earth as long and as deep as the eye could see, yawning two miles wide, with one solitary bridge to cross it. This bridge ran through the heart of Bragmout and, on the other side of the Ravine, it led to the realm of Xenothia, ruled by King Xenos.

Finally, to the West, were the cities of Damisas and Ryevale. Ryevale was the city of the King and had always shared a strong bond with Damisas, of all the realm's cities the most loyal to its King while this honour remained in the Stal family.

The Weeping Woods were surrounded by Galbraxia's rich history and, while their own factual history was not known, many stories and legends had been passed down through the generations. The thick undergrowth and dense tree population had made it easy to tell tales, but the truth would never be known, as few dared venture inside.

Arundel himself had never been within one hundred feet of the woods, let alone inside. He had ridden close once on a hunting trip with his father, who had challenged him to enter them. However, the fears of a then seven year old overpowered his desperation to show courage, and, instead of trotting into the foliage with pride in his chest and fire in his heart, he had opted to turn tail and ride away. Tears had replaced his courage at the sheer idea of facing the terrors said to live within. Now, as the rope that bound his hands behind his back cut into his skin, he wondered if his father would be proud. The rope that was tied round both his chest and the tree crushed him against the rough bark of the old oak and he wondered if he would ever have faced his fears, given the choice. He doubted it, but now he would never know.

"Help me...please help me!" he cried out again, his voice even weaker than before. His arm burned from a deep cut just above the wrist; he could feel the blood where it had dried on his fingers. His head pounded in agony. The skin had split and more blood had spilled; this time it was merging in with his tears, as they seeped from his swollen eyes, creating an oil painting of body fluids upon his once rosy cheeks. If his hands were free, he truly believed that they would be able to feel a large lump on his head, the source of the dull pain that thumped like a drum against his skull.

The longer he sat there, the weaker he felt and the drowsier he became. He had no idea how long it had been since he was first abandoned there, but, as the light dwindled, he knew that day was fast becoming night, and it was night that he feared most of all. He could almost see past the stories of human sacrifice, mystical creatures and tree roots that would work their way out from the soil to entwine you and drag you to a muddy grave. While his young imagination allowed them all to have a sense of realism, he could at least admit the possibility of their false origins, but the talk of wolves hunting at night – now that was what filled him with such feelings of dread. Wolves were the one constant of all the tales told by the children of Ryevale. It hadn't helped that, as he was banished to this location, he had heard menacing voices predicting that the wolves would finish the job. Between the smell of fear emanating from his pores and his own blood on display, he just knew that the wolves would find him sooner or later. He could picture in his mind their jagged fangs ripping through his flesh, a limb or two being carried away to feed their young. On this very night, as the sun made its way to its slumber and the moon took up its nightly post, Arundel could not shake the belief that his blood would stain the earth beneath him and the last of the Stal bloodline would be gone forever. His only hope was that he would fall unconscious before the feeding began.

He could feel his head growing heavy as it slowly sank forward, his chin driving down into his rib cage and the muscles stretching at the back of his neck. The narrow gaps between his swollen eyelids began to close, his focus slipping away. He was aware of his breath beginning to slow down, the air making a low groan when it escaped past his lips into the open. All sensation in his body began to fade away, the pain becoming a distant nightmare no longer haunting him. Maybe this was it? This might be the reprieve he was looking for. The last of the Stals, the King of Galbraxia never to be crowned, meeting his end. There would be no ceremonial send off, no rightful burial befitting a King. Instead he would die where he sat, soaked in blood and tears, his body a one-night meal for the resident wolves, any remains they didn't like left to rot into the earth of Mother Nature. Not a fitting demise, but he did not care. Not right now. As long as he couldn't feel that first bite of wolf teeth, then he would be thankful for small mercies.

The world sank into darkness. His eyes finally closed as he could feel his entire being slip away. It was over; this was the end of it all. He was ready to say goodbye to it all, safe in the knowledge he was leaving no one behind.

"SQUAWK!"

The noise startled him, his eyes opening as quickly as they possibly could in their delicate and battered state. He lifted his head from its uncomfortable resting place and eased himself back into an upright position, the rope ripping the cloth of his silk shirt. Thankfully, his appearance was the least of his worries. He began to survey his surroundings as best he could, trying to find the source of the noise that had kept him in the world of the conscious.

Still drowsy, his eyes began to play tricks on him. Wherever he looked he could see a threat, a shape of something that looked dangerous. His panic levels began to rise, his head darting from side to side. If danger was all around him, what were they waiting for? Why hadn't they made their move? He was ripe for the taking, so what was the delay? He shook his head, trying to clear his mind. Doing so immediately felt like a mistake, as the pain in his head doubled. It was as if a rock was rattling around inside his skull, bouncing off his brain with every move. But, despite the pain, it proved a worthwhile choice, since his vision became just a little clearer. The supposed dangers revealed their true identities as a wild bear became a fallen log; snakes turned into uncovered tree roots and a wolf, a bush missing a few of its leaves. Once again, he felt stupid. He was no closer to discovering that family courage, for which his ancestors and his father were known, than he was to finding a way to break his bonds.

"SQUAWK!"

Again he was snapped out of it, as the noise returned. This time he was a little more focused and so was able to identify that the sound came from above.

He glanced up, staring high into the branches of the old oak tree, at least as much as the fading light would allow him. He stared for what felt like an eternity, his eyes darting from one shadowy outline to another, his aching brain clicking into gear at each new sight, as it tried to decipher the code of what lay before him.

In actuality, it was likely that barely a minute or two had passed, yet already he was on the verge of giving up his search. The idea that life was abandoning him added to the feeling of emptiness that had burrowed deep inside of him. He let out a sigh and immediately regretted doing so, as the vibrations of his own voice sent shockwaves through his head. Still the drum pounded inside his skull.

"SQUAWK!"

It was at this moment that he found the source of the distraction. This latest outburst had given away the owner's position. About six branches above him and two to his right, partially hidden amongst the foliage, was perched a dark coloured bird. The moonlight afforded him a few glimpses of this creature: a portion of beak, a vague span of feathered wing and a beady eye that seemed to glare at him with such intent. He could not make out what species it was, but he didn't really care. For the first time since he had been tied here, he no longer felt alone. This bird, this small creature that knew nothing of his troubles, had found him in his time of need. Here he was, orphaned by the day's events, left to die within the woods that had taunted his childhood to this point, alone with no one to know of his demise. Now he had company, an ally in his struggle against his impending death, a friend to share his final moments with. He was thankful, ridiculously so, that at this time, of all the trees in these woods, this bird had chosen to take its rest upon his.

Suddenly the silence was broken again, but this time it wasn't the piercing cry of his feathered friend; instead it was the snapping of a twig not too far from his location. This was swiftly followed by the flapping of wings at some speed, as his friend made his escape into the night sky. He immediately began to mourn the bird's absence, until the thought hit him. A thought that cut him to his very core and chilled his soul, as if he had been stabbed by a blade of ice. What had actually caused the twig to snap, a foot perhaps? Maybe patience had worn thin and one of the King's soldiers had been sent back to finish the job? Or perhaps it was a paw, attached to a ravenous wolf following the scent of its prey? Neither were positive outcomes for him and so they filled him with dread.

He tried to call out, one last cry for help. But fear had stolen his words. His mouth was as dry as the summer soil, the drumming in his head picking up speed and intensity. His eyes began to blur, taking away his ability to see his impending fate. Adrenalin pumped at a rate of knots through his body, while dizziness and nausea kicked in with a double attack.

'Thank the Gods,' he thought, in the belief he was about to pass out, giving him exactly what he had hoped for.

Whatever was coming was drawing closer, since he could hear footsteps accompanied by muffled sounds, but was it the sound of two feet or four? Were the muffled sounds human voices or could they be growls? He didn't have the answers, but he felt it no longer mattered. His eyelids had become so heavy they fell shut. His body slumped, scraping down the razor-like bark of the tree. He was fading out, drifting away to another time. This was it, he thought to himself. This was the end of Arundel Stal, rightful heir to the throne of Galbraxia. At least he would get to see his father again; at least he would get to meet his mother for the first time.

This final thought comforted him. As he slipped from consciousness, voices rang in his ears. The first was soft and tender, with a feminine undertone. The second was much harder and bore a touch of authority.

"By the Gods, he is just a boy!" said the first voice. The second swiftly followed.

"Untie him at once."

2

One sunrise earlier...

"Ouch, father, that hurt!"

King Andreas Stal looked upon his son, as the young boy clutched his left arm with his right hand. Prince Arundel was his only child and the rightful heir to his throne. At present, he was merely a ten year old boy who had chosen not to wear protective training pads, and was now suffering the consequences of that decision.

He couldn't help but admire that; it reminded him of himself in his own youth. His own father had taught him how to handle a blade when he was a boy, and he had always refused to put on the pads; now here was his own son following in that same trend. Some would call it stupidity, others bravery. He would call it confidence. Young Arundel still had many fears to overcome, just like any ten year old. But when you put a sword in his hand, he felt comfortable; he felt at home. He could see that in Arundel's inexperienced eyes. He had confidence to bear a sword; he just needed the skill to use it.

"Now, now, Arundel, you could have worn the pads but you said no."

His deep voice boomed around the room, bouncing from one stone wall to another.

"A true king needs only his sword for protection."

His son's voice spoke with pride, but its soft tones could barely muster an echo.

"True enough, son. But then again, a true king doesn't drop

his sword and clutch his wound in the midst of battle."

He pointed at Arundel's sword with his own, as it lay on the floor. He watched his son lower his head, a look of disappointment upon his face. Maybe King Andreas should have felt bad for his comment, but he didn't. They were training swords, nothing more than wood painted silver, and so he knew that he hadn't actually hurt the boy, not seriously. Not only that, but he felt that Arundel needed to learn and understand the disappointment of defeat. To learn this painful lesson now might avoid him suffering defeat for real, in the future. This was a valuable lesson to learn, and within these walls it was a safe environment to learn it. To experience this for the first time upon the field of battle would be costly. The cost would likely be his life.

Arundel dropped to his knees, plunged into a frustration the King had also once known intimately. While he knew that knocking the boy down had been necessary, so too was the task of picking him back up. Holding out an ageing hand covered by a royal red silk sleeve, he offered it to his son, accompanied by a smile that suggested nothing but peace.

"Come with me for a minute."

His heavy voice now bore a softer tone. He could see the hesitation in the boy's face, as the young Prince did not know what to expect. His hand hung in the air, an invitation waiting to be accepted. Eventually, the boy reached out and grabbed the hand with his own. Nearly half the size of his, the boy's hand practically disappeared as the King wrapped his fingers around and gripped it tightly. Then, with one swift motion, he hauled the boy off the stone floor to his feet. Once Arundel was back on a vertical base, their hands parted and the King gently placed his broad arm across young shoulders.

"Walk with me."

This time, there was no hesitation as the boy followed him, doing his best to keep pace with his father's giant stride.

They made their way across the vast room towards the far side. The room was as wide as it was deep. Chandeliers, boasting hundreds of candles, were suspended by chains from the white ceiling. The walls were decorated with suits of armour and weapons of war covering many generations. Around the floor of the room itself were training instruments, made from both wood and iron, each of them designed to further the art of combat.

This room had once, a long time ago, been a very generous guest room. But that had changed under the rule of his great, great grandfather, King Athrox the Second. He was the one to turn this room into a private training room, where a king could both train, and bond with, his son. It was a tradition passed down with honour.

As they reached the far side of the room, they were now at an open air balcony that looked out across the realm as far as the eye could see. This was the one remnant of the old guest room. Stepping out into the fresh evening air, Arundel felt the gentle breeze cool the sweat upon his brow. Luxurious as silks were, they just were not designed for sweating in, he discovered, since they clung to his skin.

Stood beside his son on the balcony, King Andreas gazed upon the sight before him. The sun was in its bed for the evening, the night's watch now taken over by a half moon, nestling among a sea of stars. Fires illuminated the city of Ryevale as it stretched out below the Great Palace. He could see lights beyond the city into the realm of Galbraxia itself. He believed that some belonged to the city of Damisas; the rest he wasn't so sure about. Above him, he could hear a gentle flapping. He looked up to see a flag gently swaying in the breeze. The flag was blood red trimmed with gold and bore an eagle, wings spread, perched on the hilt of a sword half buried in the earth. This was the insignia of the Stal family and it had graced these walls for more generations than he could remember.

He pulled his attention back to his son to speak.

"One day, my son, all of this will be yours to rule and you must rule it well."

His son gave a reluctant reply.

"I know, father."

That kind of tone did not satisfy this King. He pulled at

Arundel's shoulders, turning the boy to face him. He stared at the boy who would one day be king, but the boy that stared back was not a young reflection of himself. It would be easy to question whether Arundel was actually his or not; the boy had inherited his features from his mother, for certain. His own face was rounded, a dark and heavy beard sat upon his chin and hung down in line with his collar bone, his hair thick and dark brown but at a short length that kept it by his ears. He was heavyset in build, not fat, just well built. Arundel was entirely different. His face was narrow, his hair golden and light, already down to his well defined jaw line. His chin was not yet mature enough for facial hair and his body not yet fully grown, but even still you could see he would be of a lighter and sleeker frame. These were not traits of the Stal family genetics; they were very much from the Fanardorn bloodline, his mother's. The King took hold of both of Arundel's shoulders as he knelt down on one knee, bringing them eye to eye. They stared at each other for a moment or two, father and son sharing their entire history in that very instant and looking into each other's souls. It was a rare moment, but eventually Andreas broke the silence.

"Son, do you remember what I have always told you? The same lesson my father taught me, and my grandfather taught him?"

Arundel nodded his head, his blond locks whipping past his face. However, this wasn't enough.

"Say it for me!"

Arundel let out a slight moan, the typical petulance of a small child.

"Say it."

His voice was heavier and carried a stronger demand with it, bringing the desired response from the boy.

"Belief is everything."

The boy lowered his head. King Andreas reached out and took hold of Arundel's chin, lifting his head back up.

"Yes, it is," he confirmed. The boy managed a brief smile at the relief of getting it right. The King continued, "To rule well, your people must believe in you. If they believe in you, then they will live their lives in your name. If your warriors believe in you, then they will be willing to lay down their lives for you, but for anyone to believe in you, first you must believe in yourself."

Arundel looked at him, his blue eyes full of questions. However, only one would pass his lips.

"How do I do that?"

The King's voice dropped to a softer tone as he replied.

"Well, first, you should continue to practise."

He rose back to his feet, once again looming above the young prince. He escorted Arundel back inside the vast training room to the spot where the training swords lay upon the marble floor. He watched as Arundel picked up his sword with a little more confidence than before. The boy was ready to go again and he was pleased to see it. As he reached down to pick up his own sword, his attention was caught by a loud bang of wood on stone. The heavy wooden doors to the room swung open and slammed into the walls. Filling the now open doorway were the shapes of two men. One of these men was Lord Theagran Greystone, the King's First. The role of the King's First was pretty simple: he did everything the King couldn't. If the King was unavailable, then the First dealt with matters of the kingdom. There were times when the First would even sit upon the throne in the King's absence. Just as the Stal family had sat upon the throne for many generations, the honour of the First had belonged to the Greystones. Andreas' father and grandfather had been lucky with their Firsts, loyal and kind men to the very end. However, he had not been dealt such a kind hand. He had been bitter rivals with Theagran ever since they had been of the age to speak, and now it was duty alone that had thrust them together in an uneasy co-existence. He couldn't help but notice that Theagran was wearing leathers instead of silks, covered by his silver armour that bore the Greystone crest of a snake entwined around an axe on the chest plate.

"Pardon the interruption, my King."

Theagran spoke with a sense of urgency in his voice. Standing next to Theagran was Marcasian Bavadine, Captain of the Guardians of the Crown. He knew very little about Marcasian, the man nicknamed 'The Bull', a name earned because the sight of blood sent him into a destructive rage that brought death to many.

The Bull had only been in the role for two weeks, following the untimely death of Sir Jawyn Lisendar, who had served as Captain for twenty years. It was said that age had got the better of him during a hunt, causing him to fall from his horse to his death upon an ill-placed rock. But Andreas did not believe that to be true. Sir Jawyn could ride a horse with his eyes closed and both hands tied behind his back; he had even once seen him do so. Theagran had promised to look into the matter, but for now a new Captain was required for the Guardians and Marcasian had been given the honour. The Guardians were twelve of the greatest knights of the realm who were dedicated to the personal protection of the King. The death of Sir Jawyn had left them with eleven.

"Are we at war, Theagran?" the King asked, because not only was Theagran in battle dress, but so was Marcasian.

A small black goatee decorated the Bull's lips and chin, while his long black hair was tied into a tail and hung down his back. He wore the armour of the Guardians, accompanied by a velvet cape, scarlet in colour, that was attached on the left shoulder plate and ran along the back to underneath the right breast plate. The front of the armour bore the insignia of the Guardians, two swords entwined together, a brotherhood bound together in defence of their King. His sword was sheathed upon his side.

"On the verge of war, Sire, civil war at that."

Theagran moved as he spoke, approaching with his accustomed arrogant stride. Marcasian followed, but at a distance.

"The two of you are dressed suitably then. Tell me, what civil war do you speak of?"

The King had little patience in his voice.

"It's your men, my King; they grow restless. They are warriors built to fight and conquer, yet you have given them nothing but boredom and restlessness."

"I have given them PEACE!"

The anger in Andreas' voice echoed like thunder.

"They sit on their arses getting fat and lazy, when they could be achieving so much more," Theagran said with a hint of disgust, as saliva from his mouth was launched to the floor.

"Hold your tongue, Theagran, and remember who you speak with."

He then turned to Arundel.

"Go to your room."

His demand displeased Arundel.

"But father..."

"NOW!"

He cut the boy off, his command cracking the air like a whip. He was in no mood for games, Theagran had seen to that. As Arundel dropped his shoulders in a sulk and began to run, the large, muscular arm of Marcasian grabbed hold of the boy round the neck and pulled him into his body. Arundel tried to struggle but could not break the grip of the Bull.

"Marcasian, let go of the boy at once!"

Marcasian just stared back at him, his eyes hollow and empty. All of the King's attention and anger was now focused on the Captain of the Guardians. He wasn't aware of the blade until he felt it pierce his skin just below his shoulder blades. It felt like a dull thud at first, almost like a punch from a fist. But then the burning sensation began and he could feel the trickling of his blood down his back. He dropped to his knees, the world blurred as he reached out, trying to find his son. He could hear the boy's cries, but it was the voice of Theagran that was clearest of all.

"I have waited a long time for this."

Theagran leaned close into him and with one swift movement he retracted the blade, providing Andreas with a brief feeling of release. He could smell the stench of death upon his flesh, feel Theagran's warm breath against his ear.

"You once took from me the most important thing in my life. Now know that your son will follow you into the grave because of me."

The next thing he felt was the cold blade slice across his windpipe and then he felt nothing. Arundel screamed. The King's lifeless body slumped to the floor. A pool of blood flowed from his father's throat, staining the marble. The boy's screams were swiftly silenced by Marcasian striking him on the head with the butt of his dagger. He then dropped the boy and spoke for the first time.

"What now, my lord?"

Theagran eventually turned away from his handiwork and faced his man.

"Have two of your men take the boy into the Weeping Woods and feed him to the wolves. A few cuts should be enough to give them his scent. I will address the people."

Marcasian knelt down and picked up the boy in both arms.

"What will you tell them?"

Theagran looked at the dagger in hand, the blood of the King dripping from its once clean blade.

"I will tell them that the boy killed his father in a rage and fled the city. I will tell them that the realm of Galbraxia has a new King upon the throne."

Marcasian began to make his exit, while Theagran spoke to himself softly, a terrible grin creeping across his face.

"All hail, King Theagran."

The deer stood silent, enjoying its relaxing surroundings during its search for its next meal. It had strayed far from its home, deep into the heart of the woods, seeking the next tasty treat to tantalize its taste buds. The deer did not understand the troubles of men, nor did it care. In its own mind it had no owner, no restrictions, no ties holding it back. It was as free as the wind, a creature of its own devices. All it cared for was its own survival and at this moment that involved locating its next meal. So that was what it was doing, pottering its way around the woods, scavenging for whatever it could find. The deer had very few expectations for the day ahead, but one thing it had planned for was that by nightfall it would sleep, so that it could rise another day. However, as the arrow struck its body, piercing its skin with a force that knocked it off its feet, those small expectations quickly began to slip away.

The deer was still breathing with a struggle, as Garad Danwood of Havendale emerged from the green undergrowth into the clearing where the deer lay. Garad was an agile man, his muscle supple on his slender frame. Thick black hair framed his clean-shaven face. His upper body was covered by a brown linen shirt and a battered green leather doublet over the top. His athletic legs were adorned by leathers, that had seen better days. An ancient sword hung at his waist, while in his hands a longbow made of yew wood sat proudly. A quiver of leather and animal fur hung across his back, boasting a collection of arrows matching the one which now nestled in the deer. Garad knelt down beside his dying prey, resting one hand on its rib cage in a moment of silence.

"The damn thing isn't even dead. That is five points and nothing more!"

The booming voice that broke the silence belonged to Bromon Danwood of Havendale, elder blood brother to Garad. Bromon was twice the man of Garad, in appearance. Unlike Garad, Bromon's muscle was thick and there for all to see. His arms were like branches, his legs like tree trunks. Cloth trousers clung to his thighs while a leather jerkin strained across his chest. His boots were wolf skin, while he had bearskin draped across his shoulders, both earned by the result of his own devastating hands. A mighty battleaxe was knocking against his leg as he forced shrubbery aside and joined his brother, looming over him in the same way he had done ever since childhood.

"The shot was perfect; I would like to see you do better,"

Garad replied with defiance, pleased with his efforts. He knew that when it came to the use of a bow, Bromon could not even come close to him.

"Perfect? Then why does it still breathe?"

Bromon let out a large belt of laughter at the failing of his younger blood sibling. Bromon was right and Garad hated that. There was nothing subtle about Bromon, from his appearance to his attitude, and especially when it came to gloating. He knew he wouldn't hear the end of this all day, as he took hold of the arrow. He tugged hard, pulling it from the torso of the deer and causing the blood flow to pick up pace. Still the deer breathed and he knew what must be done. As he always did with his kills, he made a silent apology in his mind while gripping the arrow firmly in his hand, ready to drive it through the throat of the deer to end its agony once and for all.

"Forgive my actions and may the Gods be gracious as you embark on your afterlife." The words rolled through his mind with ease, having been said hundreds of times before. Opening his eyes, he shifted his body weight in preparation for finishing the task, but before he could move any more, there was a loud thud as the familiar battleaxe of Bromon thumped down onto the neck of the deer, slicing through it like butter, before digging into the thick earth beneath. Garad watched the head roll away and the breathing finally stop. His anger and frustration boiled within, not for the first time when it came to Bromon.

"Damn it, Bromon. That was my kill."

He rose to his feet, wiping away the bloodstains from the arrow tip, before reaching back and placing it in his quiver.

"Quiet, little brother. As always, I was showing you how to do things properly."

There was a mocking tone in his voice as he spoke and Garad picked up on it instantly. He stepped close to Bromon, his bow nearly jabbing the older sibling in the face.

"Maybe I should show my gratitude, dear brother."

His aggressive tone was met with equal force by Bromon.

"Yes, and then I can show you my fist, swiftly followed by the floor."

Having said this, Bromon took hold of Garad by his doublet, while Garad in return grabbed hold of Bromon's jerkin. The two were ready to come to blows, as many times before.

"Do I need to give the two of you five minutes of privacy?"

The voice snapped the pair of them out of their bubble of anger. They let go of each other and turned to see its owner emerge into the clearing. The tension immediately faded away, as Arundel came into view in the clearing. Long fair shoulder length hair framed a handsome face, and a neatly trimmed blond beard concealed a chiselled jaw. A slender but muscularly toned body was covered by leather trousers, a white silk shirt and black leather doublet. Hanging from his waist was an exquisite sword of expert craft.

Arundel had grown up to become a fine man, but he had no memory of his life prior to the age of ten, when his name-parents found him in these very woods, on the far side, closer to the towns of lords and kings. They had found him bound to a tree, his body a mess of cuts and bruises. Consciousness had already left him and he had been at death's door. Why he had been there was a mystery that he could not answer.

For him, life began days later when he awoke in the small village of Havendale. His rescuers, Daros and Sylvina Danwood, were the senior elders of the village and had also become his name-parents, taking him into their family home. This made Garad and Bromon his name-brothers. Together, the three of them had become the main hunters of the village, a task that they took to with ease. While Garad was master of the bow and Bromon was destructive with an axe, Arundel could handle a sword like no other. Although his memory of his early years did not exist, he somehow knew how to handle a blade as if it was an extension of his arm.

"Last to the party as always, I see, Arundel."

Bromon followed his words with slight laughter. While he may have held some dominance over his younger brother, there was something about Arundel that made even a stubborn mule like Bromon back down.

"Well, while the two of you squabble over such minor matters, someone has to watch your back," Arundel quipped with a smirk.

"Hah, surely you wouldn't dare spill any blood on that precious sword of yours, Ari."

Garad now united with his brother. Garad had always called Arundel 'Ari', ever since they first met. Their father used to comment that he did so because he couldn't pronounce Arundel. This always angered Garad and delighted Bromon, who would remind him of it often.

"I doubt he can lift it, let alone use it!" Bromon boomed in another jibe, buoyed by the support of his blood brother.

"Razor was built for more important purposes than slaying a few animals."

Garad and Bromon laughed in unison, before Garad threw in his opinion once more.

"The fact that your sword even has a name says it all, Ari."

Arundel reached down to his side and took the hilt of Razor in his hand, easing her out of her scabbard into the light of day. The sun glinted off the blade as he pointed it towards his brethren.

"Maybe you would like to get to know her a little more personally, brother."

Razor was a fine specimen of a sword made for him by Milly, the blacksmith's daughter. Milly and her father had found their way to Havendale from the royal city of Ryevale several years ago and she had taken an instant liking to him. She used to call him her 'Prince' for a reason he never really understood. Still, Milly may have learned the same skills as her father, but thankfully she hadn't inherited his looks. She was of a sweet beauty, captivating enough, with long brown hair that fell onto heaving breasts. He had taken her to bed on several occasions, the only real intimacy that had ever appealed to him in Havendale. They bonded well enough, but he never saw it as something permanent. However, one day she surprised him with a gift: a sword crafted by her own talented hands. The blade was made from a steel that could only be found in the Forgotten Lands; he dared not ask how she got hold of it. The hilt meanwhile had the most work involved in it. Its base had been crafted into the head of an eagle, while the cross guard formed eagle wings that ran up the base of the blade. He had asked her why an eagle and Milly had told him that an eagle, stronger than any other creation of the Gods, was flying within his soul. He didn't get it, but that was just Milly. He couldn't help but feel that she knew something about his past, but even in the wildest moments of passion she never parted with her secrets. So he accepted the gift, a sword to rival any other in the land and one that had attracted jealousy within the village, especially with his name-brothers.

Milly had also told him that the bravest and most noble warriors always named their swords to build a bond between themselves and their blade. The sword felt so natural in his hand that he found naming her easy. He had chosen Razor, after the sharpness of an eagle's beak and talons.

There was a brief moment of silence between the three of them, before they all burst into laughter. They were as thick as thieves and enjoyed a good row, as much as they enjoyed their banter. Arundel sheathed Razor as Garad picked up his bow and hooked it over his shoulder.

"I will wager that the arrow did not sever the deer's head; so are we looking at five points or two?"

Garad was quick to answer in his own defence.

"The arrow left the deer at death's door, so I will settle for five."

Arundel looked from Garad to Bromon. The elder brother shrugged his mountain-like shoulders and reluctantly agreed.

"Aye, it's true; it would have been a fatal shot...eventually."

With hunting such a regular occurrence for them, they had turned it into a competition. Each would attempt the kill with their own preferred weapon. Should they complete the kill with one strike, it was ten points. A near fatal blow earned five points, while a minor wounding garnered just two points. A total miss resulted in minus five points. The competition certainly brought out the best and the worst in them and they regularly quarrelled about who exactly was winning.

"I believe that takes me ahead of you, brother," Garad was quick to point out to Bromon.

"Yes it does, if I were to pretend I had no points. But seeing as I am twice the hunter you are, Garad, you are still way behind me."

Bromon did not surprise anyone with his disagreement.

"Now that's enough, both of you. How about you get that deer back to the horses and we can return to Havendale before we die of old age out here." Ever the voice of reason, Arundel turned away from them, ready to make his way back along the path he had just come from. "Besides, I am way ahead of both of you!"

He chuckled out loud as both Garad and Bromon cursed under their breath, before Garad reached down and picked up the deer carcass, hoisting it over his shoulder, blood dripping to the floor from the open neck. The two blood brothers then followed, Bromon clearing the path for Garad and his prize as they worked their way back through the greenery of the woods.

Many believed that the Weeping Woods were as alive as the

wildlife within it. It was said that if you looked closely enough, you could see the plants moving and if you really concentrated you could hear them talking to each other. There were many rumours and stories about these woods and the three brothers most certainly believed a few of those that circulated; but, unlike many other people of the realm, they did not fear the woods.

They were back with their horses and mounted within minutes. The deer was strapped to the rump of Garad's dark brown mare. The largest horse belonged to Bromon, a strong and powerful beast built to take its master's weight, with strands of its long mane across its face to match the furry features of its rider.

Arundel rode a white stallion. Unlike Razor, the stallion was not a gift. He had found it standing guard over its dead master during a solo trip into the woods. The stallion had been tied to a tree and Arundel had made the choice to set him free, feeling that he had served his duty and had earned a life of his own; but instead of galloping off into the start of freedom, the horse had followed Arundel back to Havendale. He had chosen Arundel as his new master and they had been together ever since.

Arundel had named him Tyranos, a name the horse accepted instantly. Tyranos would not allow anyone to ride him but Arundel. Bromon would quip that Tyranos was in love with him and would sneak into Arundel's bed at night; Arundel would always reply that just because any girl Bromon had taken to his bed might look like a horse, it didn't mean others followed suit.

The journey back to Havendale wasn't a long one. They hadn't ventured that deep into the Weeping Woods this day and so, even at the calm pace they were riding, they would be home within one cycle of the day's sun. As they broke through the outskirts of the woods into the open fields, with Havendale on the horizon, they were greeted by a sight that quickened their pace. Smoke billowed from within the village, a sight not commonly seen. The calm trot broke into a gallop, all three men using their heels to fire up their horses and make a charge for home.

Questions raced through Arundel's mind as they rode forward at speed. What could have happened? Was this the result of an accident? Perhaps a hot iron dropped in the blacksmiths, or maybe a stray ember from the roasting fire? Or could it be something more sinister? His questions were answered when they found their way onto the approach trail for the village. Screams could be heard in the distance and as he approached the wooden bridge that marked the entrance of the village, a young boy came into view. The boy's skin was black from smoke as he ran across the bridge, a look of fear and panic etched across his tender young face. Arundel recognised the boy; he was Timmand, son of Timmonas the village butcher. Arundel arrived at the bridge just as Timmand was approaching. He reached out a hand, but when the boy tried to do the same, he was suddenly stopped in his tracks by an arrow that pierced straight through the back of his skull. The boy fell forward to the floor in an instant, an immediate death being the only saving grace.

Arundel looked up and saw, standing on the other side of the bridge, a man dressed in chain mail and decoration. His mail was shrouded by a cloak of blood red, his face partially hidden by a helm of silver. Upon the cloak Arundel glimpsed a partial design of an embroidered snake. Fury raged within him as he maintained his pace. The knight began to reach for another arrow, leaving a very small opportunity for Arundel to act. Holding the reins with his left hand and reaching down to his waist with his right, Arundel grasped Razor's hilt. He slid her from her sheath, the sun glinting off the blade. Tyranos picked up pace as if he realised the danger. The knight placed the arrow against the string of his bow and began to draw it back. Arundel rotated Razor in his hand and then swung with anger. The knight's arrow fell to the floor. His body dropped to its knees, while his head rolled along the muddy ground behind it. Razor had sliced clean through his neck, causing blood to spatter and a quick death.

Arundel rounded a corner, and was brought to a standstill by what he saw. Flames licked at buildings, devouring them whole. Bodies lay strewn across the grass and mud floor. People he had known, people he had shared meals or a drink or even just conversation with, now lay bloodied and dead before him. He dismounted from Tyranos and walked beside him, almost in a daze at the devastation that lay before him. He could still hear the screams, yet he did not search for them. Time had slowed to a near standstill around him. The smoke was thick in his nostrils; the heat of the flames warmed his skin. Could this be real? Suddenly he snapped back into reality, as an arrow flew past his head from behind. He then watched as it struck a knight emerging in front of him, this one dressed the same as the one at the bridge. The arrow hit the knight in the chest, knocking him off his feet. As he fell to the ground, Garad and Bromon rode up beside Arundel.

"Thanks."

Arundel meant it.

"What is the meaning of this?"

Garad ignored his appreciation, as he instead chose to ask the question they were all thinking.

"Here are three more!"

They were interrupted by an unfamiliar voice. As they looked up, seven more knights came into view. Garad and Bromon dropped to their feet beside Arundel and the three of them stood back to back, giving them a 360-degree view, while the knights formed a circle around them. All were dressed the same, bar various bloodstains that had formed different patterns on their mail and cloaks.

"I wonder if they will squeal like the others?"

The one who spoke had bent teeth and a scar down his right cheek.

"Let's just finish the job so we can get back."

The second to speak didn't suffer from the same dental afflictions as the first, but bore his own scar across his left eye.

The knights began to close in, as Arundel pressed his back firmly against those of his name-brothers.

"Ari, what say we split the pack?"

As soon as Garad spoke, Arundel knew what he meant. It was a tactic they always used to use as kids.

"Aye, Arundel, let's crack some bloody skulls!"

Bromon gripped his axe tightly, ready to back up his words, as Arundel nodded. They then waited while the knights drew closer and closer. Garad had hung his bow around his body and taken his sword in hand. Then, as the knights took two more steps, Arundel let out a cry.

"Now!"

The three of them launched forward, blades swinging, as the knights had no choice but to scatter out of the way, taking themselves off guard. Garad struck the first knight with his sword, lodging it in his gut. He then reached back and pulled an arrow from his quiver, digging it deep into the neck of a second knight. As he pulled it back out, he removed his bow and dispatched the same arrow straight into the eye of a third. Two were slain by Razor, the first with a deep gouge from shoulder to hip, and the second a swift slice across the bowels that spilt intestines onto the ground. The other two were Bromon's, his axe severing an arm of one and the leg of another, before it shattered both of their ribcages to put an end to their screams.

This battle won, it was now that they split up. Bromon and Garad set off towards the family home, the welfare of their parents a grave concern. Arundel, meanwhile, made for the blacksmith's in search of Milly. While he shared the concern of Garad and Bromon for his name-parents, they could achieve more separately. Although Milly may not have captured his heart, he did care for her; she was the only person who meant much to him, outside of his adoptive family.

Making his way down past a row of smouldering houses, his ears were met with female screams. He broke into a run, as the screams grew louder. Turning a corner, he saw two knights pinning a woman down outside the inn. One held a knife to her throat while the other was forcing himself upon her. With Razor in hand, Arundel continued his charge. The knight on his knees still thrust, turning with a dirt-stained grin just in time to see Razor come at his neck. It was the last thing he saw as his head tumbled away.

The second knight snarled and cursed, slitting the woman's

throat with his dagger, before getting to his feet. He then tossed it aside and took hold of his own sword, standing ready, beckoning Arundel on. The air was rent with the clash of steel. Arundel saw his first two swings blocked, before the knight struck him with a punch that caused him to stumble back. The knight then swung at his head, but Arundel ducked underneath it and caught the knight across the thigh. Blood began to soak through his mail as the knight staggered. Arundel went back on the attack and the knight was able to block three more blows, before a slice to the forearm caused his sword to slip from his grasp. With the knight defenceless, Arundel drove Razor forward, pushing with all his might as she sliced through the knight's ribcage and out past his spine. Arundel withdrew the blade and the knight fell to the ground. He glanced down at the savaged girl. His sorrow for her was coupled with relief that at least it wasn't Milly.

However, his sorrow would grow.

He found Milly where he had expected, side by side with her father, sword in hand, protecting their livelihood. But the blacksmiths had crafted their last blade. As father and daughter, they shared their lives together and now they shared their deaths together too. He closed her eyes and said his goodbyes. He felt the loss, but he did not shed a tear. They had been close, intimate even, but their souls had never entwined. That did not mean that he wouldn't miss her, and it did not mean that he wasn't suffering from sorrow because of her demise. In fact, his sorrow combined with anger against those who had taken her life, but also with relief that she had not suffered the same horrors as the woman back at the inn. He wanted to give her a proper burial. In fact, he would make sure that it would happen, but not yet. He couldn't, not right now, not until the village was cleared. So he set back on his path, leaving Milly behind, where she had been slain, in pursuit of the hand that had killed her. He may not have been able to save her, but the least he could do was cut out the heart of her killer with the very sword that she had crafted.

But he would not find that vengeance. Nor would he find any more knights, at least none that weren't dead or on the verge of death, but what he did find was heartbreaking.

He came upon Garad and Bromon on their knees, before burning rubble that was once their family home. Later, he would discover that his name-parents had been locked inside their home by the knights, the windows and doors nailed shut, before it was set alight. They had burned to death in a home built on happy memories, leaving behind a lasting image of sadness and horror. Even though he would not learn this until later, right here and now, he knew they were gone.

In shock, he edged closer to Bromon, driving Razor down into the mud, before dropping to his knees and joining his name-brothers in their silent contemplation. As he knelt on the damp soil, his mind tracked back, old memories and feelings flowing through him. He remembered how they had always treated him as their own flesh and blood. He remembered the tender touch of his mother, when she would treat his cuts and bruises picked up during scuffles with the village boys. He remembered the first time his father took him to council. Old man Pyceros had questioned his presence, stating that only the blood of the village chief should be in attendance and that his father only had two blood sons. His father had not faltered, nor did he delay. Instead, he replied with speed and the dominant tone in his voice they had been so accustomed to. He told Pyceros that he had three sons, who all had their right of place at council, and he would challenge any man who questioned otherwise. Pyceros had remained silent after that. They were fond memories, and now memories were all he had left. It was all any of them had left, aside from each other.

His heart also ached for his name-brothers, understanding all too well that they had lost actual blood relatives, their true parents, but he knew their hearts would ache for him too: his blood parents lost along with the first ten years of his life, now his name-parents taken from him as well.

"Arrrrhghhhh!"

The silence was broken by the agonising cry of a man at death's door. Arundel stirred from his thoughts and rose to his feet, his hand reclaiming Razor from her muddy prison. He tracked down the man within seconds, one bloody hand raised in the air, his mail stained in several places. His cloak, the symbol of his knighthood, lay torn in the dirt beside him. Arundel did not think, he did not consider his actions. Instead, he placed the tip of Razor against the knight's throat.

"Why?"

There was both anger and sorrow in his voice, as he asked the simple question. The knight stared up at him with shallow, pale blue eyes. He coughed and blood spluttered from his lips. Arundel pushed down a little harder, Razor's edge splitting skin.

"We...we were carrying out orders." The knight rasped as he spoke, a trickle of blood running down his left cheek into his ear. Again he coughed, choking on the blood, which bubbled at the back of his throat. But Arundel did not care for his injuries, only for his answers.

"Whose orders?"

The knight reached out with his hand, his fingers curling in their metal gauntlet just enough to form a point, the target being the crest upon his torn cloak. Arundel glanced at it, a snake coiled around an axe. He did not recognise it. He repeated his question.

"Whose orders?"

After another splattering cough, the knight rasped his bloody reply.

"King Theagran's."

He had his answer.

"P-p-please...show mercy."

The knight continued to stare at him, his fading blue eyes pleading for life. But Arundel did not see a man lying before him, nor did he feel any compassion. This knight, along with the others, had shown Milly no mercy, nor had they shown his name-parents any mercy. Therefore, he too would show no mercy. With one hard thrust, he drove Razor downwards, until her blade once again touched soil.

CHAPTER

4

He made one final thrust and then gave up. He withdrew himself from her and walked away over to his desk by the window. He could see the reflection of his naked body in the glass pane, his erection now limp, no use to man or beast. He had left her on all fours on the bed; he no longer had a use for her, his interest lost and never to be regained. Still, that did not stop the whore from trying. As she rolled into a seated position on the bed, she tweaked at her own nipple with two fingers and looked in his direction.

"Is my Grace not going to finish? Do I not satisfy my King in the way my King does me?"

He did not grant her a reply. Her velvet gave away the lies that her words tried to hide. Had she been so satisfied, then she would have been moist and smooth. Instead, she had been coarse and dry, the signs of a faker. Still she did not give up. His eyes remained fixed on the sights out of the window while he heard the padding of her bare feet across the stone floor. Outside daylight had given way to early evening darkness. Flames were being lit all around the city to illuminate its nightlife. From the Royal Chamber of the Great Palace, he could see that below the guard was changing over. Market stalls were closing up, their day's business at an end as the night's frolics were soon to begin. The crowds had moved away from the main square, now to be found queuing at the nearest cookery, inn or whorehouse, whichever took fancy first. Although the glass was thick and muffled out most of the outside noise, he could hear the faint clanging of iron on steel of a blacksmith still hard at work.

Inside the room, the whore was now beside him, her body pressed against his; her hand slid down his chest to his cock, gripping it tightly.

"Will my Grace not fill me up tonight?"

His lips remained closed and silent, while his cock remained limp in her hand.

"Is my King broken?"

She shook his manhood as she said this, and at that moment he felt his blood boil. He shoved her off with his shoulder and then with one hefty swing, he cracked her jaw with a vicious open hand slap, knocking her from her feet to the floor. He watched as the skin on her cheek began to darken, a small slit forming below the eye from which blood quickly began to seep.

"Restrain your whore tongue or I will cut it from your mouth and use it to finish what I started."

The aggression in his voice was raw and powerful. He could see the fear in her eyes as she touched a hand to her cheek and began to whimper. He hated to see such weakness, even in a whore. They were said to have the toughest skin of all the women in the realm, yet this one had broken with just one strike. He snarled at her and then turned away, his gaze now down upon the desk in front of the window.

The desk was littered with papers and parchments. There were letters of request from the surrounding realms, some seeking money loans, others seeking an alliance in a bid to strengthen themselves against their enemies. Other letters contained pleas, from the villages of Galbraxia to their King, begging him to spare them from his tyranny. But they were empty hopes because he was not a king of mercy. There was neither sympathy nor empathy within his cold, dark heart.

He brushed the letters aside, the light patter of paper landing on stone barely registering within these walls. Beneath the letters lay a map. This map covered the villages that bordered the Weeping Woods, all playing host to peasants and farmers, men and women so insignificant to the realm and yet such a trouble for their King to deal with.

His eyes glanced over some of the villages that now bore crosses marked over them, villages such as Nembledown and Yarsveld that had once dared to challenge their King and had burned as a consequence. It pleased him to know that they had suffered at his hand, just as he once had at theirs. His fingers ran across the rough surface of the paper, the ridges of the crosses sending thrills through him.

His fingers and his eyes then moved along the winding paths and open fields to another village, one by the name of Havendale. This one was marked by the silver tip of a dagger, pinning the map to the oak desk. His fingertips ran up the solid, cold steel blade to the handle fashioned from bone, the bone of a boar to be precise. It was coarse to the touch as he pressed it into his palm, his fingers slowly closing around it. With one swift tug, he released the steel from its oak prison and held it up to the fading light from the window. In one sharp movement, he sliced the blade down his arm, the skin splitting instantly as blood immediately began to flow down his wrist onto his fingers before dripping to the floor. In just one sweet moment, the blade had given him the joyous release that his balls couldn't. He stood there embracing the moment, feeling all his troubles and worries leave his body, if only temporarily.

The moment was broken by the sound of the iron latch on his door lifting and then the wooden bulk creaking open. This was followed by heavy footsteps and the clinking of a sword in its scabbard as Darvan Selwood of the Guardians of the Crown walked in. Darvan was a warrior new: barely five calendar years had passed since he had sworn fealty to the King and only mere skirmishes had so far bloodied his blade. Light stubble and scraggly hair attempted to hide his youth but failed. His boiled leather trousers and jacket barely showed signs of fading; his cloak was still vibrant and whole. Theagran looked upon the intruder in silence, for what must have felt like an age for Darvan. Moments earlier, this interruption would have been met with rage and violence. But the relief provided by the blade had drained that all away.

Darvan broke the silence.

"Pardon the intrusion, my King. I bring word that Marcasian approaches the West Gate."

He watched as Darvan's eyes flittered between him and the whore still whimpering on the floor.

"Open the gates. I will join you shortly."

He watched as Darvan nodded and bowed, before leaving the room as swiftly as he had entered it, the door slamming shut with a loud bang that startled the whore.

He turned his attention to her, the tears on her cheeks glistening in the candlelight. What to do with her, he wondered? Did he give her to his men for the night? Perhaps a gift for Marcasian upon his return? Or he could send her back to the whorehouse she had come from, where she could serve the city in her own way? They were all options, but not viable ones. He knew that a whore's tongue was good for two things: pleasing a man and spreading gossip. As the River Wine would flow into the night, so would her tales of the King's inability to finish. He could not let that be.

He approached her with a softer look in his eyes, tenderness in his touch as he brushed a tear from a cheek. Her gaze returned to his, the fear faded from her expression, the seductress replacing the scared little girl. He moved his fingers gently behind her head and pulled her close, their lips almost touching. But the only thing to touch her skin was the blade of the dagger ripping across her throat. He couldn't control the wave of fulfilment that washed over him as he watched the life drain from her eyes, once so pretty and green, now black and empty. As he released his grip, her body slumped to the floor, the blood which gushed from her throat now pooling beneath her. Death thrilled him more than sex ever could these days. He had once yearned for the sweet, damp softness of a woman's velvet, but now he yearned to take a life. It had consumed him, poisoned him. He didn't mind the change at all. As she gasped her last breath, he leaned over and whispered into her ear softly.

"It seems you have satisfied me after all."

On his approach to the West Gate, Theagran could see the riders nearing the city walls. There seemed to be fewer of them than he remembered, but at a distance and in the fading light he couldn't be sure. These were just some of the men that were fighting his war, a war he claimed Galbraxia had brought upon itself. When he had announced the murder of King Andreas to the people, and identified his son, Arundel, as the slayer, he had thought that the realm would rally behind him as their new King. Instead, the realm went into mourning.

After days of such sorrow, he had revealed his desire to breach Galbraxia's borders and invade the surrounding realms in a daring and prosperous expansion. He had hoped it would galvanise the people, his people, but instead it drove a wedge between them. Some of the villages united in an attempt to dethrone him in honour of King Andreas' memory. Men and women alike came out of the woodwork, with supposed links to the Stal family bloodline and claims to the throne. At a time when Galbraxia should have been uniting behind the banner of a serpent entwined around an axe in a bid to extend its lands, it found itself embroiled in civil war.

He had let the villages and the false claimants to the throne spill each other's blood before sending his army to kill off the scraps, bringing peace back to the lands several calendar years ago.

The damage had been done. Theagran's growing bloodlust had been joined by an ever-increasing paranoia. In his eyes, every village was a threat, maybe the other cities too. They were all uprisings just waiting to happen, unless he did something about it, so that is what he was doing. He looked upon it as purifying the realm. He was gradually sending his men to each and every village in Galbraxia. The instructions were clear: burn the village and slaughter a few as a warning to anyone who should come across it, and capture the rest. The captives were brought to Ryevale to be judged by the King himself. Should they declare fealty to the King, then they would join his numbers in whatever role they would best fulfil, but refusal would lead to execution for some, a life of slavery for the rest. Right now the realms of Xenothia and Carazan were vulnerable to invasion, but, in his present frame of mind, he could not take advantage of this until his own realm had been purged. It angered him greatly, which only served to increase his desire for death and suffering.

He watched as the men rode through the gate, each of them bowing atop their horse in acknowledgment of their King. The West Gate had become a sea of mares, stallions and geldings, armour, shiny new and battered old. Weapons were also clearly on display: swords, axes, crossbows, long bows and maces, all used to purify in the name of the King. As the ranks of soldiers trickled to an end, the captives then made their entrance. Three wagons filled with men, women and children stained with mud, dried blood and the Gods only knew what else. Some cried, some prayed, some just stared with hatred in their eyes. One little girl reached out a small hand through the bars, such an innocent young thing seeking help, or at least reassurance, but she would not find it, not from him.

As the wagons passed, he noticed one final entrant to the city. The soldier trotted in upon his white and brown stallion at a slow and meaningful pace, making sure to see his men safely home. His armour and cape matched that of the other soldiers, his Guardians. The battered steel plating was silver; the velvet cape was scarlet with splatters of crimson blood stained upon it, but the helm upon his head made him very distinctive. The steel plated craftsmanship of a bull's head could mean it was only one man, 'The Bull' Marcasian, Lord Marcasian these days.

Having taken his seat upon the throne all those years ago, Theagran had set about making changes to the structure of his court. Of the two major changes, the first was to dissolve the limitations of the Guardians. In his eyes, all of his men should dedicate their lives to protecting their King, not just a chosen few. So he had made his entire army his Guardians. Although Marcasian had remained the Captain of the Guardians, the title had lost its elite status. The other change was to abolish the role of the King's First. It was a role his family had held for generations; but he would be the last. Now the future generations that would follow would be kings and queens instead. With the Greystone bloodline promoted from the role of First to that of sovereign, he felt no other bloodline was worthy of the honour. Marcasian was the obvious choice, but he was needed on the field of battle. So it was that Theagran was the last of his bloodline to sit beside the throne and the first of his bloodline to sit upon the throne. Nevertheless, he was aware how these changes affected Marcasian and so had honoured him with the title of Lord. Of what lands he was Lord, was currently unknown. The City of Damisas belonged to Steward Wehrsley, Staverstock to Lord Kenton and Bragmout to Lord Tobiasin. This left slim pickings for the Bull. For this reason, he had offered Marcasian his choice of land from Carazan or Xenothia, should their invasion ever finally get underway.

"Lord Marcasian, a word."

He watched the Bull dismount, handing his stallion to the stable boy before trudging his way across the loose mud. With both hands, he reached up and removed the monstrous helm.

"My King."

He bowed ever so slightly, his armour rattling as steel ground on steel. Signs of age were beginning to appear on Marcasian's face, his skin dry and strained, his eyes tired. His jet black hair and beard were showing signs of fading, grey hairs fighting a winning battle. Still, he remained as ferocious as ever, perhaps even more so. This was symbolised by a deep scar that ran through his right eyebrow, down his cheek to his lip. A wound caused by a villager during the uprising all those years ago. A wound repaid in kind as Marcasian had severed all of the villager's limbs, leaving him alive just long enough to witness the butchery of his family by the Bull.

"I count fewer men returning than you took out. Was there a problem?"

Marcasian's expression did not alter.

"My scouts say that three villagers fought back, killing the men we had left behind to torch the village."

"Three villagers killed members of my Guardians? Tell me, Marcasian, are these three villagers now three rotting corpses?"

Still, Marcasian's expression did not change.

"No, my King. I saw no point going back."

Rage burned inside of him, although he struggled to contain it.

"Three villagers killed at least ten of your men and you didn't see the point in going back?"

Marcasian began to snarl, his lip curling up at the corner.

"Let the wolves tear out their throats and the crows pick at their bones; they won't survive the night."

They began to walk, Marcasian's stride dwarfing his own.

"Let's hope for your sake they don't survive. Tell me, what about my package, any news?"

"The girl makes good time; she should be here three moons from now."

He stopped in his tracks, the giant before him following suit. He then reached up and grabbed the gorget of Marcasian's armour and pulled him down a little, his anger perhaps getting the better of him.

"The scouts who saw these villagers, can they describe them?"

Marcasian replied with more of a growl in his voice.

"No, they did not wait around to make a sketch."

He let go of the armour. Marcasian immediately straightened himself up, clearly trying to rein in his own anger.

"Your humour disappoints me. They are scouts, their role is to observe. Clearly they have failed in their role, so what use are they to me? I want their heads by morning."

Marcasian's reply was one of a man towing the line once more.

"Yes, my King."

He wasn't quite done.

"Once word has been received that the package has cleared the Weeping Woods, I want you to take three of your best men and ride out to meet them."

He could see the sudden disgruntlement on Marcasian's face, as creases formed upon the latter's brow.

"Why in hell's fire do you want that? The girl travels with at least a hundred men; she has protection enough. Why send me to hold her hand?"

He stared straight into Marcasian's cold black eyes, meeting anger with anger.

"Why? Just in case they should encounter three rogue villagers, I would say makes good reason."

5

The sun warmed her cheek as it crept through the canopy of the trees overhead. She stopped for a moment to glance up towards the heavens, allowing her face to soak up the rays of the day's natural light source. She didn't stay still for long though. While she was keen to enjoy the day's sun, she knew that she had to keep a good pace. It was her desire for freedom that had led her out here alone; it was her family loyalty that would see her return to her travelling party.

Family was important to Thea, despite the distance that had separated her from it for so many years. She had lived at home for years, nestled within the walls of Ryevale with her mother and father, a time that had been so easy, so natural. Life as she knew it changed in her fifteenth year; her perfect world crumbled beneath her and she had no way to stop it. First came the death of her mother, murdered one cold night outside of The Velvet Purse, Ryevale's most prosperous brothel. It was a blade that had brought about her end, thrust multiple times into various parts of her torso with such anger and savagery. Her killer was chased down and put to justice by two of the Guardians later that night, but the damage had been done. Not only was her mother dead, but her good name had been soiled.

Thea wondered what had led her mother to such a place that night. The story told was that she had turned to selling herself in secrecy, her inner whore winning out over her marriage vows. Thea's father seemed to accept such an explanation, but Thea differed. She knew in her heart that the truth had been buried beneath a lie. She knew that her mother was devoted to her father, that she was as good and pure as any maiden fair the old tales spoke of, but Thea was just one voice and so her cries for the truth were muffled by the booming monotony of the lie.

Thea's grief had barely dug its trench within her heart, when her father told her she was leaving the city. Thea had never been a typical girl; she had preferred wooden swords to dolls, mud and sweat to perfumes and jewellery. This had concerned her father, who desperately wanted her to blossom into a true lady, while she had wanted to become the first female knight of the realm. With her mother gone, her father felt she needed a womanly influence in her life, someone who could mould her into the woman he was so keen for her to be. So it was that he decided to send her to the city of Staverstock and the House of Aleesona, a school renowned for making the perfect woman out of wayward girls. She had pleaded with her father not to send her there. She had begged until her throat was raw, for him to keep her at home by his side, but his mind was not for changing. Even to this day, she remembered those heart-breaking moments when her pleas fell upon deaf ears.

"Father, please let me stay with you. I don't want to go away. Please, Father, you are all I have."

Her heartfelt words had been accompanied by a steady flow of tears, but that would not sway her father. As she clung tightly to his hand in hope, his emotionless reply caused those hopes to crumble.

"My mind is made up. You leave on the 'morrow and I will hear no more of it."

He had then wrenched his hand from hers and made his exit from the room in silence, taking with him any chance for her to enjoy what remained of her teenage years. So, with a heavy heart, she showed her loyalty and devotion to her father and obeyed his command. She had set off that very next day, destined to stay away for long years, but now, in the twenty-second year of life, she found herself embarking on the journey home.

They had set out from Staverstock two weeks ago, ready for

the long journey ahead. It had been a bright sunny day, the first for several months, and she had remarked to one of the stable boys that the arrival of the sun reflected the happiness she felt, knowing she was returning home. Sister Naygova had picked out a plain white satin dress, with a rose embroidered onto the breast, for her to wear at the start of her journey, and supplied a case packed with enough dresses to keep her clothed for at least two months. Sister Caradon had provided a gold crested box of jewellery that they claimed 'illuminated her features' and would make her the beauty of Ryevale. Sister Bartol, on the other hand, had seen her off with nothing but words:

"You came here a wretch, but are leaving us a lady. Make us proud."

For many, they would have been words of inspiration, but not for her. For the past seven years, the Sisters of Aleesona had tried their hardest to mould her into something she wasn't; to change her from all that she had ever known and all that she had ever been. They had tried to wear her down, to beat her natural instincts out of her. They put special effort into her and, now she was leaving, they truly believed that they had been a success, but what they didn't know was that the one thing Thea had learned from the Sisters was how to act. She learned how to put on a show to please them. She learned how to convince them that their methods were working, that they were truly transforming her from tomboy to fully-fledged lady. It meant that they paid less attention to her.

It meant they never discovered the late night escapes she would make to the nearby village of Crackendon where she would train for hours with a sword, helped by one of the village hunters known as Maxillian. He wasn't the most highly rated of the hunters, but he knew how to handle a blade. Night after night, he would put her through her paces, treating her no differently just because she was a woman. She had been keen to learn and he had been keen to teach. In return for his skills, she had taught him how to read and write, a skill not commonly found in Crackendon. He had wanted more from her and she knew it, but she had also known that she would never give it to him. His skill with a sword was all that had interested her and was all that she took from him.

So it was that the travelling party had set off under the first sunshine in weeks; a group of sixty knights, both young and old in service, twelve merchant men tasked with trading on behalf of the Sisters, four handmaids assigned to her service, an ox-pulled wagon full of bread, hams, cheeses and wines for the trip, and little old her, seated in her carriage of white painted oak and gold trim.

Their first stop had been in Crackendon and it was here that Thea had traded some of her jewellery for a suitable sword and dagger that would help provide her own protection. Two nights later, they would stop in the town of Morkington where the dresses were traded for more suitable attire for a woman of her style. From there, it had been nothing but the open air and Mother Nature's world. The days were spent sitting inside her carriage suffering from boredom, listening to the pathetic stories of her maids and their hopes of one day kissing Samron, the baker's son. The nights were spent camped out underneath the stars with her maids incessantly huddling together for warmth. The sun had departed on more than one occasion, leaving behind dark clouds and the occasional downpour for company.

Needless to say, after two weeks of travel, she had certainly had her fill and needed a change.

"But, m'lady, there could be dangers out there. It is not safe."

Those had been the words of one of her maids, a young girl by the name of Lileth, barely into her fifteenth year, whose innocence was hidden behind a mop of dark brown locks of hair. She chose to ignore Lileth, just as her father had ignored her seven years ago, and jumped out of the carriage, as it was still moving. From what she could count, at least seven of the knights had given chase but with all of their armour weighing them down, they had been easy to lose. Her pursuers no longer in sight, here she was walking through the wildlife of the Weeping Woods on her own, finally a bit of change in her life.

Today she had donned a white chemise, navy bodice with lace, boiled leather trousers and ox hide boots, much more suitable attire than one of the dresses that had been provided by the Sisters. Her flame red hair was tied up into a bun and held in place by lace netting. Her sword was buckled at her waist, the dagger hidden down her boot. The sword was nothing special, a slightly worn blade and very plain hilt. It wouldn't win any sword of the year competitions, but she trusted it would fulfil its role when called upon.

"If only the Sisters could see me now," she thought to herself. It amused her to think of their reaction, to picture their faces and the shock that would be upon them. All of a sudden, after seven years of being trapped, the sense of freedom bubbled up inside Thea and burst out in the form of her voice.

"I will never be changed...NEVER!"

It felt so good to say that and, more so, to believe it. Her father may have something to say about it, but what could he do? Send her back? Clearly the past seven years hadn't worked, so why would another seven? No, he would just have to deal with it; at least that was what she told herself, but Ryevale was another two days' ride from here and those thoughts could wait. For now, she wanted to enjoy the freedom and beauty that lay before her. She could hear the light rustling of the trees as they danced in the breeze. The earth below her feet was solid and strong, the grass and various plants growing from it brushed against her body as she passed through them.

She was not alone as she walked. One moment a butterfly would land on a nearby leaf, the next there would be birds flying overhead. She recognised one of them to be a sparrow, or at least she thought it was. There had also been rabbits, a deer and a wild dog throughout various stages of the day. It all made such a change to her to be out on her own and to be seeing something different, something new. She felt good, she felt alive.

"Well, what do we have here?"

She watched as the owner of the voice that had just spoken emerged from the undergrowth and, at that moment, she knew that things were about to take a turn for the worse.

"A little lost are we, girl?"

The man was scruffily dressed, his tattered clothing stained with mud, among other things. But it was his face that stood out more than anything else, particularly the partially ruptured boil that adorned the majority of his left cheek.

"Not at all."

She put strength in her voice as she replied, but even so she could tell that Boil Face wasn't buying it, his mouth curling at the corners into a sneer.

"Now, now, little girl, no need to tell tales. We are all friends here!"

He chortled at the end of that remark, a sound she thought resembled a boar munching its way through its daily feed. But what really concerned her was his use of the word 'we'. Was he not alone? It was a question that was swiftly answered.

"Come on, boys. The little girl is clearly not afraid."

There was a further rustling and then, to her horror, three more dirt-stained scabs, that claimed to be men, emerged from the undergrowth and positioned themselves in front of her in a slight arc. Just like Boil Face, these three had clearly not seen a bath in a long time, evident not only from their dress but the pungent smell that assaulted her nostrils. The one, who positioned himself to the left of Boil Face, looked as if he could be quite handsome under all the grime. Surely no older than his twentieth year, she wondered how he had fallen into such lowly company as Boil Face.

"Are you sure she's not scared? She looks scared to me."

"Why, looks can be so deceiving, Brax. Isn't that right, girly?"

Boil Face had identified the one immediately to his right as Brax, a short stumpy pig of a man who held a spiked mace in his hand. She thought it best to hide her concerns as well as she could.

"Why should I fear, sir? After all, we are merely just exchanging conversation, are we not?"

"I say not. Brax is right, she is scared and I say we give her good reason to be. Let me have her."

Boil Face had held his tongue; instead it was the one next to Brax who had chosen to air his view. He edged forward, his fingers gripping a rather worn looking dagger, more likely to kill you with some form of disease it might carry than the sharpness of its blade.

"The things that old Sick Sanh could do to you, my pretty. Would you like to find out? Would you like me to make you scream?"

Sick Sanh edged his way forward while Brax, Boil Face and the handsome one stayed where they were. It was now that Thea realised her words would be of no use. It was time she put her training to the test, as her hand fumbled for the hilt of her sword.

"I would rather make you scream, sir."

Her words said and her fingers gripped firmly round the hilt of her sword, she began to remove it from its sheath. But before she could release it fully, she felt the cold tip of steel press against the skin of her neck.

"Tut tut, I wouldn't do that."

She froze instantly, her hand still gripped firmly on the hilt of her sword, but her heart beginning to pound in her chest. She felt the owner of the blade press up against her back. Although she could not see who it was, the voice indicated a male. A hand then slid round the left side of her body and took hold of the wrist of her hand still gripping the sword. The hand was rotten in places, the skin withered and dry. The nails were a mixture of yellow and brown with most of them cracked and broken, while one or two were practically gone altogether. The voice spoke again.

"Let go, little butterfly."

His breath warmed her ear and stung her nose; it reeked of rotting turnip as far as she could tell. This was an improvement from the rest of his bodily stench, which smelt as though he had spent the night rolling around in horse manure. Still, her grip loosened and he pulled her hand away from the hilt. The sword slipped back into its sheath with a gentle thud and whacked against her leg. The pain was brief, as she was drawn back to the cold steel blade pressed against her throat.

"Good little butterfly," he whispered to her in a voice meant to reassure her, yet the blade remained firmly pressed against her skin.

"Looks like Griswald Greyteeth 'as got me a pretty little butterfly t' play with."

Brax and Boil Face sniggered loudly, while Sick Sanh pleaded his case.

"Give her to me, Griswald. I ain't had me some fresh meat in days."

He licked his lips and edged closer, pushing his way through the undergrowth. The free arm of Griswald suddenly reached back around and grabbed her by the front of her bodice, pulling her back tightly against him.

"Not a chance," Griswald rasped, his spit spraying against the side of her face. His hand moved downwards and grabbed her tightly between her thighs, catching her by surprise. If only she could get herself free. In her mind she was drawing her sword and severing Griswald's wandering hand from his arm, as his blood spattered against the leaves of the foliage around them. But that was in her mind. In reality she was still trapped in his clutches with no way to break free.

"This one still 'as 'er maiden's head if ol' Griswald ain't mistaken. That means she belongs to me first."

She could hold her tongue no longer, for words were all she had left to use.

"I would rather die," she told him.

"Oh you will, little butterfly, but not until we's all had our go."

Sick Sanh piped up again.

"Seconds is mine, the rest o' you bastards gotta wait your turn."

He pointed at Brax and Boil Face, only his finger kept on moving, as she now realised that two more men had joined the group. Before she could get a proper look at the two new arrivals, Griswald let go of her crotch and grabbed her face hard, his fingers digging into her right cheek and his thumb digging into her left, causing her lips to purse. He tilted her head slightly and now his turnip breath thickened against the hairs of her nostrils.

"Do you know why they calls me Griswald Greyteeth? It's because my teeth's gone grey from gnawing on t' bones of little butterflies like you."

He began to snigger before running his coarse tongue up the side of her face. She squirmed, but he just pressed the blade a little tighter against her throat.

"There must be others, Griswald."

A different voice spoke, one that carried with it the sound of concern. Griswald let go of her face so that her head tilted back down, enabling her to see her captives again.

"What do you mean others?"

Griswald's voice did not seem to share the concern. However, now she could see that it was Brax who had begun this conversation.

"Look at her, there's no way she is out here all alone. She will be travelling with others."

Griswald did not agree.

"She looks as alone as alone can be to me."

Brax stepped forward, pushing Sick Sanh aside, so he could make his point in clear view.

"Trust me, Griswald, there will be others and they will be looking for her."

Griswald pulled Thea tightly to him, his fingers digging into the skin of her arm.

"Is that so, little butterfly?"

She wanted to nod but the blade would have scraped the skin on her neck.

"Yes, many others and when they find me, they will kill all of you."

She had hoped to instil fear in Griswald, but it didn't work. Instead he began to howl with laughter, as he pressed the blade in a little harder. She knew he had pierced the skin when a warm droplet of blood trickled down her neck.

"Is that so? Then I better gets to having you now so I can be ready for 'em."

His grip tightened and she knew this was it. She would put up a fight – that was a guarantee. She would bite, scratch, claw, kick and punch for her life. But she knew that there were at least six of them and that was just too much for her. She also knew that, while her escort would be looking for her, the chances of them finding her now were extremely remote.

Perhaps this was karma. Perhaps this was the world paying her back for the years she had spent defying the Sisters. But surely that didn't equate to this? Surely her sneaking out of a night for a little swordplay didn't deserve the horrors that Griswald Greyteeth and his friends had in store for her? Suddenly the fear Thea had tried to contain hit her hard. It took the air from her lungs and she couldn't breathe. Griswald was pulling at her hard, but yet at first she didn't notice when it stopped. She barely noticed his grip loosen. Nor did she notice the arrow as it whistled past her. But she did notice it when it buried itself right between the eyes of one of the new arrivals. Blood began to flow down his frozen face, before he slumped to the floor with a thud.

Suddenly panic was rife, but now it found home in her captors, not her. Griswald stood his ground, making sure to hold her fast while Brax, Sick Sanh, Boil Face, the handsome one and the other new arrival stumbled about, looking all around them for the source of the approaching threat. Griswald was screaming in her ear, but she did not hear him. She was too busy watching the melee unfolding before her. The fact is, while this group of miscreants might be thieves, rapists and murderers, they were clearly not soldiers. There was no organisation, no co-ordination and no control. At a time when even she knew that they should be regrouping, coming together as one to form a defensive strategy, this band of misfits were doing the exact opposite, breaking apart from each other, whilst on the edge of hysteria.

It was this lack of organisation that was the undoing of the remaining new arrival. Such panic had consumed him that he failed to see the giant axe until it was cutting through his left shoulder. The axe blade tore the man almost in two as he died in a mixture of screams and blood. Could this be her escort? She didn't remember any of them carrying axes, at least not ones as large and devastating as this one. But if not them, then who could these possible rescuers be? Brax and Boil Face had now come together, standing shoulder to shoulder, facing away from her, while Sick Sanh picked up a mace from one of the fallen. The handsome one had vanished from view, until she noticed his body face first in the grass, with an arrow in the back of his head. Brax was the next of them to die, with the tip of a sword bursting through his back, close to his spine. She was astonished by the strength and sharpness of the blade: it then ripped out through Brax's side, splattering blood everywhere, intestines spilling onto the muddy ground, swiftly followed by his now lifeless body. However, the sword was not finished, now slicing up the front of Boil Face. When Boil Face staggered round to face her, she could see the agony in his eyes, a gash to his very core running from hip to collar bone. Sick Sanh could only watch as Boil Face crumpled into a heap on top of Brax, his blood oozing from his body. She could sense the fear now in Griswald, as his muscles tensed and his breathing picked up pace. She could feel a small vibration against her back and she quickly realised it was the pounding of Griswald's heart.

Sick Sanh was a man tottering on the edge and he clearly knew it. Swinging the mace around his head, he repeatedly screamed.

"Show yourselves and die, fuckers!"

Sanh got his wish, at least the first part of it, when three men emerged from the dense undergrowth to surround him.

The first of them was an archer, a man of slender build but athletically so. In his hand he carried a bow, while upon his back he wore a quiver half covered in fur. His boiled leathers had seen fresher days, that was abundantly clear. His face was clean-shaven, with a mop of thick black hair just covering his ears. The second and largest of the three was the source of the axe. This man screamed raw power, with arms and legs thicker than she had ever seen, built of iron muscles that were required to wield such a ferocious weapon. His clothes were tight to his body and his bald head and snarl gave him a look of anger. He towered over the archer and eclipsed him in width also; but it was the last of them that held her gaze: the swordsman. His long fair hair and blond beard partially concealed a handsome face. His body was hidden beneath boiled leathers and wool, and in his hand he held a sword of craftsmanship so beautiful she almost questioned whether it were real. The hilt bore the head of an eagle while wings caressed the blade, which glistened despite the gloom.

Sick Sanh was clearly not as taken by the trio as she was. Still waving the mace high above his head, he surveyed the three men surrounding him before letting out another cry.

"Death t' you fucking dogs."

With that, he charged towards the archer. Thea watched as the archer moved with a speed and lightness of foot, the likes of which she had never seen before. In the blink of an eye, he had drawn an arrow from his quiver and loosed it in the direction of the onrushing Sick Sanh. The arrow thumped into the right shoulder of Sanh, stopping him in his tracks and weakening his grip on the handle of the mace. The weapon fell to the floor with a thud. Sick Sanh reached up to the arrow with his left hand and snapped the end off, tossing it to the ground as he smiled his grisly smile at the archer. Suddenly he staggered back a step, when the swordsman swung his eagle sword from behind Sanh and the blade sliced clean through the back of his left knee. Almost in slow motion, she watched the leg below the knee slowly topple to the floor, now severed from the thigh. Losing his balance, Sanh fell to the floor. Blood spattered everywhere. While the three men closed in, Sanh sat himself up, blood flowing from his stump and adding more stains to the grass around it. He was dying, but still he continued to screech.

"I will fucking kill all o' ya and then...then...I'll fuck the wench."

Those were the last twisted words that Sick Sanh would ever speak. The axe man brought his giant axe down into his skull, splitting his head in two. Sanh's body slumped among the flowers as the three men turned to face her. She could feel Griswald's grip tighten on her arm, but for the first time the blade wasn't so tight against her neck. Griswald was all alone and on the verge of death, and he knew it.

The swordsman broke the silence, when he spoke in a soft and tender tone that caught her by surprise.

"Let the lady go and we are done here."

The maiden could feel Griswald hesitate. If he did it once more, she would take advantage; she had to.

"Stay back or she dies."

Again the swordsman spoke.

"There is no need for any more bloodshed. Let her go and walk away with your life."

It was a fair deal, more than she felt Griswald deserved.

"You won't let Griswald Greyteeth go. She's mine, she comes with Griswald."

No sooner had he finished, than she noticed another hesitation. Seizing on the opportunity, she made her move. She stamped down hard on his right foot before driving her elbows into his ribcage. She heard a groan as she knocked the wind out of Griswald and the blade lowered from her throat. She then ducked out of the way as the archer loosed an arrow, which pierced Griswald's chest. Now she moved quickly, drawing her sword from its scabbard and thrusting it forward into the gut of Griswald. She held it there for a moment, staring into his evil dark green eyes to make sure that hers was the last face that he would see in life. Withdrawing the blade, she watched warm blood seep out and within a moment saw Griswald fell to the floor. This was the first time that she had seen what Griswald Greyteeth actually looked like. A dishevelled runt of a man, his face was littered with scars, his clothing nothing but rags, but the one thing that stood out, the one thing that really caught her eyes, as Griswald Greyteeth died right there before her, was just how grey his teeth truly were.

CHAPTER

6

It was on the eve of the third day that they first caught a glimpse of Ryevale. As the light was fading and the stars were beginning to awaken in the darkening sky, the white tip of the Great Palace emerged just above the brow of the furthest hill way beyond the valley before them. The palace towers were reaching up so high, they looked as though they could spear the moon as soon as it arose from its slumber.

It was the first time that Arundel had looked upon those white walls. Truth be told, it was so far away and so small that it was more of a tiny white blur, but in his mind he could picture those walls, an immaculate white and covered in some of the finest stone carvings the world had ever seen. He imagined depictions of the finest knights riding the finest horses, slaying dragons and saving maidens. Those were the stories he had heard when he was younger, told by some of the village children who had visited the city.

He would have to wait a while longer before he could see how accurate those stories were, for right now the Great Palace was a tiny white blip on the horizon, but despite this, he still found himself fixated by it. He had never seen it before, yet he couldn't shake off the feeling that had engulfed him. It was a feeling of familiarity, a feeling of warmth. He didn't know why he felt this way, but this sensation was dominating him. He stayed on his horse, Tyranos, his eyes transfixed on those white walls, while the last fragments of sunlight dissipated and the white walls vanished into the shadows. Yet still his gaze would not shift, until he was startled by a hefty and firm slap to the back. When he turned round, he could see Garad standing beside him, his bow hooked over his shoulder, his bloodstained hand clasping four dead rabbits, whilst the hand that had slapped his back now rested on the rump of Tyranos.

"Ari, it will be there tomorrow. Come and join us. The fires are lit and rabbit stew is in the offing."

He held up the rabbits and shook them as if to emphasise his point.

"What, no boar? You are slipping, brother."

Garad took the bait, as Arundel knew he would.

"Boar is easy, big and fat makes for a larger target. Rabbit is a skill, lest you forget that."

He watched as Garad turned and walked away, seeking out someone he could impress with his archery skills. Arundel left him to it; he was sure that Garad would find himself a serving girl, who would be much more obliging. Besides, he had plans of his own: the redhead.

Two hours had passed and the redhead had been nowhere to be seen. Lady Thea Oakwood she had called herself, three days ago, when they had saved her from the bandits. She had given them a name and a thank you, but not much more. Their eyes had met more than once, just brief glances that neither of them had planned for the other to see, but that had ended the moment they had found her travelling party. The foot soldiers had surrounded them and held them at pike point, while a knight, who had introduced himself as Sir Naven Henderley, had ridden up to them at speed. He had begun to question their purpose, until Lady Thea had set him straight.

"These brave men saved me, Sir Henderley. You should be thanking them, not accusing them."

Sir Naven Henderley clearly hated being put in his place by a woman. He sat astride his horse, wearing his perfectly buffed armour plating, with a black cape attached to the right shoulder, and the left side plate bearing the mark of what Arundel later discovered was the Guardians of the Crown. The knight's helm was suspended by rope from his horse's saddle. Even his horse wore protective armour over its face and a black silk rug covered its body underneath the leather saddle that bore the King's crest. However, all the pomp and circumstance could not hide his disdain at Lady Thea putting him right.

Eventually, Sir Henderley was able to grumble a response.

"Very well, m'lady. On behalf of the crown, I give the three of you my thanks for your bravery."

Arundel had enjoyed watching the knight squirm, before providing his own response.

"Your thanks are not needed, sir. But a share of your food and mead would be greatly appreciated."

Sir Henderley nodded and tightened his grip on his reins, ready to move on.

"Very well then, take what you need and be on your way."

Before he could reply, the redhead spoke again.

"Actually, Sir Henderley I was thinking that they could escort us back to Ryevale, where I am sure that my father would like to thank them personally. Besides, three extra fighting men would not be a bad thing, wouldn't you agree?"

There was that look of disdain again.

"We thank you for your offer, m'lady, but my name-brothers and I have other business to attend to," responded Arundel.

Lady Thea stared at him, her eyes sparkling emeralds that seemed to draw him in. Right there and then he would have gone anywhere with her if she so desired, but such a journey, merely for a thank you they did not need, was unnecessary.

"Is it such important business that you have no time to spare for your King? After all, I am sure King Theagran would also like to reward you for keeping the daughter of one of his lords safe."

He heard the words but could not respond. He was swimming in those emerald eyes and couldn't find a way out. He had heard Bromon's booming voice thunder past him, accepting the invitation, but still did not snap out of his trance until Bromon's thick hand grabbed his shoulder and yanked him back hard.

"Come, brother, we have used up enough of the lady's time for one day."

That had been three days ago. Three days of travelling and he had barely seen the redhead since. Just a few fleeting moments here and there, brief glimpses as she had stepped in and out of her carriage. They had been three long days and so, in the grand scheme of things, another two hours was barely a hardship. Nonetheless, he had given up his search and so, with a mixture of rabbit stew and mead to warm his belly, he had retired to his resting place for the night.

Unlike the rest of the travelling party, he had refrained from tucking himself away inside a tent. Instead, he had pitched up against the largest tree he could find and hung a cutting of ox hide over the branches, providing cover overhead and on both sides, but leaving the front open. He did this for defensive reasons. He had no idea where he had learned it from; it was just something that had always been in his head, ever since his name-parents had found him. By having an opening at the front, he could see his enemies approaching and would be ready for any sudden attack. Certainly, it did nothing to keep out the evening chill, but it put him at ease. He had brought a cup of mead with him and, after knocking that back, he decided to get some sleep. Laying himself down, he tucked Razor beside him and then covered himself in a fur blanket he had borrowed from one of the supply wagons. His eyes heavy with sleep, he lay there thinking of hair as red as fire.

His dream was very different. He was trapped at the top of a tower with no way of escaping, a pack of wild beasts tearing up the stairs towards the room he was locked in. He had nothing to defend himself with: his trusted sword was absent from his hand. He looked around desperately for anything he could use, but the room was sparsely furnished. It wasn't long before the beasts were at the door, banging over and over again. Slowly the door began to crack and finally burst open. As it did and the beasts flowed through the door in endless numbers, he found himself jolting awake. The stone walls of the tower had gone, replaced by the solid trunk of the tree and the ox hide, slowly swaying in the light breeze.

The night was dark but the moon was bright, accompanied

by a canvas of stars to cut through the darkness with the softest of light. Glancing round, he noticed that there was no sign of any of the campfires that had been scattered around prior to his slumber. Even his small fire had burned itself out and now it merely smouldered. He registered the slight drop in temperature and pulled the fur a little tighter around his body. He was also struck by the silence that surrounded him. The chattering, the raucous laughter and shouts of the drunkards had ceased. Not even the chirping of a bird could be heard; the world seemed at peace.

Slowly he began to slip back into his dreams, but then he heard it, the snap of a twig and the flutter of wings. He was wide awake now and he clearly wasn't alone. Slowly, he brushed the fur aside. He then grasped Razor tightly in his hand, as he edged himself quietly into a seated position. All he could do now was sit there and listen. He waited.

It wasn't long before he could just make out the sound of footsteps. They were faint, but they were definitely there and creeping closer. He continued to wait in silence, Razor in his hand, ready to greet whatever was about to face him. Within minutes it came, emerging from the left of his line of sight, nothing more than a solid shadow. With his free hand, he reached out and grabbed it firmly, pulling it towards him. The shadow fell onto his lap with a thud that jolted his body. But he kept his grip as he brought Razor up and pressed it against the shadow. He had expected a barrage of abuse, perhaps a gravelly voice cursing him. Maybe even a tussle of strength as the shadow tried to fight its way free, but he experienced none of that. Instead a shrill shriek and a high- pitched voice crying "Stop!" was all that greeted him and Razor.

The moonlight glistened on the cold hard steel of Razor's blade and his eyes followed it all the way up to the tip, which was pressed against the pale white flesh of a neck. He worked his way up the neck to a face shrouded in a black velvet cloak. He had expected to see the savage and weary face of a sword for hire, with eyes black as coal, a mouth permanently curled into a snarl and perhaps one or two scars. Instead, the face that stared back at him was one of beauty. Lips voluptuous and vibrant, skin soft as satin, emerald eyes like pools that he could swim in for hours. He knew those eyes; he had been lost in them once before. There was something else he had seen before: curling down the surface of the cloak, a lock of hair, as red as fire.

He released his grip and pulled back the hood, seeking confirmation. As the velvet hood slipped away, he saw that the one curled lock belonged to a whole head of flame red hair.

"A little lost are we, Lady Thea?"

She pulled free from him and sat up abruptly, pulling the hood back up to hide her identity.

"Please don't say my name. If they knew I was here, you would be in a lot of trouble."

Arundel sniggered.

"I think given the racket you made, they would already know. Besides, soldiers or not, I do not fear them."

She shook her head and let out a gentle sigh.

"You men and your bravado. Against one or two men you might be fine, but against an army you would be like a lamb to the slaughter. Would you really want that?"

He glanced at Razor in his hand, as he dug the tip into the earth and then looked back at those emerald eyes.

"Sometimes it's worth taking the risk."

He saw it for just a moment; her lips curved ever so slightly into a smile, her cheeks blushed a gentle red. Then, within an instant, it was gone, buried somewhere deep down beneath the surface, leaving behind the straight face of a Lady and it was one that was hard for him to read.

"I hope that your skills with that fancy sword of yours match up to your arrogance, for we may need them before the journey's end."

Her face was inscrutable as stone, making him doubt whether he had ever seen that smile, brief as it had been.

"It is not arrogance, m'lady. But I must ask, did you fight your way through the brambles in the dead of night just to insult me?"

He stared at her, hoping for the return of that smile, and her expression did alter. It softened a little, but the smile remained absent.

"No, indeed not. I must say that I am intrigued by you, Arundel. There is something about you that I find so familiar, yet I do not know you. But you are not like your brothers, that much I do know."

He nodded as he slowly rotated Razor in his hand, the tip of the blade cutting swirls in the dirt.

"They are my name-brothers since the age of ten, but our bond is as strong as blood."

"Yes, I can see that too. But what of your true parents? Your natural siblings?"

He felt himself pulling away a little, knowing that the conversation was heading down a path lost to him.

"I have no recollection of them. But if you wished to know my life story, you could have waited until daylight. So, again, I must ask you, what brings you here?"

Now Thea was the one to pull away a little, as he could tell she had become a little hesitant.

"My maid Saffrain, she tells me that we are on the outskirts of the Wendel Valley where men and women paint themselves blue."

He knew of them.

"You are talking about the Seekers."

He had heard of them but never actually encountered them.

"Saffrain tells me that they are known to hunt at night and a travelling party, such as ours, would be their ideal target for slaughter."

"Saffrain is right, to a degree. Some are known to venture out looking for prey, but only to survive. However, this travelling party would be a target for them because they hate King Theagran, and these men bear his banners."

He pointed towards her chest as her eyes followed. His finger was pointing at the crest of a serpent entwined around an axe embroidered upon her velvet cloak.

"You too wear his mark, so I can understand why you are afraid."

That hit a nerve. The soft face hardened, taking on a mask of bravado.

"I am not afraid. But I do value my life, and something inside me is telling me that I am safer here with you than if I was in my carriage, surrounded by the Guardians."

A compliment, and with it another glimpse of that heart-melting smile. He returned, with a smile of his own.

"My lady, now it is you who speaks of arrogance on my behalf; but I can't guarantee your safety."

She leaned in a little closer to him, her cheek close to his, her breath warm on his neck. She smelt sweet like honey, as her words became a little softer.

"I will take my chances. Oh, and please, call me Thea."

Suddenly, she pulled back from him. His fur blanket swiftly followed, caressing her shoulder. She clutched it tightly, pulling it against her body.

"That will keep you warm enough, m'lady; sorry, Thea."

She lay down, the fur now engulfing her, where it had barely covered his muscular frame.

"What about you?"

He pondered that question for a moment, contemplating his answer carefully. He wanted to tell her that there was room enough for two; that he wanted to bury himself in the roaring fire of her hair; to taste her. However, he opted for a safer answer.

"I will stay awake and see that you are safe, until the return of the sun."

While Thea slept, he sat and kept watch, his back pressed firmly against the tree just like when he was ten, only now there were no ties binding him. He held out until the first signs of the sun, at which point his eyes became so heavy the Gods themselves would not have been able to keep them open. When he awoke, the last shreds of the night sky had slipped away and so, he discovered, had Thea.

The party had packed up camp and got back on the move

within an hour of the sun's new life. After clearing the final limits of the Weeping Woods, they moved on into the Wendel Valley.

Unlike the previous days, Arundel found himself riding separately from his name-brothers, leaving them to their own devices, while he rode as close to Lady Thea's carriage as he possibly could. Every now and then, he would steal a glimpse of her beauty whenever she leaned out of her carriage and spared a glance his way. He was easy to spot, riding among the supply wagons, which were pulled by horses that in turn were led by men on foot. He and his name-brothers might be guests of the Lady Thea, but the Guardians did not want them around and this had been made abundantly clear. This had led to him playing a game of shadows, trying to stay as close as possible to Thea's carriage, while at the same time keeping his distance from the eight Guardians posted as the carriage's personal escort. Thus he came to be among the supply wagons.

This changed slightly when the entire party ground to a halt deep into the valley. Murmurings rumbled through the group as to the reason for this sudden stop, but Arundel ignored them all because he knew the cause. While others spoke, he sat in silence waiting. It wasn't long before the sound of hooves could be heard, cutting across the mud and grass. Within no time at all, one of the Guardians came into view, riding at speed along the train of people in front of him before coming to a stop at Arundel's side. The man looked as fresh as the daisies scattered around the inclines of the valley. His armour was shiny and showed barely a scratch; his clothing was neatly kept and a scraggly brown moustache failed to hide a young face.

"Outlander, round up the rest of your kin; you are needed."

Before long, Arundel had Bromon and Garad by his side as they rode to the front of the train. It was here that they found Sir Henderley astride his mount, his eyes a little more sunken than on their previous encounter.

"Ah good, the Outlanders. We are in need of your services, just as Lady Thea had predicted."

Arundel barely even slowed down, easing his pace just enough to say his piece so that Sir Henderley could hear it.

"Spare it, I know what is needed."

With that he continued on, leaving behind Sir Henderley, with a flushed look upon his face. As they put some distance between them and the train, Bromon turned to him.

"Care to enlighten us at any time?"

Arundel looked towards his name-brother and smiled, before pointing towards a plume of smoke rising into the pale blue sky.

"We are nearing the settlement of the Seekers."

Bromon looked none the wiser. Give him an axe and he could fight an army single handed, but give him knowledge and watch him crumble.

"Seekers? Who by the name of the Gods are they?"

It was a fair question with a lengthy answer.

"Sky worshippers. They worship the Goddess Anyeama. For centuries, they lived across the sea in the Forgotten Lands high up in the mountains, as close to Anyeama as they could be, but they were forced to abandon their home after a plague spread through the settlement and so they set out seeking a new home, as well as newly found knowledge along the way. Their journey is largely unknown, but what is known is that they arrived at the great walls of Ryevale during the reign of King Andulan III. Though his advisers urged him to turn them away, King Andulan opened his gates and the Seekers settled at last. For generations, they have served the kingdom, seeking out new knowledge such as new ways to fight, to build and to create. Every step forward the realm has made has been because the Seekers discovered something new and brought it back to share with their king."

He glanced at Bromon and Garad, as they both looked back at him with interest. Garad then spoke up.

"So how did they end up out here and why are we riding out to them?"

The smoke was growing closer with every step they took. Arundel glanced up at either side of the valley, searching for any sign of scouts, but there were none to be seen.

"Well, when Theagran assumed the throne, for reasons only

known to him, he exiled the Seekers. When they refused to leave, he had a few of them rounded up and executed to make his point to the rest. The Seekers were in need of a home once again and have settled in this valley just outside of the city of Damisas. They would have gone to Damisas itself, but Theagran decreed that anyone who gave them shelter was an enemy of the Crown. It is said that they have split into several clans throughout the valley and beyond, but this was the first settlement built. That brings us to now. To reach Ryevale we must first pass through a valley occupied by the Seekers who, due to Theagran's actions, feel nothing but hatred for our travelling companions and they hold the tactical advantage over us, courtesy of these hills. As neutral Outlanders, we have been sent to negotiate safe passage."

This ruffled Bromon's feathers.

"If these Seekers want to spill a little blood, then I say let them. Hell, I will even lend them my axe!"

Arundel leaned over and placed a hand on Bromon's massive bulk of a shoulder.

"I agree, but that is not the way it will be. You know this."

Bromon snarled, his hands gripping the reins so tightly that Arundel thought they might rip, before the axe man eventually lowered his head in surrender.

"Aye, I know. But how do you know all this?"

"Old Ramund used to teach me the ways of the world and Milly often told me tales that she had heard from her days living in the city."

Knowledge was as powerful as his sword and so he had endeavoured to learn as much as he could of both.

"Okay, Ari, if you know so much, why are they blue?"

Garad was indicating ahead of them as he spoke. Looking up, Arundel discovered what Garad was talking about.

Standing before them was a woman, who looked like she had seen at least sixty name days. Her chest was bare with two ample size breasts sagging down to her stomach. The lower part of her body was covered by a skirt fashioned from reeds. On her feet were sandals with twining that ran up her ankles. However, what really stood out was the fact that her entire body was painted sky blue; even her long, scraggy hair was dyed blue. Upon her chest, she bore two painted white eyes, with a white wing either side. In her hand, she held a wooden staff, taller than she was.

Within moments, she was joined by two more blue women, much younger and with white togas covering their bodies. The elder woman spoke, "Yorrall will see you now. He has been expecting you."

Arundel dismounted from his horse, giving her a little fuss behind the ears as he did so. Garad and Bromon were about to follow suit, when the elder woman slammed her staff into the earth with a soft thud and then pointed at Arundel.

"Just you."

Garad and Bromon were not happy, but he gave them a reassuring nod before following the elder woman.

She led him up a narrow path, worn into the hillside over time, a track of dust and stones that looked lost amid a grass sea. The path twisted and turned as it gradually climbed. He wondered if they were heading to the very top, when suddenly they emerged into a clearing cut deep into the hillside, invisible to the eye from the valley below.

As far as the eye could see, tents of every shape and size stretched into the distance. More sky blue men and women could be seen going about their business, all dressed in white togas like the two young females. Arundel glimpsed the source of the smoke, a small cook fire burning away at the centre of the tents. One skinny looking blue man was adding more wood to the fire, while a plumper blue male roasted a spit of rodent that had already been cooked for too long. This glance was as close as he would get because their path now forked off to the left.

This path was narrower and more broken than the last, but thankfully it was at least shorter. It ended in a small circular clearing, no larger than a stable. In the middle stood a dull, grey, square tent with the entrance flaps drawn shut. On either side of the entrance stood two men completely covered in a blue paint so dark it was almost black, with a yellow star over their left eye and a white crescent moon over their right eye. They wore black leather over their bodies and gripped spears tightly. The elderly woman stopped in her tracks, whilst encouraging him to continue. His right hand lowered, his fingers brushing gently against the hilt of Razor just in case things went wrong, but the two men stepped aside, pulling the flaps of the tent with them, and so he duly entered.

Inside the tent, incense and candles burned in every corner. There was no furniture, save for a wooden perch upon which a brilliant white snowy owl was sat silently, its eyes wide and keen. On the dirt floor was a wooden mat, emblazoned with the image of a beautiful woman with wings. The left side of her body was sky blue and the right side of her body was almost black. Sitting cross-legged at the end of the mat was an old looking man. He could have seen seventy name days or a hundred and seventy; it was impossible to tell. His body was shrouded in red cotton robes with the only visible skin being his hands, feet, neck and face, all of which were sky blue. His blue face was partially buried beneath white wiry hair, which came down to his elbows, and a white beard that brushed the floor. Arundel understood that this man called Yorrall was the High Priest of the Seekers.

"I know why you have come."

Yorrall's voice was coarse and withered, but at the same time strong and powerful.

"But first I must test your knowledge to make sure you are as worthy as I believe you to be. So tell me, what do you know of Anyeama?"

A test, no one had suggested there would be a test. Still, his hand eased away from Razor, her blade would not be needed here.

"Anyeama is the Goddess of the Sky, the overseer of the world. She is divided into two, her sky blue half, which represents daylight, and her dark blue half, which represents the night sky. Those of her followers who paint themselves sky blue are the workers. They are the ones who absorb the sun to brighten the world by seeking out new skills and new knowledge, before then teaching them to others. Those who paint themselves dark blue are the warriors. They embrace the darkness of the world and do what is necessary. They are your thieves, your soldiers and your protectors. When Anyeama believed she was dying, instead of passing her strength and knowledge onto her brother Travendor, the God of the Earth, she passed it onto every living creature with wings and now she lives through them."

Yorrall sat silent and motionless for a few moments, and then nodded.

"Impressive. Worthy, as I believed. Now let me be the one to impress you. Let me tell you that I know you seek passage safely through the valley for the bad company that you keep. Let me tell you that I know you cross the valley to seek a vengeance, to murder a King."

"You speak the truth; that is my desire."

Yorrall ran shrivelled blue fingers through his white beard.

"That is not all you desire. I will grant you your safe passage but first you will sit with me, for we have matters to discuss."

Arundel was uncertain what matters he was talking about. He did not know what else Yorrall could want.

"Matters?"

Yorrall nodded.

"Yes, matters of steel and eagles and hair as red as fire."

Disappointing. That was certainly one word that would describe what he thought of Ryevale, as he made his way through the dirty streets of the city. He had arrived with such high expectations, but those expectations had been washed away by one of the many buckets of slop he had witnessed being flung out onto the pavement. It seemed so long ago that they had been in the valley. So long ago since that talk with Yorrall, the High Priest of the Seekers. So long ago since he had said those words, words which had stuck in his mind ever since, only giving way on occasion to thoughts of hair as red as fire.

It had certainly made the rest of the journey a little different for him. His mind had remained constantly occupied while he rode among the supply wagons, just behind Lady Thea's carriage. As they rode for the rest of that day, so much of his time had been spent contemplating what Yorrall had told him, trying to establish an understanding of it, while wondering what he might be leading himself and his name-brothers into.

By nightfall, his concerns eased away as Thea sneaked from her carriage to lie beneath his furs, while he kept watch. That night, the conversation was more open as they became more relaxed with each other. He enjoyed her company, her sweet smell, those beautiful emerald eyes. She would play games with him, throwing out some harmless insults to disguise a compliment, looking to see what kind of reaction she would get out of him. He would play along. She was different from any other woman he had ever known. Her beauty was mesmerising, her personality heart-warming and her intelligence unparalleled. The women he had grown up with in Havendale had been simple and straight-forward, even Milly the blacksmith's daughter. With Milly, all he had to do was take off his jerkin and swing a sword crafted by her own hands and she would be in his bed for days. There were no complications, no real difficulties, it was always straightforward, but he realised now that simple just hadn't been enough. He had needed more for it to be what he truly wanted. Sex just wasn't enough and Lady Thea made him recognise that. Sure, on more than one occasion he had thought about climbing beneath those furs with her and taking her then and there, but he didn't because she was so much more than that, she meant so much more than that.

Two nights just weren't enough; he wanted more, so much more. He had been lucky to have the second night at all, the time spent with Yorrall and the slow pace of their party had delayed them enough to provide it. He wanted her, but not just for one night. He wanted her for every night and every day. He struggled with how quickly he had come to feel this way, but having spent all night with her, it tore him apart not being able to share the day together. Instead, he could only watch from afar.

Now he was riding through the dirty streets of Ryevale, with disappointment in his eyes and confusion in his mind. From all the stories he had heard, he imagined the perfect white walls of the Great Palace to be surrounded by streets made of gold and full of people living the greatest lives. He had been so wrong, a fact he had discovered the moment they had reached the North Gates. It was obvious from the designs cut into the steel that they had likely once been a great sight to behold, but now they were rusted and broken. Instead of welcoming you to paradise, they warned you that you were entering hell. Clearly, a statue had once perched proudly upon the top of the gates but had been broken off and lost, long ago.

Inside, things did not improve. The pathway within the gates was thick with mud and manure, and lined with children dressed in rags, begging for anything from coin to bread. The desperation on their faces was real and it was hard to see. A small boy approached one of the Guardians, only to receive a steel armoured boot to the face that knocked him down into the mud. Three other children then took advantage of the fallen child's misfortune, swarming around him and picking his pockets, while he lay clutching his face in agony. The scene infuriated Arundel but he could do little about it.

Things did not improve as they continued through the streets, passing through shops that were derelict and crumbling. The market place was not so much a hive of activity, but a last ditch attempt at desperation, with peasants trying to sell their worldly possessions just to feed their starving families for one more night. The only places that seemed to be thriving were the taverns and the whorehouses.

At least five fights had broken out during their journey through the city, while one working girl was chased down the street. Even the perfect white walls of the Great Palace revealed themselves to be dirty and cracked, now that he was much closer to them. Ryevale was a mess, a far cry from the wondrous world the stories had depicted. For the first time he missed home, the simple but colourful life that Havendale had provided. People had dwelt there, they had been content, but that was all gone, burnt to ashes, erased from the realm forever. Remembering that reminded him of why he was here, why they had travelled all this way. They sought revenge; they sought blood, king's blood.

"Halt where you are, Outlander."

He broke from his thoughts and tugged on the reins of Tyranos as he brought the stallion to a stop next to the Guardian known as Danyil. Danyil had blocked his path, cutting him off from the rest of the train; from Thea.

"This is as far as you go, Outlander."

He realised that they had reached the outer wall of the Great Palace, a large hulk of stone topped with spikes and a gap in the middle wide enough for a carriage flanked by two horses either side to pass through. Guards manned the gate, but had stepped aside to give the escort party access. He could only watch as

Thea's carriage passed through the gap and out of his reach. Would he ever see her again? He doubted it; his future was quite possibly a short-lived affair. So, with a heavy heart, he let her go, turning away just before the carriage vanished from his sight. Rather than hold onto that moment, he looked upon the weary and worn face of Danyil, a man who had seen more winters than he care to admit.

"Tell me, where can my brothers and I find food and shelter?"

Danyil chewed on his own gum before spitting a little blood onto the mud below.

"You wanna be trying Bella's. The food ain't worth shit, but the hospitality is second to none."

Danyil then pointed an aged finger down the street to the right.

"Wait there, someone will fetch you when the King is ready."

With that, Danyil tugged at the reins of his horse and turned away, trotting towards the wall, as Garad and Bromon drew up alongside him. Garad was the first to speak.

"They called this the City of Dreams back home, but I call it a shit hole."

Arundel nodded.

"You are not wrong, my brother. But destiny has brought us here, and destiny will be fulfilled; just not before one last hearty meal."

"Aye," Bromon boomed in response. The three men started to move off when he heard it, faintly in the distance but clear enough to make out.

"Arundel."

He could have sworn someone had called his name, but it wasn't possible, he did not know anyone here in this decaying city.

"Arundel."

There it was again. He looked at his name-brothers but they looked as confused as he felt. Perhaps there was another Arundel. Or perhaps he was not hearing right. Perhaps something entirely different was being called and he was just being a fool.

"Arundel."

There it was again and now he was certain it was his name. He looked all around him, seeking out the source, when his eyes stopped by the gap in the wall. Just for a moment, he saw a man, hair as white as snow, dressed in a gown of gold. Then the man was ushered behind the wall by one of the Guardians and was gone. The calling had also stopped and so he turned back to his brothers.

"Come, Ari, best we get a move on. Bromon grows restless," prompted Garad.

Bromon slapped his axe in agreement.

"Aye, I need tits, meat and mead, and I'm not fussed what order it comes."

Having heard enough, Arundel kicked his heels to encourage Tyranos to pick up pace and take them to Bella's.

The tavern was better than he expected. The journey through the streets of the city had severely lowered his expectations, to the point that he half expected pigs to be running wild and the ceiling to have fallen in. What he found was much more pleasing. It turned out that Bella's was named after the first ever Queen of Galbraxia, Belladina. The tavern had always catered to the higher class of citizen and was strict in its ways, from how it looked to what went on within. Bella's was always fit for a Queen, it was said, and he could see why. The stone floor was covered in red velvet rugs that, despite years of wear and tear, were still looking reasonable. The bar was built from solid oak and covered in carvings of the royal crown. The stone walls were decorated in tapestries, depicting important moments in Ryevale's history, while lanterns suspended from the ceilings supplied ample lighting. Even the furniture was made of oak, both the tables and the chairs, providing a suitable place to rest. Upstairs, he had counted six guest rooms, although they had taken just the one room for the three of them. The logic was that if the night went to plan, the likelihood was that they would never make it back to squeeze themselves into that room. A squeeze it would be too, given that the room consisted of a single feather mattress bed and just enough floor space for two adults to lie down.

Garad and Bromon were currently up in that room, while he sat here alone, or at least alone at his table. He had broken his hunger on some two day old dry bread and chicken soup. Hardly the grandest of meals, yet most likely more than many others in the city were getting, and so he was grateful. His meal had been accompanied by the sound of a drunken old stable-hand telling the barkeeper about how the city had been so different back in his day. With each example provided, a cup of wine was sunk, as if it was going to vanish, were he not to drink it right away. Eventually, his coin had run dry and then so did the wine, leading to the old man staggering out into the early evening.

His departure made for a quieter atmosphere and had left Arundel with his thoughts. Not just thoughts, but doubts. For the first time, he was actually having doubts about the possible events of the evening. To slay the King was no small matter. They were not going to receive a pat on the back and an escort out of the city. They would face a fight to the death, a fight that given the numbers likely to be involved would probably result in the death of himself and his name-brothers. For a long time, he had not even concerned himself with it for he did not fear death. Now, things were a little different. Now, he realised that, while his chances of seeing Thea again were remote, if he was dead they would be non-existent. But what could he do? He did not want the murder of his name-parents to go unpunished and he did not want to let his name-brothers down, yet in Thea he had a reason to survive. Despite being remote, there was still a chance and that gave him reason to survive. He finished his cup of mead and then began to think of Yorrall and those words. What had he meant by them? Could there be more to this all than he had realised? As a fresh pitcher of mead arrived at the table, he poured some into his cup. Swallowing it, he allowed his mind to drift back to Yorrall's tent.

"It is vengeance you seek. Vengeance for a fallen father."

Yorrall had been straight to the crux of it.

"Yes, my mother too. My parents by name at least. They were murdered by order of King Theagran."

Yorrall remained silent and motionless for a moment, before shaking his head slowly.

"No, there is more blood that stains the King's hands, blood that you must avenge."

Arundel was lost by this comment.

"What other blood? I don't know what you are talking about."

The riddle continued.

"You have merely forgotten. But what has been forgotten is not always lost. Look for the 'Golden Man'; he will guide you. Follow the books. Follow the books and you shall remember."

Yorrall may as well have spoken in a foreign tongue, for all the sense he made. Frustrated and confused, Arundel had risen from one knee to his feet, ready to start the journey back down the valley.

"Forgive me, but I don't know what you are speaking of. So if we have safe passage through the valley, I shall leave you now and rejoin my train."

"You have safe passage."

He bowed in thanks and turned away from Yorrall, heading towards the opening flaps of the tent when the High Priest spoke one last time.

"Be sure to ready your sword, Arundel, for the lost son returns to his throne and with him a storm of blood and sorrow will rage."

Again, the words made no sense, but when Arundel shot a glance back, Yorrall had lowered his head, as if in slumber. He had walked out of the tent confused and uncertain, a feeling that still hung over him as he now sat in Bella's.

It wasn't long before the entire contents of the pitcher had worked its way into his cup and then down his throat, and with it now empty, he signalled for another. He wasn't naturally a heavy drinker, but on this day he felt that he had some sorrows to drown, before he spilled the blood of the King. A fresh pitcher hit down on the table and he immediately knew that something was different. The chunky, hairy, exposed arm of the barkeeper had been replaced by a hairless yet aged hand in a faded gold sleeve. His eyes followed up the arm onto a tattered and faded gold robe.

The robe stopped at the neckline, except for a hood shrouding a face that showed its advanced years, despite the white beard trying to hide them. Dark brown eyes stared back at him beneath wisps of white hair. Arundel was the first to speak.

"You. You were the one calling my name at the wall. Why?"

The gold-cloaked man spoke softly, almost in a whisper.

"Arundel is your name, is it not?"

"Yes, it is."

"Well, when you require the attention of a person, it is customary to call their name."

He was right, but that wasn't what Arundel was getting at.

"I know that, but why would you want my attention? How do you even know my name? We have never met."

Gold Cloak glanced back over his shoulder, a sense of urgency now visible in his body language and tone, as his voice remained at a near whisper.

"I knew you once, a long time ago. The years have aged you, but only to look more like your mother than ever before. That was how I recognised you."

This caught Arundel a little off guard. Gold Cloak would not have been talking about his name-mother; they couldn't have been more different.

"You knew my mother? My birth mother?"

A slight smile formed on Gold Cloak's lips.

"Knew her? My boy, she was my second cousin."

Suddenly Gold Cloak was startled by the sound of hooves outside. He glanced past Arundel and through the small window pane.

"Guardians, curses. I can't be seen here with you, I must go."

Arundel tried to stop him, grabbing hold of his scrawny arm.

"Wait; there is so much I need to ask you."

"And there is so much I have to tell you, but not now. When the night is at its blackest, come find me. We Historians are never hard to find."

"But where will you be? I do not know this place."

Gold Cloak pulled his arm free and then tugged the hood

further over his face.

"Look for where any Historian would be, buried in the dust of time. Oh, and Arundel, you know this place better than you think. After all, you once called it home."

With that Gold Cloak turned away and crept into the shadows. But not before Arundel noticed it, just out of the corner of his eye. The back of the gold cloak bore a symbol, one you would rarely see, a tower of books, each smaller than the one below. He found himself remembering Yorrall's words, "Follow the books". The words spun round and round in his head, the entire conversation with Gold Cloak repeating and repeating. Was any of this true? What did it all mean? But there was no time to think, no time to piece the jigsaw together, for the tavern door opened and two Guardians strode in, their gaze resting upon him.

"Outlander, gather your kin, for the King will see you now."

8

"We have arrived, m'lady."

Yasilda was certainly one for pointing out the obvious. Of all the handmaids that had been gifted to her, Yasilda was most definitely her least favourite. The girl had barely reached her seventeenth year, but had gorged herself as though she had seen forty. Her portly frame struggled to hide beneath a brown cotton dress, pulled in at what waist she had by a white ribbon. Dirty blonde hair, thick with grease, clung to chubby cheeks beneath light brown eyes. Thea was not bothered about Yasilda's appearance; she did not think ill of her for it. It was Yasilda's foul character that Thea hated. She was rude, obnoxious and cold, and, while her words were pleasant, their tone clearly held disdain. As if to make her point, Yasilda pulled back the curtain on the carriage door to allow the light of the outside world to breach the inner wooden walls.

"See, m'lady. We have reached the Great Palace."

The small window did not reveal this, not directly. All she could see in that rectangular snippet was a small portion of the towering perimeter stone wall and the rare sight of a cobbled stone floor. To many, this sight would tell them very little, other than the fact that this was a place of wealth, but to her it had a sense of familiarity. Her eyes had seen this all before; she had once lived within these perimeter walls, after all. Several years had passed since the last time she had been here, since she had departed the city for her schooling. Even so, she knew that just out of sight, to the left of the carriage, would be the beautiful white walls of the

Great Palace. Despite the years that had passed, those walls would not have moved.

Suddenly, there was a light clicking sound and then the door to the carriage opened as more daylight flooded in. One of the Guardians appeared in the doorway, extending a steel gauntlet towards her. She rejected it; she was more than capable of getting herself out of the carriage. She stepped out onto the cobbles and surveyed the organised chaos that was her escort dismounting from their rides and easing themselves from their helms.

The courtyard was awash with activity. Stable hands flooded in, leading horses two or three at a time towards the stables. Squires were finding their knights and swiftly becoming laden down with all that they could carry, and a little more. Through all the chaos, through the mess of bodies moving around, she noticed an absence. Three absences to be precise, but one that mattered more than the others. The Outlanders were not in the courtyard; Arundel was not in the courtyard. Her heart sunk a little; she suddenly felt slightly empty inside. Had she seen him for the last time? She would suggest to the King that he summon them to an audience, but the King might decide otherwise. If so, then what? Would he become a distant memory? Would she only have those two nights wrapped in his furs, while he kept watch, as the one thing she could hold onto? Would she spend the rest of her life never experiencing his touch, his warm embrace? Would she be resigned to lonely nights wondering where her Outlander might be, wishing that he could be with her, just one more time?

Even if the King did choose to entertain them, would the rest of her life be any different? Certainly, she could at least see him one more time, but loneliness would still follow. She stared back towards the gate, her eyes searching tirelessly, seeking with the faintest hope that they might find what they were looking for, but no matter how hard she looked, no matter how hard she hoped, all she found was disappointment.

"M'lady, begging your pardon but your father is asking for you."

Yasilda's irritating voice interrupted her search, a search that would yield nothing. She turned away from the gate and once more took in the sorry sight that was Yasilda.

"I am surprised that he is so keen to see me, given how eager he was to send me away."

Yasilda had no idea how to reply and so she stood with her mouth open and a vacant gaze upon her face. But Thea swiftly forgot about Yasilda's face as she glanced at the sight behind.

When she looked at the Great Palace soaring up into the cloudy, overcast sky, she noticed that the brilliant white walls now looked a dirty grey. The white had lost its brilliance. There were chips in the stone, patches that had suffered the elements and never been cared for. Is this what the city had become under its King? The shining beacon of Ryevale, and all Galbraxia for that matter, was nearly extinguished. No wonder the city was in such a poor state, a fact that had not gone unnoticed as they had travelled through its streets, but why? Why had things become so desperate? What had been more important than the welfare of the city?

"Your father does not like to wait, m'lady."

She was drawn away from the once great structure and back to the less impressive Yasilda.

"Then I shall keep him waiting no longer."

Inside the walls of the Great Palace, the scene that awaited her was just as bleak as the faded white without. The first corridor, beyond the extravagant oak door, was well lit by rows of candles; however, the candlelight revealed how the great tapestries upon the walls had lost their vibrancy. Telling stories of famed battles from years past, the fabric was threadbare, and this was only the start of it. As Thea entered the Hall of Kings, her heart nearly sank.

There had been a time when this magnificent room had been the brightest in all the realm, the light of flames bringing life to the smallest of dark spaces. The sun's light gifted from the Gods would flood through the most breathtaking stained glass windows to show the room in all its glory. Soft, luscious red carpet ran from the doorway all the way up to the four stone steps that led to the platform, on which the mighty throne sat. The throne itself was a sight to behold, commonly known as the Iron Eagle; the base was formed into three legs, two of them the eagle's claws at the front and the larger one at the back being its feathered tail. The king sat within the eagle's breast while the sharp beak and piercing eyes of its head looked towards the skies. Its great iron wings curved slightly to enfold the sovereign who sat upon it. Around the Hall had stood statues carved from stone in the image of the kings of old. Generation after generation of the Stal family, all great kings of the people. They had been loved and respected and, in these statues, they had been justly honoured.

All that had changed. The brightest room in the realm now stood in near darkness. Just a few lonely candles flickered as the shadows now owned this once proud hall. What light that broke through the darkness did so only to emphasise its emptiness. Emptiness created by the absence of every statue, leaving the room bare, its history stolen. The Iron Eagle remained, but, as if hiding in the black of night, its importance had been lost. She couldn't stay there; seeing all of this filled her with sadness and anger. What had happened here? Had things really changed so much in her absence?

Thea's ascent through the Palace did little to lift her spirits. The once roaring fire of the dining hall now barely mustered a whimper, as some of her escort took seats to dine. The once rich smells that promised to delight even the largest appetite had been replaced by an odour so foul that food was the farthest thing from her mind. Still the gloom did not lift. Steps were cracked and chipped, windows broken. The paintings that graced the walls were thick with dust, their personalities lost beneath layers of neglect. Room after room provided nothing but disappointment. Her pace had constantly quickened, as if she was trying to escape the gloom, to run from it as she would a nightmare.

Her journey led her to the White Room, the library of the Great Palace. This room was huge and spanned over two floors at the rear of the Palace, joined together by an inner set of stairs. The walls were covered floor to ceiling with shelves loaded with books. For those privileged enough to have learned to read, within these walls could be found more than a lifetime's worth of knowledge, history and fantasy. As a child, her mother had wanted her to read books on the princesses and queens of old, and the gallant knights, who would rescue them and win their love. She had been far more interested in the books depicting the spoils of war. She had loved to read about how King Andolin had won the Battle of Ecrose Forge with just a handful of men, or the stories of Sir Whenton Quint, one of the greatest swordsmen ever known. While other girls her age dreamed of pretty things and knights in shining armour, she dreamed of slaying dragons and glorious victories upon the battlefield.

As she stood here now, she noticed that the White Room was not as full as it had once been. Gaps littered the once brimming shelves; books were now absent from their place of rest. All she could do was stare and wonder, when suddenly a voice from the gloom startled her.

"An empty bookshelf is a shelf failing to fulfil its purpose."

Echoing around the room, the voice startled her. It bounced off the heavy shelving from all angles as if coming from all directions; but she knew where it had originated from and in an instant she spun on her heels. There, among a stack of books, emerged a golden robe, which years were causing to lose its radiance. Covered by the robe was a man entering the later years of his existence, his ageing, rounded face framed by white hair from crown to chin. The bagginess of the robe hinted at the frailty of the figure within; yet his brown eyes showed a strength beyond his physical means. The years had taken their toll, but she remembered him even so.

"Oracle Thomas, how happy I am to see you."

She moved forward and embraced him. As her arms wrapped around him, she could feel nothing but bones and the soft padding of the robe. Releasing him, she took a step back to look at him once more.

"What has happened here? It is as if the city has withered and died."

His expression was one of sorrow and pain as he spoke.

"The King is what happened here. The throne was built by the Stals; this entire realm was brought together by them, piece by piece. Theagran can't bear that and so he seeks to erase history and start again. The texts you've noticed are missing were all those that told the history of the realm. Theagran had them burned on a night I shall never forget."

She could see the agony in his eyes.

"Where are the other Oracles?"

"Gone, I dare not ask where. When you are trying to erase history, the last thing you want around is a Historian. Only I have remained, for now, until I no longer serve a purpose, I presume."

His concern was understandable; she shared it with him.

Slowly, she walked along the aisle, taking in the empty spaces as they became more apparent.

"History can't be forgotten, no matter how much you try to bury it."

There was defiance in her words, a defiance not shared by the old Historian.

"Yes it can, I'm afraid. Generations move on and new ones continue to emerge into a world where no record of the true history of Galbraxia exists. This city is dying and its ancestry will die with it."

He bent down gingerly, picking up a book that had fallen to the floor, and then placed it on one of the shelves.

"I shall speak to the King. Perhaps I can convince him to put an end to this madness."

She started towards the door at speed, only to be stopped in her tracks by the Oracle's next words.

"You refer to him as your King."

She turned back to face him.

"He is King, is he not?"

Oracle Thomas paused for a moment and then nodded at her.

"That he is, if nothing else. Speak to him if you wish, but your words will fall upon deaf ears, I can promise you that. Theagran only takes counsel from Marcasian and none other."

She remained confident.

"We shall see."

He nodded again.

"We shall, but not tonight. The King prepares himself to see the Outlanders who rode in with you; he will be in no mood to discuss other matters."

That caught her attention. Had he really just said that? Could it be true?

"The King is seeing Arundel tonight?"

She could feel a sense of excitement begin to form inside her, just a small crumb of hope.

"Yes, his kinsmen too. He wishes to see the men who saved your life so valiantly."

That seed of excitement started to sprout inside her belly as she could feel herself starting to smile.

"But how could he know? We have not long arrived."

The Oracle began re-arranging a pile of old dust-coated texts.

"Riders were sent ahead of your party; word arrived as dawn broke. I can see this news pleases you."

She suddenly tried to hide her joy.

"It intrigues me, nothing more."

She could tell he didn't believe her.

"I have seen that look before, child. Don't think me a fool. But tell me this, how much do you know about Arundel?"

She had to think about that for a moment. She had shared his company but little else. This man had captivated her, yet she knew so little about him.

"Very little, truth be told."

The old man's body language suddenly changed; a sense of urgency and concern seemed to fall upon him.

"Then close the door quickly. Hasten, my child, because there is much you must learn."

Without questioning it, she obeyed and shut the door, ready to listen. Her father would have to wait.

Night had fallen by the time she entered her chamber. The room was devoid of childhood memories, stripped back to the bare essentials. Thea found her handmaid waiting for her inside the chamber, a piping hot bath already drawn ready for her arrival. Thankfully the handmaid was not that awful Yasilda beast, who had no doubt found herself fed and forcefully bedded by now. Instead, she had a maid by the name of Shauri. A petite girl of nineteen years, her skin kissed by the sun, thick black hair flowed down her back and around a face of natural beauty. Her breasts were generous, her body supple. She looked out of place as a handmaid; her beauty would fetch her good coin in a whorehouse, especially as she was clearly a child of the Forgotten Lands, but a handmaid she was and that actually pleased Thea. For all her beauty, one blemish betrayed it. Thea noticed almost immediately that on her left hand, Shauri's little finger had been cut off down to the knuckle. The wound had healed, so it must have been inflicted a long time past. Doubtless it came with a tale of woe, a tale she would endeavour to hear.

Shauri helped her undress before she lowered her aching body into the hot water. For the first time since arriving in Ryevale, she actually felt at ease. The dirt and dust of the journey slowly fell away from her skin, as she closed her eyes and laid her head against the steel frame.

Her thoughts started on the darkness of the once great Hall of Kings, but soon moved onto long blond locks over a muscular frame. Arundel rarely left her mind. Even though they weren't together physically, he was always there when she closed her eyes. She could feel the excitement grow inside her as she remembered how powerful he looked, wielding that sword of his. A warmth washed over her as she thought about how safe she felt under his protection. Their time together had been so short, yet the connection between them had been strong. Never had she ever felt this way before and, while these feelings were unexpected, she most certainly welcomed them. Her thoughts continued to drift. She felt joy that she would see him tonight and sorrow that it would be for the last time. Then the thoughts focused, as she contemplated everything that Oracle Thomas had told her. Could it be true? Was all of that real? It would explain the hint of familiarity she had felt from the moment they first met. But what did it mean now? Things could change; they should change; but would they?

"What will you wear tonight?"

Shauri's voice broke the silence, the foreign twang in her accent strong enough to hear. She opened her eyes and looked at the maid.

"Look in my chest; there is plenty of choice in there."

She watched as Shauri walked over to the oak strong box against the far wall. Opening the chest, Shauri sifted through a selection of blouses and leather trousers. She shook her head.

"These will not do. Your father would be very displeased with them."

Her father? She was starting to think of him that way less and less.

"Tell me, Shauri, what would please my father?"

The maid closed the lid of the chest and made her way over to the large wooden wardrobe. Inside, hanging neatly, was an assortment of dresses. Shauri reached in and pulled one out. She held it up, a dress of blue silks with red trim that hung to the floor. Thea immediately hated it, as Shauri smiled at her.

"This he would like."

The Great Palace had most certainly failed to live up to its name. As Garad so aptly put it, joy had died here and hatred had taken its place. The Guardian had escorted them up the troubled staircase of the Palace, passing floor after floor of degradation and darkness. They were being led to the very top of the tower, a room apparently called the Observation Chamber, where the King would meet them. This seemed odd to Arundel: why meet in such an obscure place instead of the Throne Room? Still, it wasn't his place to question; after all, blood could be spilt anywhere. So they made the climb and with each floor passed, Bromon's heavy breathing became heftier grunts. The three of them stayed silent until they reached the top. The stone staircase attained its summit and led them to a small hallway. Little square windows lined both sides of the hallway, all the way down to a set of large golden doors with two guards posted outside them. Night had fallen and moonlight began to creep in through the windows, adding to the candlelight high upon the walls. The ceiling had been painted like a night sky, littered with small stars all the way up to the doors. Unlike the rest of the Palace, this room actually appeared to have been looked after.

"Whose blasted idea was it to meet at the very top of a tower?" Bromon's booming voice cut through the silence like a hammer blow shattering a helm. "There was a perfectly good room on the ground floor that would have spared us such an unnecessary climb."

Garad placed a hand upon Bromon's shoulder.

"Calm, brother, perhaps now you will think twice before having extra helpings when we feast."

Arundel smiled at Garad's unsympathetic comment, while Bromon snarled.

"Perhaps you would like extra helpings of my axe blade?"

With that, Bromon drew his mighty axe and rotated it in his hands as if to show it off.

"Brother, please, I would drop you with an arrow before you could even manage to swing that toothpick of yours."

This infuriated Bromon even more, as Arundel made the decision to step between them.

"Save your energy. I fear we will need it before the night is out."

Both Garad and Bromon stared at him and then at each other, before easing off. Through all the banter, they had failed to notice that their escort had approached the two guards by the door. But now he returned and his was the next voice to be heard.

"Wait here until I return, Outlanders."

He didn't wait for a reply. Instead, he turned away from them and made his way back down the hall towards the golden doors. The guard on the left opened his door and their escort slipped through it, the door quickly closing behind him with a dull thud. The three of them turned back to face each other. Arundel's concern had not lifted.

"Whatever reason led us here, it has left us deep in trouble."

He pointed to the window as Garad and Bromon peered out in turn.

"Trying to fight our way out of the ground floor was going to be an uphill struggle as it was. But having to work our way down from the very top of the Palace, just to get to that stage makes it nearly impossible."

It was the honest truth and, more often than not, the honest truth hurt the most. Garad was the first to respond.

"There is no denying it; death knocks at our door tonight."

Bromon then nudged both of them firmly with the tip of his axe.

"Aye, she does, but I've never feared death and I won't start doing so now. As long as the King dies, then I will die at peace."

Arundel cast a glance towards the door, making sure that the guards had not heard Bromon's words. Neither of them stirred and he took that as a positive sign. He turned back to his name-brothers and placed a hand on each of their shoulders.

"We fight together, we die together. If that is tonight, then so be it."

His words carried conviction and it was matched by the glare in the eyes of his kin. An opportunity would arise, a brief moment when the King would be in reach, when his guard would be down. Maybe just a split second, the smallest of windows. It would be there and when it was, he would seize upon it, with fury and passion. Tonight two men of Havendale and their adopted kinsman would meet with Theagran, King of Galbraxia. Tonight they would spill Theagran's blood, until his body ran dry.

There were two bangs at the golden doors and both guards sprang into action, each opening their door. The escort reappeared and took two steps forward before raising his arms to beckon them.

"This way, Outlanders."

Not saying a word, the three of them began to walk forward, knowing full well that they were likely walking towards their doom. As they reached the doors, the escort held out a hand to stop them.

"No weapons. Leave them all here and collect them when you leave."

The three of them looked at each other. No weapons meant there would barely be a fight. Still, at least it meant a quick death. Slowly they removed their weapons and piled them up against the wall. Razor was the first to be placed down, followed by Bromon's axe and Garad's bow and quiver of arrows. An assortment of knives increased the size of the pile, and then they were done. With no means of protection left, the escort waved them through, but what the escort didn't know was that Arundel had a small blade hidden among the furs of his right boot. The blade had served its purpose over the years, acting as his last line of defence and unknown to his enemy. Now that blade would be used to slay a king, just as soon as the opportunity arose.

The room itself was very impressive. From the door, it formed a cylindrical shape with large windows that ran in a non-stop block the entire way round. From these windows you could survey the entire city, that and beyond on a clear day, he imagined. The floor was marbled, intersected by lines of gold that criss-crossed in several places. The ceiling bore paintings of the finest design, with several eagles soaring through brilliant blue sky flecked with wisps of fluffy white cloud. He wondered just how long that would stay untouched. A chandelier hung from the centre of the room to add to the moonlight. Arundel noticed eight Guardians lining the walls, four to his left and four to his right. Opposite the door, one area of the floor was raised, with three steps approaching it. The two corners of this platform were marked by flagpoles adorned with flags bearing the symbol of a serpent entwined around an axe.

In the centre of the platform sat a throne made entirely out of serpents, hundreds of them, entwined together to form the Chair of the King. Standing next to the throne was a man of extraordinary height. Not only was he tall, but built like a rock. His dark brown hair was pulled back into a knot behind his head revealing a scar that started above his eye and ran down his cheek. He wore a scarlet tunic depicting the same symbol as the flags, along with a white cape that ran from his right shoulder at an angle across his back down to his left hip. He was dressed differently from the rest of the guards because he was in fact the Captain of the Guardians, a man by the name of Marcasian. Arundel knew this because as their travelling party had neared the city, Marcasian and a handful of men had ridden out to meet them. During the journey, he heard many of the Guardians talking about Marcasian, the King's right hand man and sole confidant. They referred to him as 'The Bull' and told various tales about things they had witnessed him do on the field of battle, from gutting a man clean to ripping a man's head off. Just how true these tales were Arundel did not know, but what he did know was that the men feared him and that alone made him wary of the man-mountain before him.

Arundel's eyes were then drawn beyond the throne to a figure slowly emerging from the shadows. The man's face showed its years from a mass of black hair and a black beard, both of which were starting to grey. His eyes looked empty and hollow, his face expressionless. He was dressed entirely in black leathers, a black sheep's wool cloak hanging down his back to the floor. Upon his mop of hair sat a golden crown.

"You will bend the knee before King Theagran and stay that way until he gives permission to do otherwise," boomed the Bull. Theagran stepped beside him, in front of his throne.

This man clad in black was not his King, nor was he the King of his name-brothers, but on this night, for a purpose, he would bend the knee, just once. He glanced at his name-brothers and, as their eyes met his, he gave a slight nod. He then lowered himself, placing his right knee down onto the marble floor while keeping his left leg bent. As he did so, his hand brushed the fur of his boot and his fingertips found the cool edge of the blade. He slipped it out of the furs into his palm and then moved his hand back to his side. His kin followed suit and bent the knee also. He glanced over at the King and his Bull, neither of whose expressions had changed from the stony looks that they wore. He could tell this was a chore for them, an unwanted event. So why was it happening if they did not want it? That did not matter though; all that mattered was the task at hand. He clenched his fist a little, reassuring himself that the blade was still there, when suddenly the King spoke.

"To your feet, let me see the so-called heroes."

The three of them rose to their feet and again exchanged glances, as Arundel clenched his fist once more, yet again reminding himself that the small blade was in his grasp. Theagran took a step off the raised platform and then walked towards the three of them, stopping well out of arm's reach. Each step echoed through the chamber and filled the silence of the room. The silence returned when he stopped and his coal black eyes worked their way along all three of them. They then stopped upon Arundel, where they became transfixed. Those dark eyes seemed to drink him in, widening like pools that he could almost fall into. The King then took a step forward and broke the silence again.

"You have a familiarity about you, a face that I've seen before. Have our paths crossed already?"

The King continued to stare at him as his words ended, as if trying to read every fibre of his face.

"Not that I know of, Your Grace."

To call him that sat ill upon his tongue, but he had to keep up this farce for the greater end it would bring. The blade now felt warm in his hand, conducting the heat of his own flesh. Just a little closer and the moment would present itself. His fingers twitched, his hand ready to strike. The King spoke again.

"I have seen you before, be it in this flesh or another. Your familiar face haunts me, yet I can't put any recognition to its familiarity."

Suddenly it happened. As he finished speaking, the King took another step forward to get a closer look. The blade now burned in his hand, his blood pumped through his veins at an incredible rate while his muscles tensed. This was his moment; this was his window of opportunity. One swift strike to the throat and the deed would be done. He loosened his grip, allowing the blade to slip into his fingers where it could be of use. The King stared, unaware of the blade readied for him. Arundel was ready; it was time to make his move.

"Father."

The female voice broke the moment. He hesitated, his arm sticking by his side as his eyes were drawn from the King towards the owner of the voice. King Theagran turned his attention also, although he remained where he stood, within blade's reach. The voice had made it through the oak door before the speaker, although she swiftly followed. She glided in a blue silk dress with red trim that clung to a cleavage of desirable size and floated around hidden legs. The dress brushed the floor, as she moved speedily towards them. For a brief moment, his eyes struggled to take it in as he wondered who this daughter could be, the surprise of it all affecting their accuracy.

Then he saw it, the giveaway that turned his surprise into shock. As the woman walked into the embracing arms of the King, he found his eyes focusing upon a flurry of hair as red as the fires that lit the walls. He could not believe what he was seeing. Those two secret nights spent together on the road, all their conversations, their moments; not once had Lady Thea given any indication that her father was the King. Lady Thea was nothing but a lie, Princess Thea was the truth that stood before him. So, if her identity had been a lie, was her fondness towards him a fabrication also? Was it a mere act to pass the boredom of a long and weary journey? He hoped not, but he feared it to be true. He thought there had been a spark, a mutual connection, but then what did it really matter? This would be the final time he gazed upon her beauty anyway.

"I see you have already met my brave heroes, father?"

Her sweet voice broke him from his train of sorrowful thought, but it was a little too sweet, not what he had grown accustom too. All her strength, her sexual prowess, it seemed to have been replaced by immaturity. Perhaps this right here before him was the lie? He could make neither head nor tail of it.

"Barely. They are still merely faces to me."

The King's tone did not match the softness of that of his daughter. It maintained its coarse nature and lack of passion. The arrival of his daughter had done nothing to improve his mood.

"I shall introduce you, father."

The enthusiasm in her voice had not faltered, despite her father.

"If you must."

Arundel watched as Thea walked King Theagran to the start of the line, introducing his name-brothers one at a time. The King's face remained solemn and visibly uninterested when Thea spoke. The words were lost to Arundel, as he simply watched her. Even with the disappointment that currently engulfed him, he couldn't help but be mesmerised by those tender red lips, the deep heavenly eyes and the hair that warmed him like nothing he had ever known before. Before long, Thea and the King were back in front of him, although this time there was a little more distance between them. Still, the gap was small enough if the hand could strike quick enough.

"And this father, is Aramando."

"She means Arundel, Your Grace."

He found himself swiftly correcting her, as his mind slipped away from the blade once more. Had she really forgotten his name? It hurt to think so, cutting deeper then the blade pressed into his fingers. He could not dwell upon it, however, because as he spoke his name to the King, he saw it. It was so small that at first it almost went unnoticed, but he had seen it, he was sure he had. The King's concrete expression had altered. Not by much, but by enough to notice it. It was a hint of surprise, a splash of shock. Suddenly Theagran's eyes were on him as if they were trying to bury themselves deep inside him to find a hidden answer.

"Arundel, you say? Are you their brother also?"

Theagran pointed towards Garad and Bromon.

"No, Your Grace. They are my kin in name, not in blood."

There it was again, a small flicker of change in Theagran's expression. Only now the King seemed a little uncomfortable also.

"Tell me, Arundel, who are your parents?"

It was an odd question, one he had not expected. But, then again, he was used to people asking how his kinship with his name-brothers came to be.

"I do not know, Your Grace."

Still the words soured him to speak them.

"I was found abandoned in the Weeping Woods, bound to a tree and left to die, so I am told."

The change of expression upon Theagran's face was no longer subtle. His brow had furrowed, his lips pursed together so tightly the blood began to drain from them. He was almost snarling, but a look of horror in his eyes gave away more than he had hoped. For reasons unknown to Arundel, he disturbed King Theagran.

"How very unfortunate for you."

The King muttered the words quickly, not even attempting to hide their insincerity. He then wrenched himself free from Thea's grasp.

"I am a busy man with a realm to run. I must leave you now, but you are free to enjoy the splendours of Ryevale as a token of my gratitude."

Token words cobbled together, nothing more. With them spoken, the King turned his back upon them all and made his way towards the door, barking out an order as he strode with purpose.

"Marcasian, come."

The Bull quickly fell into line and followed the King out of the room. Thea spared Arundel a glance, her eyes filled with what looked like worry, but then she too made her exit from the room, the heavy doors closing firmly shut behind her.

Once the King had departed, the tension eased within Arundel's body. He realised now that they would live another night, but that also meant so would King Theagran. As the adrenalin drained from his body, he also realised for the first time that the knife intended for the King was actually digging into his own skin, with warm droplets of blood dripping onto his fingers.

"How can this be?"

The anger in his voice was undisguised, as it rasped from his throat. He opened the door in full rage and slammed it into the stone wall with a hefty bang. Walking into the room, he could feel the veins on his neck ready to burst as he looked for the nearest thing to hit. He grabbed hold of a jar, tossed it hard against the wall and watched it shatter into pieces as white powder sprinkled the floor. That had not been anything near enough to alleviate his anger, but, before he could find anything else, he heard the footsteps follow him into the room. The hulking frame of Marcasian strode into the room and pushed the door closed behind them, eliminating some of the light in the room. Theagran didn't wait for a response from the Captain of the Guardians.

"How is Arundel Stal still alive?"

Marcasian's expression remained blank as he shook his head.

"Arundel Stal died the day you became King. My men took him out to the Weeping Woods and fed him to the wolves. Gregor and Sorenson watched the wolves pick the flesh from his bones, with their very own eyes."

He could see that Marcasian believed the words he was saying, but he had just seen evidence to the contrary.

"Arundel Stal is living and breathing, kneeling before me just moments ago in the Observation Chamber. Your men are liars, Marcasian."

He hated liars, despised them. This wouldn't go unpunished.

"How can you be so sure, my King? So many years have

passed since then, he was just a boy of ten the last time you saw him."

He took a step closer to his trusted ally, his frustration getting the better of him.

"Did you not just hear what was said? His name is Arundel, he was found in the woods at the age of ten and does not have any memory of the time before that. If that isn't proof enough, he is clearly his mother's son, hauntingly so."

He waited for a response, but Marcasian seemed unable to come up with one.

"Your men lied to you, Marcasian, and in doing so they lied to me. They were too lazy to see the job through and their laziness has put us all in jeopardy."

Marcasian took a few steps back and turned away from him. He raised a large fist and slammed it into the door with a loud thud, raising dust and dirt from within the grain of the wood. Now the anger was equally shared.

"I will deal with them at once, my King." Finally, something they agreed on.

"Yes, you will. You will remove their heads and put them on display in the mess hall as warning to all your men what happens when they lie to their King."

Marcasian lowered his head a little.

"I will have it done at once."

"Before dawn breaks, no later. However, that does not aid us in the situation that now stands before us."

He was beginning to feel a little more in control of his rage, the veins weren't pulsating quite so much and his breathing had eased. For the first time, he took stock of where he was. In his fury he had stormed out of the Observation Chamber and down the stairs, stopping at the first floor he felt like and then choosing the first room he saw: this one. Such a blind journey had led them into the washroom. Lines hung from wall to wall, draped with clothes at various stages of drying. Piles of bedding filled the corners, along with jars of powders used to aid in cleaning the washing. Now he could smell the damp in the air all around him and it tormented his nostrils. Still, this was a good place for a conversation when you didn't want to be overheard. Marcasian turned back from the door towards him, his expression altered slightly to one of annoyance.

"They will die by my hand, I swear it, my King. But what of Arundel and these Outlanders? What do you plan for them?"

That was a good question, a wise question. What was he going to do about the returning prodigal son? They may have only met briefly, but it appeared that Arundel truly had no memory of his life prior to being found in the Weeping Woods. That would mean that he did not know he was the rightful heir to the throne and so, from that point of view, he was not a threat. He could just let all three of them leave the city, never to be seen again and that would be the end of the matter. However, therein lay the problem; how could he guarantee that Arundel would never be seen again? All it would take was for someone else to recognise the one time Prince, and suddenly the days of Theagran upon the throne would be numbered. He could not risk that; it was too much for him to lose. Different measures had to be taken, more drastic measures.

"Hunt them down, all three of them. They must stand trial."

Marcasian was clearly a little taken aback by this decision. In The Bull was a bloodlust that would never be quenched and he could see in the giant's eyes that his lust burnt as strong as ever on this night.

"Trial? But, my King, is that really wise? Would it not be better to gut these men quickly and quietly so their existence was never known?"

He knew the Captain of his Guardians would have an opinion on the matter, just as he knew that his Captain would voice that opinion. It was why he always sought Marcasian's counsel and his alone, but on this occasion, while he could see the point being made, he did not agree with it.

"No, there is an opportunity here that must be seized upon. The night I killed the King and had Arundel taken to the woods, I told the people of this city, of this realm, that Arundel had murdered his father and fled the city. If they remember this fact, then they will want to see Arundel lose his head for his crime and I can deliver them that. Perhaps I can finally end the civil unrest and unite Galbraxia under my banner, as it should be. Arundel Stal must die, about that you are right. But he must do so in front of the people and they must want it."

He could see that, although Marcasian had taken it all on board, the old warrior was still not convinced.

"But what if they don't remember? Or what if they choose not to care? The uprising all those years ago took place because people refused to believe what you had told them. They refused to believe that Arundel would be capable of such treachery. What if they refuse to believe again?"

A valid point and one that had most certainly crossed his mind. It was a risk, he could see that, but one he needed to take.

"Most of those non-believers perished fighting for that very cause back in those days you speak of. Others will have been burned in their homes by your men in more recent days, as a reminder of who is King and what comes of betrayal against the throne. Should any remain within these walls, I trust that my Guardians would be more than capable of laying them to rest should the necessity arise."

"I can vouch for that, my King."

Marcasian's response had been automatic, as if he had felt the need to defend the cloak that he wore and the men it entitled him to oversee.

"As I expected. But I feel their swords will barely have need of being bloodied as most in this city are loyal enough and they will want to see the would-be King punished for his crime. It will be enough to push them to my side once and for all, and then, my old friend, then we can finally look to the realms that surround us and take their lands to expand our borders."

The mention of a possible war seemed to perk up his Captain, almost causing a sly smile to break out across his stony face.

"It would be good to expand our lands at last, my King. We have an army built for war, yet the only war they have seen has been civil and highly unsatisfying. But may I still suggest that you tread with a little caution when it comes to a trial."

The King took that on board.

"Yes, you may."

Marcasian shifted himself closer to the door, the dimensions of the small room feeling more and more cramped with every moment they were inside it.

"May I also suggest, and forgive me if I speak out of turn, my King, but three men on trial for the crimes of one does not sit well with me and I doubt will do so with the people."

His Captain had a fair point there, one that had not struck him until this very moment. Arundel could face trial and execution because he was accused of murdering his father, King Andreas, but the other two? They were unknown within the city. They had played no part in that day and so they played no part in this trial. Certainly, he could label them as guilty by association, but when he was looking to galvanise the people to support his rule, he did not need to create uncertainty and complications. There was a much easier way, a way that his Captain had been hoping for.

"You are right, it will not do."

The time for talking had run its course, the time for action was now required. Theagran puffed up his chest, his anger completely dissipated, since he could now see the benefits of what had not so long ago seemed like a horror story. Composing himself – he was King after all – he addressed his Captain no longer as an old friend but as his superior, his ruler.

"Find Arundel and bring him in alive. He must stand trial for his crime. To find him, I suggest you find my daughter. Even through just a moment's glance, I can tell that she favours the Prince and so I expect them to be in each other's company."

Marcasian nodded.

"As for the Outlanders, my guess is they will be indulging in the city's more popular pastimes. Have your men tear apart every inn, every whorehouse and every card table, if needs be, to find them."

Marcasian again nodded, only this time the nod was followed by words.

"And when they find them, my King?"

He had expected such a question and he had a fitting answer.

"Tell your men to cut them down on sight; I do not want them living out the night."

The habitual stony expression on his Captain's face broke into a sadistic smile.

"As you command, my King."

With that, he watched as the huge frame of his Captain pulled open the door and squeezed back out through the archway into the corridor. He swiftly followed, closing the door behind him with a creak and a thud. It was time for him to retire to his chamber and a flagon of the city's finest mulled wine, for tonight blood would be spilt and a traitor would find justice.

Hesitation. The opportunity had been his for the taking; just one swift thrust with the blade and it would have been all over. One vicious slash and the King would have been slain. His name-parents would have been avenged. But he had hesitated, and with that hesitation the moment he had hoped for had passed him by. Their whole purpose for coming here, for entering the city, was to meet the King, so that they could butcher him where he stood. But when that opportunity had presented itself, he had allowed himself to be distracted by hair that burned like a fire in the darkness. As he had stood there, blade in hand, its cold steel pressed firmly against his skin, he could never for one moment have foreseen what was to come.

Perhaps he had been a fool. Looking back on it now, it seemed so obvious that Thea was indeed a Princess, daughter to King Theagran. So why had he not noticed it sooner? Perhaps he had been blinded by lust; he would not be the first or the last to suffer such an affliction. It had been more than that though, more than lust. His feelings for Thea were stronger than the simple desires of his groin, and so lust was not to blame, at least not entirely. It mattered not, at least not in the grand scheme of things. What mattered was that he had stood before the King; he had stood within striking distance and he had failed to strike. Both Garad and Bromon would have achieved such a simple goal; they would have struck with cruel ease. Had they been entrusted with this task, a King would have been slain this night. Instead, they had trusted him and he had let them down. As the King had walked out, very much alive, the only blood to have been spilled had been that of his own, from his palm. To make matters worse, Thea had departed so swiftly after her father, that not a single word had been spoken between them. Was that truly how their association would end? It saddened him to think so, but his sorrow would not change matters.

The walk back down the tower that was the Great Palace had been a slow one full of silence. His name-brothers were trying hard to hold back their anger and frustration, while he was doing all he could to suppress the feelings that consumed him. He could not explain himself, they would never understand. How could he tell them that his feelings for a woman had prevented him from avenging their parents? For him, the failure was a little easier to endure because they had been his parents by name only and while they had been good to him for more years than they needed to, they were not his true kin. For Garad and Bromon however, they had been their own flesh and blood. They had brought both of them into this world and, at the word of King Theagran and the hand of Marcasian, they had been wrenched from it far too early. For them, his name-brothers, it had been far more personal and so his failure to act would cut them much deeper than it did him. He could not bring himself even to look them in the eye, let alone try to explain himself. Thus they had remained in silence, right up until the moment they left the once brilliant white confines of the Palace and ventured out into the open air, stars sparkling in a dark night sky overhead.

This was where he had planned to go his own way, give them a chance to gather their thoughts before they left the City at first light. Not knowing how to break the silence, his head lowered, he began to turn right, as they carried straight on, only for a thick and firm hand to grab hold of his arm and stop him. He looked up and saw Bromon staring back at him. His glare was not as fierce as he would have expected.

"We understand."

He had not expected to hear that. Garad then chimed in.

"We were shocked too, Ari. The moment she walked in, we

were like statues, just as you were."

He could not express how relieved he was to hear such supportive words.

"I am so sorry. I could have avenged them for you, for all of us, but I failed."

Garad playfully jabbed him on the shoulder.

"No more than we would have, especially Bromon and those slow reflexes of his."

Bromon replied with a growl. Arundel looked at his name-brothers with a newfound respect.

"So what now?"

Garad and Bromon looked at each other and then Bromon spoke.

"Well, we live another night and I say we spend that night drinking until we can no longer remember it!"

Garad nodded.

"Agreed. What do you say, Ari?"

The thought tempted him, but not enough. His mind was too distracted for him to be any form of good company.

"I say, enjoy yourselves. It is on the King, after all. But my path leads a separate way tonight. I will find you again come daybreak."

Garad then placed a hand upon his shoulder.

"Perhaps you should just let her go."

His name-brother was probably right, but it was easier said than done, and right now he just wasn't ready to do that.

"I will see you at daybreak, brother."

Garad understood and withdrew his hand. Within moments, Arundel was watching them walk across the courtyard towards the outer wall, before he turned away, uncertain where the night would lead him. He hadn't been walking long when the voice grabbed him.

"Only a brave man walks these grounds alone; or a fool. Which are you?"

He turned to see a shadowy figure standing amidst the shrubbery that lined a vast area around the Palace's perimeter.

The figure took a few steps forward and the moonlight revealed a purple satin hooded cloak covering a blue satin dress. A step or two more and he could see three red curls hanging from within the hood.

"Lady Thea, or should I say, Princess Thea?"

One of the hands curled into a fist, leaving one solitary finger, which pressed against unseen lips.

"Shh. Such talk in open spaces can get a brave fool killed. Come with me to a place where the walls do not have ears."

With that, she stepped away from the shrubbery and began to walk, her cloak billowing gently behind her with every step.

Unable to utter a word, either in protest or agreement, he began to follow. Up until now, he had only seen one side of the Palace, the front. But, as Thea walked, she led him behind the Palace to vast gardens filled with fountains and statues of great artistry. The borders in their heyday would have been lush and eye catching, but in these harsh days of neglect, vibrant greens had been replaced by sullen browns, and once healthy foliage was now withered and weak. She continued to walk along a stone path partially buried by dead leaves, until she veered slightly off into a planting of shrubs that parted with ease at the pressure of her body pushing against them. Within moments she had vanished, engulfed entirely by the plants before him. Without hesitation or knowledge of what he was doing, he followed. As small branches brushed against his face and body, it took a good fifteen to twenty strides before he came out the other side. He emerged from the shrubs onto a half circle of paving stones, at the end of which stood a marble bench that still held all its original beauty. The bench was tilted so any who sat upon it, would lean back, staring up towards the sky. Beyond the bench, water shimmered in the moonlight, covered in places by an occasional spattering of perfectly formed lily pads. In the middle of the pond stood a stone statue of a young boy, gazing up with a look of awe carved upon his face.

Thea was standing by the bench. She took hold of both sides of her hood and slowly lowered it to release a cascade of flame red hair onto her shoulders.

"I call this the Moon Chair. I used to come here as a little girl when I wanted to get away from it all. I used to sit here and stare up at the moon for hours, wondering what it would be like to be somewhere else, or someone else. Those who aren't interested in the history of the Palace do not know that this even exists and these days, even despite my absence, I can tell that most aren't interested."

She slowly moved round to the front of the bench and eased herself back down onto it, tucking her legs up beside her. "Why did you think about being someone else?"

Of all the questions in his head, that was the first to pass his lips. Thea stayed silent for a moment and then slowly patted the empty space beside her.

"Won't you take a seat?"

He contemplated saying no, thinking that if he said yes he would begin something that could never be undone, but no was not the answer he wished to give, and so he walked over and eased himself down onto the seat next to her. He took hold of Razor in her sheath and adjusted her position to allow him to get comfortable. They both sat there in silence for a few minutes, gazing up at the moon that suddenly seemed to dominate the sky. Eventually, Thea broke the silence, but her eyes remain fixed on the moon above.

"Why don't you ask me the question you truly wish the answer to?"

It was a good question, but he remained coy with his reply.

"What question would that be?"

Still she did not look at him, although he glanced towards her.

"Why didn't I tell you I was the Princess?"

He didn't need to reply. He could tell she knew she was right, and so he pursued the matter.

"Why didn't you?"

There was a moment of quiet before she replied.

"For my own protection. Even though you saved my life, I did not know who you were or what ulterior motive you might have. Being just a Lady, I am less of a catch than being the

Princess. Especially a Princess whose father is a King not well liked across most of the realm."

It was a valid point, he could not deny that. He wanted to remain angry, to stay annoyed with her deceit, but he too had not been truthful about his intentions tonight and so his anger quickly waned.

"I understand, these are troubled times; you were right to be wary of anyone. You were right to be wary of me."

Thea's expression turned to one of surprise, following his reply. She shifted her body to face him a little more.

"You accepted my explanation quicker than I had expected, Arundel. What is it you are not telling me? And why was I right to be wary of you?"

He had set himself up for that question to be asked, and now he had to give an answer. He could distance himself from the truth, he could come up with a story reasonable enough to convince her, but what would be the point? This would likely be their last encounter and he did not want to leave things on a lie, especially when he now knew her truth. He took a deep breath, gathered himself and began his response.

"My brothers and I, we did not come here tonight to seek the thanks of a King. We came here to slay a King, your father."

He waited for a moment, yet her expression did not change and so he continued.

"I was ready, blade in hand, just about to take my chance when you walked in and embraced Theagran and from then on I was too distracted to fulfil my duty, a duty I had sworn to my name-brothers."

He finished and turned towards Thea, as she cupped a hand over her mouth. It was the kind of response he had expected. He had known his truth would shock her, but what came next he had not expected.

"I'm sorry."

That caught him off guard; as the two words slipped from her lips, she removed her hand from her mouth. What reason could she possibly have to be sorry?

His guilt consumed him even more. While he still wished the King dead, he was her father and that caused an emotional conflict within, made worse by the fact that she was apologising.

He pushed himself to his feet off the stone seat and took a few steps forward, trying to create distance between them so she could not see his guilt.

"Sorry? Why would you be sorry?"

He kept his back to her as he spoke, unintended harshness creeping into his voice. After a moment or two of silence, Thea spoke again.

"I am sorry that I got in your way."

Upon hearing that he turned back round to face her, his guilt washed away and replaced by shock and surprise, confounded more so by the look of embarrassment upon Thea's beautiful face.

"Did you not hear what I said, Princess? I was going to kill your father."

Perhaps that was it, perhaps she had just misheard him and that had caused the confusion.

"Yes, I heard you, Arundel. I heard you and I understand why. I understand why and if I am honest, my father deserves to meet his death by your hand."

Now he was really confused. Not that long ago he had watched Thea embrace her father as if love bound them; yet here she was now condoning his plan to murder the very same man she had embraced. His curiosity was unbounded, trying to catch up with his confusion and it caused him to move closer to the seat. He perched himself on the end and looked into those wonderful eyes.

"I did not expect such acceptance, Princess. How can you be so at ease with me wishing to kill your father, who you embraced so lovingly earlier this evening?"

She stared back at him, yet a look of embarrassment once again spread across her face.

"Please, don't call me Princess. I am not a princess. My name is Thea, and you should not believe everything you see, Arundel."

He did not know what to make of that: she was not making any sense to him.

"But you are the daughter of the King and that makes you a princess whether you wish it or not."

He paused.

"And when you embrace your father the way you did earlier tonight, tell me how else I am supposed to interpret that?"

Thea stared at him and he could have sworn there was anger in that gaze. He did not see it for long. Now Thea was the one to wrench herself away and get to her feet. She walked over to the stone edge and stopped before the pond, her back now to him.

"What is it you are not telling me?"

He asked the question and then waited for an answer, but it wasn't swift in coming. Now his confusion and curiosity were being overshadowed by frustration. He waited a little longer and then he too got up, Razor banging gently against his leg.

"I am in no mood for games, Thea. I have already let my name-brothers down tonight because I let you distract me by revealing that King Theagran is your father. Now you tell me the affection was false, but do not say why. Now you imply that I should not feel guilty for coming here tonight with the sole intention of killing your father, but you will not explain yourself. What am I to think? What am I...?"

Before he could finish, Thea had turned round and placed a solitary finger firmly against his lips.

"I know who you are, Arundel."

He tried to speak, but still that finger pressed his lips and his words never formed.

"The Oracle has told me the truth of you, of my father, of this city."

Finally she released that finger and his lips were free again. Thea took a step away from him and turned back towards the water. Moving forward, he placed his hands upon her shoulders. For a brief moment her scent tickled his nose. It was so sweet and tempting, but he pushed it aside.

"What truth?"

She turned to him, those green eyes staring deeply into his own. He could see in them the desire to be honest, to reveal the secret that was clearly troubling her, but she stayed silent and swiftly turned away again. With his hands still firmly on her shoulders, he twisted her to her right, bringing those green eyes back to his.

"What truth?"

He asked again and once more was met with silence. Finally, that silence was broken and the truth made its way out into the open.

"You are the rightful King of Galbraxia, Arundel. This Palace should be your home."

What was she talking about? What foolishness was this?

"I told you, Thea. I am in no mood for games tonight."

She shook her head.

"This is no game, I swear it."

He released his grip and stepped back.

"If it is no game, then explain yourself."

Her body shifted as if to move towards him, but then it pulled back and she stayed on the same spot.

"You are Arundel Stal. Your father was King Andreas Stal and he sat here upon the throne as his forefathers once did. You were his only child, his heir. My father was the King's First, his right hand man you could say, a position held in my family for generations. My father murdered yours and took the throne for himself. He laid the blame on you and said you had fled the city, but in reality he sent his men to execute you secretly."

He could not believe what he was hearing, the ridiculousness of it.

"It is not true."

"It is true."

She replied at speed, so quickly he hadn't expected it.

"Then if I was to be executed, how did my name-parents find me in the woods? How am I alive today?"

Now she took a step closer and it was her turn to place a gentle hand on his shoulder.

"Have you never wondered how it was you came to be in those woods, Arundel? Why you were tied to a tree?"

He had, but never for too long. The past was exactly that and he had wasted little time on it when he could never remember.

"I...I cared not."

She inched closer again.

"The soldiers most loyal to my father, under orders from Marcasian, took you out into the woods to be executed and your body left for the wolves, so that you could never be traced. However, the guards who took you were both twisted and lazy. They thought it better game to leave you alive when the wolves came to feed and it saved them the trouble of killing you themselves. But they did not wait to watch, and clearly your name-parents found you before the wolves could. I can only assume that a mixture of a physical beating and then your desire to forget painful memories, led to your forgetting all of this."

He pulled away from her hand.

"How could you possibly know all this? How could you keep it from me all this time?"

He was confused. He was frustrated. He was angry. His emotions were out of control and he did not know how to regain control.

"I did not know until this night. I was a mere babe when this happened, so I have no recollection of it. But the Oracle was present in those days. He tells me that under your father the Guardians consisted of just twelve men, the best in the King's army. Those men were loyal to your father and never believed the story my father told. My father then turned the entire army into Guardians and with the years that passed, those involved in taking you to the woods became loose- lipped and would brag about what they did in front of the original Guardians. They in turn told the Oracle and now he has told me. I couldn't let my father find out your name in case he realised who you are, so my hug was to serve as a distraction and then I deliberately said your name wrong. But you corrected it."

He did not know what to make of it. For years he had left the past buried, a memory he could never recall and so he left it be. Now all that he knew had just changed: his life had taken a sudden and unexpected turn and he was struggling to digest it all.

"I...I do not know what to say. How can all this be?" Suddenly his mind cast back to their journey here, to the words of Yorrall. The High Priest had spoken of vengeance for a fallen father; he had told him to follow the golden man, the Oracle. It seemed as if everyone had known the truth but him. Thea's voice then cut through his train of thought.

"I must take you to see the Oracle. He will tell you much more than I. He can give you back those memories you lost."

She was right. It seemed he had to stop fighting the truth and listen to what the High Priest told him. Follow the books, find the Golden Man.

"Yes, I must see him at once."

She slipped her soft, gentle hand into his and, for the first time since this conversation had begun, he felt at ease. Her touch soothed him, giving him a warmth he had never felt before.

"Follow me."

She began to walk back towards the thicket that kept them hidden from the Palace grounds, when she stopped and looked back at him.

"Arundel...I am so sorry for what my father did. You must hate me so."

He took a step closer to her.

"I could not hate you. It is not your fault. As you say, you were a mere babe, an innocent; you cannot be blamed for the actions of your father. It is I who should apologise for jumping to such swift conclusions about you. But when I saw that embrace I...I did not know what to think, what to feel."

They had inched closer and closer without realising, until now each could feel the other's breath upon their face. He looked into those eyes; he inhaled her sweet smell; her touch tingled in his hand. They both tried to speak, but not a sound came from either of them. Instead their lips touched for the very first time. Her lips were soft, slightly moist and they carried a deliciousness about them. They pressed more firmly together and his free arm slipped around her back and pulled her into him, while their hands were still joined as one. The kiss lasted for a few seconds, but it felt like an eternity, a blissful eternity. Then, as they slowly parted, he looked into those eyes one more time and he could have sworn that they smiled at him. However, when the silence was broken, they did not speak of the kiss.

"We must go now, for I fear my father will not want to see you within the city walls come morning."

They battled their way through the thicket, something that had been unpleasant enough the first time, and a return journey had never crossed his mind. Having reached the other side, they began to walk towards the Palace entrance. Under the moonlight the famed walls held a little more of the brilliance told in stories than the truth that daylight exposed.

Two Guardians were standing either side of the entrance now, spear in hand. They were motionless and hadn't seemed to notice their approach until Thea reached out for the door. Then the Guardians crossed their spears and blocked her path.

"What is the meaning of this?" she asked with surprise and frustration in her voice. The two Guardians looked at each other and then one of them spoke.

"We have been ordered not to permit the Outlander into the Palace, Your Highness."

Thea looked back at Arundel for a moment, but he could not give an answer as to why; he was as much in the dark as she. Thea turned back to the Guardians.

"But he is my guest and I order you to let us pass."

The two men again glanced at each other, but stood their ground. The braver one spoke again.

"The King's order overrides your own and he says that the Outlander shall not enter."

Arundel could tell Thea was getting agitated and, after what he had just been told, his own concern began to grow.

"This is not acceptable."

She was struggling with what to say and he could tell.

"But it is the law."

That voice did not belong to the Guardian, who had spoken

previously, nor did it belong to the other Guardian by the door. Slowly, Arundel turned round to see four Guardians behind him. They had been so preoccupied with the sentries on the door, they had failed to see those coming up behind them. He could kick himself for that, but now was not the time. One of the four was slightly ahead of the other three and the voice had belonged to him. He now proclaimed with authority, "The law also dictates that criminals must be brought to justice. Therefore, by decree of King Theagran, I am placing you under arrest, Arundel Stal, for the murder of your father, King Andreas."

At these words, all four men drew their swords. Acting on instinct alone, Arundel's hand lowered to his side and his fingers scrambled until they felt the cool, hard surface of Razor's hilt against his skin. He slid her from her sheath with ease and raised her to waist-height, while holding out his left arm to guard Thea. The Guardian spoke again.

"Do not be foolish, you are outnumbered."

Arundel looked at him and recognised that the Guardian carried himself with great confidence, and perhaps a little arrogance. He could use that to his advantage: he had seen so many men fall due to arrogance. He responded to the Guardian, "What choice have you given me?"

The Guardian lowered his head a little and they glared at each other, eye to eye.

"Very well. Seize him in the name of the King."

The three Guardians then took a step forward towards him, the blades of their swords gleaming in the moonlight. He had always been taught to take the front foot when outnumbered, to take the fight to your opponents before they could surround you. With that in mind, he charged forward.

He could tell he had caught them off guard and his first swing of Razor saw her cut through the arm of the first Guardian, splattering blood and causing his sword to drop to the floor. He then parried a strike from the second and swiftly turned to parry one from the third as well. The clash of steel on steel rang out through the night air, as he deflected several blows from both men again, keeping on his toes from side to side. The Guardian with the wounded arm was trying to recover his sword, when Arundel grabbed him and sent him crashing into both the second and third Guardians. This gave him enough time to seize the advantage and, with one swift strike, he took the second Guardian's sword arm clean off. A sweep to the right slit the throat of the third Guardian, before he drove Razor back to his left and through the eye socket of the second Guardian.

By now, the leader of the group had summoned the two Guardians by the door but Arundel had registered this. As the first spearman reached him, spear out full stretch, he stepped aside at the last moment and the spear drove into the gut of the first Guardian. Before the spearman could react, Razor was slicing his chest open and then piercing his heart. The second sentry arrived and Arundel was just able to parry a thrust with the spear. The spearman retreated and then lunged again, but this time Razor's sharp blade splintered the wood of the spear, causing it to break in two. The sentry dropped the remnants of his broken spear and tried to reach for his sword, but not before Razor pierced his gut. With five men down, the vocal leader had no choice but to get involved, as Arundel turned to face him. They began to pace around each other, when Arundel saw another wave of Guardians beginning to advance upon them from the outer wall of the Palace. The vocal Guardian had clearly seen this too.

"You will not win, Outlander. Your resistance is a lost cause."

There was no time to retort. He had to end this before more Guardians reached him. Taking a step forward, he swung with Razor, but the Guardian blocked it. He swung again and again, and the Guardian blocked each one, although staggering back with each blow. The Guardian was now wrong footed, yet made an attacking move as he swung his sword low and hard towards the waist. Arundel parried it aside, sending the Guardian further off balance. This enabled Arundel to strike, as a sweep of Razor sliced open the thigh of the Guardian, and dropped him to one knee. A second sweep opened him up from neck to breast.

Arundel saw that the next wave of Guardians was nearly upon

him as he dealt the death blow to the formerly vocal one.

But he failed to see Marcasian approaching from behind until it was too late.

He caught sight of the Bull in the corner of his eye, but never saw him swing that hulking arm of his. He felt the thud, when something hit the back of his head. For a split second, he felt searing pain surge through his skull, but then the world slipped into darkness.

"Another round, gentlemen?"

The serving girl had come up to their table, without making a sound. Perhaps it was the noise inside the tavern, or they were simply far too occupied, but, either way, there she was and the question had been asked. Garad looked at Bromon and his brother nodded, as he had expected.

"Why not?"

The serving girl leaned over to sweep up their empty jugs and Garad could not help but glance at the ample bosom that was almost falling out of the low cut bodice of her dirty cotton dress. Greasy black hair covered portions of her face, but what he could see was reasonable, at best. However, a few more drinks, courtesy of the King, and he was sure reasonable would become more than acceptable. He watched her work her way through the crowd of patrons before disappearing behind the bar. The booming voice of Bromon brought his gaze back to the table.

"You will find far better and more willing in the whorehouses, brother."

He was right, but he would not let him know it.

"Aye, Bromon, I would. But she would come at a much cheaper price and that suits me fine."

Bromon bellowed out a hefty, short-noted laugh.

"Hah! Does the King's hospitality not cover such delights?"

"If only, brother, if only!"

The serving girl returned and placed two fresh jugs on the table. This time he managed to catch her eye for just a second and he flashed her a wink. This brought a wry smile from her and, as she slipped away once more, he knew that his prospects had just risen. He then reached for his jug and raised it into the air, as Bromon did the same.

"In thanks of the King!" he cried sarcastically.

"May his reign be near its end," Bromon added.

They drove their jugs together, as drops of the precious ale splashed onto the table, before guzzling down a mouthful.

They had been in the tavern for some time now. They had not seen Arundel since leaving him at the entrance to the Great Palace, after their attempt on the King's life had failed, for which Arundel blamed himself. They had been ready, they had been prepared and it looked as if it was going to happen, but then Thea arrived and her embrace of the King was distraction enough for Arundel to miss his opportunity.

Garad knew that Arundel felt guilty that he had let them down, and he could understand why. The death of the King naturally meant more to him and Bromon, because it had been their blood parents who had been slain at the King's command, whereas for Arundel they were parents in name alone. This didn't stop Arundel caring; they had raised him from ten years old after all; but having taken charge of the deed himself and then failing to deliver, he understood that Arundel would not deal with that well.

He and Bromon had not spoken about it since arriving at the tavern. He had wanted to and he imagined Bromon did too, but the subject never came up. In all honesty, they had expected Arundel to join them after taking a little time to himself, but that had not happened, and darkness was now well and truly set in for the night. They had even lined up a round for him, but that jug still sat full and untouched upon the table. Remembering it, he gazed at it for a moment. Then, as he looked away, he noticed out of the corner of his eye that Bromon too had spared it a glance.

"The silly fool ain't coming, is he?"

Bromon never minced his words, that was for sure.

"No, I think Ari has found something better for the night."

Bromon grunted.

"Or he is too ashamed to show his face."

Bromon drank a little more of his jug. He never was one to contain his emotions.

"Now, now, Bromon; you can't blame Ari. It could have happened to any of us."

Bromon pounded his fist on the table, causing more ale to spill.

"Do not tell me to not to be angry, Garad, and do not tell me that I would make such a mistake. My blood always comes before a wench...always."

"Only because you are too ugly to be desirable, brother, not through your own choice. Ari, on the other hand, he is taken with this girl like I have never seen before."

Bromon let out a grunt.

"Pah...he barely knows the woman. One encounter in the grass does not excuse his actions tonight."

Bromon was always such hard work; he saw everything in black and white, and never grey.

"It was more than that, brother. During our journey, she took herself to his furs both nights when the Guardians were asleep."

Bromon suddenly perked up upon hearing this, as if snapped from his bubble of rage.

"Did she now? The sly devil! We will never hear him stop bragging about laying with a Princess."

Garad shook his head.

"Not even once. She lay in his furs and he kept watch, nothing more. That is true devotion, more than just a whim."

Bromon bellowed out another laugh.

"Hah, two nights and not even a sniff. What kind of a man is he?"

Bromon took another swig of ale.

"A better man than you or I, brother."

Bromon scoffed at that.

"How do you even know this?"

Now he took a swig of ale.

"I saw her the second night, and I confronted Ari, and he told me. So, you see, Bromon, his actions tonight could not be helped."

Bromon was clearly still disgruntled.

"Then who can I to be angry with, because I still have much anger in my heart?"

Garad held his hands out and indicated all around them.

"Take your pick, brother. A few more ales and any of these will be fair game."

Bromon looked around at the other patrons drinking as solidly as them.

"Fair game? There is barely a hint of competition in here. Do not mock me, Garad. I am in a fighting mood and before long, I will not care if it is even you I have to fight."

Garad saw that as a challenge.

"Calm now, brother. You have the reflexes of an ox. I could put an arrow between your eyes before you could even set your fingers upon that lumbering axe of yours."

Bromon pounded his fist on the table again.

"Mock me, do you? How about I cut your head from your body and then we can see how quick your arrows are?"

At that moment Bromon reached down beside him in search of his great battle-axe. Reacting quickly, Garad grabbed his bow from beside the table and slid an arrow from his quiver. Speed and accuracy were two key elements of an archer and he had them both in abundance. He nocked the arrow at speed and pointed it straight at the head of his brother. Then, as Bromon looked up, his axe barely off the floor, the tip of the arrow was squarely between his eyes. They stayed like that for a moment, neither of them moving, both of them waiting to see what the other did. At last, Bromon broke out into a roar of laughter that boomed through the tavern and caught the attention of many. As his laughter eased, he spoke again.

"Still quick I see, Garad. That means you are clearly not drunk enough!"

With that he put down his axe and picked up his jug, before finishing off its contents.

"Another round is in order, courtesy of the bastard King, of course!"

Garad picked up his own jug, tipped it towards Bromon in agreement and downed the rest of the ale.

He was about to raise it in the air to request another, when his eyes were drawn towards the doors of the tavern. The sound of chatter had begun to quieten and attention turned as a man dressed in full Guardian attire stepped into the tavern, helm and all. He was soon followed by five more Guardians who were dressed likewise. The first Guardian spoke to a few of the customers near him but, clearly dissatisfied with the response, pushed them aside forcibly before approaching the bar. He spent a few moments at the bar speaking with the landlord, who then pointed a chubby, hairy finger in their direction. Garad had harboured doubts from the moment the Guardian had set foot in the tavern, but now he knew such a feeling was justified. Slowly and subtly, he took hold of his bow beside him and once again slipped an arrow from his quiver. Bromon, meanwhile, had his back to it all and was none the wiser about the threat unfolding behind him.

"Ready your axe, Bromon, for I fear you are going to need it."

Bromon thought it a joke.

"Hah, have you not had your fill? We contested just mere moments ago."

Garad refrained from making an unnecessary comment.

"Not for me, brother. We are no longer alone."

His eyes stayed on the Guardians, as they made their way through the crowd towards them.

"How many?" Bromon asked.

"Six Guardians dressed for battle."

Bromon unexpectedly smiled.

"At last, some competition."

The first of the Guardians reached them and came to a stop behind Bromon. The others formed up behind him in their best attempt at a line, but the mass of customers in the tavern were making it difficult for them to stay close together, giving the blood brothers a possible advantage.

"Outlanders."

As the first Guardian spoke, Bromon pushed his seat back with a creak and then stood up, turning to face the threat.

"That we are."

While Bromon stood, Garad remained seated, wanting to conceal his readiness.

"By order of King Theagran, for aiding the murderer of a former King, you are both under arrest."

Bromon turned to face him.

"Did you hear that, Garad? We have supposedly aided a King Slayer."

Bromon turned back to the Guardian.

"Tell me, this crime we have supposedly committed yet know nothing about, what is the punishment for it?"

The Guardian remained stony-faced.

"Execution."

Bromon bellowed out another hefty laugh.

"Hah, execution you say? Well then, I guess you would allow a dead man one last drink?"

With that, he picked up the full jug that had been ordered for Arundel a long time ago. He raised it to his lips, but then flicked his wrist and sent the contents into the face of the Guardian, momentarily blinding him. Immediately, as Bromon ducked for his axe, Garad raised his bow and loosed the arrow straight into the face of the Guardian, right between the gaps left by his helm.

With that, the other five Guardians tried to draw their swords, but the tavern was too crowded and they all struggled to unsheathe them. This provided an opportunity for Bromon. Garad's brother may have been a big man and often slow, but when it came to fighting, he moved like a dancer. He drove the butt of the axe into the chest of the first Guardian, denting the armour plate and doubling him over. Bromon then raised his axe into the air and brought it down with a thunderous blow onto the Guardian's helm, splitting it open and his head with it. The

Guardian dropped to the floor and Bromon was onto the next, driving his axe through his armour into the belly. A third Guardian had his sword drawn and was moving in on Bromon, but, with his brother occupied, Garad acted quickly, loosing a first arrow into the Guardian's armpit to slow him down, followed by two more to the neck that dropped him to the floor. He then shifted his bow to the fifth and sixth Guardians. His first arrow nicked the fifth Guardian's helm and ricocheted off into the distance, but his second pierced the left eye with perfection. Bromon set about the final Guardian, hacking off a leg with one swift sweep and then bringing the axe down for one crushing blow.

All six of the Guardians were down, but the commotion within the tavern was chaotic and noisy, and Garad knew it would only bring more.

"Bromon, we must leave, and leave now."

"Agreed."

They pushed their way through the crowds and then the doorway, before stepping out into the fresh, night air. Looking all around, Garad spotted no sign of reinforcements yet. Bromon turned to him.

"What, by the Gods, was that about?"

He placed a hand on his brother's shoulder.

"I do not know. But we must assume that Ari is in the same trouble."

Bromon raised his axe, ready and eager.

"We must find him."

His brother took his bow and hooked it over his shoulder.

"Yes, we must, but for now we need to find a place to hide."

With that, he took the lead as they set off into the darkness of Ryevale.

Day had long since broken and she had barely slept. Last night, she had watched the Guardians drag Arundel's senseless body off towards the Crypt. She was then personally escorted by Marcasian himself and two of his Guardians up to her room in the Great Palace. She had been told it was for her own safety, while the other two Outlanders remained unaccounted for, but she couldn't help feeling as if in reality she was being held prisoner. Did Marcasian know that she had been to see the Oracle? Did he know what she had told Arundel? Or was it simply a case of coincidence and nothing more? She did not know the answer to any of those questions. Nor did she know the condition of Arundel. Had he been simply locked away in the Crypt? Or had he suffered a worse fate? As she lay there on her bed awake all night, she was riddled with worry: was he still alive? She feared the worst: what else could she do? Arundel had fought so bravely against greater numbers, but he had not seen Marcasian emerge from the Palace door and approach him from behind. He had been unable to stop Marcasian, as he struck him in the back of the head with the hilt of his sword. Such bravery, but it had all been in vain.

Arundel had dominated her thoughts all night. She thought about their kiss, about how much she had longed for that moment on the journey to Ryevale and now that she had finally experienced it, the fear that it might never happen again. Her anxiety that Marcasian might know the truth about her and what she knew faded away quickly, replaced solely by a fear of what may have become of her blond- haired Outlander. If Arundel was dead, then she didn't care if Marcasian or her father knew about her visit to the Oracle; she didn't care what they might do to her.

Ryevale had long since ceased to be her home and that had not changed after her return. She had never been close with her father, but now their relationship was strained beyond repair. She had no friends here, no other family. She had been packed off as a child to become a woman and find herself, but, in truth, she had lost sight of who she was until she met Arundel, until he and his name-brothers had saved her in the Weeping Woods. Those nights spent in his furs while he kept watch, they were the first real nights of her life where she felt alive, where she felt cared for. Arundel had given her warmth in a cold world and now the thought of having lost him filled her with dread.

So it was that, after waking from a light doze, she had made the decision to visit the Crypt, come daylight, to see if he was there and if he was alive. However, she was aware of the possible problems, given that there was every chance Marcasian had posted Guardians on her door. Another obstacle was the Crypt itself and gaining access to it. The Crypt had been her father's design. There were cells in the basement of the Great Palace, but only a handful, and these had always been used through history for 'special' prisoners. Otherwise, for generations, prisoners had been kept in the old gaol, which had simply been a converted stable. When her father took the throne, civil war broke out in Galbraxia and, with a rise in violent outbreaks and possible betrayals, her father had become paranoid. Therefore, he demanded a more secure method to hold prisoners. He had the old stable torn down and the Crypt built in its place.

The Crypt took years to build and many men to do so. It was dug deep into the ground, with only one access door in and out. The door itself was flat on the ground and could only be opened by key, of which only three had been cut. Inside there were no windows. Scattered torches provided just enough light for prisoners to see the basics of what they were doing, but never enough to be able to break from their cells.

The design of the Crypt was such that no Guardian remained inside; thus if anyone did escape from their cell, they would have no access to a key and would be unable to unlock the door. There wasn't even a permanent Guardian on the outside of the door. One of the Guardians would check on the door every hour to make sure it was secure, and then twice a day one Guardian would venture inside to check all was as it should be, while another stood guard outside. If entry were to be made to the Crypt, it would always require two people: one to enter, with the door shut behind him, the other to remain outside the door with the key. This way should the one who entered be overpowered, there was no key on them to open the door. A coded knock would be agreed between the two prior to entry, so that it would differ every time and the prisoners would not know it.

There were many things her father put in place that Thea disagreed with, but there was no denying the genius of the Crypt. If she could leave her room, then she would have to time her visit for just after the hourly check. As for gaining access, her only hope was that the Oracle held a key. If so, she would have to take the key in with her and take the risk. She had no idea how many prisoners were currently inside the Crypt, but Arundel was worth the gamble.

It was mid-morning when Shauri entered the room bearing a plate of bread and cheese and a bowl of fresh water. She grasped the plate, while Shauri set down the bowl of water on the side table. As meals went, it was extremely dry but having been awake most of the night, she found hunger had got the better of her and so she worked through the bread, piece by piece, and finished off with the cheese. Shauri then untied the lace bow at the back of her nightgown, and, as it slid to the floor, she stepped out of it and walked over to the bowl of water. The water was lukewarm but refreshing on her skin as she washed her face and body. Shauri next handed her a linen robe that she wrapped about herself to dry off, while the handmaid walked over to the wardrobe and opened its doors. She looked inside for a few moments, before speaking.

"Do you have a preference of dress today?"

She had only been back in the city for a day and was already sick of dresses. In any event, a dress was not suitable for a visit to the Crypt, although she was not going to tell Shauri of her destination.

"No dress today, I don't care what my father would say. Look in my trunk and you will find something more suitable."

She expected some form of complaint but none came. Instead, Shauri shut the wardrobe doors and shuffled over to the trunk, lifting its big lid and sifting through the contents inside. Before long, she emerged with an outfit that she laid out on the bed. Boiled leather trousers stained black, a cream chemise and a black bodice, rounded off with her ox hide boots. As Thea dressed, Shauri began to talk once more.

"Are you all right after last night, Princess?"

She suddenly shot a glance towards the petite girl.

"Please call me Thea, I hate being called Princess; I am merely one in title alone. And tell me, Shauri, what did you hear about last night?"

Her handmaid took a seat on the bed and for the first time seemed less strained.

"The cook told me, as he fixed your breakfast, that you had been held captive by that Outlander and Marcasian rescued you."

Her jaw almost dropped to the floor when she heard that. How quickly the truth had been buried beneath a lie, such a common practice, it would seem.

"Arundel did not hold me captive, far from it."

"But the cook said…"

She cut Shauri off before she could finish.

"The cook is wrong. I was there, after all. These walls are filled with lies, Shauri, and you will do well to learn that as quickly as I have. Now can you help me with this?"

Shauri nodded and got to her feet. She walked over and, lace by lace, pulled the back of the bodice tight.

"What did happen, Princess...I mean, Thea?"

Shauri pulled on another lace and the bodice gripped a little tighter around Thea's ribs. Could she tell Shauri? Should she tell? If she was honest with herself, it was nice to have someone to talk to; the Great Palace was such a lonely place. What harm would it do, as long as she left out key details?

"Well, Arundel and I...talked under the moonlight. We have become friends during our journey here and I enjoy his company. He was walking me back to the Palace when the Guardians attempted to arrest him, wrongly, I might add."

Shauri looked a little confused by that.

"How could he be arrested wrongly? I do not understand."

Another lace pulled tighter and Thea could feel the air momentarily squeeze out of her lungs.

"He has been accused of something he did not do, that is how."

Shauri let that settle for a moment.

"Cook said that the Guardians had it under control, but then Marcasian disarmed the Outlander with his bare hands and then made him beg for mercy."

She almost let out a loud cry of laughter upon hearing that, such was the ridiculousness of it. If there was anything she could take away from this conversation, it was the lesson learned about how quickly lies spread around the Palace and how deep the fabrications sank.

"Again, so far from the truth. Arundel was set upon by six Guardians and he slew them all. As he then prepared for more that were approaching, Marcasian came up behind him and hit him on the back of the head with the hilt of his sword. There was nothing impressive about Marcasian's actions, I can tell you that now. Arundel was the brave and heroic one and now he rots in the Crypt for a crime he did not commit."

At least she hoped he was there, alive, and things weren't much worse, as she feared. She could tell that her comments had caught Shauri off guard; the petite maid was not sure how to respond. One final breath of air escaped Thea's body, as Shauri pulled on the last lace, tied it up and then spoke again.

"How will you have your hair, up or down?"

Today's plan was definitely not one for long flowing hair.

"Up."

She then sat, while Shauri set about fixing her hair up. They did not speak another word about last night's events.

Her hopes that the Oracle would have a key to the Crypt proved correct. Although it had taken him time to find it, he did indeed possess one. He told her that in all probability it had been forgotten that he had ever been given a key, since if the King knew he had one, it would most certainly have been confiscated by now. Her visit to him didn't just produce a key; it also came with a message. The Oracle was already aware of Arundel's plight, prior to her visit, and he also knew that, if Arundel was still alive, his most likely fate would be execution. She did not ask how he got his information; she believed it best to stay silent. Instead, she listened as he told her that plans were already in place to attempt an escape, but it could not happen until the day of the execution itself, should there be one. When she asked how it would be possible, all the Oracle would disclose was that the Guardians of old remembered where their loyalties lay. So it was that she left the old library with a key in her hand and a message in her head, and set off across the grounds of the Great Palace towards the Crypt.

While the Moon Chair had been a walk behind the Palace and through greenery, the way to the Crypt was one to the left of the Palace leading from stone to soil and grass, neglected for so long that it grew up past her knees. Trousers had most certainly been the right choice because the grass would have played havoc with a dress, she thought to herself, as she made her way through the green sea. Given that the door to the Crypt was on the floor, she wondered if she would even be able to find it, since this area of land was so untended. While she knew of the patrol schedule, it had crossed her mind whether anyone actually bothered to come out here and check, if they could never even find the door.

Locating the door, however, turned out to be rather easy. After walking for some time, she came across an area of earth that was barren of any grass at all; most likely it had all died off during the building work. In the middle of this earth patch, lay a pair of circular wooden doors. Each door had a handle and a keyhole on it. The keyhole and handles appeared to be iron.

There was no sign of any Guardians around and, by her calculation, there were none due for a good while. The Oracle had only provided her with one key, which left her hoping that it would work in both locks. She knelt on the doors themselves and slipped the key into the first lock. She turned it to her left and heard a clicking sound. She then pulled the key out and slipped it into the second lock. It fitted, so that was a good start. Turning it left, she again heard a clicking sound. She then stood up and slipped the key into her right boot, before preparing herself for the hard part. She leant over, grabbed one of the handles and began to pull. For a few moments, the door was as heavy as anything she had ever experienced and it barely even moved, but then, becoming much lighter, it suddenly pulled up and open, as if it were stretching up to the cloudy sky overhead. She gave herself a moment to catch her breath, and then set about the second door with similar success. With both doors open, she could see that on the inside there were also handles and keyholes. Beyond the doors, the daylight enabled her to see the first four stone steps that led downwards, but from there on, there was nothing but total darkness. For a brief moment she hesitated, but then she remembered those nights that Arundel watched over her; she remembered that kiss; she remembered how he made her feel, and she took her first step forward. As she reached the fourth step, she was past the entrance and could see the first of the lit torches, the flame guiding her along the next few steps. Before she ventured on, she reached up and pulled the doors closed above her, a much easier task than opening them had been. Then she locked them both.

After that, one step at a time, she carefully made her way

down the stairs. Every so often, there would be a torch, the flame of which illuminated just enough of the stairs to lead her to the next. She could feel a surprising coolness in the air, a slight breeze that indicated ventilation had been built into the Crypt somewhere. She had not bothered to count how many steps there were, but it was certainly more than a few. As she approached what she believed was the eighth torch mounted on the wall and stepped into its light, she could no longer see steps ahead. The floor appeared to level out and this was swiftly confirmed when she took a few more steps forward.

Although the darkness gave away little, it wasn't long before she emerged from what must have been the end of the stairwell corridor and into the main chamber, for now she could see various torches mounted on stone pillars that led off in three different directions. With the stairwell behind her, she could now take the route straight ahead, to her right, or to her left. Which one to choose? How would she even know where to begin? After much consideration, she opted for straight ahead and took her first steps in that direction when she heard it for the first time. Her first instinct was that it was a moaning sound, a sound not necessarily surprising in a place like this, but, as it became more consistent and she listened more intently, it began to sound more like muffled speech. It didn't help that it echoed off the walls, making it impossible for her to distinguish any words at all. However, because the corridor branched off into three tunnels, she could at least tell which direction it was coming from, to her right.

Now a dilemma faced her. Could it be that there was more than one prisoner down here and they were talking to each other? Could it be that a prisoner was talking to himself? Or could it be that someone else was visiting down here? Perhaps a Guardian was in here, after all, and they had just failed to stick to the rules of leaving a Guardian up top. If it was the last explanation, she could not risk being seen and so thoughts of heading back up to the surface sprang into her mind. Then she realised that the one factor, which made conditions so difficult down here, was also something she could use to her advantage, and that was the darkness. If what she had seen so far was anything to go by, she should be able to get very close to the source of the noise and remain hidden by the dark. So it was that she opted to go right, instead of back.

As she made her way down the right hand tunnel, she kept herself among the shadows, but close enough to each torch to be able to see. The longer she walked, the louder the sound got, until eventually she could tell by the tones that it wasn't just one voice, but two. The tunnel remained straight the entire way without deviation, and as her walk continued, the muffled voices were slowly becoming a little clearer and she could pick out the odd word, although those words on their own made no sense at all.

The Crypt had clearly been built to a regular design with every pillar and every torch seemingly an equal distance apart. Therefore, it was easy for her to notice the change up ahead, when it came into view. She could see far enough to what appeared to be the final torch mounted on a pillar, but then, just to the left of that torch, she could see another flame, which she reasoned should not be there. Her steps became more tentative and she buried herself further into the shadow, as she came ever closer to the extra flame. Now, random words became whole sentences and the voices seemed familiar. One of them, she believed, was Arundel, helped by the fact she expected him to be down here. The other, while she recognised it, she could not quite place. The unknown voice spoke.

"You should have died."

The voice she believed was Arundel's then replied.

"I did."

There was a pause and then Arundel spoke again.

"Who I once was died that night."

She continued forward at a slower pace and more warily. She could now see the extra flame was being held by a figure robed from head to toe in what she assumed was black, since it blended so well with the darkness. The face was obscured by a hood. The unknown voice spoke again.

"Do you still claim to have no memory after all this time?"

Arundel responded, "It is no claim. I was reborn in my tenth year of life."

She had reached as far as she could and set about taking up a spot in the darkness. But as she did so, she failed to see the broken bit of stone until it was too late. Her foot kicked it. It bounced along the floor, making a quiet clink that within these walls boomed loudly. She held her breath and buried herself deep in the shadows, when suddenly the hooded figure turned towards her direction. With the head facing into the light of the flame, she could now see enough of the features to determine who it was. How could she have been so stupid? How could she have not recognised it straight away? She desperately held back a gasp, as her father's eyes sought out the source of the noise. After a few moments, he turned back to the cell.

"You aren't alone down here after all, Arundel. It would appear the rats have come to join you."

Arundel did not respond. Her father then spoke again.

"What sickens me the most is that even after all these years, you look just like your mother."

Arundel responded.

"Did you murder her too?"

This seemed to provoke anger from her father. He drove one fist into the bars of the cell and shouted loudly, "Never! "

Silence followed for a few moments and the anger seemed to ease from his voice, when he spoke again.

"Murder her? I loved her. No, Arundel, you were the one who murdered her when she gave birth to you. You took her life as she gave you yours and I will forever hate you for it."

Did she hear that right? Had her father just told Arundel that he loved a woman other than her mother, his wife? Clearly, Arundel picked up on it too as he replied.

"You loved my mother? But what about Thea's mother?"

Yes, what about her mother?

The King responded.

"She was nothing but a mere consolation prize, a wife picked by my own father. I never loved her, I could never love anyone else but Lady Hytheria Fanardorn, your mother. She should have been mine. Your father did not deserve her and I never forgave him for stealing her from me. For years, I dreamed of my revenge, until the night I slit his throat right before you. But even his death did not ease my broken heart."

She could not believe what she was hearing. After all these years, her father had never truly loved her mother. She had always seemed a little unhappy, but Thea had never understood why until this day.

"Thea's mother was nothing but a burden to me. She had always made me weary, but after I killed Andreas, she became a liability. She knew what I had done and could not accept it. Her nights were spent drinking heavily in any tavern that would take her and while I was glad she was absent, I feared she would eventually speak the truth. So I had Marcasian deal with her one night, as she staggered out of the Howling Witch, a fitting tavern name that night. He then dumped her by a brothel to make it look as though an unsatisfied customer had taken out his discontent on her. As the Queen, the shock of her death and the demand for enquiry would have been too great a risk. But a Queen moon-lighting as a whore, that was a scandal that everyone was happy to bury, without question."

She was shocked, stunned. She wanted to scream out, to yell with the full force of her lungs. She wanted to take that flame and drive it into her father's black heart, but she could not reveal herself, could not let him know she was here. So instead, she remained silent and still, while tears trickled down her cheeks.

"Are you learning yet, Arundel? Do you understand that I will do anything to keep what I have? I had no hesitation in sending you to your death when you were ten years old, and I have no hesitation in doing the same now. The people of this city have been hardened by years of civil war. They have embraced me as their King and accepted you as a murderer, and they will be glad to see you punished for your crime. You will be left here to wallow in the darkness, knowing that your death is imminent, while my Guardians track down your Outlander kin: I guarantee, they will be found. Then, in three days, I will have you executed before my people, but first I will make you watch the death of your kin, so that you will die knowing I have taken everything from you that you have ever held dear."

She could feel her heart pounding. Already devastated by the truth about her mother, she now faced losing Arundel in three days. She had to do something, anything, to stop that from happening. Arundel, meanwhile, gave his response.

"I do not fear death. I have courted it enough in my life."

A cackle seemed to slip from her father's tongue.

"Good, well you shall be bedfellows with death soon enough."

With that, her father turned away from the cell and began to walk down the tunnel in the direction of the exit. Her instinct and desire was to head straight over to Arundel, but she knew through experience that the walls would carry their voices and alert the King. So she waited. She waited in the darkness, her tear-stained cheeks damp as she wiped them dry. Then, when she felt it was safe to do so, she moved from her hiding spot and with the little light left, she made her way to Arundel's cell.

"Arundel!" she cried out. There was a moment of silence and then a reply.

"Thea, is that you?"

"Yes."

She was so relieved to hear him again, even though she had just been listening to him speak. Her hands fumbled across the bars until they found his, and she slipped her fingers between his.

"What are you doing down here?"

She wanted to give an answer to that. There were so many things she wanted to say, to share with him, but she now knew that she did not have the time.

"There is no time to explain that now, Arundel. I only have three days to get you out of here."

He gripped her fingers more tightly.

"Do not risk yourself for me. There is no escape. I could not bear you suffering because of me."

She brushed that off; it was her choice to make and she had already made it.

"I will speak with the Oracle. He will know what to do. I will save you, Arundel; I will save you."

CHAPTER

14

He had no idea how much time had passed. Down here, deep underground, there was no day or night, just constant darkness. He had been told by King Theagran, that he would be left down here for three days before his public execution, but he could not say how long it had been since that conversation. For all he knew, it could have been three hours or it could have been three days; there was just no way of telling down here. However, he guessed that one day had passed since then, and he had Thea to thank for that.

Moments after his conversation with Theagran had ended, a brief exchange with Thea had taken place. He had been given no food down here and, before departing, Thea had said she would arrange for her handmaid Shauri to bring some down for him the next day. He was told that he would know it was Shauri, and not a trick, as she was missing a finger. True enough at some later point, a young female, shrouded in a faded brown hooded cloak, appeared at his cell bars. She did not speak a word, but as she passed him through food from a bucket she carried, he saw the stump where a finger had once been. Her silence was coupled with a swift exit, as soon as the last item of food had been handed over, and it meant he was unable to ask what day it was.

Thankfully, the quality of the food more than made up for the quality of the service. Thea had sorted him a decent helping of breads, cheeses and berries, along with a few strips of boar and chicken. It was more of a delicacy than he had often enjoyed during his days back in Havendale, where food had been scarce in winter, and almost as hard to find some summers. Shauri had also left a bucket of water by his cell, within arm's reach, and given him a small cup to scoop it out with.

He should have been concerned that a Guardian might catch him with all of this, but he had not been aware of a single one, since he had been down here. There was a risk that when they came to take him for his execution, they would find the goods and question how he got them, but in such dark surroundings, he was confident he could hide any remnants. This was because a large portion of the cell remained unlit by the single flame upon the pillar in the middle of the walkway. Only when he ventured near the bars, could he enjoy some of its light, and this was just enough for him to relieve his bladder and bowels, nothing more.

At the very least, it should have made sleeping easy, given that he could take up position in utter darkness with no disturbance, coupled with the sheer boredom from having nothing to do. However, his lack of physical activity saw him use up little energy and prevented him from getting overly tired. So he dozed upon occasion, or at least he thought he did. With no way to keep track of how much time had passed, he did not know how long he slept each time he drifted off, but it felt like a series of light naps, rather than heavy sleeps. This, he imagined, was a bonus, as far as his captors were concerned. Simple things, such as a severe lack of light and the absence of time, were enough to drive a man crazy, without even realising it. He imagined that was why Theagran had told him he had only three days before his execution, because it would leave him sitting here knowing his death was imminent, but never knowing exactly when.

All he had to keep him occupied was the food he had secretly been given, and his thoughts. Thoughts about his blood parents, parents he knew nothing about, parents who had once been King and Queen of this decaying city. A father, who had been betrayed and murdered by his rival; a mother, who had died while bringing him into this world. He knew little about his blood parents except for their demise and he would prefer to know nothing rather than that.

His thoughts also turned to his name-brothers, Bromon and Garad. Such valiant warriors, brothers in every way, bar blood. He thought about how he had let them down on the night he could have cut out the heart of the King, the heart of Theagran. He thought about how his past and their association with him had put them in grave danger. But he also thought about the fact that at the time of his conversation with Theagran, they had yet to be caught. He clung to the hope that they still remained at large. Given his failure, he would gladly sacrifice his life for them to live.

Then, of course, he thought about Thea. With a tingle, his nostrils recalled her intoxicating scent. His eyes remembered how vibrant her own eyes of emerald green had been. He remembered her beauty; he remembered hair like a roaring fire. He remembered her spirit, her laugh and the way she tried to hide her softer side but often failed. He remembered that kiss. If his life was to end soon, then he was glad that it had not ended before that kiss. Their time together had not been long, but to him it had felt like a blissful eternity and having had to wait all his life for a moment such as that kiss, he would gladly wait a thousand more lifetimes to experience another.

He was asleep when they came for him. He had not heard them approach, but was jolted awake, when they banged on the bars of his cell. His eyes took a few moments to adjust, not so much to the darkness, but to there being a disturbance to the light from the mounted torch flame. He edged himself up to a seated position and realised that a few pieces of bread remained beside him. Under cover of darkness, he pushed them into the straw that covered the floor and tucked them out of sight. His eyes then moved to the bucket of water by the bars of his cage, but there was nothing he could do about it. Thankfully, the new arrivals had either not noticed it or just didn't care. He could count four Guardians in total, unless more were waiting further down the tunnel. He could not make out any more detail, aside from their Guardian garb. The one closest to the bars then spoke, "Death awaits you, Outlander."

The Guardian beside him unlocked the cell door and pulled

it open. He stepped aside and the two at the back entered the cell, carrying rope. Approaching him, they grabbed his feet as the lead Guardian spoke again.

"Do not try and resist, Outlander. Your death is to be seen by the people, not down here in the shadows."

He had contemplated putting up a struggle, but with no way of defending himself, he knew it would be pointless. The only gain would be to deprive Theagran of the pleasure of executing him in front of the city, but he knew that the King would have Thea present and, if he were to die, he would rather do so looking at her, one final time. So he remained co-operative, as they bound his ankles first and then took separate lengths of rope and bound each wrist. They then helped him to his feet, whereupon he discovered they had left enough slack in the ankle rope for him to walk slowly. The two Guardians held a wrist rope each as they stood either side of him, giving them control of his arms. He shuffled out of the cell into the tunnel, where the lead Guardian took up a position in front of him, while the last Guardian shut the cell door and then positioned himself behind them. In silence and at little speed, due to the restrictions on his ankles, they negotiated the passage. The stairwell was a task in itself but, with help, he was able to make the climb back to the surface.

As they reached the wooden doors, the lead Guardian banged a fist on them four times and they all waited a moment. Then the doors began to open and the sunlight flooded in. It pierced his eyes like a fire. After three days of darkness, the bright sun was too much for him to handle so quickly, but he was unable to raise an arm to shield his eyes. Instead, all he could do was wince and look away. The next part of the journey he made with his eyes mostly closed, only opening them narrowly every now and then to try and let them adjust. Walking blind, of course, made things even harder going, when coupled with his ankle restraints. On numerous occasions, he felt the yank of the ropes on his wrists and then his body lurched forward, as they pulled him on.

Eventually, his eyes settled and the light no longer burned them. As he looked about him, he realised that they had been joined by two more Guardians flanking the lead Guardian. The grass surrounding his prison has given way to cobbled stone and the vast open space around them was now enclosed by run-down buildings on either side. This had once been his home, these had once been his streets, yet he had no recollection of them, no idea of where he was in the city. He had expected to see people watching him pass in the street, yet there was no one to be seen. He found this odd, but he quickly shrugged it off.

He paid little attention to the buildings they passed. Not only did he have no memory of them, but he also found he had no interest in them either. Instead, he just stared at the Guardian directly in front of him, particularly at his waist. For there, swinging by his side and clinking into his armour, was none other than Razor. Even with his weakened eyes, he could not mistake the hilt shaped like an eagle's head with its wings caressing the side of the blade. He did not know the name of the lead Guardian, but he did know that he was a thief. He had wondered what had become of his sword, and now he had the answer. Razor had been claimed by someone who did not deserve her and that infuriated him. So much so that he almost forgot that he was about to be executed, as he concentrated instead on his property being in the possession of this undeserving thief.

However, his mind was soon dragged back to the scenario at hand, as the narrow street opened up into a vast square. He remembered this square from when they had first arrived in Ryevale. Entering through one set of gates to the city, a path led straight down into this square which, when he last saw it, had been full of people going about their trade in a thriving market. From here, narrow roads branched off in different directions, making it the unofficial hub of the city. In the middle of the square stood a stone fountain, topped by a marble warrior, resting upon his shield. On the shield was a crest too faded to be seen, but water spurted from the centre of it into a large triangular base. Various stalls had been set up all around the fountain last time, but not today. He could not see the stalls at all; in fact, it was hard to see much of the fountain, due to the sheer mass of people that had gathered. Now he knew why the streets had been deserted during his walk here: the people had already made their way to this point, ready and waiting for him to arrive.

Further on from the fountain, at the furthest point from the path that led to one of the gates, stood a wooden stage. This had not been there previously, and he could only imagine it had been erected just for him. Upon a temporary throne, on the stage, sat King Theagran. Beside it was a less impressive chair, upon which Princess Thea was sat. Standing beside Theagran was the giant of a man that was Marcasian, in full battle dress, his bull helm beneath his arm. A wooden stump was positioned in the middle of the stage and next to it, bearing a rather large axe, with his face covered by a black mask, was the executioner. He knew that stump was for his head to rest upon. However, he could see no sign of Bromon or Garad, and he took that as the only positive in this bleak picture before him.

As Arundel and his escort party made their way towards the stage, the crowd began to jeer and hiss and boo. Angry fists were waved in his direction and wild hands clawed at him as he walked. He could feel what he assumed was spit spraying his skin, while his escort dragged him away from the angry crowd. Theagran had been right; the people were baying for his blood, no questions asked. The first item to hit him was a cabbage that thumped against his chest and fell to the floor. Next, some form of rotting fruit hit his neck and exploded on impact, soaking him. Other missiles followed, some hitting and some missing as the path became littered with food. In a city that was starving, he questioned their reasoning for throwing what little food they had, but then that was their mistake to make. He was able to shrug it all off until a coin cracked against his skull. The impact took him off balance and the pain immediately seared through his body. He stumbled and had to be caught, before he crashed to the floor. His escort held him up and then pushed him back to his feet, as he fought through the pain to regain his footing and continue. The crowd became even more raucous, until he was led up the steps and onto the wooden stage. He could feel the warmth of his own blood, trickling from his skull down his cheek.

He glanced towards Thea, her red hair flowing over a green dress that almost matched her eyes, but she could only turn those eyes away from him, as she was clearly trying to hide her tears, not from him, but from her father. He then moved his gaze onto Theagran, who sat with a crooked smile etched upon his face.

He could not look long, before he was dragged away. He felt a boot drive into the back of his right knee, forcing him to kneel in front of the stump. The Guardians holding the ropes that bound his wrists stayed by his side, but walked far enough away so that the ropes pulled his arms out tightly and he could not move them.

The crowd continued to jeer and hiss until the loud booming voice of Marcasian echoed through the square.

"Silence!"

Within moments, the din turned to a murmur, and then the murmur became silence. Sadly, he could not see Thea because she sat behind him, but he could see Razor at the belt of the lead Guardian, who was still very much in view. Marcasian spoke again.

"You are all here today to bear witness to the just execution of a man who not only murdered his father, but murdered our King."

The murmurs surfaced again for a moment, but instantly faded.

"Arundel Stal murdered King Andreas in cold blood and then he fled the city like a coward to avoid facing justice, justice that this city, and you its people, demand."

He would never have taken Marcasian for a speaker or a wordsmith; it wouldn't have even crossed his mind. So he was sure that these words the Bull spoke were not his own, but even so, as he delivered them, they were having the desired effect.

"Fate has delivered him back to us. He returned to this great city seeking more blood. Arundel Stal did not return to receive justice, but once more to murder a King."

The crowd gasped as they heard this. Clearly, this information had been held back for extra effect.

"But while King Andreas was an easy victim for Arundel, King Theagran most certainly was not. King Theagran could never fall for such an act as this, and so Arundel was foiled in his plan. At last, Arundel finds himself facing the justice he deserves."

The crowd let out a cheer at the mention of that. He did not remember these people; he had no memory of how Ryevale had once been, but he could see that those gathered here today were Theagran's people, either through choice or circumstance. None of them questioned a thing; there was no concern or consideration that this might not be the truth. All he saw was a bloodthirsty mob, bitter and twisted from their lives under a cruel King. Again, Marcasian spoke.

"Arundel Stal, by order of the Crown, you are guilty of Regal Murder and attempted Regal Murder. For these crimes, you face the only sentence justifiable for your actions…death. Do you have anything to say?"

He was surprised at that question. He had not expected them to give him any opportunity to speak, given that he could speak the truth that he knew, but then he could see that the truth mattered not here. No matter what he said, none would believe him. However, he was not going to stay silent.

"Your minds are already made up about me, so my words would be lost upon you. But as a warrior of my village, I ask that the warriors' code is honoured, and that I die by my own sword."

He looked toward the lead Guardian who carried Razor at his side. Marcasian followed his gaze for a moment and then turned to the executioner, who still stood clutching his axe. The executioner walked over to the Guardian and examined Razor for a moment, before turning back to Marcasian and nodding. Marcasian responded.

"So be it."

Marcasian next turned his attention to the Guardian.

"Hand it over."

He could see the reluctance on the Guardian's face as he pulled Razor from her sheath and passed her to the executioner.

The executioner then gave the Guardian his axe to hold, before making his way to the chopping block. Again, Marcasian spoke.

"Ready him."

With that, the Guardians holding his wrist ropes pulled him forward so that his head rested upon the block. He found himself facing the executioner. The executioner slowly moved himself into position, doing nothing with speed but simply precision. It seemed to take an eternity, as everyone watched on in silence. Suddenly, before the executioner had even lifted Razor, the silence was broken.

"Long live King Arundel!"

Murmurs suddenly started among the crowd once again. Above the murmurs, another voice could be heard to shout, "Arundel is innocent!"

The murmurs were growing louder. Another voice shouted above them.

"Theagran is the true murderer."

This was swiftly followed by another voice.

"Arundel is the one true King!"

With this, it sounded very much like chaos had resumed. The noise from the crowd was deafening, with arguments breaking out everywhere.

"Guards, bring me order!" Marcasian barked, but as the moments passed Arundel assumed it had not been achieved, since the uproar was as loud as ever before. He wished he could see what was happening, but he was still being held down tightly by the ropes with his gaze fixed upon the executioner. Marcasian approached the executioner and grabbed him by the shoulder.

"Do your job, do it now."

Marcasian then retreated, as the executioner set himself and raised Razor high up into the air. He contemplated closing his eyes; at least that way he would not see it happen, and the pain would last mere moments before he felt nothing. Instead, he chose to keep them open, to stare death in the face. If he hadn't done so, he wouldn't have seen the arrow strike the executioner in the chest. With the noise from the crowd, he could not hear the cry of the executioner as the arrow buried itself in his flesh, nor could he see the grimace of pain, covered as the man's face was by the black mask. Despite the arrow, the executioner still had Razor held high until a second arrow struck deep in his temple. The executioner froze for a moment, letting Razor drop from his grasp, before he fell to the floor with a loud thud. Razor landed by the executioner's body and remained in Arundel's view.

Suddenly, he felt the ropes on his wrists go slack. He glanced up to see that, stunned by the death of the executioner, the Guardians holding them were scouring the crowd for the archer. Seizing his opportunity, he lunged to his right and reached out a hand, grabbing hold of Razor's hilt. With swift movements, her sharp blade cut the rope on his arms and ankles, with ease. Realising this, the first guard was on him within moments. Arundel parried his strike and then sliced him open, just beneath his armour across the belly. The second guard then attacked. Arundel rolled out of the way of his sword before sweeping Razor across his ankle. Blood spurted up as the Guardian thumped to the floor. Arundel jumped to his feet and, with one strong thrust of his sword, pierced the wounded Guardian's throat. He turned to look for Marcasian, but the Bull was in the thick of the crowd, where fighting had broken out everywhere.

Thea and Theagran were nowhere to be seen, their seats empty, as they had probably been ushered away the moment trouble began. He couldn't think about that now; he needed a plan of action.

He felt something hit his shoulder with a small thud, and he saw a stone fall to the floor. He turned round to see Garad standing by the side of the stage, beckoning him over. Behind Garad, Bromon was making good use of his axe on nearby members of the crowd. Arundel started to move towards them, when his path became blocked. The man standing in front of him was the lead Guardian that had retrieved him from his cell.

"Going somewhere, Outlander?"

The Guardian then smiled and reached down to his sheath, only for his hand to find nothing but air. Of course, that sheath had been holding Razor, but now Razor was back where she belonged. The Guardian had just enough time for the smile to disappear from his face, before Arundel drove Razor into his body and then finished him off with a hefty sweep that separated head from neck. Arundel dropped off the stage beside Garad and Bromon, and gave them both a solid pat on the shoulder.

"It's good to see you alive, brothers."

Garad hooked his bow over his shoulder.

"And you, Ari. But let us save the reunion for after we've escaped."

Bromon plunged his axe into the side of his nearest assailant and then turned to them both.

"Aye, this melee could be our aid."

He was right. In the chaos of fighting, no one was paying them any attention. With haste, they began to push their way through the crowd, in the process keeping an eye out for any of the Guardians. Eventually, they reached the end of the skirmishes, and of the square itself. Garad then grabbed Arundel by the arm, and pointed to a wooden rail at the start of the pathway to the city gates.

"Our escape plan."

Tied to the rail were three horses. He had seen healthier looking horses in his time, but they would do. Arrows suddenly began to rain down on them and Arundel glanced back into the chaos to see that a unit of Guardian archers had arrived from one of the side streets. The name-brothers ran as fast as their legs could carry them, until they reached the horses. There was no time to untie them, so Arundel used Razor to cut the ropes, before mounting one that was black with brown flecks. He hooked Razor into the saddle and kicked his heels, once he had seen Garad and Bromon were also mounted on their horses. They rode hard towards the gates, fearing that at any moment they would close. Focused on the gates, he never saw the arrow bury itself deep in Bromon's back, nor did he see the two arrows strike his horse. As he reached the gates, noting to his surprise that they were still open, he stopped when he realised that only Garad was with him.

They turned back round to see Bromon some distance away, lying on the floor and trapped beneath his dying horse. Just beyond him a number of the Guardians, led by Marcasian, were running at speed.

"We must go back for him," Garad shouted with urgency, but his voice betrayed him because they both knew they would never make it to him in time.

"We can't help him, Garad."

Someone had to say it. They wanted to save him, but instead they had to watch as the Guardians reached him and surged past. They all kept on running, except for Marcasian. With so many Guardians blocking their view, they lost all sight of Bromon on the floor. However, once the oncoming Guardians drew closer, Arundel saw it.

"No!"

Garad let out a loud cry and tried to spur his horse forward, but Arundel reached out and grabbed him.

"It's too late."

While his hand had hold of Garad, his eyes were fixed on Marcasian, as the Bull stood, with one arm raised in the air and Bromon's head in his grasp.

Arundel wanted to let Garad go. He wanted to ride with him into the oncoming Guardians and seek revenge, but their deaths would achieve nothing here. So instead he had to try to calm Garad down, which in itself was proving difficult. All the while, the Guardians were getting closer. Suddenly, someone emerged from their left, a face shrouded by a hood, but Arundel could see enough to realise he did not know him.

"Go, you must go now. We will close the gates."

There was no time to ask questions. Instead, he turned to Garad, grabbed both of his shoulders and shook him fiercely.

"We must leave, Garad. Live today, avenge Bromon another day."

Garad stared at him and his eyes surrendered. He reluctantly turned his horse, before Arundel slapped its rear to cause it to break into a gallop out of the city. Arundel then glanced back at the unknown helper, who barked one final command.

"Go, my King! Go now!"

With that he urged his horse on and made his way out of the city, the loud clang of the gates closing behind him the last thing he could hear.

15

They rode hard until the light began to fade. Their concern had been that Marcasian would get his men mounted and on their trail, and so they aimed to put as much distance between the city and them as possible. The obvious option would have been to return from where they had come, but the Guardians would know that and most likely follow that route; so it had to be avoided. Damisas had been another option, since it was the closest city to Ryevale. Again, this would be a risk, because surely the Guardians would also think to look there. In addition, being the second city of Galbraxia, it would be loyal to King Theagran. Doubtless, word of what had happened would swiftly reach Damisas, making it just as hostile as Ryevale had been. So that too had to be avoided. This led them to ride south of Damisas into unknown territory, in itself a risk, but the least risky of all their options.

So it was that they had spent most of the day on the southern path where the open prairie stretched as far as the eye could see, for a long time affording them no cover at all. Thankfully, as the light began to fade, trees started to come into view. At first, it was just a handful scattered here and there, but then the clusters grew bigger into what could only be described as small islands of trees. There was no sign of these thickets meeting to form woods, from what Arundel could see, and so they chose the thickest one, in which to bed down for the night. They were able to tie up their horses near the middle of the cluster out of sight of any passersby, before picking their spot to make camp for the night.

Barely a word had been spoken since the journey began, and

that did not change while they carried out their designated tasks. Arundel set out to gather wood for a fire, while Garad was left to hunt with his bow. Arundel found his task an easy one, given their surroundings, and before long he was back at their chosen spot, using flint to spark a fire. As the flames took hold and grew, the natural light left them completely and yet Garad had still not returned. It reached the point where Arundel was about to go and search for him, when his name-brother emerged from the undergrowth with a string of squirrels over his shoulder. Garad dropped his catch at Arundel's feet and then leaned his bow and quiver against a tree. They both set about skinning the squirrels and skewering them with sticks, before mounting them over the fire. Still the silence remained.

Eventually it was Garad who broke the silence, much to Arundel's surprise.

"We are headed south. If we continue on this path, I believe we will end up at the hills of Alvern and the city of Staverstock built within them. At least, that is what mother told me as a boy."

At the mention of their mother, the sheer scale of recent events really hit Arundel. This had all began because his name-parents had been murdered by Marcasian and his men, on the orders of King Theagran. Then, while in Ryevale, he had become aware of his forgotten past, of his blood mother who died in childbirth and his blood father who had been slain by Theagran's very hand. And, of course, while escaping from the city, his name-brother and Garad's blood brother, Bromon, had fallen to Marcasian. So much loss, and all because of those two evil men. Now here they were, in the middle of nowhere, with no clue of where to go or what to do, and they had not spoken a word of the day's events. He could not let that continue.

"Garad, we need to talk about today, about Bromon."

"I don't have to talk about it, Ari." That answer was blunt. "One day I will, but not now. I just can't."

If that was what Garad wished, then he would not pursue the matter. He knew the conversation would come, but he would leave it for when Garad chose to have it. He switched his attention to the fire for a moment and checked on his roasting squirrel, when Garad spoke again.

"What we do need to talk about is why your head was on the chopping block, Ari. What was it Marcasian said? Something about you murdering your father, the King? Now that requires some explanation."

He was right, it did require an explanation, even though it was still raw to him as well. So, as they both set about eating squirrel, he told Garad all that he knew; of his parents being King and Queen of Galbraxia, his blood line sitting on the throne for hundreds of years; of Theagran murdering his father and the attempt on his life by some lazy and sadistic soldiers. He laid it all before Garad, who listened intently, without interruption. Then, when he was finished, Garad finally added his comment.

"So, after all this time, I have been living with the true King? Milly would have given you more than a sword, had she known she was lying with royalty!"

For the first time that day laughter broke out between them and it felt right. After a day full of sorrow, it was good to be able to end it with a slight lift, and end it they did, as the rest of the squirrel was packed away for the morning, and they both slipped into the world of slumber.

The next day began with a meal of squirrel and berries freshly picked by Garad, once his troubled sleep had ended. They discussed pushing on south to discover whether Garad was right and the city of Staverstock was there. The concern was that the city would most likely be loyal to Theagran and, if word had not already reached that city, then it soon would. It was the same concern they had had about Damisas yesterday, and it would probably be true for every city in the realm. Their best hope would be one of the villages, since it was the villagers who always suffered the King's wrath and thus felt little loyalty towards the King. They had no idea how far away the nearest village would be, and so they decided to stay put for another day or two; they would gather as much food as they could carry, before setting out in search of a new home. Consequently, they spent the day hunting and scavenging, with a couple more squirrels and one rabbit added to the pile, as well as a mixture of berries and nuts. The animals were skinned, cooked and cut up into strips to make them easier to transport and eat, when the time came.

Conversation between them had been at a minimum, partly due to their separating in order to gather food with more speed, but when they were together and they did speak, it was not about Bromon. Garad asked questions about Thea and contemplated what life could have been like for Arundel, had he grown up in the Great Palace of Ryevale. Effectively, he did everything he could to avoid mentioning the death of his brother. Arundel did not push him on it.

The conversations did get him thinking, though. Not so much about life in the Palace, he had never thought about that, but he did think about Thea, every single day. He wondered if she was still in the city and if she was safe. He wondered whether she knew that he had escaped, or if she had been told lies. Surely the whole city would know, and it would be impossible to keep a secret like that, but then, if she did know he was still alive, was she thinking about him? For days, he had feared never seeing her again because of his expected death, but now here he was alive and well, and yet he still faced the horror of never seeing her again. It was enough to drive a man crazy with frustration.

As night drew in, they sat around the fire, tucking into another squirrel feast, and began to talk about the days when they used to hunt freely in the Weeping Woods. Garad led the conversation.

"We used to leave the village for days, claiming we could live in the woods forever."

It was true: how foolish they had been.

"That's right, we did. We spent so many years wanting to get away from the village and now here we are homeless, wishing we could go back. How things change, huh?"

Garad nodded, picked up a small pebble and tossed it aside.

"Mind you, now we know why you wanted out of the village, Ari, what with you being a Palace boy and all."

Garad let out a small smirk, which was encouraging to see.

Arundel leant over and jabbed him in the shoulder, with his fist.

"You're never going to let that go, are you?"

Garad shook his head.

"Not in this lifetime, or the next."

Garad shoved him for a moment and a friendly scuffle was about to ensue, when Arundel heard it. For a moment he questioned whether he had actually heard the sound, or if it was just in his mind. It had seemed real, real enough to suddenly put him on high alert. He took a step back from Garad and began to look into the darkness all around them.

"What is it, Ari?"

He remained silent for a moment, he had heard the question, he just wanted to make certain in his head. His eyes continued to search the darkness, as he spoke again.

"Can you reach your bow?"

Still he kept his gaze off his brother and waited for a response. After a moment or two, Garad replied, "Yes, I think so, why?"

Clearly Garad had not heard it. This, again, cast doubt. It led him to question his ears, but he was certain he had heard it, faintly, somewhere out there in the dark, a cough, a human cough.

He slowly edged over towards the nearby tree, where he had left Razor in her sheath, propped up against the trunk. He had just about got his fingers around her hilt, when he felt cold steel press against his skin. Looking towards his cheek, he could just make out the spear tip and part of the shaft that stretched out into the night.

"Garad, if you have your bow, now is the time to use it."

The response came behind him.

"I'm not in a position to do that, Ari."

Guessing that Garad was in a similar predicament, he made the decision to act. He threw himself backwards to the floor and rolled through, pulling Razor with him. As he completed one turn, he was able to haul himself up to one knee, while sliding Razor out of her sheath and holding her towards the threat. Even now, all he could see was part of a spear that faded into the dark night. He turned round to see Garad on his knees, two spears digging into his back. These also seemed to come from the darkness.

"Sorry, Ari."

Arundel shook his head.

"Don't apologise. If it is bloodshed they want, then that is what they will get, because I will not go down without a fight."

He rose to his feet and held Razor up by his side as he continued to look around, in case any spears attempted to move.

"That will not be necessary."

The voice came from the darkness. He did not recognise it, although the accent was familiar. He had heard it somewhere before. He wasn't quite sure where, but he knew that it wasn't in Ryevale.

"Who are you?" Arundel shouted out, still frantically looking around.

Suddenly, the shadows appeared to move for a moment until the firelight reached far enough to show a slim figure. As the figure drew closer, Arundel could clearly see the whites of the eyes. Finally, when the figure was fully illuminated by the flames, he could see it was a man.

The man wore a black leather singlet, with all exposed skin painted dark blue. The only break in the darkness was the yellow star painted over the left eye and the white crescent moon painted over the right eye. The man was slim, but even through the paint Arundel was certain he carried more power than would first appear. Having joined an image with the accent, he remembered where he knew it from. This man was a Seeker, just like those he had encountered in the Wendel Valley when they had travelled to Ryevale with Thea and her escort. Judging by his body paint, he worshipped the side of Anyeama, Goddess of the Sky that represented the night. The man spoke.

"Our High Priest Yorrall has sent us to aid you. My name is Urag'Ki and these are my men."

He held his hands out and the spears lowered from Garad. As Garad got to his feet, they watched five men slowly emerge from the darkness, all painted in the same way as Urag'Ki. As they gathered about the fire, Urag'Ki named them all, pointing at them in turn. "Shalrog…Kurantchi…A'Lmun…Pitroch and Zaz'Te."

Each man bowed slightly as his name was mentioned. Arundel and Garad acknowledged them all and then Arundel felt it best to return the gesture.

"I am Arundel and this is my name-brother, Garad."

Urag'Ki spoke.

"We know who you are, Arundel, son of Andreas. You are the one true King of Galbraxia. We would not have been sent to help those who we do not know."

Arundel eased Razor back into her scabbard and gestured towards the fire.

"Please take a seat. We have little in the way of food and no water, but we offer you what we can."

Urag'Ki, Pitroch, Kurantchi and Shalrog all sat around the fire, while Zaz'Te and A'Lmun positioned themselves in opposite corners of the clearing as if on guard duty. Urag'Ki spoke again.

"We thank you, but let us offer you some refreshment."

With that Kurantchi and Pitroch removed what appeared to be bags made of bear fur from their backs. Kurantchi produced apples, bread and slices of deer meat from his bag, while Pitroch produced two skins of water, which he swiftly passed around. Arundel hadn't realised just how thirsty he was, until the liquid touched his lips. Eventually, he passed the skin on to Garad before speaking.

"How did you know we were here?"

Urag'Ki worked an apple round and round in his hands.

"The High Priest foresaw the attempted execution and your escape. He sent us to spy on the borders of Ryevale to watch for your exit from the city. But we arrived after you had fled and the city was placed in lockdown. Thankfully, your trail was easy for A'Lmun to track, and we were swiftly in pursuit, albeit almost a day behind. It was just luck that you have stayed in this one place for a day, that we have found you so soon."

So Yorrall had foreseen it. This actually provoked anger within him.

"If Yorrall had foreseen it, why didn't he warn me when I saw him? He was full of cryptic advice then, why couldn't he tell me this? Our brother is dead and that knowledge could have prevented it."

Urag'Ki placed a hand on his shoulder.

"We saw your loss, but Yorrall could not have prevented it. His visions can occur years ahead of time, or mere minutes. This one visited him that very morning."

That swiftly took the aggression out of him.

"I'm sorry."

Urag'Ki shook his head.

"There is no need, we understand grief."

Garad suddenly interrupted, the skin of water still in his hands.

"Wait, you said you saw our loss. What did you mean by that?"

Urag'Ki turned his attention to Garad.

"Some things are best not known."

Garad's grip visibly tightened on the flask.

"He was my brother, I must know."

His voice was stern, filled with anguish. Urag'Ki turned to Arundel, as if for reassurance, and Arundel nodded slightly. Urag'Ki then turned back to Garad.

"Your brother's body hangs from the city wall as a warning and his head is on a spike above the city gates."

Garad exploded, throwing the skin hard against a tree, as he shot to his feet. He clearly did not know what to do, what to say or how to cope. Arundel stood up and walked over to try and comfort his name-brother, but Garad pushed him away.

"We can't leave him like that, Ari. We've got to get his body back. He deserves a proper burial."

Arundel placed his arms on Garad's shoulders and this time his name-brother did not resist.

"I know, but we will never get near the city, not now."

He could see the despair in Garad's eyes and he wished he could give a better answer, but, at present, they were wanted men and it just wasn't possible.

"We shall go."

Urag'Ki's voice caught them both by surprise, and they slowly turned to face him.

"I will leave A'Lmun and Zaz-Te here with you, and the rest of us will retrieve your brother's body."

Garad pulled away from Arundel and walked closer to the Seeker.

"Can you do that? What if you are seen?"

"It is nearly a day's ride back to Ryevale. We will leave at first light and then wait for the fall of night. We work best in darkness; we will not be seen. We will get your brother back."

Now it was Arundel's turn to speak.

"Do not leave your men here, if having fewer numbers puts you at risk. We will be fine."

Urag'Ki shook his head.

"The High Priest says you are the one true King, the one man who can restore order to the realm and reunite it under one banner. You are to be protected at all costs. My men stay."

That was the end of that argument. Urag'Ki would not be moved.

So it was that come first light, Urag'Ki, Pitroch, Kurantchi and Shalrog all set off for Ryevale while Zaz'Te and A'Lmun remained behind.

The day passed slowly. Once again, they tried to occupy themselves with hunting, but their thoughts were on Bromon, and nothing more. Eventually they took a chance and began to build the burial pyre. Zaz'Te and A'Lmun helped, and the extra hands made much lighter work. Naturally, Arundel feared that this could be a wasted effort, should Urag'Ki and his men fail to recover Bromon's remains. However, he kept those thoughts to himself, as the building of the pyre seemed to give Garad a purpose. Day turned into night, and the pyre was complete. The effort of building it did not provide the sleep Arundel had hoped for, and a restless night followed for both him and Garad. Finally, as light began to break Arundel drifted off into a welcome sleep that was eventually broken by Zaz'Te.

"They're back."

Arundel had no idea how long he had slept, as he dragged himself to his feet, but the sun was already burning brightly high in the sky. Pitroch was the first to clear the trees, spear in hand and nothing else. Then came Kurantchi, who seemed to be carrying something behind him, something wrapped in a large deer hide. As Shalrog followed, Arundel could see he was carrying the other end of the deer hide. Finally, Urag'Ki cleared the trees and gave Arundel a nod. Garad then led them to the pyre, while Arundel approached Urag'Ki.

"Thank you."

Urag'Ki let out a gentle grunt and followed up with, "Welcome."

They waited until day began to fade, before lighting the funeral fires. Arundel left Garad to have some final words with his brother, before they all gathered round the pyre. Bromon was a warrior and he was given a warrior's funeral. Sadly, they did not have his axe to accompany him, but they made do as best they could with wood and stone. Garad said the prayers traditional to his village, but Arundel remained silent. He stood and watched the flames engulf first the pyre, and then Bromon's body. He felt the heat gently toast his skin, he saw the flames dance yellow and orange and he silently said his farewell to his name-brother. Arundel then slowly walked away, leaving Garad and the others behind. He walked to the edge of the clearing and, leaning against a tree, he looked out into the darkness. He thought of his parents, both name and blood. He thought of Bromon, of Garad. He thought of Thea. What did he do now? Where should they go? He did not have the answers.

"In a world where we lose so much, we must hold onto what little we have and never let go."

Arundel turned to see Urag'Ki standing beside him. He too was gazing out into the darkness.

"What do you mean?" Arundel asked.

"You have lost so many of your kin, but you have not yet lost her. The High Priest says there is destiny in her emerald eyes, and in your reflection. It is time for the one true King to rise up and take back what is rightfully his."

Now Urag'Ki turned to face him.

"And save his Queen."

Arundel let out a sigh.

"How can I do that? How can I be the saviour that Yorrall claims I am, when I am a fugitive throughout the realm? What should I do next?"

Urag'Ki stared at him intently.

"You must go to Damisas."

Arundel sighed again.

"The second city of Galbraxia? They will kill us as soon as we walk through the gates, or just hand us over to Theagran; we can't go there."

Urag'Ki moved a step closer.

"Damisas is not loyal to the serpent. Within the confines of her own walls, the eagle will always fly."

16

"Where is it?"

Marcasian asked the question with a growl in his voice. When he awoke this morning, he had not expected this. When he addressed his men responsible for that night's watch, he simply wanted to find out if there had been any sightings of the Outlanders, a question to which he could already guess the answer. As he had expected, the answer was no from all of them. When he then asked if there was anything else to report, he was doing so more out of habit, than expectation. There was never anything to report and he had expected this morning to be no different. So when Jerothen, who had been in command of the watch last night, told him that he needed to take a look outside the city gates, it had caught him off guard.

He had met Jerothen in Antolin Square where the execution of Arundel Stal had failed to take place. Abragias Stal was the first King of Galbraxia, crowned so after he led the very first defence of the city against marauders from across the Tavernia Sea. His victory sealed his seat upon the throne and, following his death, a statue of him was erected in the middle of the Square; it later became a fountain. Marcasian hated that fountain, just as he hated all the Stals of every generation. It was a hatred passed on to him by his father and his grandfather, and one he had embraced, even if they had never truly explained to him why. Sometimes for a boy growing up poor, it was very easy to hate without need of a reason.

Days ago, the Square had descended into chaos when rioting

among the people had enabled the Outlanders to escape. There were no outward signs of that chaos now. The market stalls had swiftly returned, and this very morning were preparing to open for business. However, the memory of the chaos remained. The execution stage was still in its place, with gallows swiftly built upon it, and now twenty of the rioters hung from those gallows, as a warning. How long they would remain there would be up to the King, and, at the moment, the King was in a foul mood.

Marcasian walked with Jerothen from Antolin Square, down the path towards the main gates. As they approached the gates, Marcasian noticed six of his Guardians lined up by the perimeter wall, standing to attention.

"What are they doing?" he asked.

Jerothen pointed at them.

"Those were the men, tasked with the watch over the city gates last night. They are waiting for you, because I am sure you will wish to speak with them."

Jerothen then gave a signal with his hand toward the gates, and they started to open. Dust kicked up and was caught in the breeze, as the gates parted and then clunked to a heavy stop. They began to walk through.

"I am in no mood for games this morning; tell me what it is I must see," Marcasian commanded.

Jerothen stopped in his tracks and pointed up.

"Look above you."

Marcasian stared at the spike above the gates where the fat Outlander's head had been mounted. Only the head was no longer there. The spike remained, its tip stained with blood, but the head was gone. He turned to Jerothen.

"The body?"

Jerothen replied, "Gone as well."

Marcasian stared at him intently.

"How can they be gone? How can a head and body just disappear? Could it be one of our own?"

Jerothen shook his head.

"I doubt it; the gates did not open at all last night."

"What explanation did your men give?"

Jerothen's expression did not change as he gave his reply.

"They could not explain it. They state the body was there as light fell, and was gone as light returned. They do not know how it happened."

Marcasian had heard enough. How could six men be in charge of the gates and not one of them hear or see a single thing? He struggled to believe it and he certainly didn't accept it.

He made his way back through the gates at a speedy pace and approached the waiting line of men. As he reached the nearest Guardian, automatically he pulled his arm back and drove his fist into the man's head, knocking him to the floor. Turning to face the other five, he thundered:

"Six of you and no one saw a bloody thing? You were on the night watch, so what the hell were you watching, for a body and head to go missing, right in front of you?"

The Guardian on the floor was trying to get back up, but Marcasian raised his foot and drove it into the Guardian's head, flooring him once more. The skin on the Guardian's forehead split and blood began to trickle from it.

"I do not accept such negligence. The King does not accept such negligence. You have all neglected your duty and that is an offence that will not go unpunished."

He then turned to face Jerothen.

"These men are not fit to be Guardians. Strip them of their garb and take them to the Crypt."

Jerothen looked at the Guardian bleeding on the floor.

"All six of them?"

Marcasian thought about that a moment. He then pulled out his sword and drove it through the throat of the sprawled Guardian. As his blood spattered onto the dirt, his body squirmed for a moment and then stopped. The Bull withdrew his sword and wiped the blood off on the Guardian standing next to him.

"All five of them."

With that, he walked away, as Jerothen gave out instructions and the five men were seized.

The stairs of the Great Palace were never a joy to ascend, especially when bound for the very top, as he was this morning. But it was even worse today, when he was going to have to tell the King that the Outlander's body had been taken. For years, Theagran had been paranoid, ever since the Civil War when you never knew who would betray you at any time. But the discovery that Arundel was still alive had added fuel to that fire because he had found that his own men had lied to him. Thus, when the execution day came and some in the crowd had called out in support of Arundel, which led to his escape, the sense of paranoia increased and Theagran withdrew himself to his throne room atop the Great Palace. He had remained there ever since. This news would do nothing to ease the King's concerns. Once Marcasian reached the top of the stairs, he took the brief walk down the corridor and knocked loudly on the door.

"My King, it is Marcasian. I come with news."

Sadly, it was not good news. The King's voice could then be heard.

"Enter."

He pushed the door open, with moderate force. As he entered, he saw the King standing at the large window looking out onto the city. Shutting the door behind him, the Bull was asked by his King whether the news was about his daughter, by any chance.

This caught him off guard; he hadn't expected that. Why would it be about Thea?

"Your daughter, Sire? Why would it be about her?"

His news could wait, especially given its bad nature. Clearly there was something he had missed and he wanted to know what. The King continued to look out the window.

"I had a visitor this morning, a fat pimple-faced girl who says she is one of Thea's handmaids."

"That would be Yasilda, my King."

He knew her, more intimately than he cared to admit. But a man has needs and sometimes it's more about making sure those needs are satisfied, than who you get to satisfy them.

"Well, this Yasilda tells me of the whispers that come from my daughter's chamber. She tells me that Thea, on more than one occasion, has spoken of Arundel in a romantic context. She says that when it comes to Arundel, my daughter can't be trusted."

There was a moment of silence and then the King spoke again.

"Have you heard of this?"

For the first time that day the King turned to face him, a look of anger in his eyes.

"It is the first I have heard of it, Sire. Perhaps she is more like her mother than you thought."

Theagran strode over to the nearest candlestick and shoved it over, in rage. His voice turned to a shout.

"My own daughter! I can't trust the people of this city! I can't trust my men and I can't trust my own flesh and blood. Who is there to trust in, but you, Marcasian?"

That was a good question, but he ignored it, to offer some solace instead.

"Perhaps it is not true. Perhaps Yasilda has heard nothing but the foolish whispers of women."

A look of contemplation crept across the face of the King.

"Perhaps. I must know for certain. In these troubled days, I must know if my own kin can be trusted, or if stern action must be taken."

The King walked towards him with more of a spring in his step, buoyed by the possibility of a false truth.

"You must speak with this Yasilda. Tell her that if she wishes to stay in favour with her King, then she will spy on my daughter and report back to you, and you in turn will report back to me."

He knew the kind of girl that Yasilda was and he knew that this would not be a problem. She had no real loyalty, except to herself. It would get her killed one day, but for now it would keep her alive all the while it helped the Crown.

"Right away, my King."

He turned to leave, momentarily forgetting why he had gone there in the first place, until Theagran's next words stopped him in his shoes.

"Marcasian, if you had not heard the rumours about my

daughter, then what bad news were you bringing to me?"

Ah yes, he had not passed that news on. He wished there was a way he didn't have to, but it was unavoidable. He turned back round to find Theagran almost upon him, those cold, black eyes staring right at him. There was no way to go about this, other than to be blunt.

"It's the body of the Outlander, my King."

Theagran's face twitched a little, almost flitting between curiosity and a hint of anger.

"What about it?"

He took a moment's pause and then answered.

"It's gone, taken in the night. We do not know by who."

He watched as any hint of curiosity slipped away from the King's face and the anger turned into rage. Theagran walked over to a nearby table, containing plates of food and chalices of wine, and with one hefty sweep of his arm, he sent it all crashing to the floor. The clattering of metal upon stone echoed around the walls. The noise took a few moments to cease. The King stood for a moment, hands on hips and his back to Marcasian, as he breathed heavily. He then broke the uncomfortable silence.

"What of the men who were on watch? Did they not see anything?"

"No, Sire."

Another pause.

"And what of those men now?"

"One is dead, the other five are being escorted to the Crypt as we speak, Sire."

Theagran slowly turned back round to face him.

"They die at dawn. I will not have any more failure."

Marcasian nodded.

"Yes, my King."

He started to turn to leave, but again Theagran's words stopped him.

"Arundel must be found. Gather some of your best men, those you can truly rely on, and have them split up into scouting parties. I want them to scour the whole of this miserable realm until they find him and bring him back to me, so I can mount his head upon my wall."

Marcasian already knew some suitable candidates, including one the King had not mentioned.

"What about me, Sire? Shall I lead one of the scout parties?"

Theagran stepped closer to him and peered around him for a moment, as if seeking a hidden spy.

"No, I need you here with me. Someone that I can trust has to remain."

Marcasian nodded.

"As you wish, Sire."

With that he turned and this time made his way, uninterrupted, back to the door and out of the throne room.

CHAPTER

17

Dawn was breaking, when they came upon the high walls of Damisas. The city was a perfect circle, from what he could make out, with walls so high that he could not see beyond them. He noted the tops of the walls and the spikes that lined them, making it difficult for any man who would venture to scale such a height and climb over the top. As they approached, Urag'Ki gave a signal with the flame of his torch. Slowly, the gates opened a little, just enough for them to pass through. It still felt like a bad idea to Arundel, when their horses were trotting towards the opening. At worst, he expected to be cut down by the masses on entering through those gates, and at best, he expected to be seized and sent straight to Ryevale and the waiting hands of King Theagran. More than once during the journey here, he had expressed his anxiety to Urag'Ki, but the Seeker, with few words, had vowed that the concern was not necessary. Urag'Ki's confidence had not settled him and so, as they rode into the city, one hand was resting firmly on the hilt of Razor.

However, to his surprise, no blades or arrows pierced his skin; no hands tried to grab him and pull him from his horse. In fact, for the first part of the journey, there had barely been so much as a glance their way. This enabled him to take in his surroundings, which like the welcome or lack thereof, were also unexpected.

After the disappointment of Ryevale and the degraded city hidden within such lavish walls, he had anticipated a similar sight behind the unremarkable, towering dark walls of Damisas. However what he found was very different. The cobbled streets were being swept as they rode in, while the brick of the buildings looked fresh. The faces of those passing by wore smiles and the rich smells of roasting meat and boiling vegetables tantalised his nostrils. Ryevale had felt like a city that had had the life sucked out of it and was on the verge of death; Damisas, on the other hand, was vibrant and full of life. He couldn't believe how different things were here compared with Ryevale; why would such decay be allowed in the greatest city, but others flourished? He had asked that question of Urag'Ki but was simply given a response that answers would come.

Their entrance into the city had gone pretty much unnoticed, but the journey through it did not stay that way. Once the gates were some distance behind them, he heard a young voice cry out.

"It's King Arundel!"

On hearing this cry, crowds began to form around them. His initial pleasant impressions of the city had led him to remove his hand from Razor's hilt, but now his hand drifted back to its resting place upon the eagle's crown. With every step, the crowd grew bigger, but the atmosphere did not seem hostile. In fact, more men, women and children fell in behind them as they rode, and, before long, cries of "All hail the King!" broke out with gusto. He cast a glance back at Garad, who shrugged with uncertainty. He then switched his gaze to Urag'Ki, who appeared totally unfazed by it all.

So they rode on, the large crowd in tow, until they reached a rectangular building within the heart of the city. Stone pillars lined the perimeter of this impressive edifice, while the roof had been carved into what appeared to be wings. As they came to a stop, he had expected to see guards approach and surround them, but none came. In fact, as they dismounted, not even the crowd moved any closer. Instead, the only ones to approach were stable hands to take away the horses. A short and slightly portly man, with a brown shaggy beard and scraggly hair, then emerged from the doorway of the building. He wore a tattered old cloth robe, with markings too faded to be identified upon it. The man approached them with a wide smile, holding out open arms. As he drew ever closer, he began to speak.

"I had heard the rumours and lived with hope; but never in my wildest dreams had I thought them to be true."

Before Arundel could react, the man wrapped those arms around him in an unexpected embrace. The embrace did not carry strength with it, but was firm. The man had a musty smell about him that did not please, but it was over as quickly as it had begun, and the man stepped back, straightening down his robe with a brush of his hands.

"Forgive me, I hug you like a long lost brother, and yet I have not even introduced myself. I am Barrington Wehrsley, Steward of Damisas."

Barrington took a bow as Arundel began to speak.

"And I am..."

But he was cut off by an excited Barrington.

"No need to introduce yourself, for you are Arundel Stal, the true King of Galbraxia."

It still did not sit right to hear that. How could he be a King? The first ten years of his life were a forgotten memory. He was simply an adopted son of a village elder, a hunter and a lover, not a ruler. Garad stepped forward and leaned into him.

"How does it feel to be popular for a change, Your Highness?"

He jabbed an elbow into Garad's gut, causing his name-brother to take a step back.

"Please, just call me Arundel."

Barrington smiled.

"It would be my pleasure."

Barrington then placed one hand on Arundel's shoulder, while pointing towards the entrance of the building with his other hand.

"May I suggest we step inside? We have plenty to discuss."

Arundel turned to look at Garad who held up his hands.

"I will wait here with Urag'Ki. Just don't forget about me, Your Highness."

It was good to see a flash of Garad's humour, in the light of recent events. He gave him a nod and then turned back to Barrington.

"Lead the way."

Barrington clapped his hands together with joy, and began to walk towards the pillars that lined the outside of the building. Arundel followed.

Beyond large stone doors he found a vast hallway, with staircases to right and left, leading up to a second floor. Two doors opened out from beneath the stairs, while one solitary door stood before him. The walls were decorated with tapestries of various scenes that he did not recognise; some were battles, while others he could not make out. Candles provided illumination and there was a warmth within these walls that he had not felt back in the Great Palace. He did not have much time to stop and stare though, as Barrington walked straight over towards the solitary door before them and gestured for Arundel to join him. Arundel obliged and, as they stood side by side, Barrington pushed the door open and held out a hand, indicating for Arundel to enter.

"Welcome to the Equalitarium."

Arundel took a few steps inside a large room that was entirely circular. The walls were lined with purple banners trimmed with gold, that bore the symbol of a set of scales of justice; but what stood out was the seating. A stone bench ran in an almost complete circle in the middle of the room. There was just a small break in the bench to enable people to walk inside the circle. That was all the furniture that the room contained, yet it was enough to grab his attention and intrigue. He took a few steps forward and ran his fingertips over the stone bench, surprised at how smooth it felt to the touch. Barrington's voice broke through the brief silence.

"How well do you know your history of Damisas, Arundel?"

He glanced back towards the enthusiastic Steward.

"I do not know this place at all. I have no memory prior to my tenth year and, in the outer villages, little is spoken of city life or the realm as a whole."

Barrington walked over to him, wearing a broad smile, as he placed a gentle hand on Arundel's shoulder.

"Ah, then let me be the one to give you a history lesson, if I may."

Arundel nodded.

"Please do."

Barrington's smile seemed to broaden. He stepped forward a little and, taking a seat on the bench, let out a quiet grunt.

"There was a time when Galbraxia and the realms around it were nothing more than woodland and open grass, inhabited only by nature's gifts. There was also a time when the Forgotten Lands were known by another name, a name lost over time in these parts. But in those days, the Forgotten Lands were torn by war, victims of a bloody campaign of destruction led by the warlock known as Gruldock the Insatiable. Having become the leader of his people, he had earned the title of 'Insatiable' because he was not satisfied with what he had and always wanted more; this desire drove him to wreak devastation, in order to make all of the lands his own to rule. Foreseeing a future of nothing but suffering, a wizard named Xoumarin led a group of hundreds, or even thousands so the legend tells, of the survivors, and they fled across the sea to settle upon these shores. They were the first people of Galbraxia, and they set about building two cities, Ryevale and Damisas, although back then they did not hold those names. Xoumarin had split the people into two groups, in order to build the cities, each led by their own master builder. One group built a city designed for beauty and the other built a city designed for survival.

"It was then decided that to settle down, one most suited would need to lead the rest, to set guidelines and rules for them to live by. Naturally, they turned to Xoumarin, but the wizard was ageing and wished to see out his days in peace, so another was chosen and given the rule of the realm as the Uncrowned King.

"For a while, life was good, but then their troubles of the past caught up with them. Gruldock the Insatiable had conquered the Forgotten Lands and then, staying true to form, decided to cross the sea himself and conquer those who had fled him. The journey across the sea tired his men, however, and so when their campaign began, the settled people were able to enjoy small victories over Gruldock's men. But Gruldock had not been so dominant merely by luck and he soon set his sights on the weaker city that had been built for beauty."

Arundel could guess which city that was.

"Ryevale?"

Barrington nodded.

"The very one. The city fell within a day, and without many losses for Gruldock, who then turned his attention to the second city, besieging it. However, this city held out for months on end, and Gruldock became ever more angry. His anger saw him make mistakes, and enabled Xoumarin to lead the people once again, this time to fight back against the invaders. Xoumarin and Gruldock would battle face to face in a fight leading to the death of them both. But heavier losses were sustained by Gruldock's men, who succumbed to defeat on the battlefield. The survivors fled, including blood relations of Gruldock, and they founded the realms that surround us. The survivors of Galbraxia's founders returned to a life of peace, but the Uncrowned King had perished in the sacking of Ryevale, and with Xoumarin also dead, the survivors had no leader. They tried to live this way for a time, but while the people enjoyed a form of equality, factions began to form and, instead of thriving, the realm started to struggle. Chaos took over, and so it was decided that the people needed a King, to guide them when needed. So a great tournament was held to find the most suitable man to lead the realm, a man with the heart of a warrior. That tournament was won by your ancestor, Abragias Stal and, through his victory, he became the first true King of Galbraxia."

Despite having no memory when it came to any of his family, it still filled Arundel with a sense of pride to know that his own ancestor was the very first King. Barrington continued.

"King Abragias set about laying down rules for the realm to restore order. With the people organised, he had Ryevale rebuilt. It would still stand out as the foremost city of beauty in the realm, but would also be far more defensible, should another invasion take place. However, believing that would not be enough, he had Damisas fortified. The walls were raised to the heights you see now and designed to be impenetrable. This very building, erected as the home of the Lord of Damisas, was designed at such a height and in such a location that it could not be seen or easily targeted by any attackers on the other side of the great walls. A tunnel was then dug between the two cities, so that, should Ryevale fall, the King and his family could flee to the safe haven of Damisas. This tunnel is a much quicker route between the two cities than above ground, due to its direct nature, but was never truly needed as an escape route, and so has been forgotten by most."

This intrigued Arundel.

"Does the tunnel still exist?"

Barrington smiled.

"Yes, it does. The people of Damisas have maintained it as best we can, over the generations, because we have always believed that one day it would be required. But, as a precaution, in case the tunnel was used by those for whom it was not intended, Damisas itself is full of secret tunnels and passages to help protect its people."

Arundel was even more intrigued. But curiosity gave way to contemplation, as he began to think of Thea; ideas started to form that perhaps he could use the tunnel to see her again. But he tried to push those thoughts aside and focus on what he was being taught. In addition, from the moment he had walked into this room, he had been keen to know its purpose.

"You mentioned that this is the house of the Lord of Damisas."

Barrington nodded.

"That it was, and now it is my home."

He slipped in his question, with ease.

"Then what purpose does this room serve? I have never seen anything like it."

Barrington seemed pleased the question had been asked, and very excited to be able to answer it.

"This room is where the Lord would hold court with the people of the city. If they had an issue they wished resolved, they would come here to speak with the Lord. But here in Damisas, we not only believe in justice, but also in equality. In our eyes, the

King rules over the realm, but after him and his royal blood, the rest of the realm is equal. We all hold different roles in the realm, but none of us is above or below the other. The role of the Lord was to look after the people of the city, and that is what he would do. But when they spoke with him, they would do so as equals, hence no head chair, no throne, no platform, just one circular bench where everyone is the same."

Arundel liked the idea of that. He had only known village life and had heard the rumours of tyranny outside the village. But even in the village, there was a hierarchy that had to be adhered to, a pecking order dictated to everyone by their families. To hear about equality was refreshing. Still, though, he had questions. For the first time in his life, he felt that he was getting some answers, some understanding of where he came from, and he thirsted to know more.

"If this house was built for the Lord of Damisas, and you state that you are not the Lord, but the Steward, what happened to the Lord?"

The smile faded a little from the face of Barrington. Sadness seemed to creep into his eyes and suddenly it felt like the tale might not end so joyfully. Barrington took a breath and began to speak, only now in a softer tone.

"My cousin Arianna was born to Broderick Wehrsley, Lord of Damisas. At a young age, she married your uncle Alun Stal and so, when Broderick died, Alun became Lord of Damisas. Together they had a son named Brodus, and were very much the toast of the city. But when news spread of your father's death, alleged to be by your hand, and of Theagran taking the throne, everything changed. The realm descended into civil war, with several trying to lay claim to the throne through distant bloodlines, while others just wanted it for themselves.

"Alun, though, had the true rightful claim in your absence, and was pushed by many here to fight for it. Many in the realm rallied behind him, and, at first, he and his followers enjoyed a taste of victory.

"But the Guardians had the numbers, experience and

weaponry to put them in control, and eventually Alun was killed in battle by Marcasian. This left Damisas vulnerable, and, with Alun dead, his followers had no claim to fight for and the rebellion was over. Theagran sent Marcasian and his men here to take control of the city. Every one of our soldiers was taken to join the Guardians so that we would have no means to fight again. Several of the Guardians, under the leadership of Sir Dafryl Vain, remained here to oversee us and make sure we did not try to raise fighters again. Arianna and Brodus were executed, to end the bloodline of Lords here, and their bodies were hung up for weeks to serve as a warning to us all. I was made Steward because I have no interest in women and will never father children, so there was no risk of future blood vengeance. Theagran believed that when I die, this city would consume itself.

"But behind our high walls, we have secretly begun to thrive. With the able men gone, there was little to no trouble here and soon Dafryl and his men became bored. Time wore on and Theagran forgot about us, so those men dwindled in numbers as, one by one, they returned to Ryevale. Eventually, only Dafryl remained, until death came to claim him, and we have been unwatched ever since. We have managed to build a small army of the sons who were too young to take to Ryevale, but who have since grown to adulthood with anger in their hearts; but they are not well trained. Our trade links with the realm flourish; we have good connections with the Seekers, and eyes and ears from village to village, to help keep us informed. Theagran has become so consumed by his own paranoia, he has forgotten about us. Our dream is one day to make him regret that, and pay for all he has done. We hope that you can be the one to make that possible."

That caught him off guard: he wasn't expecting such a comment.

"Me? Why me?"

Barrington edged closer, a sense of caution about him now. He glanced around him, as if to be sure no one was listening, and then he spoke.

"You are the rightful King. Most of us in this realm know you are innocent, for we have been spared the poison that rots Ryevale. Stay here and we will keep you safely hidden, and, in return, I ask you to train our men, make them into real warriors. Then, when the time is right, tour the villages and I guarantee that they will rally to your cause. Unite the realm and take back what is rightfully yours."

The passion built in Barrington's voice as he spoke, a glimmer of hope replacing the sadness in his eyes; but so much had happened, so much had changed, that right now Arundel did not know what to think, or who to trust.

"I...I don't know."

That was the best answer he could give at present, and not the one that Barrington wanted to hear, but it was all he could offer. Barrington, however, responded more optimistically than expected.

"You don't need to decide now. Let us settle you into a room, get some warm food in your belly and a good night's sleep for your head, because tomorrow is another day."

Barrington rose to his feet and placed a reassuring hand on his shoulder, before pointing with his free hand towards the door. They began to walk towards it, when it suddenly opened and an unknown, thin, pale-faced man came in.

"Pardon the intrusion, but we have Guardians passing through the gate wishing to search the city for...well...for..."

He didn't finish the sentence, but instead turned his gaze towards Arundel. Urgency suddenly seized Barrington, and he spoke with haste.

"See to it that Arundel's companion is hidden away; do so now."

The man nodded in agreement and made a swift exit. Barrington turned round, but their eyes did not meet. Instead he was looking beyond Arundel.

"Follow me...quickly."

Barrington began to walk, and Arundel had no choice but to follow. Barrington stayed silent for a moment, as he moved across the chamber, until he reached the opposite curve of the dome. He then ran his fingers along the stone and pushed hard a few times, when suddenly a secret door opened in the wall beside him.

"In here, quickly. You must stay out of sight. If they find you, that will be it for all of us."

Arundel had no choice, but to agree. He did not know if Barrington could be trusted, or his people for that matter, but right now he had to believe that Guardians were in the city, and he had to believe that Barrington was trying to keep him safe and alive. So with that, he walked through the open door into a darkness that engulfed him completely. Barrington pushed the door shut behind him. Now all Arundel could do was wait. Wait to discover if Barrington was truly friend, or foe.

18

For the first few days after Arundel had fled his own execution, the world had been a blur. The city had been put into lockdown and she had been ushered to her room by order of her father, allegedly to keep her safe. Yasilda had been assigned to her, on a permanent basis, as a second handmaid to work alongside Shauri. Again, she had been told it was to look after her, but she knew that it was to keep her locked up, providing two people to get her anything she needed. It was just another part of her father's paranoia, and she knew it.

During the years she had been away, she would hear whispers of how the King was becoming irrationally suspicious of those around him, after the Civil War that had torn Galbraxia in two for so long. Having been around him for just a few days, she could clearly see that it was true. Now she was experiencing it first hand, and it made her feel like a prisoner.

However, that realisation did not truly sink in until the fifth dawn. Up until then, so much had been going on that she just hadn't been able to settle, to get her head straight. She knew that Arundel and Garad had made it out of the city, and that Bromon hadn't. Shauri had told her about what they had done to poor Bromon's body, and it was Shauri who had told her when the body had gone missing. It was this news that had given her hope, for the first time, that Arundel was still alive; this was the news that had brought the world back to a normal pace for her. It was also around this time that Yasilda had started trying to spend more time with her.

For those first few days, Shauri had been more in favour as her chambermaid, as it were, while Yasilda fetched and carried. Now, Yasilda was trying to spend time inside the room and that did not sit right with Thea. She did not trust Yasilda; no one did. Everybody knew that she had given herself to Marcasian time and time again, and in her eyes anyone who would choose to lie with that man, was not one to put your faith in. Despite her doubts and concerns, she had been left with little choice. Confined to her room, Yasilda and Shauri were her only real contact with the outside world, and so she had become reliant upon them. All she could do was what she felt was right, and so, as best she could, she would assign Yasilda the unimportant tasks and would keep her at a distance.

Come the seventeenth dawn, her boundaries were widened, at least to an extent. She was told that it was still too dangerous for her to go outside, by order of the King, but now she could have the freedom of the Great Palace. She asked for more information than that, but the soldier sent as a messenger did not oblige. It was only a small victory, being granted access to the rest of the Palace, but a victory nonetheless. Her newfound freedom had come as a relief to Yasilda as well, although she would never admit it. The problem with Yasilda was that she had no patience and no work ethic. Shauri did everything with ease and a smile on her face, and she would never treat her chores as work, no matter what. Yasilda, on the other hand, moaned and complained, and would drag her heels the moment she could no longer be bothered to do what was asked of her; that would happen very often and very quickly. So now that she could move about the Palace, Yasilda could escape and hide for large parts of the day and that suited them both well.

On that seventeenth dawn, Yasilda made her exit with the messenger, while Shauri stayed and helped Thea dress. Despite the improvement to her circumstances, she had chosen a black woollen dress that hung to the floor and a black lace headdress that covered her face. Shauri had been surprised that she chose a dress, but Thea had done so with a purpose. Once she was ready, she stepped outside her room, and, for the first time in over two weeks, she felt different air upon her skin. Shauri joined her, asking the most obvious question.

"Where are we going, Princess?"

A good question with an answer the maid had not expected.

"The Worship room. Let us make haste. I feel I should not linger like this."

Shauri did not reply, but her expression clearly demonstrated her agreement. So they made their way down two flights of stairs and along the corridor until they reached the Worship room.

Tight shut, the door was stiff to open, which told her that it had not been used in some time. Again, she was not surprised because, since her return to the city, it had been clear that Ryevale was running short of both faith and belief. She did not stay in the Worship room long, just for enough time to light a candle in late mourning for the loss of Bromon and then another to carry her hope that Arundel was alive and well, and would stay protected. The two candles barely cut through the dust and cobwebs in the cold black room, but even so, she felt better for lighting them. She knew her father would not be happy with it, if he found out, and so they swiftly made their exit and headed back to her room for her to change. The dress was swapped for the more familiar trousers and chemise, with leather jerkin; and then she set about walking every floor of the Palace, just because she could, after being confined to one room for so long. In that time, she shared some small talk with Shauri, all the time being careful what she said, given who might be listening. Most of what was said was just typical nonsense, but there was a moment when Shauri checked they were alone, before sharing her suspicions about Yasilda. Shauri believed that Yasilda's presence in recent weeks had a hidden purpose, most probably linked to the fact that Thea had been around Arundel. To be honest, it made sense to her because a paranoid King who knew that his number one enemy had been in contact with his own daughter, would be overwhelmed with suspicion as to how deep that contact had run. Although she had no proof of this, she decided she would continue to act as if Yasilda could not be trusted, and would keep her cards close to her chest when Yasilda was around.

With every floor of the Palace covered, they then made their way to the library. As she entered, her eyes darted about with eagerness, only to be met with nothing but partially bare shelves and the remaining old books, slowly gathering dust.

"Oracle Thomas, are you here?" she called out. Nothing but silence came in return. She checked over both floors, but there was no sign of the old man and his gold cloak. For the first time that day, she felt disappointment. She had been waiting for this day of extended freedom to come, in the hope of speaking with the Oracle and finding out if he had any news of Arundel. Now the moment had come, the emptiness of the library left her feeling slightly numb. She had thought of Arundel, day and night, since he had made his escape. At last, she had believed she would be a little closer to knowing if he was safe, but instead she felt further from that knowledge than ever before. She slumped into the nearest chair, causing a little dust to puff into the air, as Shauri placed a comforting hand upon her shoulder.

"Patience, Princess. He shall return, I believe."

Thea looked up at her handmaid and saw a glimmer of hope in her eyes that she longed to have herself.

"I hope you are right, Shauri. I can't bear to be in the dark much longer. I know that the Guardians have not found him, otherwise they would have paraded his body by now, but I do not know what has happened to him."

Shauri scrunched her remaining fingers softly, rubbing the skin of Thea's shoulder almost like a massage, as she spoke again.

"He has lived outside these walls most of his life, Princess. The realm will not be so harsh to him."

She knew Shauri was right, but the uncertainty made it difficult to cling to such belief.

"I have leave to step outside these walls, Princess. Let me walk the city and see what tales are told."

Thea placed her own hand on top of Shauri's, whose skin felt rough in places from much manual labour in her short life.

"I would appreciate that."

Shauri then nodded gently, and swiftly walked out of the library, leaving Thea alone. She decided she would wait for a while, just in case the Oracle returned, and since she was in a library, it made sense to read. She would have chosen to study a little history of the realm, but as those books had long been burned, she was left with much less choice. She settled on a book entitled 'The Magistar & The Beast', and returned to her chair. The tale was set in the Forgotten Lands and was quite hard going, but it served its purpose to pass the time. She wasn't sure how long she spent in the library, but as the light began to fade, she decided her time was up. Folding the corner of the page, she placed the book on the nearest shelf, so she had reason to return the next day, and then made her way back to her room.

That night, Shauri brought very little information back with her from the streets, which only served to add to the frustrations of the day.

The next morning, she returned to the library with renewed hope that she would see the Oracle, but he was still absent. Once more, she buried herself in her chosen book. Three more times the sun rose and set, and her days were spent in the library alone, with no sign of the Oracle. With each passing day, Arundel occupied more and more of her thoughts; the continuing lack of information about him was taking its toll on her. Yet another day passed, and once more she found a library devoid of its Oracle, as she settled down with her book. She was getting closer and closer to the book's end, as the day wore on, and her mind drifted from the words upon the page to thoughts of how she would pass her waiting time when she was done.

"May I interrupt, Princess?"

The voice startled her from the page she was on. She lowered the book to see the familiar garb of the Guardians. Beginning to panic, her mind raced to find a reason for the soldier's presence. Then he spoke again.

"Forgive me, I did not mean to startle you."

His politeness caught her off guard, more than his opening

sentence had. The Guardians were many things, but polite was not one of them. Her eyes moved up the armour to a face that was well worn from years of experience. His crinkled pale skin surrounded powerful blue eyes. His black hair was losing a battle against grey, and stubble adorned his sharp jaw. The soldier may have seen many years, but he still looked a formidable warrior. She regained some composure and replied, "What is the reason for this interruption?"

Her response was defensive: she couldn't hide that. Sitting in the library was not something that should get her into trouble; however, her actual motives for being there, were they to be discovered, could lead her down a very difficult path. So, just to be safe, her guard was up.

"The reason is your safety, Princess."

She had not expected that answer, but perhaps she was misreading it, and he meant he was there to put her safety at risk. She did not sense that was the case, the complete opposite in fact. Being in the presence of her father's soldiers always left her feeling uneasy, but this weathered man had a somewhat comforting presence about him. She looked at that face again and wondered if it looked familiar.

"My safety? Do I know you, soldier? And how might your interruption affect my safety?"

The soldier shifted his body and shook his head a little.

"My apologies for my manner, Princess. My name is Sir Winstan Charrington. I am a member of your father's so-called Guardians of the Crown, but once held leadership of the true elite Guardians, under King Andreas Stal."

That was where the familiarity came from. She remembered him from her very young days, before her father had sent her away to be moulded into a lady.

"Very well, but what do you have to do with my safety?"

Sir Winstan took a few steps away to the door of the library and looked out into the corridor momentarily, checking both ways before glancing back towards her.

"I have been sent by Oracle Thomas."

That immediately caught her interest, and she darted to her feet, before hurrying across the floor towards him.

"You have spoken with the Oracle? Where is he? Can I see him? I have been waiting for days to speak with him."

He checked the corridor again and then once more turned back to face her. He moved forward, ushering her away from the door and further into the library. His voice lowered a little.

"I last spoke with him on the day of his departure. He told me to keep an eye on you. He said that when you were released from your room, you would most likely venture here seeking him out. He asked that if you did so for more than three days in a row, I should intervene and steer you away."

All of a sudden, she was full of questions.

"Where did he go? Why can I not be here for more than three days in a row? Why would he send you?"

She could tell that Sir Winstan was anxious to be gone and reluctant to answer her questions.

"Now is not the time, Princess. All can be explained later."

She had been waiting long enough; she was not going to wait any longer.

"I am sick of waiting, Sir Winstan. As your Princess, I demand some answers."

Sir Winstan shifted his body weight and moved a little closer.

"I do not know where he has gone. Not knowing meant there was no chance of me ever telling the wrong people, if circumstance forced it. As for your presence here, Oracle Thomas said that, while the odd visit would not stand out, even the most foolish of your father's men would find it odd and suspicious to see you spend your time here, every day. As for the rest, that can wait. What matters now is that you leave this room and don't come back, not for another seven nights. On the eighth night, when darkness falls, you can return and you should find Oracle Thomas here, all being well. But do not come back before then."

She shook her head.

"I won't."

Sir Winstan backed away from her towards the door, where

he glanced into the corridor again. He then turned to her.

"I shall take my leave now. You must do so shortly after, so we are not seen to do so together. These walls have eyes, Princess, more than you may realise."

Before she could say another word, the ageing soldier stepped out into the corridor and slipped out of sight. She gave herself a moment or two to settle herself, before taking a seat. She would continue with her book a little while longer and then depart, as requested.

The following days were painfully slow to pass, yet at least she was waiting with a target. So she battled her way through the days, rediscovering the Great Palace inch by inch, to keep herself occupied.

At last, the eighth night finally arrived. She waited until Yasilda was gone and the Palace had quietened down, before slipping out into the darkness of the corridors. Carrying a small candle of light with her, she made the familiar journey back to the library. As she approached the door, she could see that it was slightly ajar, but no indication of light inside. She hoped beyond hope that this was not another disappointment. Reaching out a hand, Thea pushed the door open slowly, just enough to be able to slip inside without noise. She took a few steps, moving the candle around in order to try and see if anyone was nearby, with no joy. She then called out softly, "Oracle Thomas, are you here?"

There was a moment of silence, and then a response from the darkness.

"Come to the upper floor."

That gave her hope, and so she carefully found her way to the stairs and climbed them, one by one, until she reached the upper floor. She moved the candle around again and at first could still see nothing.

"Where are you?" she whispered.

"Look again."

She moved the candle once more and then saw the figure, sitting in the corner shrouded in shadow. She began to walk towards it and, as she got closer, the light began to flicker off a golden robe. Holding out a hand, the figure pointed towards a vacant chair and she slipped herself into it.

"I am so glad to see you, Oracle, but why are you sitting in darkness?"

There was a moment of silence and then Oracle Thomas replied in a low, soft voice.

"The game has changed, Princess. These are now days of secrecy and caution. My absence goes unnoticed, as it always has, but now my presence is scrutinised more than ever."

She was confused, what on earth was he talking about? Suddenly, questions just leaked out of her.

"What do you mean? Where have you been? Why was Sir Winstan helping me, when he is a Guardian? And what has become of Arundel?"

Oracle Thomas held up his hands, indicating she should calm herself.

"Arundel is very much alive."

"Oh, thank the Gods."

A huge wave of relief washed over her upon hearing that and, for the first time in a long time, she was able to relax. So much so that she withheld any more questions for the moment, enabling Oracle Thomas to continue.

"He is in Damisas, along with his brother, Garad. They have been there for some time. A war council has been formed and plans are being made to recover the realm from the tyranny of your father and put the rightful King upon the throne. I have been in Damisas, as part of that council, and will continue to be. As for Sir Winstan, he was loyal to the Stals. He never believed the lies Theagran told, and over the years has learned the truth when it was not known that he could hear it. He and the remaining original Guardians are still loyal to the Stals, to this very day. In fact, there are several among the ranks of your father's Guardians who also share that loyalty. But these dark days have forced them to remain silent, through fear of death. Your father has his suspicions, that is clear, because those men are the first to be sacrificed in battle, when the situation calls for it. But he needs their strength to fight for him and, until Arundel returned, there was no living Stal that they could have rallied behind, making them no threat. But as I say, the game has changed, and Sir Winstan is very much a friend."

She was trying to take it all in, but all she could think about was how relieved she was that Arundel was alive and how desperately she wanted to see him. She rose from the chair and paced for a moment, piecing it all together, before speaking.

"I must see Arundel, Oracle. I must. How do you get to Damisas unseen?"

Oracle Thomas leaned forward in his chair.

"There is a secret passage that runs between the two cities, built as an escape route for the King. There are two entrances from this end. The first is right here in this room. The second is hidden behind a false wall within some stable buildings, outsidethe Great Palace's perimeter. That is a much bigger entrance, that enables horses to access the tunnel, something I highly recommend."

Without even thinking, she asked her next question.

"Could we get there tonight?"

Oracle Thomas eased his ageing body from his chair and walked towards her.

"I assumed you would ask that, which is why I had you come here as soon as night fell. By foot, it would take us most of the night, but, by horse, it is much swifter and would provide you with some hours of darkness, before you would need to return."

"Then we must go at once. I have waited long enough."

He nodded in agreement and made his way past her. She followed him down to the lower level, and then over to the middle section of the bookcases. Oracle Thomas moved apart the books on the third shelf. He reached across the shelf. She heard the sound of a lever, and then a section of the bookcase separated from the rest by moving inward. Oracle Thomas pushed it in further and this provided a sufficient gap for them to slip through. After that, he pushed the bookcase back into place behind them. The light from Thea's candle broke up the darkness enough for her to make out a stone wall to her right. Searching around, Oracle Thomas located a torch, which he lit from the candle. Within moments, a much stronger flame lit the darkness and she could see they were in a small, stone room with a flight of steps that ran directly down. Oracle Thomas led the way down the steps. She lost count how many there were, once they had gone beyond the number of steps within the Palace itself, and she knew they were now underground.

Eventually they reached the foot of the steps, and continued along a stone passage. Now they were walking forward, instead of down. Neither of them spoke; thus, silence accompanied them for the start of the journey, but that was later broken by the distant sound of horses, echoing off the walls around them.

It wasn't long before they came across the two horses, which had been tied to a brass ring fixed to the wall. The horses were saddled and ready. They stood by a second pathway that, she assumed, led off to the stables the Oracle had spoken of. From here, it appeared that the tunnel became a lot wider, probably wide enough for three or four horses to be ridden side by side. She imagined that was to enable the King's escort to ride with him, if he needed to escape. As they mounted the horses, Oracle Thomas spoke for the first time since being in the tunnel.

"Are you sure this is what you want?"

She responded with certainty.

"There is no time to waste. I am seeing Arundel tonight."

With that she took hold of the reins and kicked her heels, and they set off into the darkness towards Damisas.

CHAPTER

19

It had been a busy few weeks. Arundel's initial doubts about Barrington Wehrsley and his loyalty had vanished. He had hidden from the Guardians the day he arrived, and Barrington, true to his word, had not given him away. Then, once Theagran's men had departed, Barrington saw to it that he and Garad were given rooms inside the Lord's House and they spent the night feasting well, something they had not done for some time.

The rising of the new sun had seemed like a fresh beginning for him. While he still found it hard to accept the idea he was a King, he at least liked having walls around him and a purpose, once again. Barrington had shown him round the city and introduced him to several key figures of the community, those that had helped it flourish with their different trades. Steel was plentiful, as were food, silks and wool, to name but a few tradable items. The city worked for itself, everyone playing their part to keep it strong, and they all appreciated that which was done by others. It made for such a productive atmosphere, something he found vastly different from Ryevale and its state of decay. Seeing it all had made him eager to play a part himself, and Barrington had already identified that role for him.

At the end of the tour, he was introduced to Damisas' secret army. Their numbers totalled around a thousand, give or take, a range of ages and generations. The eldest were those who had been mere children the day that Theagran had taken all able fighting men. Then came their sons, and their grandsons. Some of them were decent fighters and good hunters. Some were raw but had potential, and others were simply inexperienced and weak. However, all could improve, given the right guidance, and while he wasn't sure that he was exactly the man to give them that guidance, such was the task Barrington had set him. So after another day of settling in, he, along with Garad, set about taking the fighting men of Damisas and turning them into an army, capable of regaining the realm. It was going to be a tough task, but one that he had already begun to enjoy, from that first day.

Very quickly, though, a problem was discovered. Most of the men had spent their days working with the sword and very few had any ability with a bow. That was where the women of Damisas stepped forward. Plenty of them were as keen to fight for their realm as the men, and saw archery as the perfect way. Around one hundred women joined the small ranks of men, and were then taken aside and trained, independently from the rest, by Garad. That left the others for Arundel to train, and this he did every single day. However, while the role offered him a positive distraction, every day his mind would drift to thoughts of Thea and to wondering whether he would ever see her again. He hoped beyond hope that he would, but, under the circumstances, he feared the worst.

Training the troops was not the only distraction created for him, however. Barrington had also set about creating a war council, which met in the evening, whenever it was felt that matters needed to be discussed. This was Barrington's way of showing that he and the city were ready to take a stand and fight for their King.

On this eve, after another day of swordplay, Arundel found himself sitting at the latest meeting of the war council. The council was comprised of the same men, each time. Naturally, as its founder and Steward of Damisas, Barrington was present. Garad was also a clear choice to sit on the council, as was Urag'Ki. He and his men had opted to stay in Damisas to act as a liaison between the city and the rest of the Seekers. Then there was a man named Darwin Eckleton. Darwin had been in charge of the secret army for several years, doing his best to train them. Even though

Arundel had the task of bringing them up to scratch, he was the King, and kings did not run the army. So he had appointed Darwin Captain of the army, given his knowledge of them, and they had taken to calling themselves Restorers of the King. It wasn't exactly a title that would stick, but it gave them motivation. Besides, who was he to argue with that?

The final place on the council belonged to a man whose absence this evening was very noticeable. That man was Oracle Thomas. The Oracle had made his way to Damisas from Ryevale a few weeks ago, via a secret tunnel that ran between the two cities, and had stayed ever since. Arundel had spent a lot of his free time with the Oracle, learning the history of his family and the realm, and gaining a better understanding of what it was to be a king. He had to admit, even after the history lessons, he wasn't really sure that he was the right fit for King, but the true King he was, and, for the first time in his life, he had a responsibility, and he had been raised to accept responsibility, when it belonged to him. So he worked hard to be a worthy pupil of the Oracle's teaching, learning all he could. However, he was well aware there was so much more to take in. With the Oracle absent from this sitting of the council, he wondered if he would get another chance.

"Theagran's men have extended their search even further. No village will be left untouched as they try to find Arundel," Urag'Ki reported. Although he now spent his time within the walls of the city, he remained in constant contact with his scouts who travelled the realm far and wide. "For now they just search, no killing. But that will not last much longer, if the search continues to be fruitless. That I guarantee you."

Barrington cleared his throat, before joining in.

"No doubt of that. I have seen what violence Theagran's paranoia can lead to. The people of Galbraxia remain strong for now, but we need to give them some hope to keep them that way. We need to give them..."

Hesitation kicked in as he stopped mid-sentence. Arundel did not need to hear the rest, because he already knew what would follow.

"Me. We need to give them me."

Barrington reluctantly nodded.

"Yes, my King. They will have heard you are alive, and the fact Theagran's Guardians are searching for you will naturally confirm the rumours. But I feel seeing you in the flesh is what they really need to rally their spirits."

Arundel couldn't disagree with that; in fact, he had contemplated it for some time now.

"That sounds great, but in case you don't remember, Ari is a wanted man. He can't just stroll out the gates and go on a village tour."

Garad was blunt and to the point, as always; Arundel expected nothing less of his name-brother. He had also noticed that since the loss of Bromon, Garad had become even more protective of him. Most likely, it was his way of trying not to lose the remaining family he had. Urag'Ki now chimed in.

"Garad is right. The King can't just step outside, unprotected. If he is to leave the city, then I will leave with him."

"As would I," Garad added, almost embarrassed he hadn't said it first, "But it will need more than the two of us to keep Ari safe. I know how much trouble he can get himself into. I've protected him my whole life."

Arundel suddenly looked at Garad and was surprised to see him keep a straight face while saying that. He couldn't help but respond.

"Your memory is somewhat fractured, brother. The one in trouble was always you, and the one doing the saving was always me."

Barrington clearly wasn't in the mood for brotherly banter.

"Nevertheless, the three of you would not be enough for my liking. We have waited too long for the true King to save us. I will not risk your life now. If you are to go, then you must have a larger escort. Darwin, how ready are your men?"

Darwin adjusted himself in his chair, preparing to speak for the first time.

"They are progressing at speed, but I would not yet have full faith in them to carry out such a task."

"How long do they need?" Barrington asked. Darwin took a moment to mull it over.

"I would hope to have them ready before the cold sets in."

Barrington thought about it for a moment and then spoke.

"In that case, I suggest we wait. Let the Guardians continue their fruitless search, while our men prepare themselves. But as soon as their training is completed, I feel you must venture out of the city, my King."

Arundel accepted that proposal.

"Agreed."

With that decision made, Barrington moved discussions on to the anticipated good harvest.

The meeting had gone on longer than necessary. A war council without a war is just a council, and that, effectively, was what the meeting had been, a council meeting. While he knew the trading strength and stock levels of the city were important, for him it was an area that wasn't really his strength. So it was that he was glad when the meeting had run its course, and he could retire to his room for the night. Once in his room, he began to unwind as best he could. If he was honest, he was itching for the day to come when he could set out on his journey to the villages. While he appreciated the hospitality of Damisas and he enjoyed his work with the soldiers, he was hungry for a little action. With Thea sadly nothing but a warm memory for him, and Oracle Thomas now seemingly absent and unable to continue his teaching, he was left with much unoccupied time. Thus, the chance to get out among the people, running the risk of some swordplay, appealed to him. However, with the men not yet ready, that would have to wait, and another day's training beckoned, once the night's sleep was complete.

He began to undress and ready himself for his slumber, when suddenly there was a knock at his door. He wondered who on earth it could be at this time and naturally assumed it would be Garad, a beer in hand, looking to share old tales. It wouldn't be the first time, but tonight he just wasn't in the mood for it. Walking over to the door, he grabbed the handle and pulled it open.

"I'm not in the mood tonight, Ga..."

He stopped before he could quite finish, as the man standing at the door was not the man he had expected. Instead of the youthful exuberance of his name-brother, there was age and wisdom, wrapped in a gold cloak.

"Oracle Thomas."

The old man nodded his headed slightly.

"My King."

Where had he been? Why was he not at the meeting, but here now?

"Your absence at the war council was noticed tonight, Oracle. Where did you go?"

The Oracle did not answer for a moment, as if trying to pick his words carefully.

"I was off bringing you a gift, my King."

Before Arundel could ask what he was talking about, Oracle Thomas stepped aside to reveal another figure, standing in the shadows behind him. This figure was also shrouded in a long robe, only one more costly and sumptuous, made of sapphire velvet and embroidered with ivory silk flowers. Between the large size of the robe's hood and the darkness of the corridor, it was difficult to make out many details of the face. However, he could see the eyes, and those stunning emerald greens instantly grabbed his attention.

"Thea?"

A sweet familiar voice replied, "Arundel."

Was this real? Had he gone to bed and drifted into this dreamy slumber? Out of view, he subtly pinched himself and when the world around him did not change, he knew this was real. He was so taken aback by the surprise, he barely noticed Oracle Thomas slip off into the pitch black of the corridor. Instead, he was too busy bumbling around, like a young boy talking to a girl for the first time.

"Where are my manners? Please come in."

He took a step aside and the figure walked into the room. He was still struggling to believe it was her, as he pushed the door shut. But then, when he turned around, he saw the hood fall back, and the familiar, fiery red hair spill over gentle cheeks. Words could not describe his joy at seeing Thea again. Not stopping at the hood, she unfastened the robe and slipped it off, before laying it over his chair. What he then saw really surprised him. Thea was wearing a red velvet dress that hung to the floor, while the bodice more than emphasised her impressive breasts. Seeing this surprised him, because he knew how much Thea hated dresses.

"Things in Ryevale must be grave, if you are still being made to wear dresses."

She looked down at herself, as if to remember what she was wearing.

"It was all I had available, and I had not expected to ride a horse through an underground tunnel, when I set out earlier."

She came closer to him.

"Do you like it?"

Now he too moved a little closer.

"The garment matters not to me, Princess. It's the woman underneath that I appreciate."

Thea blushed, as the two were even closer. Her voice became softer.

"I'm not a princess anymore, my King."

Even closer still.

"I am not officially a king."

They were so close now that they were almost touching, when the moment took over and their lips met. He pursued the kiss, something he had wanted to do for some time, and to his delight, Thea returned it, with equal passion. That was the end of any form of self-control. Having believed he would never see her again, now that he had her, he would not waste another second. He wrapped his arms around her and she began to run her fingers through his hair, as their tongues now met.

His fingers fumbled at the lace on the back of her dress, without much success. The passionate embrace saw them stumble around the room, allowing him to snatch hold of his knife, which he then used to cut the lace. He began kissing her neck as he pulled at the top of the dress, easing it from her shoulders. Her fingers clawed at his bare chest, as her dress fell to the floor. Underneath the dress was a silk slip and he pulled it up her body and over her head, to reveal her naked frame beneath. His hands caressed her skin, before his lips found her nipples. Thea moaned softly. Her hands untied the cord on his trousers and then pushed them to the floor. Their lips soon became locked again, as he lifted her up, her legs wrapped around his body. He carried her over to the bed and lowered her onto the mattress. As their tongues danced and their fingers interlocked, he slipped himself inside her to unite their bodies as one.

20

Several cycles of the moon had passed since Thea had first appeared at his chamber door. The plans for him to head out into the realm and rally the villages behind him were put on hold for longer than had been anticipated by the war council. Damisas' secret army was filled with brave and honourable men and women, eager to prove themselves for their King, but they still lacked training and, admirably, Darwin would not let them out into the field until he was completely confident they could protect Arundel. So they waited, and they trained, and they worked, and they worked, to become the best-organised fighting machine that they could be. During the day, Arundel continued to work alongside them, sharing what knowledge he could. He also felt that by training with them, they would actually want to protect him and not just feel required to do so. That was important to him because, even now, he didn't feel like a King; he felt like one of the people, as he always had, and he didn't want to lose touch with that. From what the Oracle had taught him, Theagran had never understood or cared about the people he ruled, as result of which most of the realm despised him, while the people of Ryevale had become poisoned by his hate. Things needed to change and the hopes of many were pinned on him to change them; he could not do that, if he lost sight of who he was. So he worked with the soldiers by day, and, by night, spent his time with the woman he loved.

Unfortunately, he was restricted to seeing Thea at night only, and it could not be every night, either. For Thea, every night she sneaked out of the Great Palace, along the hidden tunnels into Damisas, she was putting herself at risk. They both knew that if she did this every night, soon enough she would raise suspicions. Consequently, their moments together were fewer than he would wish, making him treasure them even more. His nights without her were lonely, while the nights they spent together made him happier than he could have ever believed; he could not deny the fact that he wanted more. Heading out into the villages would only extend the absence between them. However, by the time the secret army's initial training was completed to Darwin's satisfaction, the bitterness of winter had set in, bringing snow and ice that would keep them within the high walls of the realm's second city.

Word reached them from their spies within Ryevale that even Theagran's Guardians of the Crown had suspended their search for him and Garad, and retreated home to let the winter pass. Galbraxia had ground to a halt. Arundel used this time wisely, not only by savouring every minute of his evenings with Thea, but also by learning more about his family history and the history of the realm from Oracle Thomas. The Oracle wanted to teach him, as best he could, how to lead and how to be a King, but Arundel had never been one to learn through talk. His skills with a sword, both on a hunt and in a fight, had come from actual practice, from putting himself in the necessary environment, where he did not merely survive, but thrived. He worked out that if he were to ever take his place as the true King of Galbraxia, then for his reign to be a success, things would have to happen in a similar way.

While the winter had been harsh, it had not lasted long and soon, a little warmth had returned to bring about a thaw. As the snow melted away, he had made the decision that, once the ground was sufficiently soft to ride, they would set out. The villagers had waited long enough and should not have to wait any longer.

And so, here he now was, sat upon his horse, riding through damp and slightly overgrown terrain. A heavy set of furs protected his body from the icy chill that still cut through the air. His final day before departure, his final morning with Thea, had been one that would change his life forever, but his mind could not think of that now, not as he sat here riding out in the open.

Arundel was flanked by Garad, Urag'Ki and Darwin, while thirty men and women of the Damisas army filed in line behind them. He had decided that the title of 'Restorers of the King' was not necessary, because, in his eyes, they were the army of the people and so should be identified as such. Garad was always going to accompany him on this journey, and Darwin, as the Captain, was naturally going to lead his troops in their first real test.

Urag'Ki had been the surprise addition to their party. He could have returned to his people, but had wanted to stay and maintain a link between his fellow Seekers and Damisas. The time spent in the second city had brought him and Arundel closer together. Arundel had never really had any friends, not true ones, just his name-brothers to rely upon, but in Urag'Ki he had formed a bond that he had never known before. He had found a friend that he could trust with his life, a rare thing in his life so far. Their cultures were different, very much so, but they shared their differences to help each other learn, and at times those differences provided a humour that could not have been planned for. They would spar together, drink together and tell stories together, but, as far as the stories were concerned, his could never compare with those of Anyeama's finest warrior. So it was that when their departure was announced, Urag'Ki volunteered himself, swearing to protect the King and his friend.

So far their journey had taken them through the villages of Farrindorr, Cassmera and Dandringham. Each had seen their fair share of hardship during the winter freeze but, as with his own village of Havendale, experience had kept them prepared for such events and they had coped. The reception in Dandringham and Farrindorr had been warm from the start, as the locals rejoiced in the realisation that the rumours of a Stal King had been true. They were offered overwhelming hospitality, with as much food and drink, as well as other goods, as they wished to consume; but Arundel and his party did not want to deprive the villages when they had little to spare. Instead, they shared goodwill and a breath of fresh hope before moving on, knowing that when the time came he would have their support.

Cassmera, however, was a little different. Upon their arrival there, the atmosphere had been almost as frosty as the winter that had just passed. The first few villagers they came across quickly scattered, disappearing into nearby homes without so much as a word. The first words to come their way were not words of encouragement, but instead throwaway comments, suggesting they leave. They had no intention of doing so, not yet, not until they understood why things were different here. They had slowed their mounts to walking pace, and more than once, he spoke out loud that they were here in peace, but still no one would come forward to speak with them. He was beginning to wonder if they would ever get a response, when a young girl stepped out into the path in front of them. The girl had a grubby face, partially hidden behind scraggy light brown hair, with tattered cotton clothes covering a malnourished body. Despite the visible weakness in her body, she stood strong and defiant before them, not intimidated by those that approached her.

Arundel held up a hand to signal the party to stop and Darwin quickly barked the order to the soldiers.

"Stay here," he told them quietly, before dismounting from his horse. Beneath his furs he wore a mixture of chain mail and light armour, something he was still struggling to get used to: the extra weight caused his feet to sink into the sodden mud beneath his feet. Slowly, he made his way over to the girl, who did not move at all. On reaching her, he dropped down to one knee.

"What is your name?"

The girl showed no fear as she replied confidently.

"Sara."

He gave her a smile.

"It's nice to meet you, Sara. My name is Arundel."

Sara nodded slightly.

"Yes I know. They say you are our King, our true King. Is that so?"

A bold question, he admired her spirit.

"So I am told, but between you and me, I don't feel like one."

For the first time, he saw a slight change in her expression, a slight crack of a smile forming upon her lips as if the innocence of youth was momentarily trying to break free.

"Tell me, Sara, why do your people not want us here? Other villages have been welcoming, but here is very different. Why is that?"

This time Sara hesitated, for the first time visibly unsure whether to say any more. Thankfully, she decided she should. In a soft tone but with a hint of an inner strength, Sara began to explain.

"Other men have come, searching for you. They searched our homes and threatened that if they find out we had been helping or hiding you, then we would suffer. We had so little food to survive through winter and they helped themselves to a lot of what was left, leaving us to starve. And then before they left, they...they..."

Suddenly her voice began to waiver and that hidden strength disappeared, as she struggled to complete the sentence. Arundel guided her back on track.

"What did they do?"

Sara battled with the words for a moment longer, before finishing.

"They made an example of Hector."

"What example?"

Sara did not speak a word in reply. Instead, she slowly took his hand in hers, her skin soft against his rough palm, and began to lead him along the path towards the village square. He wondered what he was about to see, when all became clear as the square came into view. A temporary lynching post had been erected and hanging from it was the rotting corpse of Hector. Birds of all kinds were pecking at the loose flesh while flies hovered about, in vast numbers.

"Why do you leave him there?"

Sara lowered her head a little.

"They said we would be punished if we took him down."

He stood there and stared at Hector, at what had become of him, and in that warning, he could see just how cruel and violent this impending war was set to be. He was interrupted in his thoughts by the sound of footsteps behind him. He turned round to see that Garad, Urag'Ki and Darwin had joined him. He turned to Darwin.

"Have him cut down and given a proper burial."

Darwin nodded.

"At once, my King."

He then turned away and headed back towards the soldiers, barking out orders, while Sara began to speak in a tone of rising panic.

"If you do that, we will get punished: they will kill us all."

He knelt down in front of Sara once more, and brushed a reassuring hand against her cheek.

"No, they won't. You have Damisas to protect you now. We will protect you, I promise."

As a tear rolled down her cheek, he could see both fear and relief in those once innocent eyes, and then, when he wasn't expecting it, Sara wrapped her arms around him.

"Thank you."

Before they had left Cassmera, he had spoken to all who would listen, spreading the word of hope and unity that this journey was all about. He had also asked Urag'Ki to send word to his people, to have them let Damisas know that rations needed to be dispatched at once. As they left the village, the atmosphere still carried a chill to it, but it had warmed somewhat from their arrival. Cassmera had done him good; he had needed to see this. The joy of Dandringham and Farrindorr had perhaps made him a little complacent, when they had presented such a pretty picture. Cassmera had reminded him that war was not pretty, anything but. It was ugly through to its core, and he realised that many innocents would suffer during its course.

With those villages long behind them now, three turns of the moon had passed, before the outline of Antolina had appeared on the horizon. The moon had turned once more, and now they were approaching the entrance. The village was surrounded by a wooden wall, standing no higher than his chest, and smoke billowed from chimneys into the grey sky overhead. They had slowed their mounts to a walk, but as they reached the entrance, it narrowed too much for them to stay on horseback and so a full dismount took place. As they entered on foot, Arundel began to feel uneasy. While the reception in Cassmera had been frosty, at least there had been people around to flee or curse. So far, he had yet to see a single soul: Antolina appeared to be abandoned. He was so busy looking around him, that it took Urag'Ki to point it out, before he noticed the deep, heavy footprints that scattered in all directions in the mud. After Urag'Ki had dropped to a crouched position to study them for a moment, he glanced up at Arundel with a troubled brow.

"These prints are too deep to be villagers. Those who made them were heavy, likely clad in armour."

"Guardians."

Garad said what they had all immediately thought, and his reaction was to take hold of Razor's hilt and draw her from her sheath. As they all followed suit, Darwin was next to speak.

"I fear we may be too late, if the silence is to be trusted."

He had feared the same, but did not say it.

They began to walk again, this time with more caution and, as they did so, he wondered whether the soldiers behind him were about to face their first real test. Silence continued to hang in the cold air for a while longer, until they neared the centre of the village. Then he heard the voice for the first time. He could not make out the words, but, by the sound of the voice, he could tell that it was speaking to someone or something, with a stern purpose. Maybe there was hope for the villagers yet. Darwin had begun organising the troops, shifting them from two long columns into several shorter ones that now formed human walls on either side of him.

Within moments, the picture became clearer. The villagers were all on their knees by what appeared to be a memorial stone of some kind. They were surrounded by twenty armour-clad Guardians, by rough count, with one more Guardian standing before them, shouting out. The words had become a little clearer now, and Arundel could tell that the speaker was talking about them hiding something. The problem was that his words becoming clearer meant that the shouting man could also now hear the sound of rattling armour. He stopped mid-sentence to turn round and see them. His silence did not last though, as he pointed towards them and roared, "It's him, it's Arundel! Your King wishes him dead! Let us not disappoint!"

With that, the men surrounding the villagers began to advance towards them, while their vociferous leader positioned himself just behind.

"Hold your positions! Protect your King!"

Darwin was the one to shout now, making sure his troops stayed focused. Twenty one versus their thirty four, those were good odds for his new warriors to test themselves against. No sooner had he thought that, than the situation changed. Having been silent as a tomb for so long, Antolina suddenly became awash with activity, when more Guardians began to emerge from within the cottages all around them. He did not bother to try and count. It was clear they were now outnumbered, and chaos was about to rain down upon them.

The world suddenly became mostly a blur, with only what was near him remaining in focus. The closest thing to him happened to be a Guardian approaching at some speed, sword raised in anger. He reacted quickly, blocking it with Razor as the blade swung down towards him. He then drove his forearm into the helmet of the Guardian, stunning him momentarily, before thrusting Razor through his throat and causing blood to spurt in all directions. When the Guardian fell to the floor, another took his place. Arundel ducked under a wild lunge and sliced Razor up the man's back, splitting it in two. An arrow whistled past his head, straight into the eye of another Guardian, and he saw Garad shrug in the distance, before turning his bow on another target. The sound of clashing swords and pounding armour rang out all around him, as he worked his way through the melee. He found Urag'Ki and two of their soldiers trading blows with a group and so he waded in, slashing and hacking with Razor, until the group were no more. Slowly, the hectic scene began to calm a little, the numbers dwindled and the mass combat became pockets of fighting. One of those pockets involved Darwin, who was in the process of ending the vociferous leader's shouting permanently as he parted his head from his neck. Arundel then ran Razor through a Guardian in the mud, before looking around him to consider the situation. The Guardians were all dead, but, unfortunately, so were five of their own. Nonetheless, the Damisas soldiers had passed their first test with flying colours, and he watched them proudly, as they rejoiced in their victory. The sound of cheers was suddenly replaced by a loud cry.

"Over there!"

He looked towards the path that led out of the village and saw a Guardian on a horse, galloping towards the gate. "Leave it to me."

He was pleased to hear Garad's voice, confirming that his name-brother was still alive. At the same time, he was not surprised to hear him claim the shot. Garad then raised his bow and lined up his target, before letting loose an arrow. The arrow glided through the air and then pierced the Guardian's left shoulder. The Guardian slumped forward, but managed to stay on his mount, and they could only watch as he rode out of the village and out of sight.

CHAPTER

21

"Arrggh!"

She couldn't help but let the groan of pain slip from her lips, as the wood cracked against her arm. She had padding on, but all that served to prevent was bruising. It could not prevent pain. She would have hoped that the blow would have been enough to avoid a repeat. Thwack, thwack.

"Arrrggh!"

She was wrong. She had managed to block the first two swings, but they put her off balance and left her open for the third swing to crack against her other arm. She could kick herself for that, but reasoned she was taking enough hits as it was.

"Again."

Sir Winstan Charrington spoke with a soft but firm tone, as he readied himself for another round. He had his wooden training sword raised and ready, and so she shook both arms to rid herself of the pain, before raising her own sword. She remembered back to her days in Crackendon, training with Maxillian, and in a way this could have been seen as a backward step. With Maxillian, she used a real sword; there was no other choice. Here with Sir Winstan, all combat was with a wooden training sword. The only time she would get her hands on steel was when she went up against the training targets. However, there was a reason for the training swords. Maxillian was a young boy, who was self taught in basic swordplay, something she had easily been able to handle. Sir Winstan was a trained knight of the highest order, and had been so for most of his long life. Within a few nights of practice with

Maxillian, she had become his equal, but with Sir Winstan, she had been training for some time now and it was still the case that if they used real steel, she would be missing limbs, at the very least.

The training had encouraged her to feel such respect for Sir Winstan, even more than she already did. He was a professional of the highest level and he made it look so easy. She could see why he had survived so much bloodshed over the years, and felt relieved that, by his own admission, his loyalties lay with the Stal bloodline, and not her father. After they had met for the first time, Sir Winstan had gone out of his way to make sure they would see each a little more regularly, so that he could keep a protective eye on her.

At that time, the rules constraining her freedom in the Palace were still quite strict. However, she was well aware that she was getting on the nerves of most guards, because she would walk circuits with Shauri around the Palace every day. Her reason for this was purely because she wished to discuss matters that she did not want Yasilda to hear, and Yasilda was far too lazy ever to go on walks. The fact that it annoyed the guards proved to be a bonus. All the time she walked around, they had to stay alert, and none of them wished to do so, being in a role that they clearly did not want. The guards had recently gained more control themselves, due to the fact that her father, increasingly paranoid, had secluded himself on the top floor, ever since Arundel had not been found. Meanwhile, Marcasian, who should have been giving the orders and running things with his usual iron fist, was preoccupied leading a small team to carry out his own investigation into who in the city had betrayed the Crown, by keeping Garad and Bromon hidden.

All of this created a window of opportunity. Seeing the reluctance of the other guards, Sir Winstan had volunteered to become her personal guard, thus taking the pressure off of the rest. Marcasian would never have allowed it, but he was too busy to notice, and so it was agreed by unanimous decision. This opened up more opportunities because, with her own personal guard supposedly to keep watch on her, she was able to venture out into the grounds of the Palace. She would talk with Sir Winstan and listen to his stories of the days of old when the Guardians of the Crown were simply twelve of the finest knights assigned to protect the King, in the days of Andreas Stal and his ancestors. While Oracle Thomas had taught her overall history of the realm, Sir Winstan taught her the more personal history of individuals.

To begin with they would barely leave the perimeter of the Palace on their walks, but then as winter arrived and the cold air began to bite, the Guardians reduced their presence outside; so their walks would venture further and further out into the grounds. Occasionally, he would even accompany her to Damisas, on her late night visits. He had wanted to meet Arundel, the man he had not seen since he was a boy of ten. However, at the same time he did not want to intrude on the little time she had with Arundel, and so he would just wait, always putting her first. She enjoyed the freedom she had gained, she enjoyed the knowledge that she was learning and she enjoyed having someone around in her life, who was more of a father figure than her actual father was. On more than one occasion, she had told Shauri that she wished Sir Winstan had been her father and would talk of how her youth might have been so different; but then, had that been the case, she would not have met Arundel and so those thoughts were bittersweet.

The training had been Sir Winstan's idea. He had kept the idea to himself for some time, not even hinting at it. Then the snow came, and with it some changes in arrangements within the Palace. Some of the Guardians' squads had still been out searching the realm for Arundel, when the first snow fell and cut them off from a return to the city; presumably, they were dead, unless they had been able to find sufficient shelter. Those who remained in the city did not wish to brave the cold and the thick white blanket of snow on the ground, unless they had to. Marcasian and his team had based themselves outside of the Palace walls in the heart of the city, to make their investigation easier in the tough weather.

Even Thea had to admit the weather was too extreme for her outside walks to continue. She had been facing up to another period of being trapped inside the Palace, when Sir Winstan approached her one morning and said he wanted to show her something. Following him into the old throne room with all its dust and cobwebs and darkness, she was not sure what he could show her that she hadn't seen before. When he led her behind the old throne, she started to think this was nothing more than a ruse to pass a little bit of time. But then, when he pushed one of the bricks and a small doorway opened into a secret passage, she was shocked. Discovering there was a secret passage in the library had been surprising enough, but this just amazed her. She had never realised how many secrets lay in this old Palace. Without considering possible risks, she followed Sir Winstan into the passage and closed the door behind them. He explained that this was another passage built to protect the King, should he be trapped in the throne room. The passage led to the outskirts of the Palace, in the opposite direction to the one in the library. There was a choice of two different sets of stairs: one led out just inside the Palace grounds, and the other outside the city wall, into open fields.

Guiding her by torchlight, Sir Winstan chose the first set of stairs and led her up to a wooden door. Fishing for a key from his gauntlet, he unlocked the door and pushed it open. The door led them into a building she had never seen before. The cold hit her like a thousand tiny blades piercing her skin. Sir Winstan walked over to one of the corners of the room and picked up some logs, which he placed in a small fireplace. Before long, he had a fire roaring. As the temperature crept up and her skin began to warm, Sir Winstan told her that this was the training house for the old Guardians, the elite twelve. No one else knew it was here, and that was done for a purpose, because the best of the best, the official protectors of the King, needed to prepare and train and plan in secrecy. The largest room with the fireplace was sparsely furnished and designed for hand-to-hand combat. There were three other rooms off of it. One contained training targets of different shapes and sizes for solo training. In the second room was an old oak table with twelve chairs around it, so that planning meetings could be held there, when necessary. All of the training equipment, from training swords and pads, to real steel swords and shields and armour were housed in the third and final room. Sir Winstan explained his logic to her, stating that if Arundel was to push his claim for the throne, then war was coming and, given where her allegiance lay, she would need to be able not only to protect herself, but also to be of use in battle. She told him about her days of practising with Maxillian, and how she could already handle a sword, and he simply laughed. At the time, she thought he was being somewhat rude and arrogant, but now, after many days of training together, she understood why he had laughed.

"Again."

Sir Winstan gave the command and once more took his stance. This time, she decided to go on the offensive, swinging blow after blow with her training sword, but Sir Winstan blocked each blow with ease and it began to frustrate her. Slightly losing her control, she aimed with a wild swing, which he ducked, before he then drove a shoulder into her body and knocked her over. She hit the cold hard floor with a hefty bump, once again the pads barely masking the jolt of pain that surged through her body, and before she could gather herself and react, the tip of Sir Winstan's wooden blade was pressed against her neck. She let out a grunt of exasperation, before Sir Winstan lowered his sword and offered her a hand instead. After a moment, she took it and he pulled her back to her feet. A dull pain still throbbed in her lower back. She unclipped the strap around her chin, pulled off the protective helmet she had been wearing and dropped it to the floor as strands of hair, drenched with sweat, flopped down and clung to her cheek.

"What is wrong?"

That soothing voice of Sir Winstan broke the silence, no trace of the previous demanding tone.

"Nothing is wrong."

She meant that when she said it, yet she wasn't sure she

believed it herself. Clearly, Sir Winstan did not believe it, as he scoffed and spoke again.

"You don't fool me, Princess. You have been far better than this for weeks; your head is not right today. Nor has it been for the last few days."

If she was honest, there was something playing on her mind, but she was hesitant to say it because she did not want to appear weak to this brave old knight. So instead, she tried to change the topic of conversation.

"I have told you, don't call me Princess. We both know that I am not a real princess."

Sir Winstan placed a hand on her shoulder.

"Whether we like it or not, your father sits on the throne as King and so that makes you a princess. Therefore, I will refer to you as such. We do not want to give ourselves away by my using your name."

He was right and she knew it. It was a snap reaction to try and avoid the question, and obviously it had failed.

"So, come on, Princess, what is distracting you?"

Her avoidance tactic a failure, she took a deep breath and decided to proceed with the truth.

"I haven't heard word of Arundel since he left Damisas to tour the villages. They were supposed to stay in contact with the city, and Oracle Thomas would then keep me updated, but I have not heard a single piece of news."

As the words slipped from her lips, worry flowed over her in a strong wave.

"That is not unusual, Princess. It is hard to maintain communication when you are out in the realm. With so much travelling and so much to do in the villages, I imagine they are just too busy to try and send word."

That gave her a small measure of reassurance, but not enough for her liking.

"I understand that, but those soldiers have never seen real combat before and we both know that more Guardians have been sent out to find him."

She sat down, in the hope that it would ease her stress in some way, but it didn't. Sir Winstan took a seat next to her, with a slight groan of age.

"They will protect him and, from what I hear, he is very capable of protecting himself. They will be fine, Princess. He will soon return, and nothing will have changed."

He had been right about many things, but on that he was wrong.

"Things have already changed."

This seemed to catch the curiosity of Sir Winstan, who shot her a quizzical glance.

"How so?"

She probably shouldn't say, but she had let things go a little too far already and so she decided to tell him what she had only shared with Shauri until now. Sir Winstan sat there and listened, as she took him back to the night before Arundel set off to the villages.

She had awoken with a slight nudge to her side. Her eyes slowly opened and then adapted to the darkness and vague moonlight that tried to illuminate it. With that, she realised that Arundel was sitting up beside her. Not only that, but it was still some time until morning.

"What's the matter?" she managed to stammer in a croaky voice that was not yet ready to be active. He leaned in close, their noses almost touching, as she felt his warm breath upon her skin.

"I have something I want to show you."

He followed his words up with a tender kiss and the early wake up was forgiven. Having dressed, she was then led out into the cold early morning air, over to the stables, where she mounted Arundel's horse and slipped into the saddle, behind him. With her arms wrapped around him tightly, to her surprise they made their way through the city, to the main gates, and out into the realm. Just north of the city was a small lake and it was there that they rode. A path that had clearly been worn down over the years led them all the way down to the shore, where the remnants of a stone bench could be found. They dismounted and she took a seat on the ruined seat, while Arundel tied up the horse, before joining her. By now, the hint of dawn could be seen pale in the night sky.

"Very well, I have to ask, what is it that inspired you to bring me here at the crack of dawn?"

He wrapped one of his powerful arms around her and pulled her in close.

"Old folklore, so I am told, tells a tale of this lake. It is said that when the wizard Xoumarin brought the pilgrims of the Forgotten Lands to these shores, he also brought some of the more magical creatures with him, including a pair of unicorns, one male and one female. However, during the war with Gruldock the Insatiable, the male unicorn was killed and the female fled, never to be seen again. Or, at least, never to be seen by most. However, some say that the female unicorn found her way to this lake, and that this is where she stayed. Those same few claim that, occasionally, as dawn breaks, the unicorn comes to the water's edge to drink, just over there on the opposite side. It is said that this bench was built as an observation point to watch her. Of course, there is no proof that any of this happened, or that unicorns even exist. But, as this is our last night for a while, I wanted to share this special moment with you."

How could she have argued with that? This man, this fantastic man, never stopped finding ways to amaze her. She tried to find the words to show her appreciation, but in the end opted for a kiss full of love. They sat there for a while, wrapped up in each other, watching out over the water as the sun started its climb towards the heavens, its reflection gracefully spreading across the water. Then, all of a sudden, she heard a noise coming from across the lake. The faint sound of rustling, perhaps the snap of a branch. At first, she wondered if she was hearing things, but Arundel's change in body language told her he had heard it also. She slipped from his arms and pushed to her feet, taking slow quiet steps towards the very water's edge in order to get the best view possible. She heard the noise again and then a beam of emerging sunlight showed her enough of the opposite shoreline to spot movement among the bushes. The excitement washed over her and, for a moment, she was a young girl all over again. Even though she knew the story was probably just that, a story, part of her wanted to believe and was excited by that belief. She stood there, silent and still, and watched as something came nearer. Anticipation built and built; could she really be about to see a mythical creature?

Suddenly, the greenery parted and something started to emerge. She strained her eyes as hard as she could until they focused in on the creature breaking free from the thick growth to find the water. Unfortunately as the animal grazed, she could see that it was clearly not a unicorn, but a deer. A gentle laugh escaped her, when she realised how silly she had been to allow herself to believe in such foolishness. Even so, despite not being the lady others expected her to be, she could still appreciate the beauty that was before her. Not just that, but she could appreciate the man who had wanted to share it with her.

"I want more of this."

She spoke quietly, almost a whisper as if no one was meant to hear, yet Arundel did.

"So do I."

His voice was just as soft, and she could hear the emotion that coated it. She could feel him move close behind her, but she did not turn round; her gaze remained on the deer, which momentarily looked straight at her, before taking another drink.

"I don't want to be without you any more."

This time she spoke a little louder, now that she knew it was a real conversation. Again he spoke softly.

"I am done with having to let you go."

She always hated leaving; it wrenched her heart every single time. She wanted to stay, to be a part of his life every single day, and she hoped, with all her heart, that he wanted the same. He spoke again.

"If I am to be King, then I want you forever by my side as my Queen. If I am to die, then I want to die knowing that my heart belongs to you."

That caught her off guard, but in a pleasant way.

"What are you saying, Arundel?"

Moving her gaze from the deer, she turned around to find Arundel bent down on one knee.

"Thea, would you do me the honour of being my wife?"

Sir Winstan had listened to the whole story in silence as it ended on her saying yes. He hadn't been quite so engrossed as Shauri, who had been full of high-pitched squeals of excitement, but he had taken it all in, she could tell. After a moment or two of silence between them, he finally spoke.

"When is the wedding?"

"The date is not set yet. We will work that out when Arundel gets back, if he gets back."

She hated having that doubt, but it was impossible not to. "And what then, will you continue as you are?"

She had never once considered doing that.

"No, I will live in Damisas with him, and be free from my father and this poisoned city."

Sir Winstan grunted in contemplation, and then pushed his tired body into gear, to get back to his feet. He picked up both training swords and offered one to her.

"If you are to marry and leave this city, then war will come in swift response, a war from which you will not be safe. Clear your mind, Princess, for our training is now more important than ever before."

A thick mist hung over the land this early morning. The sun had risen, but swiftly vanished behind the dense, grey veil that was slowly engulfing the city. Despite the poor visibility, the guard posting atop the walls was still required and so, on this morning, two of the Guardians kept watch above the main gate. They were both wrapped up well to keep out the chill that still hung in the air, along with the damp hidden within the mist. Neither wanted to be there; they saw no point, especially when they could be somewhere far warmer, like their beds. The first guard stood and stared out into open land beyond the city walls, and, mist or no mist, just like always he saw nothing. The second guard leaned his back against the wall and was carving into a small piece of wood, with his knife. As he worked, his slightly shaking hands slipped and suddenly caused a cut he did not want to make.

"Bugger."

He cursed. He took a closer look at his carving and then tossed it aside.

"Bloody ruined. It's too damn cold; my hands won't stop shaking."

The first guard turned away from the empty scene before him, to look at his partner for the shift.

"Nazeth, how about you try focusing on your job instead? You are supposed to be keeping watch, so, you know, that means actually watching."

The second guard pushed off the wall to stand upright and sighed, as he turned around.

"What's the bloody point, Tomei? When have you ever actually seen anything that wasn't an expected arrival? All the times we have done this posting, have you ever seen a threat? Have you ever had to raise the alarm?"

Tomei thought about that for a moment, and then shook his head.

"No."

Nazeth waved his arm, as if to emphasise his point.

"Exactly. Bloody pointless. We could sleep, if it weren't too damn cold to do so. We will never see anything."

He turned away from the outer fields again and began scouring the floor for his carving, deciding that maybe he could rectify the mistake. As he bent down and began to grope about the dirty floor, silence fell upon them for a few moments until Tomei spoke.

"What's that out there?"

The second guard didn't even bother to look up, and just continued his search.

"Yeah, yeah, very funny. I wasn't born bloody yesterday, you know."

His companion did not back down.

"No, seriously, there is something out there in the mist, and it is getting closer."

Nazeth's search was proving fruitless and so, reluctantly, he chose to call the first guard's bluff. Rising to his feet, he looked over the wall out into the mist.

"Come on then, where is it?"

Tomei pointed directly forward.

"Just there."

He looked forward and couldn't see anything. He squinted to try and improve his focus but all he could see was mist. "You bloody fool, there isn't anyth..."

He cut his sentence off, as he suddenly saw it. A dark shadow moving within the grey, getting bigger as it drew closer.

"What is it?" Tomei asked. The answer was he didn't have a clue, so he kept watching hard, not wanting to make an assumption in case he was wrong. Slowly, the shadow began to emerge from the mist. The first thing he could make out was the head of a horse. Then, when he saw the glint of armour, he decided to take no chances.

"Raise the alarm!" he shouted.

Tomei ran over to the alarm bell and grabbed the rope, shaking it vigorously as the bell rang out loudly. Nazeth kept his eyes on the mist, waiting for more horses to emerge, but none came. Once the lone horse cleared the mist completely, the guard could see a soldier in armour slumped forward, an arrow buried into his shoulder. He then noticed the crest of a serpent entwined around an axe upon the draping over the horse.

"Open the gate!" he shouted, with urgency. "It's one of ours!"

Marcasian had just finished with Yasilda and pushed her aside on the bed. She was panting, with a broad smile on her sweat stained face. While she ran her hands through her scraggly hair to wipe the sweat from her eyes, he sat on the edge of the bed and looked at her in disgust, nothing more. If he was honest, he couldn't stand her. She was ugly, had a terrible body and every time she spoke, it made him want to crush her skull in. However, there was one thing she was good at, one thing she was of use for, and so he kept her around for that purpose, a purpose he had once again just used her for.

It was a good way to get his frustrations out, to have some form of release when he needed it, and lately he really needed it. For a long time now, even through the harsh snows of winter, he and a small team had been working their way through the city, trying to find out who had betrayed the King by housing Arundel's kin. So many people had been spoken to and grilled at length, while others had been dealt with in a more violent manner. Yet they were no closer to the truth, no closer to a confession, than they had been when they first began. He knew someone was culpable, but he just did not know who and it angered him greatly. When this enquiry had started, the guilty were going to be put on public trial. Now he had reached the point that if he found the culprit, he would kill them then and there with his bare hands, just to put an end to this miserable investigation. His anger was at such a pitch, that he had contemplated wrapping his hands around Yasilda's fat neck and squeezing hard, so he could listen to her choke, while he watched her pathetic life drain from her eyes. As a spy, she had so far proved more than useless. He knew in his gut that there was something about Princess Thea that could not be trusted, and was sure that Yasilda would be able to pick up some information. Yet the best she would ever manage was the city gossip that served no value, filtered with her moans that Thea walked a lot and she didn't like walking. It was ludicrous really that he allowed her life to continue, but a man's needs were a man's needs and so, for now, she lived. She moved up behind him, running her fingers over his chest and leaning in close to his ear.

"Ready to go again?"

He brushed her off and stood up.

"Get out."

Yasilda rolled herself awkwardly off the bed, as he walked over to the window to keep his distance from her, to stop himself lashing out.

"Have I displeased you?"

He didn't bother turning round; he was done having to look at her for today.

"Get out."

He could hear her whimper a little, while she gathered her clothes together. He didn't know why she bothered being upset; they both knew there would be another time, just not at the moment.

Out of the window he stared at the mist that seemed to engulf the castle, and wondered what irritations the new day would bring. Behind him he heard Yasilda open the door and scurry out, only for the sound to be replaced by that of heavy footsteps. He knew that one of his men was approaching, but he did not shift his gaze. A few more footsteps and then they came to a stop, replaced by a voice that sounded both hurried and stressed.

"Sire, the King demands an audience with you immediately."

Still he stared out of the window.

"Does he now?"

The tone did not change in the soldier's voice.

"Yes, Sire. It is urgent."

It must have been urgent for the King to come out of the self-imposed hibernation he had vanished into of late. It would be more drama and grief he was sure, yet another irritation to add to his collection. He turned to face the soldier.

"Let me get dressed. "

The soldier briefed him, as best he could, on their route back to the Palace from Marcasian's temporary home within the city. One of the Guardians, who had been sent out to search the villages for Arundel, had returned with an arrow in his shoulder and a message upon his lips. He had returned alone. The message was unknown, at least to the soldier. Reaching the final few steps of the Palace, the soldier waited, while Marcasian completed the walk up to the doors, which were promptly opened for him. As he stepped inside, he could see the wounded soldier slumped on the floor, partially against a wall, but having to lean forward because of the arrow buried deep into his shoulder. He could tell by the look on his face that he was in pain and reasoned that there was every chance he could be at death's door. He then moved his eyes away from the soldier to the throne, which was empty. Standing behind it, all in black with a tarnished crown upon his head, was King Theagran. His skin was looking pale, unsurprising given how much time he had been spending tucked away in here. He had lost a little weight, as well, and his skin was looking tired and aged, but his eyes burned with as much evil as they had ever done.

"You sent for me, my King."

Staring at him from behind the throne, Theagran stood there for quite some time and said nothing.

"I was told it was urgent."

Still the King stood there staring, as if he had never seen him before. The soldier on the floor then let out a groan of pain and this seemed to snap Theagran to life.

"This so-called warrior encountered Arundel in the village of Antolina. Only Arundel was not alone, he had men with him, men who did not appear as simple rogues, but knights."

That surprised him.

"How many?"

Theagran moved from behind the throne and walked towards him.

"He says twenty, maybe thirty. Although some had died during the fight."

Now he was intrigued: where had that lost boy found himself twenty or more knights?

"Did they bear any crest to give an indication of where they came from?"

By now, Theagran was right beside him, and he could see that the King's once thick black hair and beard was starting to look somewhat grey and thin.

"He says they bore one crest, that of an eagle upon a sword which you and I both know is the crest of the Stal family."

He replied with a grunt, he didn't need to be told. Theagran walked past him and over to the door, as if to check no one was listening.

"I thought we had rid ourselves of that wretched bloodline, and now here we are with one of them trying to build an army and take my throne."

The soldier let out another groan of pain, which reminded Marcasian about the patrol the soldier would have been a part of, before being shot by an arrow.

"What of his men? If he came back alone, where are they?"

The ageing face of Theagran curled into a snarl.

"Dead. He says they are all dead. They came up against Arundel's little band; they had more men, and they all died except for him. He couldn't win the battle, and he couldn't die in it; what kind of soldier does that make him?"

He pointed a finger of disgust at the soldier on the floor and then shot Marcasian a glance that did not need any accompanying words. Without saying anything, Marcasian walked over to the soldier, slipping his knife out of its sheath as he moved, and with one swift movement, he sliced across the soldier's throat. The death was quick, just a few garbled murmurs and he was gone, his blood soaking his clothes and the floor around him. Marcasian wiped his knife and placed it back into its sheath. Theagran shuffled over to the throne and took his seat, a troubled look upon his brow.

"We must cut the head off the snake, before it grows any bigger. If Arundel gathers more men, then he may actually become a danger. He must be found and he must be killed. I want more men sent out and this time there is no mercy for those pathetic villagers."

That sounded more like it; something he could finally get behind.

"Let me lead them, my King."

Theagran shook his head.

"No, I need you to stay here and keep things in shape."

He wasn't taking no for an answer, not this time.

"With all due respect, my King, I have spent an age on a fruitless search for the traitors within the city; the men here have run themselves. But you sent others out without my leadership, and look what happened: they were slaughtered by lesser numbers. Let me lead them; let me end this for you. My thirst for slaughter needs to be quenched, so let it be Arundel's blood that quenches it for me."

Theagran sat there in silent contemplation for a minute or two, before breaking that silence.

"As you wish. But I want there to be bloodshed. I want them all to feel my wrath. Burn those villages to the ground, smoke him out and lead him right to you, and then cut him down where he stands. I want you to come back with his head on a pike and his heart in your blood-stained hands, do you understand?"

Oh, he understood perfectly. His hands gripped the hilt of his sword with eagerness.

"Yes, my King, as you wish."

23

Thirty-four of them had left Damisas to tour the villages; twenty-nine of them had returned. The fight in Antolina had cost them five lives, all of those belonging to the squad of soldiers that had escorted them. The argument would be that those five lives were worth the cost, since they had defeated a squadron of Guardians of greater numbers. It had been the perfect first test really, and the war council would be delighted, without doubt, but to Arundel, every life lost was because of him and weighed heavily on his conscience.

Following the fight, they had stayed for several days, to help settle the village down, before continuing on the tour. They had made it to eight more villages, before their low rations forced them to turn about and head back to Damisas. The tour had, generally, been a success, with most villagers either pleased to see them from the start, or warming to them by the time the visit was over. They had all suffered under the rule of Theagran, having all previously lived well under generations of Stals, and so, naturally, they were eager to see a Stal upon the throne once more. Food was scarce for many of them, and he had pledged to help them where he could. The heavy snow of winter had caused some damage and so he and his soldiers had helped with repairs during their stay. Some of the villages even had volunteers willing to join up and fight alongside him, but he urged them to stay and protect their homes, thanking them for their courage in the process. So, yes, a success would be a fair assessment of the trip.

When they returned to Damisas, he had expected it would

be simply to stock up on rations, and then head out again. However, it was decided by the war council that another trip should be held off for a while, as things could become more risky if the Guardian, who had escaped from Antolina, ever made it back to Ryevale. So it had become a case of as you were, now that they were back in the city.

The first night back had been spent bathing and sleeping, letting his body ease down for a night. Word had not yet reached Thea that he was back, and so she was not there with him that night. However, he was told that she had been visiting the city during his absence. She now regularly travelled with an old knight named Sir Winstan, who she had briefly told him about. Sir Winstan was a loyalist to his father, Arundel had been told by Thea, and Arundel had therefore been keen to meet him, but it had not been possible yet. It appeared that Sir Winstan had not wasted his time during the visits, making recommendations on the training set up for the soldiers and also on the defensive duties required for the city. All of these suggestions had been taken on board, and were evident every day, as the soldiers went about their duties, with impressive organisation.

Thea had also made the most of her visits in his absence, meeting with the city dressmaker and making some other arrangements for the wedding. By some he meant all, because everything had been organised and only required his return, for the date to be set. Now that he had returned, he was told it would be in a few days. Some he knew, like Garad, would have run for the hills on hearing all this, but not him. He could not wait to marry Thea, to have her as a part of him, for the rest of his days. He would do it today if he could, but that was not the agenda and although he was the King and had the power to overrule such decisions, he decided to leave it all to the war council.

It was a new day, the sun had broken through the grey cloud and, for the first time in many months, there was a warmth in the air. Not much, but enough to take the edge off the cold chill that cut through to the bone, when it could. The moon had taken its turn forty-four times since their return to Damisas, and life had resumed its previous pattern The story of the fight had been told in homes, taverns and on the training field for days, as those who had taken part boasted about it, while those who had remained behind, wished they had been there. Spirits were high and the city continued to thrive, while avoiding suspicion from the throne.

Arundel had visited the families of those five, who had died on tour, and expressed his condolences, along with his honest words praising their bravery and how they were an inspiration to others. He had also personally overseen the organisation of rations to be sent out to the villages. He wanted to make sure that this took place, otherwise he would not be a man of his word. If his word meant nothing, how could he expect people to support him?

On a happier note, Thea had visited several times. Those evenings, short as they were, meant everything to him and reminded him why this war was worth fighting. Last night had been the most recent of such evenings, when she had reminded him that their wedding was merely days away. She had told him that the regime of the Guardians back at Ryevale remained lazy, especially since Marcasian had not been seen for some time and their numbers seemed fewer. The only concern was that with Sir Winstan as her personal guard, Arundel had been cut out of the loop completely with regard to military tactics. He was so preoccupied with making the most of his time with her he didn't pay sufficient attention to the hidden warning signs. He should have done, but he hadn't, and it was moments like that which always made him question whether he was suitable to wear a crown. With the arrival of day had come the departure of Thea, and now he was left waiting until the next time, which could quite possibly be their wedding night.

For now, he needed to occupy his mind and, with his presence no longer required at training with the troops, finding that distraction was not so easy. Garad would have been a natural choice, but his name-brother had found his own diversion in a woman named Eliya, one of the archers who had travelled with them to the villages. The two of them had grown very close and were certainly enjoying the early days of a new relationship. He would not deprive them of that, not today. He would also try and hide his jealousy that Garad could be with her any time he pleased, something he wished for with Thea.

Oracle Thomas would have been another option, but he had taken to teaching the children, sharing his vast knowledge with them, and Arundel felt that was far too important to interrupt for no real reason. So here he was, sitting outside what was now the Sky Temple; it had been converted after they had first arrived because of their close relationship with the Seekers. While waiting for Urag'Ki to finish his prayers to the Goddess Anyeama, Arundel ran a smooth stone down the blade of Razor to make sure she was sharp; this also kept himself busy as he waited.

Eventually, his friend emerged from the temple, as always painted head to toe in a deep dark blue. Only this time, he had bright yellow stars painted on his chest in the form of an owl. Urag'Ki had told him before that it represented his family and each family had their own star design. It was done so that when they prayed, Anyeama knew which family she was to bless and watch over. Urag'Ki walked over and took a seat beside him.

"An absent heart making for an idle mind?"

He rubbed the stone down Razor's edge once more. "Something like that."

Urag'Ki began to unwrap some thread he had around his wrist, another act carried out for prayer. It would be wrapped tightly to cause pain, so that he would remember his own vulnerabilities and could then ask Anyeama to help him overcome them.

"Anyeama teaches us that when two souls are entwined, they will share eternity together. Your soul is entwined with Thea's, my friend, and you will share eternity with her, whether it starts in this life or the afterlife."

He certainly hoped it would start in this life.

"Thanks. The day she leaves is always tough, especially now I'm not required in the barracks anymore."

Urag'Ki placed a consoling hand on his leg and squeezed it a little.

"Anyeama always has ways of answering our woes when we need her; your Gods must surely do the same."

He shook his head.

"I don't have any Gods, not since I was a boy, so I am told."

Others might have been shocked by such a confession, but his bond with Urag'Ki had become strong enough for the latter not to be affected.

"Then you must rely on the people you protect, to answer your woes instead."

That reply did not exactly ease him.

"My King, my King, you must come quickly!"

The voice startled them, emerging from nowhere, riddled with panic and urgency. He turned to see one of the men assigned to guard duty, running towards him as fast as his armour would allow. The lad, who could have seen no more than seventeen summers, was still learning the ropes of his new role in the people's army and it showed in his lack of composure.

"What is the matter, lad?" he asked, in an even voice, aiming to calm the boy, but it did not work.

"You must come to the gates quickly, my King."

Realising he would get no further information, he rose to his feet and sheathed Razor, before following the boy swiftly through the city, towards the main gates.

By the time they arrived, a crowd had gathered, made up of a mixture of civilians and soldiers, the latter trying to keep the former back to create space. As Arundel worked his way through the masses into a gap, he could see that the huge gates of the city were open. A stream of villagers, covered in soot and blood, were making their way through, some limping, some being carried. Many carried all the possessions they could fit into their arms, and not a few were in distress. One of them, a male in his middle years, clothes torn, left eye shut and the left side of his face stained with blood, spotted Arundel and dropped to his feet before him. In a broken voice, the man began.

"My King, please, you must help us."

Arundel held out a hand and helped the man back to his feet, puzzled by the scene before him.

"What has happened?"

A knot of villagers had started to build around the man now, and continued to advance, despite the man doing all he could to stop himself being pushed away.

"Marcasian and his men," he stammered. The strength of the crowd overpowered him and he was swept away, shouting out as loud as he could before the distance became too great. Arundel was just able to hear the words.

"It's all gone!"

Within moments, the man was out of sight, as the soldiers stepped in to help guide the villagers away from the gates. Arundel was so taken aback by it all that he had not noticed Urag'Ki by his side, until his friend spoke.

"The people have given you an answer."

The rest of the day was spent helping the villagers. Getting them into the warm, fed and watered, was just the beginning. They had all been temporarily set up in the City Hall that was once upon a time used for city council meetings. It had been a long time since one of those was held, ended by the tyranny of Theagran, and sitting empty and unused, ever since. Today it had found purpose again. By the last count he had heard, two hundred and thirty-three people had made it to the city from various villages. The man that had spoken to him had come from the village of Tepal, the last one they visited on their tour. Many of the others were from villages Arundel and his army had not yet reached, which was why he was not recognised by them when they came through the gates. The volunteers who had taken on the task of looking after them were collating a list of names and villages; once this was done, they would start housing these survivors.

Meanwhile, despite the late hour, he had been summoned to an emergency war council meeting. The usual attendees were there, with Barrington Wehrsley looking as though he had scrambled out of bed, while everyone else, after a long day's graft, looked eager to get to theirs. However, bed would have to wait as Barrington was detailing all the information that he had.

"The final head count is three hundred and seventeen, from a total of five villages. They all tell a similar tale of how Marcasian and a large number of Guardians, between one and two hundred, depending on who you ask, rode into the villages, killing on sight and burning dwellings to the ground. A few were spared in each village to spread the word that they were doing it because of you, and that it will keep happening until you are handed over, dead or alive."

Barrington was clearly anxious, as he continued, "At the moment, we can cope with the numbers. We have empty accommodation, because we lost so many to Theagran all those years ago. But if more keep coming, we will struggle both to house them and with rations."

Darwin chimed in, with some authority.

"We must ride back out at once and meet this force, head on. They have started at the villages closest to Ryevale, and are clearly working their way out. It would be easy to determine their next targets."

Oracle Thomas then calmly added his point to the debate.

"That is what they want. Marcasian is baiting Arundel because as far as he knows, he has the numbers and, let's face it, he is right."

"The wedding is in just a few days. We can't delay that. A King needs his Queen," asserted Barrington.

"With all due respect, the wedding will have to wait. Lives are at stake and we must act now," Darwin responded sharply.

Oracle Thomas then spoke again.

"This is war, and pivotal moments require pivotal decisions. We are on the cusp of one of those moments and we must choose wisely."

Arundel had sat there in silence, listening to it all, each point in turn, hearing what they all had to say. To be honest, he didn't need to, because his mind was already made up. Before he could say anything, Garad piped up.

"Don't you think Ari should be making this decision? He is the King after all."

With that all eyes switched away from each other and fell upon him. His decision could remain in his head no longer. "We ride at first light. While I respect your considerations towards my personal life, Barrington, the wedding must wait. We have been travelling the villages, promising to protect them. Now that they are actually under threat of extermination, we can't just sit by and do nothing. I will take one hundred of our soldiers with me. I do not want to strip the city of its resources, and we will need to start training those villagers who are able and wish to fight. Train them while we are gone in the hope they can be as ready as can be upon my return."

Barrington looked worried.

"But one hundred, when they could have up to two hundred? With those odds, you won't make it back."

Darwin was keen to defend his own.

"We were outnumbered before and were victorious. We can do it again."

That seemed to do little to ease Barrington's concerns, as he turned to Oracle Thomas for support.

"Oracle, surely you can see that this is suicide?"

Oracle waited a moment before calmly replying.

"It could be, I agree. But Arundel is right: if we do nothing, then we will lose this war anyway, because how can we represent the people of the realm and not defend them? I have faith in our King and I have faith in those who fight for him."

Oracle had been Barrington's only hope. They all knew Garad would side with Arundel, were he to be asked. On hearing Oracle's response, all resistance drained from the Steward's face. Arundel turned to Darwin.

"Let the soldiers sleep for tonight, but wake them early and make sure they are ready to ride by break of dawn. We have no time to waste."

Darwin nodded.

"Of course, my King. They will be ready and eager."

Of that he had no doubt. He then turned to Oracle.

"You have the task of telling Thea the wedding is delayed. And, seeing as you are in support of this, tell her it was your idea!"

There had been no exaggeration by the villagers who had made it to Damisas. In fact, their words had probably not done the devastation justice. Arundel and his soldiers had not seen all of the attacked villages on their journey because of the route they had taken, but, with the few they had passed, it most certainly hit home just how brutal the Theagran regime could be. Each village had been burned to cinders, mere piles of ash and partial structures all that were left to indicate that a community had ever existed at the location. As for the villagers who were not able to get away, theirs was a tale of horrific woe. Their bodies had been piled up high and left there to rot. The smell was horrendous and caused more than a few to lose the contents of their stomachs. These bodies were once innocent people, going about their daily lives and just wanting to live well and in peace, but now they were nothing more than a feast for flies and any wildlife that would stumble upon them. Arundel had wanted to bury them, to give them some form of dignity and respect, but time was not on his side.

The aim was not to follow Marcasian's path, in the hope of catching him up, but to cut around the Guardians in order to get ahead and be able to confront them that way. It had been worked out that the village of Godstone was their best bet to achieve this aim. If they could get there before Marcasian did, then they could set themselves up ready to defend it, but that meant that time was against them and they could not afford any delays. This is why they could not bury the dead, as much as he wanted to. Urag'Ki sent word out to his people, in the hope that they would carry out the task, but with the amount of villages that had been attacked, it was no swift job.

So they continued on their journey, maintaining a fast pace, which from a distance would have been impressive to see, given the size of their party. The cold remained, but otherwise the worst of the weather held off, making the journey a little easier.

The route they had picked was designed to avoid any possible encounter with Marcasian, bearing in mind their numerical disadvantage. The more sensible option was to set up in the village and hold the tactical advantage, and so that was the aim. However, the risk was always that their paths could collide at any time and one night they thought it had happened. They had made camp for the night and those not on guard duty were settling down, when one of the guards on watch raised the alarm. There had been a mass scramble, as those at rest grabbed what armour and weaponry they could in preparation. Had it been Marcasian and two hundred men, they would have been slaughtered, of that he was certain. Instead it had been a group of Seekers, led by Shgrog'An, coming to update Urag'Ki on their actions and what they had seen. The victims from two of the villages had already been laid to rest in the earth; in time, the others would be too. For now, they chose to stay with the party to travel to Godstone, and Arundel was never going to turn down an extra twenty fighters. That was the closest they had come to an encounter on their journey and, after one more night, Godstone emerged from the morning haze.

Upon arrival, they found a village in fear, but one very much alive and unoccupied. They had no idea how long it would be before Marcasian arrived and so they set to work straight away. Wooden spikes were carved and dug into the ground all around the village, while archers were posted to every possible vantage point. Garad and Eliya took it in turns to run shifts to make sure the eyes of the marksmen and women up high stayed sharp and focused. Mounted patrols were run around the outskirts of the village by a team of four. They were split into two pairs and walked in opposite directions so that two sides were always covered. Shgrog'An and his men had stayed at Godstone, but were carrying out scouting missions in rotation, in the hope they could spot Marcasian early and give them a warning. However, it was not the Seekers who were the first to spot Marcasian and his Guardians, but Eliya. She watched them appear in the darkness under torchlight, and with all the ferocity she had, she raised the alarm.

With the first light of morning, came the realisation of the threat before them. Marcasian had lined his men up along the green grass just outside of arrow length, showing his strength for all to see. He had clearly realised that Godstone was protected. Eliya, by her best count, could say that the number of two hundred wasn't far off and Arundel knew that meant the numbers were definitely against them. However, as planned, the tactical advantage was on their side. The spikes made the entrance to the village neither easy nor swift. The Damisas archers up high were a difficult target for any archers Marcasian might have on the ground; in addition, if the Guardians charged, they faced a high risk of death before they even reached the village gates. Marcasian would have recognised their best chance was a battle on the fields outside Godstone, and that scenario was not going to play out any time soon, if Arundel had his way. Therefore, there was little surprise when Marcasian, along with two Guardians, slowly rode forward towards Godstone, stopping close enough that they could be heard and far enough away from his own men for it not to be a trap.

"I request a meeting with Arundel Stal."

There was a possibility that it could still be some kind of setup, a lure to get him out in the open, but he had to take the chance in order to find a way to end this standoff. Therefore, he ignored those who said he should not go outside. Garad naturally wanted to accompany him, but he wanted his name-brother to stay with the rest of the archers, in case he needed his eagle eye. Darwin was another who wished to join him, but if the worst were to happen, the army needed a leader, and so he commanded

Darwin to lead the mounted swordsman into a line among the spikes, but otherwise stay back. Urag'Ki, on the other hand would accept no excuse to keep him back. Thus, as the gates opened and Arundel rode out to meet with Marcasian, Urag'Ki was riding right alongside him.

Arundel had gone for full regalia, with the red and white cloth bearing the Stal crest draped over his horse. He wanted Marcasian and his men to see that he was acknowledging his right to the throne and was proud of his heritage. They rode at a slow pace, enabling them to break the tension with a brief conversation.

"Just in case we die, I wanted to tell you something. Do you remember Thea's handmaid, Shauri, who sometimes accompanied her to Damisas? The one missing a finger? She has a tender heart when it comes to you. Thea says that, after all she has been through in her life, she is extremely brave and would not disappoint a warrior such as yourself."

Urag'Ki did not change expression or angle of sight as he replied.

"Anyeama teaches us that bearing the scars of our past makes us strong and it is an honour to share a life with such strength."

Now he shifted his gaze, turning towards Arundel with a slightly puzzled look.

"What I do not understand, is why you tell me this now, at this very moment."

Arundel shot Urag'Ki a brief smile.

"Because no good man should die, not knowing that he will be mourned."

Urag'Ki replied with a grunt and a slight nod, and then turned his gaze back to Marcasian.

Before long they came to a stop before the giant hulk of a man and his two associates, who both carried flags bearing the serpent entwined around an axe that represented Theagran. Marcasian was decked out in full armour; his helm, shaped like a bull's head, hung from his saddle. The scar down his eye and cheek looked raw and angry in this cold.

"You asked for me, Marcasian."

The big man growled a little, before speaking.

"I don't do small talk. I have no desire for it."

That was good, because neither did he right now.

"Then make your point and let us part."

Marcasian shifted his body slightly.

"I have been sent here personally to see to your death, but we find ourselves at a standstill. We both know that I have the numbers, but that you have the territorial advantage, leaving us at a stalemate. Nevertheless, I am a man of my word and seeing to your death personally is what I intend to do. So I have a proposal."

He was intrigued to hear what this proposal was.

"I'm listening."

Marcasian stared straight at him.

"You and I, one on one, a dual to the death. Returning to Ryevale with your corpse is all I need today. Your men need not die. For you, my death would leave my men without a leader, and they would flee rather than fight without guidance. Only one man has to die today, not hundreds. Do you agree?"

He glanced at Urag'Ki, and got very little physical response in return. Urag'Ki already knew how this would go, and would show no surprise.

"I agree."

Marcasian's mouth broke into a twisted smirk, at the swift response.

"Then let us waste time no longer."

With that he dismounted from his horse, removed his helm from the saddle and placed it on his head before handing the reins to one of the Guardians behind him. Both Guardians then rode back to join their ranks. Arundel followed suit, climbing down from his saddle and handing the reins to Urag'Ki, who rode back towards Darwin and the rest. As he turned back round to face Marcasian, he was met by a gauntlet to the head.

He staggered backwards, the blow having caught him off guard; a second blow dropped him to one knee. Marcasian then drew his sword and swung it down towards him, but Arundel was able to move, partially blocking it with his own gauntlet as he did. Now he was off balance and Marcasian managed to shift his body enough to drive a knee into Arundel, knocking him onto his back. Arundel was fumbling by his side, grabbing Razor's hilt and trying to free her from her scabbard but the angle prevented it. Marcasian then drove his sword tip down towards Arundel, but he was able to move out the way as the blade cut into the dirt. Thinking quickly, Arundel drove a fist into the back of Marcasian's knee, buckling it. This enabled him to get to his feet. He then began to draw Razor and was able to bring her up just in time to block another swing by Marcasian.

The sound of steel on steel rung out, as they clashed again and again. Marcasian was using his size and strength advantage, putting Arundel on the back foot, so all the latter could do was stay on the defensive and block blows. However, although this giant of a man had such an advantage in domination, Arundel was the quicker of the two. He parried three more blows and then ducked a wild swing before driving the hilt of Razor into that bull's head helm, causing a dent. This clearly caused Marcasian some discomfort, as it was pressing against his skull. The big man tried to adjust his helm, enabling Arundel to make an attacking move. He lunged forward, but Marcasian blocked the thrust with his own sword and then caught Arundel with a hard punch, that caused him to stagger back.

Now Marcasian went on the attack and swung with his sword once, twice, three times, all of which were blocked by Arundel. A fourth swing was also blocked, but took Marcasian slightly off balance. This enabled Arundel to drive Razor's hilt into the bull helm again, causing another dent. Marcasian let out an angered roar of pain and pulled the helm off, hurling it at Arundel. The helm caught him in the body and enabled Marcasian to move in, swinging blow after blow that Arundel struggled to block. Marcasian aimed with another wild swing that Arundel evaded and then, seeing an opening for the first time, he swung Razor at the thigh of Marcasian, her sharp blade cutting through his armour with ease. Marcasian let out a cry and grabbed at his thigh as blood began to trickle down the armour plate.

The giant man became enraged and lunged towards him, a limp now in his stride. But his anger made him clumsy and Arundel was able to parry his sword away and then slice Razor across the breastplate of Marcasian, causing another cry of pain as he fell to his knees in the mud. His sword dropped from his hand and his breathing became heavy. As Arundel slowly circled round to the front of Marcasian, he could see blood rapidly staining the breastplate. He looked him in the eyes. Marcasian managed to find some words.

"Do it. Finish it."

Needing no more encouragement, Arundel raised Razor up into the air ready for a finishing blow, but as he lifted her up, his eyes caught sight of his own men, charging towards him at speed. Confused, he turned round too late as the pike thrust into his chest. The pounding blow drove him off his feet. The pain didn't really register until a moment later. The Guardian on his horse had not let go of the pike and it caught in his armour, pulling it until the wooden handle snapped. He could feel the warmth of his own blood spread across his chest, as pain throbbed uncontrollably. His senses began to desert him for a moment, his vision became blurred and he found himself disorientated. Even through the blur, he was able to see enough to roll to one side, just missing the arrow as it thumped into the dirt. He tried to get to his feet, but with great difficulty as pain shot down his arm and rendered it useless. Noise surrounded him, such a din it was hard to ignore. Then he saw them, pair after pair of armour-clad legs surrounding him. This was it; this was the end. He thought of Thea, of how much he loved her, how much he would miss her. His time had come, and he was as ready as he could be.

But the blades did not strike. Nothing attacked him. The lights did not go out. Instead, his ears slowly settled to hear words that he was so grateful for:

"Protect your King! Protect your King!"

CHAPTER

25

Ryevale had become a difficult place to live in, of late. For Yasilda it was never the greatest, not given the life she had led for so many years. However, things had certainly taken a turn for the worse since Marcasian had returned. When he had departed the city with two hundred Guardians in tow, some sixty days ago, the mood had been reasonably buoyant. For the first time since Arundel had fled his own execution, it felt as though the unrest would be nearing an end. Villages were going to be pulled into line and the so-called true King would be eradicated from this world, taking any form of rebellion with him to the grave. The tension in the city had eased, with many just waiting for the rebel King's carcass to be put on display in the City Square, as a signal they could all breathe a big sigh of relief. Then the day came that changed everything.

Marcasian did indeed return, as did some of his men, just as was expected, but what they hadn't expected was how few men returned and, more so, the condition in which Marcasian returned. He had been laid over his saddle, his helm missing, his armour split and stained with blood. Beneath some pieces of armour, wounds had been bandaged, as best they could, and then covered back over with the steel, to protect them from the elements. He was barely conscious and appeared to be at death's door when some of the Guardians on their post raced over and took him down from his mount. They rushed him off to the city infirmary, calling for both doctor and priest.

It was thought that King Theagran might have accepted this

outcome, had the return been accompanied by news of Arundel's death. This was not to be the case: as word spread that he was last seen wounded, but still alive, a dark cloud encompassed all. Theagran was said to have killed two Guardians in a rage, and then ordered the city gates to be closed indefinitely, before vanishing back to his throne room, where he had been hiding away.

Uncertainty descended over everyone. This defeat had not been expected and, with Arundel still at large, the people began to worry about what might happen next. He had been painted as such a monster by Theagran, that some people actually believed Arundel would sneak back into the city, to slit their throats in their sleep. Personally, Yasilda didn't care. Marcasian survived his injuries and, after a few days, was released from the infirmary to his room under her care: that was all that mattered to her. No one else had wanted to look after him, through fear of his rage, but she was used to it; in a strange way, she liked it, if truth be told.

Marcasian may have escaped death, but he still suffered from infections, during the healing process. While asleep and in his worst fevers, he would talk, or sometimes shout, about what had happened. From what she could piece together from those ramblings and from the talk she had overheard among some of the Guardians, Marcasian had challenged Arundel to one to one combat. The Bull had been on the point of losing, when his men surged forward on the attack to save his life. Arundel was stabbed with a pike before his own men came to his aid. During the subsequent fighting, the Guardians lost many men and so turned tail and ran. She knew that if this were all true, an enraged Bull, such as she had never seen before, would emerge from his sick bed.

But, for now, he was a weakened Bull and so she tended to him as well as she could. She would wash him, change his dressings, feed and water him, provide him with his medicine and even arouse him, just because she could. She would have read to him too, but reading was something she had never been very good at. In fact, there were a lot of things she wasn't very good at, and she knew that people had noticed. She was well aware that she was often labelled as fat and thick and ugly by many in the city; she had heard it all her life, but she didn't care what they said because she didn't care about them. She didn't care about anyone, but herself and Marcasian, and she did not care who she hurt, or how, in order to please him and herself. Pleasing him was at the top of her agenda; with him nearing recovery, she desperately wanted to provide him with something that would put her in a good light, but what?

The only thing that mattered to him was Arundel, finding and killing him. One attempt to kill him had failed, and another would be difficult because no one knew where he was hiding. For so long now she had been given the task of spying on Thea, in the hope it might bring useful information, but she had brought him nothing. She was just as bad at being a spy as she was everything else. The truth was, Marcasian could have been up and about by now, leading the Guardians once more, but his pride was hurt and his drive lost, and so he would just sit in his room, his rage building and building, but not yet unleashed. There seemed little she could do to alleviate the situation. She would offer herself to him and he would take her, rougher than ever before, but still he would not leave his room. She had almost given up hope, when one day she stumbled upon the beginning of the answer she was looking for.

The cold had eased and the sun warmed a blue sky spattered with wisps of white cloud. She hated the cold, but loved the sunshine, and so she had ventured outside to pick some flowers for Marcasian's room. He would hate them, naturally, but she liked brightening up the otherwise cold, hard, stone chamber, as best she could. Normally she would stay within the immediate perimeter of the Palace because she was too lazy to do more, but Selise, one of the Palace rats that worked in the food hall, had spoken about some wild purple flowers that grew further out, in the long grass of the Palace grounds. 'Palace rats' was the unflattering name given to the poor girls of the city who were neither highborn enough to live well nor pretty enough to whore themselves for money. Instead, they found their way to the Palace, where they took on the work no one else wanted, in return for somewhere to stay, and then gave themselves for free, to anyone who wanted it. Yasilda had been one herself, until Marcasian had bedded her and then claimed her for his own. Selise had not been so lucky, although she was favoured by many of the Guardians who were stationed in the Palace. As regards the flowers, Selise had no idea what they were, but Yasilda liked the sound of the purple and so there she was, hiking her way into the long grass.

She had searched and searched for some time with no luck and was about to give up, when she heard voices. At first, she was too far away to identify anything other than that they were female voices. She moved closer, as quietly as she could, and as she got nearer, she narrowed it down to being just two different voices. Still she crept forward, knowing she could not go much further before her heavy footsteps would give her away. One step at a time, she moved as quietly as possible until she came to a stop. Not because she had been heard, but because the words had become clear and the voices recognisable. Somewhere, a little further ahead of her, Thea and Shauri were hidden by the tall grass. She crouched down at first before eventually sitting down, to take the weight off her feet. The conversation was nothing much of interest, just a talk about dresses, until Shauri said something that caught her attention.

"I can't believe you are getting married tonight!"

Now Yasilda was interested.

"I know, it has been so long in coming, I can't believe it has finally arrived."

How had she missed out on this before? She listened as Thea continued.

"From the moment Arundel proposed, I have been waiting for this moment and now it is finally here. I just wish we could leave now and not have to wait until night falls."

Yasilda could not believe what she was hearing. Now Shauri spoke again.

"I bet Damisas will look wonderful. I am told they celebrate weddings in style there."

She had heard all she needed to hear. Trying to contain her excitement in case she gave herself away, Yasilda struggled back to her feet and then began finding her way back to the Palace.

As she made the climb up the Palace stairs, panting and feeling the burn in her limbs from so much activity, she could have kissed Selise. If she hadn't mentioned those flowers, then Yasilda would never have heard that conversation. And now here she was, on her way to Marcasian with the news that Thea was going to marry Arundel tonight in Damisas! She was so excited, it made her feel giddy. Such news would put her in Marcasian's good graces for a long time to come, she just knew it. One thing had vexed her this entire journey back: how did Thea get out of the City? The gates were always locked and guarded, as was the Palace. So how was it possible? She had tried to push the question to the back of her mind and focus on how pleased Marcasian would be with the news, but she just could not keep the question away.

As she reached the right floor and began to walk towards Marcasian's room, she stopped in her tracks, coming to the realisation that what she had wasn't enough. While it was extraordinary information, it would be even better if she could report back just how Thea was getting in and out of the Palace unnoticed. That extra piece of information could be vital and she knew it. She suddenly knew what she had to do: she would have to try and follow Thea tonight. That in itself created a new puzzle for her head to struggle with. If she followed Thea and let her leave, how could she make sure that Thea returned? After all, the information would be excellent, but if she let Thea disappear forever, that would be held against her despite everything else she had discovered. She needed to think of a plan. She had to put her brain to some use and come up with an idea, but there was no way she could do that on an empty stomach. Taking in a few gulps of air, she began to walk down the stairs towards the food hall.

Lunch was being prepared as she arrived in the hall and, while the majority of tables were currently empty, the room was filled with delicious smells. Salted potatoes, a mixture of vegetables and meat pie were all tantalising her nostrils. She wasn't sure if the meat in the pie was beef or lamb, but she was leaning towards lamb. Letting her senses indulge in the aromas for a moment, she then found Selise, who managed to sneak out a ready cooked pie, before dragging her over to a far corner table so they wouldn't really get noticed. Selise dished her up a large portion and, as she cut into the hard pastry, the warmth and mouth-watering smell hit her. Once the first mouthful had been consumed, her taste buds quickly confirmed what her nostrils had suggested: it was lamb. She sat there shovelling in forkful after forkful, only half listening to Selise talking about her night spent with one of the Guardians named Talin. Her mind was occupied instead with trying and failing to come up with a plan. She just couldn't think of anything, unsurprisingly really, because plans and clever thoughts were not a strength. After several failures, she decided to take a break from thinking and gave her full attention to Selise, who had seemingly moved on from her sexual exploits of last night.

"Aren't you just fed up with all the panic and fear around here? Everyone comes in here looking miserable and talking about that Arundel guy, as if he is the devil himself. Aren't you just sick of it?"

To be honest, she hadn't really been bothered of late.

"I'm too busy with Marcasian to notice. He is far more important than all this drama. It bores me really."

It did bore her, yet here she was getting involved because she suddenly had some information to give!

"I don't know why they can't just end this nonsense. You know what I would do?"

She didn't, and, to be honest, she didn't care.

"No, Selise."

She knew she was about to be told anyway.

"I would take a large number of the army to all the cities and make a register of everyone living in them. That way you know who is already there. Then I would leave men in each city to update the register whenever people leave or arrive. That way I reckon you would flush him out. If he is a so-called King, then I would bet you all the gold in the vaults that he is hiding in a city, not some rat-infested village."

It took a minute or two for the words to sink in. It took a further few minutes for her brain to awaken and piece it all together. Then, like a lightning bolt, it struck her. She had a solution. For the second time that day, she felt like she could kiss Selise. All she had to do was tell a lie and hope it was believed. She needed to make Thea think that Marcasian was marching the Guardians to Damisas tomorrow to enforce a city register, conducting a thorough search. That way, Thea would not be able to stay there tomorrow and would have to come back. At least that was how she hoped it would go. Now she had the plan, she needed to pass the lie on, but she could not tell Thea direct, not without raising suspicion. Since Marcasian had returned, she had not stepped foot near Thea's room, let alone spoken with the Princess, and to do so now would be too obvious. No, her best option was to tell Shauri and make it seem accidental. The message would soon get back to Thea. That was the plan, and now all she had to do was wait. Thea never attended the food hall: Shauri would always come and collect food enough for both of them, to take back to the room. So she just had to sit here and wait for Shauri to arrive. In the meantime, she convinced Selise to steal another pie and then sat back, like a predator awaiting its prey.

Yasilda was on the verge of dozing off, when she caught sight of Shauri entering the hall. She sat there and waited, watching as the little handmaid collected two portions of food, and then she made her move. As Shauri negotiated her way through a growing crowd, both hands occupied carrying her tray, Yasilda pounced. She moved at some pace for her, appearing frantic as she bumped herself into Shauri. Amazingly, the young maid struggled briefly for balance, but managed to rescue the tray from falling, with very little spillage. Her tone of voice was less composed, however.

"You idiot, Yasilda! What the hell are you doing? I nearly lost everything."

She took a couple of pretend gasps and then put on a voice

that she hoped would sound a little stressed.

"Sorry, Shauri, I, er, I am just a little flustered at the moment about tomorrow."

At first, there was no reaction, but then she could see a small glint of interest in Shauri's eyes.

"Why? What is happening tomorrow?"

So far the plan was working.

"It's Damisas. Marcasian… It's…No, I shouldn't say anything. Forget I mentioned it, and I am sorry I nearly spilled your food."

With that, she maintained her panicked state and started to walk away, praying to herself that Shauri would stop her. "What about Damisas?"

She smiled to herself: the bait had been taken.

"What is happening to make you so worried? You can tell me."

Yasilda put her smile away and her panicked face back on, before turning round. She then grabbed Shauri by the arm and pulled the young girl aside, away from everyone else.

"I will tell you, but you must promise to keep it a secret." Shauri nodded, a look of concern now etched on her face.

"I promise."

Yasilda looked all around her to make sure no one was listening and then spoke quietly, almost in a whisper.

"Marcasian is leading a large number of the Guardians to Damisas tomorrow. They are going to search the entire city forcibly and create a register of everyone there. Then he is going to leave men behind to keep track of everyone who comes and goes. It will happen at every city, to make it impossible for Arundel to hide."

She could see the slight concern on Shauri's face, even though she was clearly trying to conceal it.

"Oh, that seems a bit extreme. Still, if it works, then that is what matters, I guess."

Yasilda could hear the false optimism in Shauri's voice and could see that she was now itching to get away. She was going to make it easy for her.

"I mustn't say any more. I have to get back to Marcasian. No one apart from him and the King know about this, so you must promise me you won't say anything, not even to Thea." Shauri nodded unconvincingly.

"I promise."

With that, Yasilda made her exit from the hall and hid herself, as she watched Shauri hurriedly scurry towards the stairs.

As night fell, darkness engulfed most of the Palace, apart from the odd burning torches scattered around. While light danced and flickered on parts of the wall, the shadows dominated and hid within them a secret. Yasilda was tucked away in the darkness, keeping watch on Thea's room, waiting. Her wait was long, but ultimately rewarding. As time ticked by and the guard patrols stopped, the door opened with a slow, subtle creak and out stepped both Thea and Shauri, dressed in hooded robes. She let them walk on a few paces before beginning to follow, tiptoeing as quietly as she could, scarcely daring to breathe in case she was heard.

As she followed down stairs and along corridors, she became so confused by the darkness that she lost her bearings. Never losing sight of her prey, she began to worry that she would not be able to find this place again come morning, but then a landmark appeared. In the distance, a dancing flame showed her enough to see that the library was in sight. Just as she was trying to make sure she would remember to walk past it tomorrow, she saw the two women turn, push the doors open and enter the library. She was shocked by this, and a little concerned. Had she heard wrong? Perhaps they were not going to Damisas tonight. Late night reading made no sense to her, but neither did entering the library to try and leave the Palace. She stopped at the door, wanting to wait long enough for Thea and Shauri not to be directly on the other side, and then gripped the handle and turned it softly. She pushed the door open as gently as she could and, when she could see enough to know no one was behind it, she stepped inside.

Yasilda began to weave her way between the dark rows of

shelves, nearly tripping over a pile of books at one point. A strange scraping noise then broke the silence, although she couldn't identify it. She had no clue where she was going, and hardly any visible light by which to see. It was possible she had doubled back on herself, but she couldn't be sure. She was getting frustrated and growing more concerned that she might bump into one or both ladies, when suddenly she saw it. Turning past a four-shelf rack, which was overloaded with books, she found herself in a short aisle with another bookshelf at the end of it. Only this bookshelf was moving, or at least part of it was. She squinted hard through the dim light to try to make out what was going on, and then realised that part of the shelving unit was a secret door, which had just closed shut.

The moment she found out that Arundel had been injured, her heart sank. There she was, preparing to wed the man she loved, and he was out in the realm hurt, possibly dying; and there was nothing she could do about it. Oracle Thomas had sent word to her via Shauri but, unfortunately, giving very little detail. At the first opportunity, she had made her way to the library to speak with the Oracle in person, but he could shed no more light on the matter. The Seekers had brought back word, from the villages, of Arundel's injury and their impending return. As soon as he heard this news, Oracle Thomas had left Damisas in haste so that he could tell Thea. While she wanted to leave for Damisas there and then, she could not. She was expected at a dinner with her father and unfortunately had to sit through it, putting on the best false front she could, whilst her mind was riddled with fear and concern.

She left for Damisas the following night and, upon her arrival in the city, was met by Urag'Ki, Arundel's closest friend, indicating that the party had already returned. Urag'Ki explained what had happened, as he led her to Arundel's chamber. Arundel had been fighting Marcasian in single combat, but the moment it had become clear Marcasian was losing, the Guardians began to charge at Arundel. In response, the Damisas soldiers counter-attacked, to protect him. Since they were reacting to the charge of the Guardians, the latter were a pace ahead. Before Arundel's army could reach him, he was stabbed in the chest by a Guardian's pike, which snapped off. However, the Damisas forces were then able to form a protective wall around him, to prevent any further injury. During fierce fighting, the Guardians sustained the heavier losses, and fled the battlefield, taking a badly wounded Marcasian with them.

Arundel's army headed back to Damisas, bringing Arundel with all speed. Urag'Ki explained what had been told to him by Barrington, once they had returned and Arundel was being treated.

It would seem that Arundel had been a lucky man, saved by his armour, which was unlike any the Guardians possessed. In the early days of Galbraxia, when the first settlers were at war with Gruldock and his army, they had brought over skills with them that were learned in the Forgotten Lands. They used a steel like no other in their armour, and layered it in such a way that made it extremely hard to penetrate. Such steel-making techniques were unknown in Galbraxia, but the layering method had been passed down from generation to generation of blacksmiths in Damisas. While Arundel's armour was not quite as impenetrable as Gruldock's would have been, it was still extremely tough. The tip of the pike had just pierced the skin, but had not gone deep. The impact had done the most damage, cracking a rib and causing heavy bruising. The method of forging and design of the armour was believed to have resulted in fewer casualties for their soldiers, than the Guardians. Hearing all this had calmed Thea considerably, but her emotions were still high, so that when she finally stepped into Arundel's chamber to see him lying upon his bed, she flung herself into his arms. Tears trickled from her eyes.

Time healed Arundel well, much more quickly than Marcasian, who had suffered far greater injuries at Arundel's hand; her King was on his feet in a matter of weeks. Now that all seemed a blur, so long ago and so unimportant. For now something greater awaited her. With the sky dark and the moon up high, here she stood, ready to make the walk to her wedding.

The night was perfect. The dark sky was clear, with a blanket of stars twinkling brightly. It had felt as though she had counted every one of them twice over, while she waited for the word to start her walk. There was a warmth in the air, and an air of quiet expectation hung over her, just waiting to be broken by the approaching merriment. Her dress was perfect. A white vision, the bodice of twined lace cut across her breasts perfectly, her snow white shoulders left bare. The lace then gave way to silk at her midriff, flowing into the train that ran behind her. White lace covered her lower arms and a lace veil hung over her face for the moment. In Damisas, the tradition was for the bride to cover her face with a veil bearing the symbol of her house. Her face would remain concealed until midway through the ceremony, when her husband to be would say his vows and declare that he was taking her from her family house to form one of their own. The veil would then be removed to symbolise the bride relinquishing her family name, ready to take her new one. When Thea had heard this, her heart sank a little. Given all that was happening, all that she knew, how could she wear her father's crest? How could she have the serpent entwined round an axe crafted into her veil? She hated her father; she wished she was not related to him. So she made the decision, with the help of Oracle Thomas' historic knowledge, to have her mother's house crest upon her veil instead. Therefore, her veil had been beautifully adorned with a mare, encompassed by a crescent moon.

Another issue she had faced was the question of who would give her away, since it clearly could not be her father. Her first choice had been that Sir Winstan should have that honour. In the short time she had known him, he had been more of a father figure to her than Theagran had ever been. It would have meant so much to her if he could give her away, but ever since he had been removed from his role as her personal guard, she had been unable to get close to him, and there was no way he would have been able to leave Ryedale. This had left her somewhat short of options, with both Garad and Urag'Ki part of Arundel's wedding entourage. Since Oracle Thomas was leading the ceremony, he was another option out and she had been beginning to think there would be no one to do it. So she was extremely grateful when Darwin offered his services. He had come to her, almost nervously, as if expecting to be turned down, yet she had embraced him with a hug of genuine thanks; and now he stood by her side, in full battle dress and a cape bearing the crest of his King's house, the eagle upon a sword. She was ready;, she had been ready for a long time and now she just wanted it to begin. At that moment, the faint chords of an organ could be heard and Darwin offered her his arm.

"It is time, Princess."

With a deep breath, she linked her arm with his, and took that first step.

The route to the ceremony had been lined with fire torches that added to the warmth. She had known it was going to be designed that way, but had underestimated how impressive it would look. She had also underestimated how many people would be present. Since it was so deep into the night, she had expected a low-key affair, with only a select few there to witness it. However, the street was bustling with onlookers and the cheers that sounded, as she stepped out onto the path, had really caught her off guard. It felt as though the entire city had come out to share in her moment, and she couldn't help but smile. The walk was a short one, but it felt so much longer.

The ceremony itself was taking place in a building known as the Temple of Unity. It had been built for the sole purpose of marriage between men and women, but when Barrington took over, he made some changes in recognition of his own sexual preference. Marriage between anyone, be it man and woman, man and man, or woman and woman, was now welcomed in the Temple. It didn't have to be marriage, because unity meant more than that. Some would come here to take vows of eternity, but not as a married couple. Friends would also come here to reaffirm the bonds of their friendship, which they believed would last a lifetime, and some broken families had come here to repair their damaged ties.

As the Temple came into clear view, she once again admired its beauty, shining in the moonlight. Built of marble, it was a brilliant white, streaked with veins of light pink. Around the outside of the square building ran columns on which were carved garlands of roses climbing from bottom to top. Once she had ascended the steps, two of the city's soldiers opened the doors for her. She heard loud cheers from the crowd behind her, as she stepped through the doors into the Temple corridor. The corridor was lined with marble statues of couples, one of Barrington's additions. The organ music was louder now, echoing off the walls, and she could feel a slight tingle to her skin and tremble of her arms, in her excitement. At the end of the corridor, a second door was opened and she stepped through into the ceremonial hall. Row upon row of seats lined either side of the aisle, and, to her surprise, they were full. She had no idea who was sitting there or how they had managed to get a seat, but what she did know was that they were all looking at her, with eyes of wonder.

At the end of the aisle, was Oracle Thomas standing by the Union Altar. Behind him rose the large Hands of Unity statute, two large hands entwined for eternity. She could see Garad in the same battle dress as Darwin, and then, beside him, stood Urag'Ki, who looked as he always did, because for the Seekers, there was no such thing as ceremonial attire. And then beside him, in his own individual battle dress and wearing a crown of white gold, was Arundel. As she walked towards him, she couldn't help but marvel at how handsome he looked. He had never worn the crown, even though it had been made for him soon after his arrival in Damisas, since he just didn't feel right with it on. But he wore it now and he looked triumphant.

As she reached the Union Altar, Darwin leaned in and wished her good luck before taking his seat. She then turned to face Arundel. He took her hands in his and she found herself getting lost in those loving eyes of his. The organ, which dominated the right hand side of the Temple behind the Hands of Unity, reached a crescendo and then fell silent. Arundel leaned closer and whispered, "You look beautiful."

He straightened back up, readying himself for the ceremony. Although generally, dresses were not her choice of clothing, and she never really regarded herself as a beauty, on this day, at this moment, she did feel beautiful.

Oracle Thomas then began the proceedings.

"Today we all join as one to witness this union by way of

marriage between Arundel Stal, the true King of Galbraxia, and Thea Greystone. It is a union born of love that binds these two, both in this life and the next. Their union is one that was built underneath the stars and carries such a strength that they wish to declare it for all to see and embrace. Upon this night, we all shall bear witness as a King gains his Queen."

She hadn't thought about that. Marrying Arundel had been purely about her love for him; she had barely given a thought to the fact that she would become a Queen. The ceremony continued. The crowd watched on in impeccable silence, as they exchanged their vows and rings, and then Arundel removed her veil, releasing her from her family of old, so they could start a new family. The last act was for Arundel to place the Queen's crown upon her head and then seal it with a passionate kiss. At this, the crowd rose from their seats, with raucous applause, to send the couple on their way to Arundel's chamber, and there consummate their marriage.

She was where she wanted to be, lying in Arundel's arms, her head resting upon his chest, rising and falling with every breath as she listened to his heartbeat. Thankfully, this was finally going to be a regular occurrence. They had decided that, after the wedding, she would move to Damisas. They knew that her disappearance from Ryevale would cause an uproar, but the time for action had almost arrived. Plans were being put together to launch an offensive against Theagran and his Guardians, ideally out in the field of battle, because, despite Ryevale's defensive weaknesses, a siege was the least desirable option.

Initially, they had planned for her to move straight away, but that plan was delayed by a day after Yasilda had shared Marcasian's plans with Shauri. Marcasian and the Guardians would be coming today to register all who lived in the city. Not only would they have to hide Arundel, but also the army, their weapons and armour, because by law these were banned. The last thing they needed was to have to hide Thea as well. So it was decided that she would return to Ryevale before dawn, be seen for one more day while registration took place and then return the next night. The hope was that the time taken by Marcasian and his men to reach the other cities for registration would give them enough breathing space to piece their plans together. It was with a heavy heart that she dragged herself from her husband's arms and proceeded to get dressed. Arundel then escorted her down to the tunnel entrance, where she found both Shauri and Oracle Thomas waiting for her, already on their mounts. It had been decided that the Oracle should return to Ryevale too, for similar reasons. Arundel took her in his arms once more, and then they shared one final passionate kiss before they had to prise themselves apart.

"This will be goodbye for the last time. The next time we say hello, it will be forever."

Her heart melted as he said those words because she wanted nothing more. She stared at him for as long as she could, almost refusing to release his hand as their fingers gripped each other's.

"The light is against us, my Queen; we must make haste." Oracle Thomas was right and she knew it. She had too much to lose to risk it all now. Reluctantly, she released his hand from hers and urged her horse forward to start the journey ahead.

Oracle Thomas remained silent for most of the journey, unlike Shauri. Her handmaid could not stop talking about the previous night's events, ranging from how beautiful the ceremony was, to how she managed to steal some time alone with Urag'Ki. She would not say more than that, even though it was clear she wanted to. Thea didn't mind the conversation: it helped pass the time and she was enjoying remembering all that was good about the ceremony. Eventually, it seemed like Shauri was just about to crack and reveal all about her night with her Seeker, when Oracle Thomas interrupted.

"We have arrived."

They had reached the entrance to the stables. They tied the horses up to the brass ring outside the stable entrance for them to be collected later, and then finished the rest of the journey on foot, as always. Reaching the bottom of the stone steps, Oracle Thomas led the way, finally breaking his own silence as he began to share his opinion on the day's registration at Damisas. Reaching the top of the steps, he pulled the secret lever and the hidden door began to open. Oracle Thomas then stepped through into the library still talking, only to stop mid-sentence. She wondered why he had gone quiet so abruptly, but then as she stepped into the library herself, she discovered the reason. She could only gasp as she saw the room filled with Guardians, as far as the eye could see.

"Seize them!"

The raging voice thundered from the shadows. Two Guardians grabbed her, one either side, as she tried to struggle. Oracle Thomas and Shauri were also held captive. She could feel her heart racing. Fear swamped her body. Tension gripped her. Her breath came fast and heavy. She knew who the voice belonged to, even before his face was revealed; she would recognise her father's voice anywhere, especially his angry voice. True enough, he emerged from behind a row of Guardians, predictably followed by Marcasian. What did surprise her, though, was when she saw Yasilda follow Marcasian, a broad smile upon that hideous face. How could they have known? What would happen now? So many questions, with likely very few answers. She could feel the pain of gauntlet fingers digging into her arms, but it barely registered right now; instead, her alarm was growing with every step that her father took towards her.

Eventually he came to a stop in front of her. He stared straight at her, those evil eyes burning a hole right into her, yet he did not say a word. He just stared and stared, leaving her uncertain if she should say something first. But even now, even in this desperate moment, she just could not find it within her to speak to him. The feeling, it seemed, was mutual because after a few more moments of intense staring, Theagran took a step to his left, to where Oracle Thomas was standing.

"Well, what have we here? I thought you were dead, old man. I thought you had been wiped out with the rest of your kind. But here you are alive and in the flesh, so it would seem not."

He turned his head to look at Marcasian a moment, before

turning back to Oracle Thomas.

"Still, that is easily rectified."

Thea never saw the knife being drawn; she simply saw Marcasian thrust his arm in front of Oracle Thomas and then she saw the Oracle's skin split in two, as blood began to gush from his neck.

"No!" she cried out in sorrow, as the Oracle was released by his captors so that his body could fall to the floor with a thud. He lay there, his eyes open and looking straight at her, while a claret pool formed around him. In her cries of anguish, she had wriggled so much that she had nearly broken free of the Guardian's grip on her. She could then only watch in horror as Marcasian handed his bloodstained knife to Yasilda, and the useless traitor walked straight up to Thea. Yasilda's odious breath almost burned Thea's skin, when she raised the knife to Thea's throat.

"I have been dying to do this for a very long time."

Yasilda smiled smugly as she spoke and Thea braced herself for the blade to start to pierce through her skin. But, instead, Yasilda pulled the blade away and turned towards Shauri, driving it deep into her gut.

"No!"

Once again, this was all Thea could cry. Yasilda brutally plunged the knife into the body of Shauri, over and over again. Thea lost count of the number of times the knife pierced her, as Shauri's severely punctured body slumped to the floor. But Yasilda still did not stop. In anguish, Thea struggled until she suddenly felt herself pull free from the arms that held her. Reacting without thinking, she grabbed the sword from the sheath of the Guardian who had been holding her right arm and drove it straight down into the head of Yasilda. The Guardian's slow reactions then kicked in, and they pounced on her, knocking her to the floor as Yasilda's body collapsed on top of Shauri's. In the fall, she hit her head hard upon the stone floor, immediately causing her vision to blur and the room to start spinning. Consciousness began to slip from her, but not before she heard her father say, "Take her to the Crypt."

How drastically things could change in one night. One minute she was getting married beneath the light of the moon and then, as the sun was getting ready to rise, she had been taken prisoner, after witnessing the slaughter in cold blood of two of those closest to her in this world. She had been so happy, finally married to the love of her life and ready to move so she could be with him forever. Her life was finally falling into place; at last she was wanted and had a place she knew she could call home, only for it all to come crashing down, with one betrayal. Well, betrayal might not be quite accurate. She had never been close to Yasilda, she had never confided in that wretched girl and never once considered her a friend or ally. So in that sense, Yasilda had not actually betrayed her. Yasilda had somehow discovered the truth about Arundel, the wedding, Damisas and the secret tunnel, and then she had scurried off to Marcasian to tell all. Yasilda, the stupid girl who was hated within the Great Palace, who cared for no one but herself and the Bull, had destroyed Thea's life with one whisper. She should be readying herself for the next chapter of her life, she should be packing her belongings in order to move them to Damisas with a spring in her step and a song in her heart. Instead, she found herself slumped against a wall, sitting in the dirt, deep underground in the dark bowels of the Crypt.

The last time she had been down here, she had come to visit Arundel, and in doing so, had overheard his conversation with her father. That was the day she discovered the truth about her mother's death and Theagran's part in it; that was the day that any form of bond that may have existed between them had been cut asunder. Now she was the one confined within a cell and she knew that Arundel would not be coming to visit her.

The darkness was all consuming; it dominated everything down here. It had been noticeable before, but in the corridors when she was last here, there had been the benefit of some torch light. Here, in her cell, the light barely broke through, and so her eyes had little to focus upon. She could not tell if it was still day, or if night had fallen. She had no idea how much time had passed since she had been locked in her cage; that was one of the problems down here, you had no sense of time. She had come to in the cell, having been knocked unconscious moments after killing Yasilda, and with no one there to tell her, she had no idea how long she had been senseless.

As far as she knew, she was alone down here. There were moments when she thought she could hear faint screams, the odd voice crying out, but when she listened hard, there was nothing but silence, and she began to wonder whether those screams were inside her own head.

It still hadn't truly sunk in that both Oracle Thomas and Shauri were now dead, that she would never see them again.

Oracle Thomas had shared so much of his wisdom with her, he had taught her so much about her own family, about Arundel and his past. He had opened her eyes at a time when Theagran wanted them blinkered. He had shared with her the truths that Theagran had tried to erase from the world, when he had stripped the libraries of their history. He had been the driving force behind Arundel's uprising, the one who had planned this rebellion. He had given so much for the cause, at enormous risk to himself, and now he had paid the ultimate price by giving his life.

Shauri, on the other hand, held more of an emotional attachment. She may have served as Thea's handmaid, but, over time, Thea had come to see her as the little sister she never had. They had spent every day together; they had confided in each other. Shauri had known little things about her that she would never dare tell any other. Shauri had suffered so much in her young life and Thea had hoped finally to give her the life of freedom that she deserved, once they were in Damisas. Instead, all she had given her was a premature and violent death. She could feel the raw anger and hurt build up inside her, as she remembered Yasilda, out of control, full of rage. How Shauri must have suffered in that moment, even for such a short space of time. It gave her a small comfort that she had been able to take Yasilda's life from her, to give Shauri some form of retribution, even if she did not know it. While it had felt good, it did little to alleviate the situation that she was now in.

As she sat there alone in the darkness, she faced total uncertainty. When Arundel was down here, he was awaiting execution. He had known that from the start. Although in the end, with help, he was able to escape, he did not know that would be the outcome while he was lost down here in the Crypt. The executioner's chopping block had been calling him, and now she feared it was calling for her. There were moments when she tried to convince herself otherwise, clinging to the small hope that life would go on. After all, if Theagran had wanted her dead, he could have done it there and then, alongside Shauri and Oracle Thomas. Yet her life had been spared and there surely must be some reason for that. The problem was, in some ways, she knew her father too well, and this was why she struggled to convince herself that she had a future. Theagran was a paranoid man, forever suspecting treachery, and so when anyone actually dared to betray him, he made an example of them. She knew that, by marrying Arundel, Theagran's sworn enemy, she had committed the ultimate betrayal and although she was his flesh and blood, Theagran would not let that go unpunished. Her best guess was that her execution would be public. In that way, Theagran would send a message to all who served under him, that even family connections would not stand in the way of punishment for treachery. She knew in her heart that this would be the case; she just needed to come to terms with it, until she found out her fate.

Sitting had switched to blind pacing, stumbling through the shadows with swift turns, due to the small size of her cell. She had nothing else to occupy her mind, nothing to distract her from the sorrows and concerns that had dominated since she awoke. Every now and then, she would shout out, partly to see if someone else was actually down here, and partly just to do something different for a moment, to break up the boredom. Even that had become a routine and, once again, she could not escape everything being the same. Eventually, she laid herself down in the corner, curling up in the hope that sleep might come and take hold, to free her temporarily from this nothingness.

She lay there, and she lay there, and finally her eyelids began to feel heavy. They were starting to close, when she heard it. The noise was probably not that loud, but in the deathly silence of the Crypt it boomed from one wall to another. Something had clunked against one of the bars of another cell. Some wood perhaps, or possibly a stone, she could not say, but her guess would be that whatever it was had not happened intentionally. If it had been intentional, there would have been more depth and ferocity to it, whereas this was more like a flick. Perhaps a foot brushing passed an unseen object, knocking it into the bars. Suddenly, at the thought of that, she rolled over to face the bars, wondering once more if she really was alone down here. She peered intently through the darkness to see if there were any changes, if anything looked any different. The darkness all looked the same, just as it had done since the start of her incarceration. She was about to give up and roll over when she noticed it, faint at first, but it was there. A small glimmer of light began to dance off the walls opposite her cell. She sat up with a jolt, staring as the light grew brighter and brighter, illuminating more of her surroundings with every passing moment. It had to be someone approaching with torchlight, she could not think of any other explanation for it, but who? Did anyone actually know she was down here? Maybe the executioner was ready and the Guardians were coming to collect her. Maybe someone else had come down to gloat at her fate. Or maybe she was about to discover that she had a secret friend in the Palace who wanted to help set her free. Unfortunately, she doubted it was the last, not now, not after everything that had happened.

With the light now at its brightest, she could almost feel the warmth of the flame as it came into view, along with the person holding it. At that moment her heart sank and she almost wished for the shadows to return, so she could hide among them, as the all too familiar voice spoke.

"You look so surprised."

Her father stood before her, his now grey scraggly hair tucked back beneath his crown, his grey beard, dirty and matted. The skin on his face looked worn and tired, as age was clearly starting to take its toll, together with the recent stresses as his grip upon the realm had been slowly loosening. To be honest, she was surprised to see him; he was the last person she expected.

"What, no words of welcome for your father? For your King?"

She had nothing to say to him, nothing at all, and so she remained silent.

"You betray me, and yet you have the gall to give me the silent treatment. How dare you, Thea!"

His betrayal ran far deeper then hers: she was not going to buckle and so she remained silent.

"I guess I should not be surprised, not given what I now know."

He took a moment's pause, as he moved a little closer to the bars.

"All this time I have been hunting Arundel down, seeking out the man who is trying to ruin all that I have built, and he has been hiding right under my nose in Damisas. Not only that, but he has been fucking my daughter, my only daughter. How much of a fool you have both made me look, just so you can please yourself."

For the first time, she felt the desire to speak, to set him straight, to stand up for her relationship.

"Arundel is my husband, my King."

She could see from the snarl that curled his lips and the glare in his eyes, that the comment enraged him.

"I am your King. Arundel is a traitor and you are nothing

more than his whore. Do not try to persuade yourself otherwise."

She would not let this go now.

"I would not expect you to understand love, because you have never felt it. But to label Arundel a traitor is nothing more than an insult and a lie. There is only one traitor in all of this, and he is standing in front of me."

She had hit a nerve. With a dull thud, Theagran slammed a fist against the bars.

"Lies! Nothing but lies from a traitor who betrayed his King with his own false claim."

She couldn't stop herself now. If these were her last moments, her last words, then she was not going to hold back.

"How could he lie about something he did not remember because as a boy of ten you had him left to die? Arundel did not tell me the truths of your past, the Oracle did. It is not Arundel who betrayed his King, you did all those years ago, when you killed Arundel's father. Arundel is the true heir to the throne, he is the true King of Galbraxia, and you have simply stolen the throne and now hold it hostage."

She could see the rage continue to build within him. For years, he had ruled through fear, and so no one dared speak to him in this way, let alone challenge him. He was not coping with it well.

"You will hold that tongue, Thea, or I will not be held responsible for my actions. You are my daughter and I am your father, and it is about time you started to respect that and learn your place."

He was actually spitting on certain words, his anger was so intense.

"I know what you did to Mother."

She could not avoid the topic any more.

"I heard the words from your very mouth, as you stood where you are now and told Arundel. I know what you did to her, and I will never forgive you for it. You are a lot of things, Theagran, but you are not my father. I have no father."

She waited for the explosion, for him to lose it altogether, but instead he turned away and started to walk off down the corridor, taking the light with him. Just as the shadows began to return, Theagran turned round and marched back to her bars.

"You are a traitor to the Crown and have been found guilty of treason. The hangman's noose will not serve as justice enough for treason by blood and so in two days the fire will be lit. Make the most of this time, Thea, because it will be your last."

He said no more, but walked off and this time kept walking. With him went the light, and the darkness regained its stranglehold on everything. So now she knew, death awaited her. Not the noose, clearly such a swift exit was not enough for her betrayal. She was to be burned at the stake, a slow and agonising end. For a moment fear overtook her, but then it was pushed aside by her recognition that having to live without Arundel was not living at all.

And so she found herself accepting death.

The warmth of the night had carried through to the morning and felt as though it was slowly on the rise. By the afternoon, the sun was burning brightly in the sky at its peak and Arundel could feel it upon his skin as he stood on the ramparts of Damisas near the main gates. Looking out onto the fields outside the city, he could see the approaching Guardians on the horizon, as had been expected. Thea had made them aware that Marcasian would be bringing some of the Guardians with him to carry out a registration of the city today, with the intention of leaving some behind so they could monitor comings and goings from then on. That was something they just couldn't allow. There was no way they could continue to prepare for the planned assault on the throne if Guardians were based within the city walls once again. Something had to be done and quickly. Despite having received very little warning, the war council had managed to come up with a plan.

Thea had volunteered to return to Ryevale for one more day, to avoid the risk of having to be hidden from Marcasian. As far as she knew, they were going to have to hide Arundel and the entire army as well, in order to keep suspicion away from the city, and go along with the registration. In fact, that was not the plan. Arundel had let her go because he wanted to keep her safe. There was a chance that their strategy could go horribly wrong and lead to their deaths; were that to be the case, he did not want her to be discovered and suffer the same fate. So, with a heavy heart and just a brief sleep after their wedding, he had said goodbye and watched her ride through the secret tunnel back to Ryevale.

There had been no time to wallow after that, no time to rest, because they had to work with haste to put the plan in place. For a while now they had been eager to initiate an attack, to face the Guardians head on and try to end this war and Theagran's reign. However, they knew that their best chance of doing so was on the field of battle, not when Theagran's army was hidden inside Ryevale. Certainly, they could besiege the city; after all, it had not been built to withstand such a situation; but that would take time and resources, and they did not have sufficient of either to gamble with. The question they had been stuck on was how to draw the Guardians out into the open for such a battle. It was felt that the arrogance of Theagran's army, coupled with a lack of tactical sense, might be the key, with the Guardians fully believing they would win and having no need to stay within the city walls. Since that was not certain, they had remained hesitant. Now the Guardians were coming here, into Damisas, and likely to be split up into small groups. If the information Thea had been told was correct, then the Guardians would be entering every single building in the city, in order to see who was there, and complete the register. Being separated into smaller units would provide the perfect opportunity for the Damisas force to seize upon.

That had, therefore, driven their plan. Instead of hiding the army away completely, they were suited up and scattered in numbers among several of the buildings within the city. They would be waiting there for the Guardians, in order to slay them out of sight, and in doing so, drastically reduce their numbers. The remaining Guardians would be locked inside the city, unable to flee, and, it was hoped, with no chance of survival. Expectations were high that the plan would work.

The design of Damisas' high, fortified walls meant that when standing on the rampart, you could watch the outside world or aim an arrow through gaps built into the wall, but still be protected since the wall continued to tower above you. As Arundel stood at one of these gaps, he could watch the approaching Guardians, knowing that even their best archer would have great trouble trying to hit him with an arrow. With the protection in place, he watched and he waited. Given the speed of the horses the Guardians were riding, it wouldn't be long before they would reach the main gates and then he knew that it was in the lap of the Gods as to what would happen next. One way or another, he hoped this would end today, or at least as much as was possible without Theagran's presence. With the uncertainty of whether he would survive the day, his mind repeatedly drifted back to last night, to the wedding ceremony. He remembered how beautiful Thea looked in her dress. He remembered her flame red hair and those emerald green eyes, how intoxicating he found them. He remembered her soft skin, her warm touch. He remembered just how much he loved her, and, in doing so, it reminded him how determined he was to survive the day, so he could be with her again. That outcome was not in his hands, not as things stood. He did not know whether that moment in the tunnel, when her hand slipped from his and she rode away into the darkness, was to be the last time he ever saw her. He hated the thought that it could be, his hand suddenly clenching the hilt of Razor as he told himself that he must not let it be. Today was not the day for good men and women to die, not if he could help it.

Eventually, he was joined on the rampart by Urag'Ki, Darwin and Barrington. Since he had the important role of leading the archers, Garad would not be there. The archers were to be divided into two units, one led by Garad and the other by Eliya. They were spread along the top of the city walls to give them the best vantage points, but for the time being they were clustered at the points where the walls provided the maximum cover to hide behind. It was necessary for them to be concealed, because if Marcasian entered the city and saw archers on the walls, alarm bells would surely ring in his head, telling him that something was not right. For this plan to work, they could not afford any mistakes, no matter how small.

"Here they come, like lambs to the slaughter."

Barrington spoke with confidence, too much confidence for Arundel's liking.

"That is the kind of talk that will lead us all to our deaths."

On hearing this, Barrington looked surprised.

"Why so negative, my King? Our plan is perfect. It will surely bring us closer to victory."

Arundel looked at him for a moment. For a man who had seen such devastation and failure in his lifetime, he was amazed at how over-confident Barrington was now.

"Nothing is perfect. This is war, Barrington, and war never goes to plan: the Oracle has taught me that. We have already experienced that out in the villages, and could well experience it again here today."

Barrington continued to look stunned.

"But we were victorious out in the villages. Does that not give you confidence in those that fight for us?"

Arundel stepped away from the gap in the wall and came a little closer to Barrington.

"I have confidence in our soldiers, Barrington; there is no question of that. But I am wary about this scenario, as anyone should be, because we are banking on every element falling into place, as planned."

Barrington was now scratching his head. Arundel could tell that the Steward did not wish to argue, but at the same time his excitement was making it difficult for him to accept a more cautious approach.

"Their numbers will be divided, and they will not expect anything. Marcasian won't bring the whole army, but we can make a huge dent in their numbers, and take out Marcasian as well. Without him, Theagran will surely fall."

Arundel could sense he was getting nowhere, but was struggling to leave it there. He was about to continue his argument, when Darwin interrupted, making the point on his behalf.

"I would suspend your confidence, Barrington; things may not be as we expected."

No sooner had Darwin uttered those words, than Arundel returned to his gap in the wall. As he looked out, he could see just why Darwin was concerned. The Guardians had stopped some distance away from the gates and lined up in rows. They were in arrow's reach and close enough to be identified, especially Marcasian, but not close enough to appear as though they were waiting for the gates to open. "Why do they stop?" Darwin asked, the concern in his voice obvious. It was a good question. Arundel was trying to think of an answer, when Urag'Ki moved up beside him.

"Look at their numbers. Over the years we have scouted them many a time, and I would say that the greater part of their army is out there."

It had occurred to Arundel that their numbers seemed large, but not knowing how many Guardians there were in all, he had been unable to appreciate the significance of this until Urag'Ki had just spoken. There was something else that stood out to Arundel.

"From what we have seen in the villages, they are in full battledress as well."

Urag'Ki nodded in agreement. Barrington then spoke, but now his confidence was transformed to concern.

"What are you saying?"

Urag'Ki answered for him, perhaps a little more bluntly than he would have done.

"That is not a registration party out there, it is a war party." The concern in Barrington visibly heightened and he began to panic a little.

"What do we do?"

Another good question, one he could not really answer. "What can we do? They are out there and we are in here. Until they make a move, we do not know their full intention or what their plan is."

Barrington started to pace back and forth, an action that was little help to anyone else.

"There's movement."

It was Darwin's voice that interrupted again and Arundel could see very quickly that he was right. Marcasian and four others, all on horseback, had broken away from the ranks and were trotting forward towards the gates.

"You need to talk to them."

Barrington was surprised to hear Arundel say that.

"I do? Why? And say what?"

Arundel needed to calm him down a little.

"Take a few deep breaths, get control of yourself and put on your best official voice. Just ask them how you can help them, something like that."

"Yes, my King."

Barrington then took a few moments to compose himself, by which time Marcasian was coming to a halt.

"Marcasian!" he shouted out, "This is Steward Barrington Wehrsley. What brings you to Damisas?"

Marcasian spoke with conviction and authority and what he said caught them all by surprise.

"Steward, I am not here to speak with you. I am here to speak with the man you have been hiding all this time: the false King. Arundel, I request an audience with you."

They all looked at each other in shock. How could Marcasian suddenly know this? Was he simply guessing, in the hope he might catch them out? What else did he know? So many questions, yet they all remained silent, and so it was Marcasian who spoke again.

"Come on now, Arundel, why so shy? We have already faced each other in combat. Why hide away from a conversation? I know you are in there, just like I know that last night you married King Theagran's daughter."

That last sentence caught him like a slap in the face. Now he knew this wasn't a wild guess: Marcasian knew the truth, at least some of it. He stepped forward towards the gap, shrugging off Darwin, who tried to stop him.

"What do you want, Marcasian?"

Straight to the point, there was no use in wasting time. Marcasian adjusted himself in his saddle.

"Ah there he is, the false King himself. What I want, Arundel, is what King Theagran has wanted for some time now: you."

Marcasian pointed up in his direction.

"You wanted that the last time we met and it wasn't exactly working out for you then, until your men stepped in to save you. Do you really want a repeat?"

He could see Marcasian laugh at that comment, and then wag a finger.

"You misunderstand me, Arundel. I do not want another fight. What I want is for you to come down here and hand yourself over to me. Your execution is long overdue." Arundel was not backing down.

"Why would I do that?"

There was no laughter this time; Marcasian's face remained deadly serious.

"Because if you don't, your new wife will burn at the stake by nightfall, the day after tomorrow."

That comment hit him like a knife to the heart. That was how Marcasian knew: they had Thea captive. Arundel was confident that Thea would never have betrayed him, so there must be more to it than that. But his mind wasn't thinking straight. All he could think of was that Thea was in danger because of him. He turned away from the gap in the wall and began to hasten towards the staircase leading down to the gates.

"Where are you going?" Darwin called out to him.

"You know where I am going," he shouted back.

Now Barrington chimed in, "You can't, otherwise we lose everything."

He ignored that. He was thinking about Thea, nothing else. Once again he felt that his actions showed why he should not be King. He took the first few steps down, and then felt a hand grab his shoulder and yank him back hard. He turned round to see Urag'Ki standing there.

"Not now."

He tried to brush the Seeker off, but his grip was tight.

"You must not go out there."

Arundel shook his head.

"If Thea is still alive and there is a chance that I can save her, then I must take it."

Again he tried to pull away, but Urag'Ki was not letting go. "If you go out there, they will kill you, and then they will kill her anyway, if they haven't already. You know this is true. She has married you. Theagran will never let that go. You know this, Arundel."

He didn't know what to say, but Urag'Ki continued.

"If you go out there, you don't just kill yourself and her, you kill all of us. If you die, this realm dies. All of those who supported you, we all die. It is the truth."

He could feel his heart breaking. He had contemplated never seeing her again as a result of his death, but not the other way round. Living without her just wouldn't be living. "Then what do I do?"

Now Urag'Ki placed his free hand on Arundel's other shoulder.

"You fight. We all fight. We have started something, and we must see it through, be it to victory or death. Thea would want you to fight to your last breath for the people, and you know it is true."

He did know it; they had even talked about it, once before. Thea did not want to be the reason for the deaths of thousands of innocents. She would not want Arundel to walk away from this, having promised so much. But, at the same time, he could not give up hope that he could rescue her. He just couldn't do that.

"Then we fight. But if there is another way to try and save her, we will do it no matter how much people protest." Urag'Ki nodded.

"Agreed."

Urag'Ki then released his grip and they both walked back up the stairs towards Darwin and Barrington, when Marcasian could be heard calling out again.

"I can wait here all night, Arundel. But mark my words, Damisas will fall this night and you will meet your executioner, whether you come willingly or not."

For the first time in a few minutes, he was thinking rationally as Darwin suddenly spoke up.

"How can he say the city will fall? Even that fool knows this city was built to withstand any attack."

Darwin was right: Marcasian would know the city was impenetrable. Arundel spoke again.

"If he knows that I am here, that Thea has been coming here and that we are married, what else could he know?" Suddenly Barrington jolted with alarm.

"The tunnel!"

Darwin quickly added, "That would make sense. They can't penetrate it from the outside, but the tunnel would enable them to do it from the inside."

Darwin was right too, and, with no time to waste, Arundel snapped into life.

"Barrington, sound the alarm. We need our men out of the buildings and to the tunnel. Dar…"

He was suddenly cut off by loud screams and cries for help. He realised they were too late.

"Darwin, Urag'Ki, with me. We will have to hold the tunnel until reinforcements arrive. Barrington, raise that alarm! Get us those soldiers!"

He didn't wait for a response. He set off as fast as he could, drawing Razor from her scabbard as he ran. Nearing the bottom of the staircase, he could see several Guardians cutting their way through the crowd, who were all unarmed. They were scattering in various directions, but he could tell that some were heading for the gates.

As he reached the solid ground, he set off for those who were running towards the gates, only to collide with a Guardian he had not seen. The clash caused him to lose his footing and stumble, but he managed to prevent himself from falling over. The Guardian swung at him with his sword, but Arundel was able to parry it away with Razor. Now Arundel had regained his balance, he could parry another cutting thrust from the Guardian, and then, out of nowhere, Urag'Ki appeared, slicing his blade across the back of the Guardian. Arundel was then able to drive Razor into his throat.

"Thanks!"

Urag'Ki nodded at him.

"We must get to them before they reach the gates."

Arundel pointed at those running in the distance.

"If they get the gates open, Marcasian will march his army right in."

Urag'Ki disagreed.

"Leave them to the archers when they arrive. If we don't stem the flow coming through that tunnel, we will get overrun from within, and all will be lost."

Arundel nodded. They started sprinting towards the square, where the tunnel entrance could be found.

Their journey was hampered by those Guardians, who had already made it through. Quickly, Arundel and Urag'Ki joined up with Darwin and helped him fend off another three. They then separated to spread the fight and Arundel warded off a sword, before slicing its owner across the chest. A further assailant came up on him, swinging an axe, but Arundel ducked and swept Razor across his legs, cutting both of them off, with ease. He spun on his heels and drove Razor straight into the chest of one more Guardian, who was rushing towards him. Withdrawing her quickly, he parried a strike from another Guardian and then slashed him across the throat.

For a moment, there was a pause in the onrush of Guardians, enabling him to check on both Darwin and Urag'Ki, who likewise had been fending off attackers. The respite was going to be short lived. Glancing towards the entrance to the tunnel, he saw that what looked like a multitude of Theagran's soldiers had now poured out into the daylight and were charging towards them. He readied himself, Razor in hand, knowing full well that the three of them against the approaching large numbers would be a fight they would struggle to win. The numbers were too great to count, but it was clear that the odds were not in their favour. They had no choice though, but to stand, and fight, and hope.

Arundel braced himself, as the Guardians came closer and closer, when suddenly they seemed to stop. In fact, not only did they stop, but they were turning round, as there was some sort of commotion behind them. At first, he struggled to see what was happening, but evidently Darwin had realised.

"They are fighting themselves."

It sounded ludicrous, but as bodies moved around, his vision became clearer and he could see that Darwin was right. "Some of them have cut off their drapes; they no longer wear Theagran's crest."

Darwin's vision was impressive; Arundel had no idea how such detail had been picked up so quickly. Again, after a few moments, he could see that Darwin was correct.

"Our fight is not over yet."

He need not say any more than that, as both Darwin and Urag'Ki clearly understood what he meant.

Advancing at speed to join in the melee, Arundel made the decision to target those still wearing Theagran's crest. As he reached the group closest to him, he began swinging left and right with Razor, connecting time and time again to try to cut a path. Steel slashed everywhere around him, while he was working hard to try and avoid it. Someone clattered into him from behind, causing him to stumble briefly. He turned round, swinging Razor with ferocity, only to find his swing blocked by a hefty blade. He was set to swing again, when a voice spoke over the noise of fighting men.

"Stop, my King!"

He then looked down the end of that hefty blade to the man holding it and realised it was Sir Winstan, Thea's former guard and one of his father's loyal elite knights. Immediately, Arundel felt a sense of relief: he had seen the knight briefly on a few previous occasions, when he would collect Thea to take her back to Ryevale. He also knew that Sir Winstan had made training and defence recommendations for Damisas during his visits. He could see that Sir Winstan was one of those who had cut off his drape. He wanted to speak but wasn't sure what to say.

"My men have this under control, my King. Those gates are open and you must get them closed before Marcasian reaches them." He glanced round and could see that the Guardians without drapes were holding their own, and one or two of his soldiers had now arrived to join the fight. He turned back to see that Sir Winstan was right: the gates were wide open. One Guardian had climbed up inside the gatehouse, while what looked like twenty to thirty more were on the ground, surrounding the ladder up to the gatehouse, to protect the man inside. He turned back to Sir Winstan.

"Thank you."

There was no time for further pleasantries. He had to get those gates closed.

He began to run as quickly as his armour allowed him, watching as the Guardians around the ladder prepared for his arrival. Once again, he knew he was facing impossible odds, but he had to try. If Marcasian and his army reached those gates, then all could be lost. So he ran and he ran, Razor gripped firmly in his hand. Then, suddenly, he saw arrows strike five of the men, several in each, dropping them to the ground. Another wave of arrows took out six more, while the rest began to scramble, trying to find some cover. He looked up to see the archers running along the battlements, either side of him, Garad leading them on one side and Eliya on the other. Another flurry of arrows eliminated a further four Guardians. Arundel's pace slowed, as he saw the opportunity to shout out some orders.

"Garad, move all your archers to the gates, and take out as many of Marcasian's riders as you can."

Garad gave a signal that he understood. Arundel then turned to Eliya.

"Eliya, to the gatehouse, get those gates closed. I will deal with the men on the ground."

Eliya gave her own signal that she understood.

He turned his focus back on the Guardians before him and tried to up his pace again. More arrows flew, dropping another ten Guardians. Not what he had asked for, but he was grateful for them. The remaining Guardians were in disarray, trying to prepare for him, but at the same time trying to avoid arrows. They had split up, leaving enough gaps between them for Arundel to take advantage. As he reached the first Guardian, he ducked a wild swing and drove Razor straight into his gut. He withdrew her in time to parry the swing of a sword and then take out its owner with a slice across the face. Two more approached, only for the body of another Guardian, pierced full of arrows, to fall down onto them. Arundel now knew that Eliya had cleared the gatehouse. There was suddenly a loud creak and the gates began to shut, distracting the remaining Guardians. This enabled Arundel to move in, striking down one with Razor, before barging another into the unforgiving iron gates. He slashed and ducked and thrust, and, soon enough, none of the Guardians were left standing. One was on his knees, trying to hold in his intestines with bloodied hands, as Arundel strode up behind him and finished the job.

Battling to catch his breath, he turned to look at the gates, where he could see Marcasian and his men now approaching. But the gates were shutting, the gap had narrowed too much and Marcasian reared his horse to a dramatic stop, just before them. The two of them glared at each other, knowing that this would resume another day. Arundel continued to look into those hollow eyes of Marcasian, and did not break his stare for a second as the iron gates slammed shut.

CHAPTER
29

There was very little time to allow the dust to settle. By the time the fighting had ended, light was starting to fade and Arundel was not in a patient mood. Darwin was quick to organise a few of his men to assess what damage had been sustained and what work needed to be done. Having watched the gates close, Arundel had made it back up onto the wall to see Marcasian and the remains of his army, riding off at speed. Wounded horses and dead men, amid a litter of arrows, covered the grass just before the gates: the archers had performed well.

Within a short time, further tasks were allocated as he gathered with Darwin and Barrington near the tunnel entrance, which was now guarded by six men. Arundel ordered that all fighting men and women were to be fed at once, after which they were to prepare their armour and arms. An early night for an early start was ordered. Any civilians who would not be fighting the following day or who were not involved in feeding or preparing armour and arms, were to be tasked with burial detail. Their own dead were to be buried in accordance with normal custom in Damisas. The bodies of the dead Guardians were to be taken outside of the city and buried in a mass grave. His final demand was for an emergency war council to be held as swiftly as possible.

Darwin and Barrington had then gone their separate ways to implement those orders, while Arundel made for his chamber to pause and reflect. All he could think about was Thea, and what fate she might have already met. If Marcasian was being honest and she was still alive, then he imagined that she was trapped in the deep, dark bowels of the Crypt. However, he was not oblivious to the possibility that she was already dead, and that Marcasian had been bluffing, in the hope it would lure him out. Either way, he felt helpless. The not knowing was killing him, while sitting here helpless was simply burying him further in a very dark place. When Urag'Ki had stopped him from handing himself over, he had told his friend that the first opportunity that arose, they would try to save her no matter what. Well, they had survived Marcasian's planned attack and now, as far as he was concerned, an opportunity had presented itself. After such a long period of talk and brief skirmishes, the time had finally come to act. Whether the council agreed or not, tomorrow Damisas was going to war.

"I think we all know where this meeting is going, so I suggest we get down to details."

Barrington was quite blunt for a change, and, to be honest, he appreciated it. He was also grateful to Garad, when he had knocked on his chamber door to tell him the council was assembled. That gave him something positive to do, instead of wallowing in despair. Now as he sat here, he did so in front of a larger council than there had ever been before, despite the absence of Oracle Thomas. The usual councillors were present – Barrington, Darwin, Urag'Ki and Garad – but they had also been joined by Eliya, Sir Winstan and a soldier named Crauss. Sir Winstan had been asked to attend to shed light on what had happened earlier and in turn to share some knowledge. Eliya and Crauss were there for tactical reasons. Given that Eliya shared the lead of the archers with Garad, while Crauss had been given charge of the foot soldiers, it had been deemed necessary that they be present for any vital tactical information they would require, ahead of the impending battle. With everyone listening, Barrington continued, "Arundel, we all know that you desire to go to war tomorrow; that has been made clear. The council discussed it, prior to your arrival here tonight, and you have our full support."

That certainly made things easier. He was going to do this, whether they had supported him or not, but it was easier with their backing. He felt he had to give a response.

"I thank you for your support. I am aware that some doubt will be cast upon my motives for this, questions may have been asked as to whether I am doing this for Thea and not because it is the right time to make our move. Well, some of that would be right, because I am doing this for Thea. If there is a chance, no matter how small, that we can save her then I am going to take it. But at the same time, I do wholeheartedly believe that this is the right time to strike. We have sat on our hands for so long, wondering when an opportunity may arise to bring an end to this war, and I believe that opportunity has presented itself to us today. At the very least, we have been given a warning. We survived today, but for how long can we keep on just surviving? We must finally meet Theagran's Guardians on the field of battle and bring an end to this bloody affair."

He looked around the table to gauge a reaction to his words. To his surprise, he saw no obvious objection. Thankfully, Darwin broke the silence.

"Our King is right. We were lucky today. The assessments of the damage have been handed to me. Inside the walls, fifty-two civilians died, along with one hundred and sixty-three Guardians, and twelve of Sir Winstan's men. Outside the walls, one hundred and thirteen Guardians died and only thirty of their horses survived, twenty-two of which were rounded up, while the rest fled. Although those figures appear to show a favourable outcome for us, in reality they flatter us. Our forces were scattered, and there was no way Urag'Ki, King Arundel and I would have held the Guardians on our own. If it had not been for Sir Winstan and his men, the three of us would have perished and Marcasian would have entered the city with full force. Damisas would have fallen."

Now there was a reaction: Barrington had clearly not contemplated such a terrible fate to be possible, despite what had happened today, and was about to express his view. However,

Arundel intervened swiftly to pick up where Darwin had left off, turning to the old knight.

"Darwin speaks the truth, Sir Winstan. Without you and your men, we would not be sitting here right now. We thank you for what you have all done, but I must also ask why you did it?"

It was the question that had been on everyone's lips, but they had clearly been too polite to ask. He needed to know. He had plans for Sir Winstan, but before he could put them into place, he needed to know exactly where his loyalties lay. Sir Winstan cleared his throat and began to speak.

"For generations a Stal has sat upon the throne as King of Galbraxia, a Greystone has been his First and then twelve elite knights have formed the Guardians of the Crown, the King's personal guard. That role also often passed from generation to generation of the same household. I served under your father, King Andreas, and my father served under your grandfather. The people of this realm were loyal to your family and were prepared to lay down their lives for their King. It was Theagran who appointed Marcasian as a Guardian with us Guardians of the Crown. Although, as we now know, deception was *their* objective, the rest of us have remained true. That loyalty has never been lost; the same goes for many of those who served in Galbraxia's army. But over the years since Theagran stole the throne, lives have been lost and fidelity to the Crown was lost with them. Theagran was no fool. During his Civil War, he would always use those of us, who had served your father the longest, as his sacrificial lambs. Thus, through death by natural causes or by being in the front line, the numbers of those loyal to your family have dwindled.

"A mere one hundred and thirty-seven of us remained at the start of this day, and all of us were assigned to the tunnel attack, along with one hundred and sixty-three Guardians loyal to Theagran. This did not surprise me, because the most casualties were expected to come from that attack and, as always, we were expendable. Three hundred of us were sent into that tunnel, but those one hundred and sixty-three Theagran loyalists that led the charge had no idea that we planned to show our true loyalties and betray them. We saw two possible outcomes for our plan. Either we would all die, and do so at least knowing that we had fought for the right cause, or we would live to join your ranks and help you free the realm. Thankfully, for most of us, it is the latter.

"I served your father, my King, and then, for too long, I was forced to serve a mad man. But now, if you would have me, it would be an honour to serve you, the true King of Galbraxia, as it would be for my men."

Sir Winstan bowed his head a little, as if awaiting Arundel's judgement. Arundel reached out a hand of comfort and placed it reassuringly on Sir Winstan's shoulder.

"I wish I could remember you from my childhood, Sir Winstan, but those memories were stolen from me. Oracle Thomas told me that you were very loyal to my father and a great knight, and so I would be proud for you fight alongside me."

Sir Winstan lifted his head and nodded in thanks, since no more words were needed on the matter.

"But I must ask you, Sir Winstan, what of Thea and the Oracle?"

This was something else he needed to know. He hoped that Sir Winstan could provide some information about Thea that might give him some hope she was still alive.

"The Oracle and the young handmaid were slain in cold blood." At these words, Arundel glanced at Urag'Ki. Although he knew that it was part of his friend's culture to hide his emotion, he understood very well that beneath that stern face the news of Shauri's death would have had an impact. Sir Winstan continued, "Queen Thea was taken to the Crypt and, from what we heard, sentenced to death for High Treason. What Marcasian said is true, to the best of my knowledge: in two days, she is to be burned at the stake. At the time we departed from Ryevale, work had only just begun on building the pyre so it is unlikely to be ready by tomorrow."

While Arundel's heart sank at the thought of the fate that seemingly awaited his Queen, he could at least take a crumb of comfort from the knowledge that she was probably still alive at the moment. Meanwhile, he wanted to mourn the death of the Oracle, a man who had taught him so much about his past and his heritage. However, the immediate prospect of waging war the next day meant his mourning would have to be delayed, as Eliya suddenly spoke up.

"Forgive me for my insensitivity with the news we have just received, but if we are to take to the field of battle tomorrow, we must be as prepared as we can possibly be." She had his attention because he could not disagree. Eliya then turned to Sir Winstan.

"Can you tell us how many in number Theagran has and what we can expect to be up against? Any information would be greatly appreciated right now."

It was a valid question. Arundel realised that he needed to put his personal emotions aside for now and focus on the task at hand. If they were to be successful, then it was paramount that everyone was pulling together. He looked up at the old knight, who was clearly pondering for a moment or two, before giving his response.

"If the figures we have heard tonight are accurate, then Marcasian lost two hundred and seventy-six men today. Your previous two encounters with his men out in the villages took roughly a hundred Guardian lives, give or take a few. Even with those losses and the defection of my men today, Marcasian will likely be able to lead nearly two and a half thousand men."

That number hit the council hard, very hard.

"How many do we have?"

Sir Winstan posed the question and Darwin provided the answer.

"With the addition of your men, we have just over a thousand."

There it was, the reality of the situation. They were heavily outnumbered. For the first time tonight, Urag'Ki spoke.

"I shall send word to my people; they will wish to join the fight. That should give us another five hundred, if all the clans can be reached."

It was a help, undoubtedly, but still left a considerable gap.

Eliya spoke again.

"So they outnumber us by possibly a thousand or more. Those are difficult odds. We have had some success until now, but surely this fight could be beyond us?"

She had said what everyone had been thinking, but had not dared to say. Everyone that is, except for Sir Winstan, it would seem.

"Battles have been won with greater deficits than that, history tells us so. It is not always about quantity, if you have the quality."

Sir Winstan adjusted himself in his chair, immediately taking control of the meeting and in his element, able to use his expertise and experience, which were his strengths. These were strengths that Arundel knew he would be foolish not to use.

"We may not have the numbers, but we have fresh soldiers who are fighting for a purpose. From what I have seen and what I have heard, your men and women have been trained well, and from the whispers I heard among the Guardians, you also possess the better armour and weapons."

Darwin proudly stepped in.

"That we do courtesy of ancestral knowledge that has been passed through generations."

Sir Winstan resumed his speech.

"Exactly, knowledge is power, as the Oracle would say. Theagran has tried to erase history and in doing so, much important knowledge has been lost, weakening his own cause. He has an army that has become complacent over time, because it has had so little to do. His soldiers do not train, they do not learn, it would be hard to say that they even care. For too long, they have not faced any resistance, so that they look upon life as easy. They have no true generals, very little skill on the fields of war because they neglected those with experience, such as my men and myself. They will fight because they are told to, and will have very little guidance in doing so. You, on the other hand, will all fight because you need to, as your very lives depend on it. Your army is fighting not just for its own freedom, but for the freedom of the realm. Never underestimate such motivation. Not only that, but

Marcasian is arrogant and so are his men. He will believe, without a doubt, that they will be victorious and, therefore, he will not guard against any possible risks, whereas you are all aware of the possibility of defeat, and will therefore prepare yourself properly. Fools rush in, and Marcasian is most certainly a fool."

Sir Winstan took a pause.

"If we make the right decisions and show a little patience, we can win this. Marcasian will hand us the victory, whilst blinded by the belief he is bringing us defeat."

Sir Winstan spoke with such conviction, such passion that it was hard to not be inspired by it. Arundel had already known in his heart and his head what needed to be done: this speech just reaffirmed that. But before he could say anything, it was Garad who followed up the words of the wise old knight.

"If we don't try tomorrow, we stand on the edge of defeat anyway, now that Theagran knows Ari is here. I, for one, would rather die on the battlefield a free man, than be forced to live whatever life might be left, like a slave."

Arundel had heard enough.

"It is now or never. If Marcasian is as arrogant as Sir Winstan says, then I have no doubt that he will leave the safety of the city walls to face us. With the right organisation and leadership, I have faith that we can win. That is why, Sir Winstan, I would like you to lead us out there tomorrow. Darwin, Eliya, Garad and Crauss will work with you to organise their units as you direct. With your experience and knowledge, we would also be fools not to utilise you."

Sir Winstan appeared a little surprised at Arundel's proposal, but took it in his stride.

"I will do as you ask, my King. But we can't just arrive at Ryevale and make it up on the spot. We must have a plan in place. Therefore I suggest we make ourselves comfortable, as best we can, because it is going to be a long night."

Sir Winstan wasn't wrong. They planned and plotted long into the night, making sure that all the bases had been covered as far as possible, and that everyone knew their role. A few hours' sleep followed, before they roused themselves at first light to brief the soldiers. Breakfast was swiftly consumed by all, and then they were ready to depart from the city. It was a sight to behold, when a thousand strong, dressed for battle, filed through the gates in disciplined ranks. Crowds of civilians waved them off, uncertain who, if any, would return. Foot soldiers, mounted cavalry and archers all moved in unison, ready and willing to lay down their lives, in the name of freedom. The banner of house Stal was held high and billowed in the early morning breeze, as they marched, ready to try to return the one true King to the throne of Galbraxia.

Very little was said on the journey; after a long night of plans they were all talked out and eager to get on with proceedings. Every single one of them knew that they could very well be marching to their death, and such a thought kept them all in a subdued mood. The quickest path took them briefly into the Weeping Woods, skimming the edge of Galbraxia's most prominent woodland, before bringing them to the entrance to Wendel Valley. The last time Arundel had come to this valley, it had been in the company of Guardians, back when he had thought Thea was a daughter of a Lord, not of Theagran; back when he had never even considered she would become his Queen. In fact, at the time, he had not known his true history or supposed destiny. Instead, his purpose had been to assassinate a King, with a high chance of losing his own life in the process. Passage that day had not been easy; in fact, Arundel had met with the High Priest to request that they be let through, such was the animosity between the Seekers and the Guardians. Today, however, was different. Today, their passage was easy: it was welcomed, it was cheered.

On reaching the head of the valley, they were joined by all the clans, increasing their strength by a good five hundred, as a wash of dark blue filtered into their ranks. Words of thanks, followed by guidance and tactics, were swiftly passed onto the clan leaders and Arundel found himself buoyed up by their hunger and eagerness to fight. By the time they had cleared the valley, the clans had gone on ahead and their numbers were five hundred lighter once more, at least for now. The Seekers were their surprise element and, if all went to plan, would have a pivotal role to play.

Despite all the plans, despite the splendour of the army before him, throughout the journey this still hadn't felt real. What they were about to do and what they were about to face, still hadn't quite sunk in. Ryevale came into view on the horizon for the first time, but still it didn't really sink in. In a way he was grateful for that, because it took the edge off the journey, kept a little ease within him. Even as night fell and they set up camp using the contours of the land to hide them from the watchers on the city walls, reality hadn't quite kicked in. His mind was too busy, fearing that this delay was risking Thea's life, that by camping until morning they would be arriving at the city on the day of her execution, which might be too late. However, he knew that Sir Winstan was right, when he said they would need a night's rest after a day's march to make sure they were fresh for battle in the morning. He couldn't argue against that, and so he didn't. Instead, he lay all night praying they would not be too late, his mind never even contemplating the battle that would come in a few hours.

At daybreak, they moved on to a stopping point on the open fields. The city was within reach and, for Arundel, the situation changed. This would be their fighting ground, this would be where they would begin their last stand. As they lined themselves up with excellent organisation, Arundel watched the city of Ryevale come to life. From being empty, the walls were now brimming with archers, lined up almost shoulder to shoulder. The city gates then opened and Arundel saw the Guardians pour through them, in numbers far greater than their own. Swords, spears, axes, maces, horses, shields were all on display, as Theagran's men, led by Marcasian, showed their full strength.

At that moment, for Arundel, it became very real indeed.

"Their greater numbers, as we know, give them an advantage over us, but they also have another advantage that Marcasian will exploit: the city. Marcasian will not bring his archers out onto the field; instead, he will pack them onto the city walls, giving them a better line of sight and better angle, than our archers will be afforded. From the distance where we will line up, our arrows will not be able to reach, leaving us with a problem. It will also put us in a vulnerable position when steel meets steel. I can tell you all how Marcasian will play this, because I know the man he is. Most leaders in his position would wait for us to attack first. We are the 'invaders,' for lack of a better word, and so we would be expected to be the ones to strike first. But not Marcasian. Marcasian will want to make the first move, since once his foot soldiers have set off, ours will be a pace or two behind. By the time both sides collide, the fighting will be closer to our line than his, and this will keep our archers from advancing close enough at least to get a shot at his cavalry. It will also make us sitting ducks for his archers, and he will rain down arrows on us, happily sacrificing his own men in the process, because he knows he can afford to do so. He also knows that you won't just sit back and watch your men die, and that you will charge into the fight, where, if his archers don't kill you and the rest of our men, then his mounted will. That is how he will see it, and his arrogance will prevent him from believing anything else could happen.

"But he does not know that we will have the Seeker clans, and he does not know that we will be coming with our own strategy.

It is vital that our men are mobile first. By the time his army has left the city, our foot soldiers need to be on the move. They need to protect themselves from Marcasian's archers, and get our archers close. We need to hit their numbers, and hit them hard. If Marcasian sees that things aren't going his way, his patience will run out and he will lead his mounted into the fight, putting distance between them and the city. This is where the clans come in. They can then advance, pouring a trail of oil along the front of the city and setting it ablaze. The smoke will hamper the vision of Marcasian's archers, thus protecting us, and enabling the clans to enter the city and clear the walls. The rest, well, that comes down to flesh and steel on the battlefield."

That was how Sir Winstan had painted the picture last night in the war council and, so far, he had not been wrong. Watching the city walls become enveloped in archers and seeing the vast numbers pour out of the city gates, it would have been easy to become distracted by fear and concern. But there was no time for that. As Sir Winstan had advised, Arundel's men needed to be on the move before the Guardians had even settled, and so, as the Guardians marched out of the city to line its walls, Crauss and Eliya had been organising frantically, ordering the foot soldiers into four columns lined up in two rows of two. Each column was shaped like a rectangle and carried long shields. Those round the outside held their shields out before them, or to their side depending on their position, while those in the middle held their shields flat above their heads to form a protective roof, as it were. Just enough gaps were left for them to be able to see. The Guardians were still taking up their positions when Crauss' foot soldiers began to march towards the enemy.

Sitting upon his horse, Arundel watched as the four columns moved with perfection. He could see Marcasian and others beginning to panic on their lines, trying to ready their own foot soldiers. Before they could muster them, the sky suddenly darkened with the first wave of arrows flying over from the city walls. Arundel saw his men stop and lock their shields together to protect themselves against the oncoming storm. Shields were pierced left, right and centre but, as the last arrow fell, it seemed as though all of their foot soldiers got back to their feet, maintaining their organisation with the small vision gaps between shields, and they set off again. Marcasian had scrambled his men enough so that they too were now on the march, but he had lost a lot of ground. A second wave of arrows then blacked out the sky as, once again, Arundel watched his soldiers lock their shields together to keep from harm. This time, however, a few in each column remained on the grass while the rest rose back to their feet and continued to march.

The Guardian foot soldiers were getting closer, when suddenly a cry went up from Crauss. The soldiers at the front of each column dropped to one knee and those in the middle lowered their shields and then dropped to a knee also, revealing archers hidden among them. The archers in the front two columns took aim at the approaching foot soldiers and let loose, slaying Guardians before they could try to protect themselves. The archers in the back two columns took aim at the Guardian archers on the city walls. Thankfully, they were now close enough to reach and, as the arrows loosed into the air, Guardians dropped from the city walls.

The foot soldiers stood up and their march began again, while the Guardians were hampered by their losses. The march lasted mere seconds, before a third wave of Guardian arrows took flight. The columns stopped and locked shields once more, while the arrows littered their ranks. Cries of pain and screams of anguish could be heard as more of the Damisas force fell, with shields dropping in scattered areas of each column. As the last arrow struck home, Arundel's soldiers stayed organised and stuck to their task. They took a knee once again and the archers let loose their own second round of arrows, finding their targets in approaching Guardians and again slowing them down in the process, while more Guardian archers fell from the city walls, revealing further glimpses of daylight amongst their lines.

So far, they had inflicted more damage on the Guardians than they had received, but that changed when the fourth wave of

Guardian arrows briefly blackened the sky before raining down upon Arundel's soldiers. This time they caused far more chaos, exploiting the gaps created in the last round. Arundel could only watch and listen to the screams of his soldiers as the arrows struck home. For the first time, disorder hit their ranks and as they started getting back to their feet, all four columns had lost their shape because of the casualties they had just taken. The Guardian foot soldiers, although slowed by their own dead and wounded, were nearly upon his stricken soldiers and, with another round of arrows likely to come their way, Arundel was ready to charge. Sir Winstan clearly sensed this and placed a gauntlet against his chest plate.

"No, my King, not yet."

He struggled to deal with that.

"But they are about to get slaughtered."

Sir Winstan remained calm. At that moment the voice of Crauss could be heard, bellowing across the field.

"Regroup as two! Regroup as two!"

The message clearly reached his men, and Arundel watched the remnants of the four columns scramble together to form two slightly larger columns. They managed it, just as the first line of Guardian foot soldiers reached them. As the shields locked in place, Guardian blades ricocheted off them.

"We must lure Marcasian into the fight. The moment he charges, their archers will no longer be able to fire random arrows for fear of hitting him. They will have to take specific aim and that will lessen their threat, until our friends in blue can light the fires."

As Sir Winstan spoke, Arundel watched the Guardians trying to hack their way through the tough shields that were protecting the soldiers behind them. They were making little headway when a fifth round of arrows cut through the air and rained down upon them. The shields once again became littered with arrows, with some finding a way through the battered steel, but many a shaft also cut down the Guardian foot soldiers that had been trying to break down the shield wall, leaving them on the grass and mud in bloody heaps. When the Guardians had first set off, they could have afforded such a loss, but not now, with their numbers already drastically reduced by Arundel's soldiers. Sir Winstan pointed out Marcasian in the distance, as the Bull was pacing his horse back and forth, visibly impatient and seemingly itching to move forward.

"We are so close."

As Sir Winstan spoke, Arundel watched as the front line of the columns used their shields to push back the closest Guardians to them, before then taking a knee. Once again the shields held above their heads lowered and the remaining archers loosed their arrows. One column took out another wave of foot soldiers, while the other column targeted the archers on the city walls, causing more to fall to their death. Crauss' quick thinking and the soldiers' quick actions upon his orders had enabled them to regain the momentum and, suddenly, Marcasian's initial forces were looking heavily depleted. The Bull had clearly seen enough and, within moments, his entire mounted force was on the charge.

"Now we ride, my King'.

Sir Winstan spoke with passion. He put spurs to his horse and began a charge of his own.

"Charge!"

The cry ripped through the air, as Darwin shouted at the top of his lungs. Arundel was already on his way, just like Sir Winstan. He glanced back, and could see the rest were following, with Urag'Ki the closest. Returning his gaze to the scene before him, he could see that it had descended into the chaos of hand to hand combat, with both columns now broken up. He could only hope that Garad was still alive, amongst all the carnage. Marcasian and his men had reached the fight, causing Arundel to use his spurs to push his horse harder. He released one hand from the reins and took hold of Razor's hilt, easing her from her scabbard. Within moments, he was charging into the fray, swinging left and right, as Razor's blade cut through steel and flesh. He had barely managed to slow down his horse, when the arrows struck it, two to the body and three to the neck. The legs of his horse suddenly buckled and it lurched forward, throwing him from the saddle.

He fell and hit the ground hard, shockwaves coursing through his entire body; the force then rolled him through the blood-stained mud. He clattered into a pair of legs as he rolled, knocking down whoever they belonged to, and eventually he came to a stop, courtesy of an arrow-filled body, which he thumped into. The pain was instantaneous, and seemed to pulse through every fibre of his body, but he was in one piece, and the pain would have to wait.

He had lost his grip of Razor as he had rolled, but she was, thankfully, within reach. Turning over, he grabbed her with one hand and then just managed to scramble out of the way, as an axe came driving down towards him. The axe dug into the mud with a thud, stunning its handler. This gave Arundel enough time to swing with Razor, slicing through both ankles of his attacker and causing him to fall to the floor as his legs separated from his feet. The Guardian cried out in pain but those cries were silenced, when Arundel drove Razor into his head. Arundel started to get up when someone crashed into him, flooring him. The Guardian, who had hit him, stumbled but remained on his feet and, when he realised who was on the ground beneath him, he swung hard with his sword. Arundel managed to block the blow and reset himself, before a second swing came in. He blocked that too, but knew time would run out, all the while he was stuck on the floor. The Guardian swung, with blow after blow. Arundel was finding it harder to defend himself, when suddenly the blows stopped and the Guardian's head fell away from his body, which slumped to the ground. A blood soaked Urag'Ki came into view and he extended a hand to Arundel, who took it, and the Seeker helped him to his feet. Suddenly, Arundel pushed Urag'Ki aside, just avoiding a lunging spear. Arundel cracked Razor down onto the spear, shattering it before thrusting her into the gut of the attacking Guardian and doubling him over. Urag'Ki finished the man off with one swift blow, and then they quickly found themselves separated again, fighting with different men in different directions.

It was certainly hard going. With so many people, blades

swinging, arrows flying, it was absolute mayhem. He found himself stepping over bodies, both living and dead, adding to the corpses with almost every swing or thrust of Razor. The air was filled with the cries of death and pain, of the grunts of straining muscles and the clash of steel upon steel. He lost count of how many he had slain: there had simply been too many in the melee. His adrenalin was fuelling his body, muting the pain from the fall. He barely noticed the cuts accrued so far, from battle. There was so much at stake, not just for the realm, but also the chance he could save Thea, and that gave him motivation enough to keep on going. Thick smoke caught at his throat and he glanced towards the city, where the walls had vanished behind thick, grey plumes. The clans appeared to have succeeded in the first part of their mission, and the Guardians' arrows had stopped, for the time being. He had noticed that some of the Seekers had even joined the battle, satisfying their lust for revenge against Theagran.

He was trying to get some idea about which way the battle was going, when his eyes fell upon Marcasian. Despite being covered in blood, the Bull was cutting his way through anyone he came into contact with. He was always going to be a massive threat in this battle, and so he was proving to be. Arundel knew Marcasian had to be stopped. He set off towards the Bull, fending off any who tried to block his path. As he drew closer, Marcasian spotted him and shrugged off his own attackers to walk forward himself. Arundel remembered their fight before; he remembered how, even though he had been winning that day, Marcasian's ferocity had made him an enormous challenge. This time round, Arundel was far from fresh. The Bull came closer and closer, the sounds of his grunting audible. Arundel gripped Razor tightly, and was doing his best to set himself, preparing his body for the test that was about to come. He then drew Razor back, readying himself for the first blow, when an arrow suddenly hit Marcasian, piercing the armour of his leg. Marcasian stopped for a moment, wincing, as he grabbed the arrow and pulled it out of his leg. He flung it aside, and took another step forward, when the second arrow hit, this time piercing his chest plate. A third arrow then struck his chest plate and, for the first time, Marcasian began to stagger. When two more arrows hit, one in his gut and the other in his thigh, Marcasian dropped to his knees. He wobbled there, his eyes burning with rage, but his body was incapable of the fight needed to get back up.

Arundel approached him, and Marcasian on instinct swung with his sword, only for Arundel to block it and then slice Razor down, severing the sword hand. Marcasian cried out in anguish, as blood began to spurt. Marcasian clutched at the stump and spat his words towards Arundel.

"Do it, end it."

Arundel was happy to oblige and lifted Razor above his head for the killing blow, when a voice cut him off in his tracks.

"No, Ari, he's mine!"

Arundel turned his head to see Garad approaching, covered in cuts and also blood, some his own but mostly belonging to others. His bow was in his hand: now it was clear who had fired the arrows. Arundel lowered Razor, as Garad approached him.

"I owe it to Bromon. Let me finish him."

Arundel nodded and took a step back, while Garad wrapped his bow over his shoulder and grasped his sword. Garad then turned towards him for a moment.

"Get to the city! Save Thea! Go Ari, go!"

Arundel didn't need telling twice. Scouting around, he located the first available horse still alive, and grabbed its reins, before mounting it. At the kick of Arundel's heels, the horse broke into a gallop, and, as he rode towards the city, he just caught sight of Marcasian's head falling to the ground.

31

He weaved the horse through the battlefield, where the blood-stained grass had become littered with bodies. The distinctive sound of steel upon steel still rang through the air, but was mixed with the blood-curdling cries of the wounded and dying. From the saddle, he had a clearer view than on foot, and it seemed to him that the battle was going well, but he had little time to take stock properly. He slashed Razor down the back of one Guardian in fierce combat with a Damisas foot soldier, as he rode through the devastation of conflict, edging ever closer to the city.

Ryevale's walls were all but hidden behind a screen of thick grey smoke and dancing yellow flame. The fire had begun to spread across the grass, and would surely participate in the fight soon enough, but he had no time to stop and help. Instead, he kept his eyes focused on the smoke before him, watching as the light breeze blew wisps away just enough for him to see beyond. When he caught a brief glimpse of the city gates, he knew exactly where to head. Drawing ever closer to the smoke-screened walls, Arundel saw that some of the Guardians were fleeing back to the city, most likely in the hope of sanctuary, but sanctuary they would not find.

He held his breath as he rode into the smoke, saving his lungs as best he could from the suffocating air. The heat intensified with every stride of his horse, and, on entering the city through the smoke, he found out why. Some of Marcasian's men, who had been carrying oil, had been killed and their cargo spilled across the pavement of the city into the nearest buildings. Fire had begun to spread beyond the walls and the civilians were running in panic.

As well as the red and yellow of the flames, a shade of dark blue dominated this side of the city walls: the Seeker clans were fighting their way through those who had fled the battlefield. One Guardian tried to grab Arundel's boot when he rode by, in an attempt to pull him off his horse. Arundel thrust out with his leg, causing the wounded soldier to tumble into the nearby flames, which devoured him alive.

Still Arundel did not stop, as he rode through the cobbled streets of the city. Sir Winstan had tried to explain to him last night how he could find the pyre in the city square, but that complex explanation escaped him now and he simply rode blind. Unfortunately, the main city gates were not the ones he had fled from on the day of his execution, the ones that led straight to the square. That would have been too simple. His twists and turns at times led him down dead ends and his frustration grew, but then came a beacon to show him the way. As the fires of the gates fell further behind him, he realised that there was a separate plume of smoke, rising into the blue sky deeper into the city. While he thanked the guidance that it brought him, he also feared for what it might mean.

The smoke was getting nearer, but his horse was beginning to tire. While it may have still been alive when he found it, it wasn't unscathed. An arrow had snapped off in its rump and the wound was gradually taking its toll. Its pace slowed drastically, and, as the opening to the city square came into view, the horse slowed to a stagger. Realising its plight, Arundel decided to dismount and finish the journey on foot. Climbing down momentarily distracted him and he failed to see the pitchfork, before it was too late. The slightly blunted points scraped along his armour, before digging into the ribs of the horse. The horse shrieked and bucked its legs, and then, as the pitchfork was withdrawn, the horse stumbled and fell. Arundel turned in time to fend off a second thrust of the pitchfork, an enraged citizen at the end of its handle. He parried the thrust away and drove Razor into the civilian's chest, slaying him where he stood.

Arundel then began to walk, as fast as his weary body and heavy armour would allow him, towards the entrance to the Square. As he neared it, two more civilians emerged from buildings, one holding a lump of wood and the other some form of blade. The one with the wood swung it but Arundel blocked it with a gauntlet, the wood shattering as it hit the steel of his armour. The second then lunged with his blade and caught Arundel in his side between the plating on his armour. The pain was instant and he could feel the warm blood begin to trickle. He swung wildly with Razor, missing both men. His first attacker then grabbed hold of him by his armour and tried to pull him off balance. Arundel stumbled as the one with the blade lunged at him once again. This time, Arundel was able to kick him back before thrusting Razor into the gut of the man who had hold of him. The man's grip gave way and Arundel ripped Razor out through his hip, causing his intestines to spill to the ground, followed by his body. The man with the blade lunged again but now Arundel parried the blow and sliced Razor straight across his chest. Flesh ripped and blood spurted. The man staggered and fell backwards into a wall.

Arundel could feel the pain screaming out, but he pushed it down deep inside, as he once again hastened towards the entrance to the square. Each step was heavy, each movement pained him, but none of that mattered as he walked into the square. The heat hit him first and then he saw it.

The wooden pyre dominated the centre of the square due to its sheer size, both in height and width. Heavy logs made up its base, while thinner, longer branches formed a spire on top of it. Arundel momentarily stopped in his tracks. His eyes took in the flames, licking away menacingly at the wooden structure. The pyre was engulfed in fire and, from this distance, he could see little beyond their wicked dance. His body sprang to life again, and he rushed forward, trying to shield his face from the heat, while desperately seeking out what the flames were hiding. Closer and closer he came, the heat warming his armour as the flames cracked and hissed, occasionally leaping towards him. He was so close he could almost touch it, when he finally saw their secret. As the fire burned ferociously, at its heart was the body of a female, blackened and blistered.

The shock hit him like a thunderbolt, rocking his body from within. Razor slipped from his grasp and fell to the floor with a dull clang. Arundel dropped to his knees, as tears began to trickle down his cheeks. His heart felt as though it was breaking into a thousand tiny pieces within his chest. He had vowed to protect her forever, to keep her safe from their wedding day until his very last, and yet he had failed. He hadn't even managed one day. She was his everything, his Queen, and now she was gone. As he knelt there on the cobbled stone, he was watching his future, his very reason, literally burn away in the flames. He could not imagine life without her. He could not contemplate the idea of going about the rest of his days, knowing he could never share a single one of them with her. Once again, he felt he was not fit to be King. All they had done today, so many lives trying to fight for the freedom of the realm, suddenly meant nothing to him. Without Thea, in that moment he could not give a damn about the realm and those living in it. Without Thea, he no longer cared about his own life. The fight drained out of him, his will to continue evaporated. He was done; he had nothing left.

"You!"

The voice cut through the silence with menace. Its rasping, coarse tone was easily identifiable. Arundel's head lifted and he began to scour the Square until he found the source. The stage, upon which he had been so nearly executed many turns of the moon ago, still stood prominent at one end of the Square, not too far from the pyre. Just beyond it, to one side by the line of the buildings, Arundel could see the hulking frame of Theagran. Black leathers adorned his body with no armour in sight, most likely because of his arrogant assumption that victory would come easily. His black hair was now grey and had thinned; a tangled mess, it hung around his face. Theagran had a sword in his hand and was making his way towards Arundel, yet Arundel did not move. But the anger within him was rising, flooding through his body and fuelling his muscles. With every step Theagran took, every word he spoke, Arundel could feel his fight returning.

"My city burns because of you," Theagran rasped. "My daughter burns because of you!"

The hatred in his voice was not hidden.

"I should have killed you myself, the night I killed your pathetic father."

Arundel was breathing more and more heavily. His veins were starting to pulse and his fists clenched inside their gauntlets so tightly, it felt as though he might dent the steel.

"My daughter betrayed me for you, Arundel, and now I can send you to hell to join her!"

Theagran was almost upon him now, when Arundel finally snapped. His rage erupted like a volcano within him. He grasped Razor, plucking her from the cobbles before exploding to his feet. His muscles suddenly felt invigorated, the armour as light as a feather, as he charged at Theagran, who clearly was not quite sure how to react.

Once Arundel reached the false King, he swung Razor with all his might, only for Theagran to parry her away. Anger consumed Arundel; it took complete control as he swung again and again, only for Theagran to parry each and every blow. Lack of accuracy was causing his wild swings to fail, but he did at least put Theagran on the back foot. The sound of steel against steel pierced the air time and time again, as Arundel fought with everything he had to avenge his Queen. Theagran staggered back more than once and, so far, had failed to do anything other than defend himself, as Arundel's blows rained down upon him.

At one point, Theagran lost his footing but was able to block another blow, before scrambling up the wooden steps onto the executioner's stage. Arundel followed Theagran onto the stage and aimed with another wild swing, but this one lacked power, so that Theagran once more parried it away. The problem was that Arundel had been fighting most of the day against many foes, while Theagran had not lifted a finger. Arundel's rage had fuelled his adrenalin, and it was that adrenalin which had enhanced his attacks until this point. However, as the adrenalin slowly drained, the aches and pains of his body came flooding back and suddenly the labours of the day began to tell.

Arundel aimed with another swing but again it was weak and this time, having parried it away, Theagran for the first time countered with a swing of his own. Arundel managed to move out of the way, but without warning the momentum of the fight shifted. Arundel's arms became weary, his armour suddenly felt like dead weight and his breathing became laboured. Theagran lunged forward with another thrust, followed by another and another, that put Arundel on the back foot. It was all that he could do to keep blocking them away with Razor. He needed to dig deep, he needed to get back on the offensive and so after blocking yet another swing from Theagran, he aimed with one of his own. It was erratic, however, and Theagran was able to move out of the way, before thrusting with his own sword.

The blade slipped between plates on Arundel's armour and sliced through the skin on his left side, just below the ribs. The pain was instantaneous and winded him. As he stumbled, Theagran spotted his opportunity. He aimed with another thrust, which Arundel, through the pain, found a way to block, but this time Theagran followed it up with a shoulder barge, knocking Arundel off his feet. He fell down onto the wooden platform with a thud, and a burning pain engulfed the wound by his ribs. Razor fell from his hand and hit the planks, just out of his reach. The pain in his side blurred his vision, as his eyes began to water and his head began to swim. He could just about make out Theagran, lifting his sword high and then driving it down towards him.

Arundel pushed through the pain and rolled out of the way, just in time, as Theagran's sword plunged into the wood of the platform with a crack, splintering it. The sword was temporarily stuck. Arundel sought to take advantage of this and crawled towards Razor. He reached out a gauntlet and had just got his fingertips on her hilt, when Theagran's foot suddenly kicked her away. Arundel could only watch, as Razor was sent flying off the platform back onto the cobbled stone floor with a clang.

Theagran's foot then shifted and, before Arundel could react, it connected with his head. The force of the kick rolled Arundel over onto his back.

Momentarily, the world seemed to go black. His head began to throb, as his vision returned, and he could feel warm blood trickling over his lips from his nose. He mentally prepared himself for a second kick, but none came. As his body began to revive, he rolled over to see Theagran trying to remove his sword from the platform, where it was embedded.

The cut in his side burned and his head was pounding like a drum, but he ignored this to work his way to his feet. He then charged at Theagran, driving his whole body into the grey-haired tyrant, with a hefty thud. The force took Theagran back several paces, and they both crashed into the temporary throne upon which Theagran had sat on the day of Arundel's near execution. The throne splintered and tumbled down, as they both fell with it.

Arundel could hear that Theagran was now starting to breathe heavily: during the fall, he had rasped out a cry of pain, when he took the full force of the breaking throne. Arundel had ended up on top of the false King. He slowly shifted his body so that he was astride him. With punch after punch, he began to pummel the head of Theagran, each blow filled with anger and hatred. His gauntlet had come off in the tumble, but he did not care, as his knuckles collided with the bone of Theagran's skull. Theagran's face began to crack and blister, and Arundel's knuckles became bloodied by a mixture of Theagran's blood and his own.

He had Theagran trapped, he had him beaten, but a desperate man can be forced to do desperate things and Theagran did just that. His hands fumbled along Arundel's body before he pushed his fingers into Arundel's wound by his ribs. The pain was immediate: Arundel howled out loud and reared his body back. That enabled Theagran to hit him in the face and then throw him off. Arundel's side felt like it was on fire and had become so tight, he struggled to move. He managed to roll onto his front and started pushing himself onto all fours. Clutching at the wound and trying to will away the pain, he began to get to his feet, when

Theagran cracked him in the body with a piece of wood from the throne. The force caused him to stumble, and the stumble twisted the wound. Another surge of pain coursed through him and made him dizzy enough to lose his footing and fall back down.

"To think my daughter threw it all away for you," Theagran rasped. Arundel tried to get to all fours, only for Theagran to connect with a kick that just caught his head and rolled him backwards across the platform.

"It makes me sick to think that my own flesh and blood would betray me for someone as pathetic as you."

Theagran's foot connected yet again and rolled Arundel even further, pushing him closer to the edge of the platform. The world was spinning, his focus flittered in and out, as pain consumed him, and it only got worse when Theagran delivered yet another kick. This time, as Arundel stopped rolling, he found himself right at the platform's edge. The cobbled floor wasn't very far below the platform, but it would hurt if he fell, he could tell that. Theagran rasped once more, "Your disgrace of a father was not worthy of your mother, as you were not worthy of my daughter."

Theagran then aimed with another kick, but this time Arundel found something extra inside him to grab the foot, just before it connected. He then cracked his arm down onto Theagran's knee and he could have sworn he heard it snap, as Theagran cried out with a hellish scream and fell onto his back. Arundel wanted to capitalise on this, he needed to, but he was struggling to find enough energy within him to do so. Instead he lay on his back, sucking in as much air as he could, trying to give his senses enough time to settle down and return to him. He could hear Theagran's mutterings of anguish, but the false King was currently out of his line of sight. Arundel gave himself a moment longer, trying to take advantage of Theagran's now possibly shattered knee, before he began to move the dead weight of his armour to get to his feet.

Once he had managed to stand up, he heard the sound of a man's rasping cry. Arundel turned round just in time to see Theagran lunge at him, with as much force as he could muster.

When Theagran's body crashed into his, all of the air escaped his lungs and his wound screamed. The world seemed to slip away, as they both fell off of the platform and onto the cobbled stones, with a thump that shook him to his core.

After the initial landing, they rolled in different directions, with Arundel finding himself on the edge of the pyre. He could almost feel the flames licking at his skin, he was that close. He wanted to move, to get away from the fire, to get himself ready for whatever was to come next, but he couldn't. His wound had become unbearable, his lungs were devoid of breath, his ribs felt as though they might be cracked. He could feel his legs, but they didn't seem to want to move just yet. It was as if his body had temporarily shut down, to deal with the trauma it had suffered.

What he failed to see as he lay there was that Theagran had been crawling his way over to him, but Arundel didn't find out until it was too late and the false King was on top of him. It took a moment for Arundel to notice the dagger in Theagran's hand, and his arms found enough life in them, just in time for him to raise them up and block the dagger by grabbing Theagran's wrist. But Theagran had the better positioning, being on top, and he was slowly overpowering Arundel, pushing the dagger closer and closer to his face. Arundel gave everything he had, to try and push the arm away, but he was losing the battle. He could feel the tip of the dagger pressing into the skin of his cheek. It began to break through the skin, when Arundel found some life in his legs and lifted one up, before pressing it against the damaged knee of Theagran. Theagran cried out in pain and Arundel could feel his arm loosen, enabling Arundel to push it back, lifting the blade away from his cheek. Thinking quickly, he then thrust Theagran's hand into the flames of the pyre. Theagran let out a shrill shriek and dropped the dagger into the flames. Seizing the opportunity, Arundel shifted his body weight with a sharp jolt, and threw Theagran off him. The false King landed in the flames, but then fell out of the pyre onto the cobbled stones, crying out in pain as his leathers set alight. Arundel dug deep and pushed himself to his feet, before staggering over towards the stage where he found Razor.

Theagran was writhing on the floor, desperately trying to put the flames out, with little success. In the frenzy of his anguish, the false King stumbled up to his feet, frantically looking for salvation from the flames, but instead he found Razor's sharp, cruel blade, as Arundel plunged her straight into Theagran's black heart. Arundel then eased her back out from his adversary's chest, and watched the false King collapse onto the cobbles and the flames start to consume his body. The cries had stopped and silence fell.

Arundel was slumped against the stage staring at the pyre, at what was once his Queen, when the first of his men arrived in the Square, led by Sir Winstan, who had seen better days. Despite his wounds and the mess of his armour, the old knight was alive and kicking, as he instructed some of his men to find water and put the pyre out. He then hobbled over to Arundel and perched next to him.

"I am so sorry, my King."

Arundel remained silent. He had nothing to say, nothing at all. What could he say? His Queen was dead; he had been too late and had failed to save her. Sir Winstan, however, had more to say.

"The battle is over, my King. We are victorious."

That barely registered with him. He should have been elated, he should have been jumping for joy, but with Thea gone, he felt nothing.

"It is hard to assess the damage, but we have rounded up those who surrendered and begun to treat our wounded. I see you have taken care of Theagran. Now you truly are King of Galbraxia."

What kind of King was he when he could not keep his Queen safe? He continued his silence, concluding in his head that he needed to get away from here, he needed to leave this god-forsaken city and the poisonous people who lived within its walls, and never come back. Riddled with pain, he began to walk slowly away from the stage. Sir Winstan followed him.

"My King, several parts of the city are currently engulfed with fire. Once the pyre is out and Thea cut down, we must start engaging our men in putting out the fires."

Arundel stopped in his tracks, for a moment. For him, that was not a must, far from it. The men and women who had fought for him had done enough, they had given their lives to save the realm, and he would not ask them to risk more to save this decaying city. He glanced back at Sir Winstan for a moment, and then turned away to start walking again.

"My King, the city?" Sir Winstan called after him. Finally, Arundel broke his silence, but not his pace.

"Let it burn."

He hadn't waited for the pyre to be put out and Thea to be cut down. He couldn't watch such an event; he had already seen enough. He would forever have to live with the heartache of knowing that he did not get to her in time, that he failed to save her. The thought of another day without her cut through him worse than any blade could, and every inch of his body felt the pain. He had left Sir Winstan to marshal the task, leaving him strict instructions that once it was finished, he would withdraw the soldiers from the city. Arundel cared not for those who remained inside the burning city. As far as he was concerned, leaving it to burn was the best choice. Theagran had spent years poisoning every element of the once great Ryevale and this had been so apparent when Arundel had originally visited with Thea. Everyone within the city walls had been loyal to Theagran, and he could tell that they would not change, even now that the false King was dead. They deserved to be left to the flames: the realm would be the better for it.

So Arundel had left with the first wave of his surviving army, escorting the wounded from both sides. As he first rode out of the city, he gazed at the carnage from what had been the biggest battle in recent history. The field was littered with bodies from both sides, as well as horses, in various stages of decomposition. The grass was stained red in places and the mud had become something of a quagmire underfoot. Cries of agony could still be heard from all points, as he had reached the temporary medical post that had been erected. The post was designed to identify who would be in a condition to make the journey back to Damisas, and who was in urgent need of immediate medical care: for the latter, that care was provided as best as possible. Working his way through the rows of wounded, he was offered treatment for his own injuries more than once, but each time he turned it down. There were those in far greater need than he, and so he let them get the attention they required.

It was at the medical post that he had found Urag'Ki tending to one of his own who was at death's door, a door he swiftly slipped through. Urag'Ki said his prayers, closed the clansman's eyes and then rose to his feet. They embraced as the true friends they were, relieved to find each other alive. They exchanged their news, when they found a corner to converse in. Arundel told Urag'Ki about Thea and his fight with Theagran. The Seeker did not necessarily agree with his decision regarding the city, that had been obvious, but he did not question it. Urag'Ki then told Arundel what he knew. It turned out that one group had already begun the journey back to Damisas with some of the wounded, and among them were Garad and Eliya. Garad was bruised and bloodied, but other than that fine. Eliya had taken an arrow to the thigh, but it was believed that if they could get her home quickly enough, she could be healed. It was not known how many of their numbers had survived the battle, but Urag'Ki did know that neither Darwin nor Crauss were alive. Darwin had been killed by Marcasian during the Bull's rampage, while Crauss had fallen victim to a stray arrow. Arundel would mourn the loss of both: it seemed to be a day for such grief. That was the ugly side of war; the glory of victory always came at a high and bloody price. He knew that on this day many good men and women had died in his name.

Urag'Ki also told Arundel that around one hundred and twenty Guardians had surrendered and been taken prisoner. They, too, would soon be on their way back to Damisas to await the King's decision on their fate: his decision. Those were the kind of tasks that awaited him, now that he was officially the King of Galbraxia, but he could not think about that, not in that moment.

He just wanted to get back to Damisas and lock himself away, shutting out the world for a night, so he could mourn his Queen in the way she deserved. He spared one final glance towards the city that his family had ruled for generations, watching as fire slowly consumed it, and then he began the journey back to Damisas, leaving Ryevale behind him, forever.

Damisas, as a city, rallied with the return of its heroes. Every available nurse and doctor worked around the clock to treat the wounded. A temporary infirmary was created in one of the halls in order to deal with the overflow of patients. Graves were dug at an alarming rate and those who had not fought temporarily took over the guard duties from those who had. Everyone who could work was doing so, in one way or another.

Yet amongst all of the chaos, the city still found time to give Thea a funeral fitting for a Queen. Her body was to be wrapped in fine silk sheets and placed in a small wooden boat that was lined with wood and leaves to burn easily. A shroud bearing his family crest, the one she had adopted the day they married, would be laid over her wrapped body. The boat was to be pushed out into the lake, where he had proposed to her, and a flaming arrow would then be fired into it to set the boat ablaze.

That was the plan for her funeral, but at this point her body was being washed and wrapped in silks. Every fibre of his being had told him to stay away, to wait until the funeral before he saw her again for one final time, but his heart couldn't wait. He wanted to speak to her one final time, a one-sided conversation that he did not wish to have at her funeral, in front of so many others. A conversation that was between them and no one else. His heart naturally overruled his brain, so he had made his way to her final resting chamber.

As he reached the chamber door, he stopped for a moment, taking a few deep breaths before pushing the door open. Stepping inside, he saw her body lying on a preparation table while two elderly females were tending to the silk wrappings. He had been told that the two women had once been nurses and so knew the role well, and they had been more than happy to offer their services in this time of need. Thea's head and her upper torso had been wrapped tightly, as had the right arm. The rest of her remained uncovered, her charred black skin flaking with every touch made by the silk. He struggled to comprehend that this was once his beloved wife, this burned shell. He took another deep breath and closed the door behind him. The smell of burned flesh hung in the air, assaulting his nostrils: just one more dagger in his already fractured heart.

The two women had stopped to look at him briefly, but neither spoke a word. Their eyes showed their sorrow, before they continued with the task at hand. One was finishing the wrapping around Thea's torso, while the other was preparing to begin on the exposed left arm. He took a step closer and, lowering his eyes, he started to speak.

"I was supposed to take care of you; I was supposed to protect you. I failed you."

He paused for a moment, trying to hold back the tears.

"It's strange the path life can lead us down. For years I had enjoyed the company of women, but never once had I given my heart to one. I guess my missing childhood haunted me more than I cared to accept, leaving an absence in my heart that no one could fill. That is until I met you."

He paused again, a lump forming in his throat.

"That day in the woods, when my eyes fell upon you for the very first time, I knew there was something different about you, and I was immediately drawn in. Then, as we spent more time together, I could see the great woman that you were. Your kindness, your bravery, your quick wit and sharp tongue blended with an innocence that could only be admired. You wore your heart on your sleeve and were bursting with passion, and I found it impossible not to be swept up by it. For so long my heart had been locked behind iron bars with the key lost, and yet along you came and suddenly I had my heart in my hands offering it to you."

He glanced at the two women, but neither looked his way as

they chose to continue their work. It made things a little easier for him. He carried on.

"Our time together was not enough. There was so much we had left to do, starting, at the very least, with simply being able to share every day together. But Theagran took that from us and I could not stop him. I failed you, Thea, I fai..."

His words came to a sudden stop and his mind drifted from them, catching up with his eyes, as they had made a discovery. The woman working on the uncovered arm had begun to wrap it, and to do so she had to lift the arm in the air. As she did so, the hand came into view in the corner of his eye. At first, he just noticed the flaky black fingers burned in an outstretched position as if they were reaching towards him; then he noticed something out of place, something that just wasn't right. The thumb and first three fingers were as expected, but the little finger was not. His eyes focused more closely on the little finger, as he realised through the charred mess that the top of the finger down to the knuckle was missing. Why would they have cut off part of her finger? It made no sense to him. His puzzlement was added to by the nagging feeling that he had seen such a thing before. He stared and stared, at the mutilated finger when suddenly it hit him. When she was a slave, Shauri, Thea's handmaid, had had the little finger on her left hand cut off down to the knuckle. Could it be coincidence? Surely not. For the first time since he had stormed into the square a moon's turn before, he suddenly found himself hoping that Thea might still be alive. Urgency coursed through his body as he pulled himself together. He should have said something to the women, but he was suddenly in a hurry and so his words stayed within him. Pulling the door open, he hurried out of the room.

Heads turned as he strode through the streets to the holding cells, walking at a pace so quick that it must have almost looked as though he was running. They would likely have wondered what on earth was going on, but he did not care. He had a purpose and no time to waste, and that was all that mattered. Entering the gaol house, he made his way down the stairs to the lower level where the guards stepped aside to allow him into the main block of holding cells. Each cell was full to the brim as defeated eyes fell upon him in the dim light. He came to a stop in what was roughly the middle of the block and then spoke loudly and sternly, so that all could hear.

"I know that Queen Thea was not burned upon the pyre. I know that she is still alive. Who will tell me where she is?"

His voice boomed off the walls, yet he got no response. In fact, some of those watching eyes turned away from him.

"Theagran is dead. Your loyalty towards him means nothing. I stand before you now as your true King and I am asking for the truth. Where is Thea?"

Again, the cells fell silent, as more eyes turned away from him. He could feel his anger and frustration building and was set to walk out to think of a new plan, when a voice crackled through the silence.

"Aye, she is still alive."

The words were like music to his ears and he begun to scour the cells to find who had spoken.

"Who said that?"

Again he looked and this time he could see a hand waving through the bars of a cell to his right.

"Over here."

Arundel wasted no time in making his way over to the cell as the Guardian came into view. His armour had been stripped from him, leaving behind a cloth garment stained with a mixture of blood and dirt. Light brown shoulder length hair was matted and dirty and framed a face that showed its age. His skin was a dark brown, except for a small white scar that cut into his upper lip. The Guardian spoke again.

"The name's Skaragot Tyne and I can tell you that you are right. Thea still lives."

Arundel moved a little closer to the bars of the cell, despite the stench of musty sweat assaulting his nose.

"Where is she?"

Skaragot adjusted himself against the bars.

"She was taken to the port to be sold to slavers in the Forgotten Lands."

He had not expected that answer, and so it caught him off guard.

"Slavery? I thought the port had closed and been cut off from the rest of the realm many years ago?"

Skaragot nodded.

"Aye it had. But there is a small path that leads through it, which only a few of us know about. The port has remained open in secret, trading with the Forgotten Lands in black market goods and slaves. Theagran made good business for years, selling captured villagers for trade and then using the money to buy black market goods. It was with those goods that he bought the loyalty of those who lived in Ryevale."

Arundel couldn't quite believe what he was hearing. How had this not been known here in Damisas? Or if it was, why had nothing been mentioned? Surely Oracle Thomas must have known? Skaragot continued.

"Theagran wanted to kill his daughter for marrying you, but he realised the price she would fetch was too good to ignore. So he had her dead handmaid put on the pyre to confuse you if you ever found it, and dispatched Thea off to the port to be sold."

Arundel suddenly gripped hold of the bars, hope burning brightly inside him.

"Would she still be there?"

He hoped for the right answer.

"Depends who was in port. It could be that no slavers were in port and so she waits there. Or it could be that she has sailed the sea already."

Arundel already knew what he was going to do next, but for a moment he weighed up what he had been told.

"How do you know all this?"

Skaragot picked at something in his teeth briefly, flicking whatever it was away through the bars before replying.

"I was one of Theagran's traders. I used to help transport the slaves to the port and then bring back the black market goods."

"So you know the path?"

Skaragot nodded.

"Of course, would have been useless at the job otherwise."

Arundel eased his grip on the bars and took a step back. "How do I know you are not lying?"

Skaragot sniggered.

"What would be the point? You said yourself, loyalty to a dead King is pointless. Besides, I don't want to stay in this shithole forever. If I lead you to the port and help you with the quay master, then I hope that in return you will let me go as a free man."

Arundel stood there for a moment, contemplating what had been said, before turning away from the cell and walking at a quick pace back towards the entrance. On reaching the steps, he was approached by one of the soldiers in charge of the cell.

"My King, is everything all right?"

Arundel stopped to speak with him.

"I want that man cleaned up and waiting on a horse for me by the time lunch is served. Also send word to Sir Winstan that I need a horse and my armour made ready for me and I must speak with him."

The soldier nodded.

"At once, my King."

Arundel then made his way back out into the morning air.

"This is not a wise decision, my King."

Sir Winstan voiced his concern, as he helped Arundel fit the final plates of his armour.

"The realm has just experienced a massive upheaval and it needs its new King to sit on the throne and lead it into a new world."

Arundel checked that all was fitting properly and then turned to face Sir Winstan.

"I know that."

Sir Winstan pressed on.

"To do so means you staying here, my King. Let me go in

your place and I vow I will bring back your Queen or die trying."

Arundel placed a reassuring hand on Sir Winstan's shoulder.

"I appreciate the offer, but I need you here. No one knows this realm, or the ways in which it was ruled by my father, better than you. I am making you Warden of the Realm until I return."

Sir Winstan gave him a look that was a mix of pride and concern.

"But you are the King, the people need you."

"I am the King and every good King needs his Queen. I need my Queen. I have every faith in you, Sir Winstan. You can lead the realm into a brave new world, until I come back."

Sir Winstan clearly realised there was no changing his mind and so he changed tack.

"Make sure you do return, my King. It is about time a Stal sat upon the throne again."

Arundel did not respond. Instead he just gave an understanding nod to the old knight, before holding out a hand as his horse was brought over to him.

Turning to mount his horse, Arundel caught a glimpse of Skaragot, who sat upon a horse just ahead of him. Arundel settled into the saddle, as Sir Winstan took a few steps back. He was about to urge his horse forward, when a voice interrupted him.

"Going somewhere, Ari?"

With that, Garad rode up alongside him to his right, dressed in fresh leathers, with his quiver strapped to his back alongside his new bow. Urag'Ki rode up to his left, looking as he always did. The Seeker turned to Arundel.

"Did you really think we would let you go without us?" Arundel glanced at them both in turn, cracked a smile and spurred on his horse.

Arundel will return
in two more installments of
this epic journey:

PERENAYSIA

A journey to the Forgotten Lands plunges our heroes into the
heart of a rebellion against the Master Curator, the overseer of
an ancient order. Magical creatures, wizards and witches all
have a part to play in seeking to restore peace and justice there,
as well as aiding Arundel in his quest.

THE WAR FOR GALBRAXIA

With its King absent, Galbraxia is under threat of invasion from
the descendant of an ancient enemy. With the realm at risk, who
will save Galbraxia?